P9-BBQ-206

STEVE ALTEN

Based on a story by Steve Alten and Nick Nunziata

VARIANCE
USA
10/2010

ISBN: 1-935142-16-X
ISBN-13: 978-1-935142-16-4

Published by Variance (USA)
www.variancepublishing.com

Library of Congress Catalog Number: 2010934993

Visit Steve Alten on the World Wide Web at:
http://www.stevealten.com
You may also e-mail Steve at meg82159@aol.com

Cover Design by Erik Hollander, www.hollanderdesignlabs.com
Interior Artwork by John Toledo
Interior Design by Stanley Tremblay
Printed in the USA

10 9 8 7 6 5 4 3 2 1

Dedicated with love, to my teachers

Eliyahu Jian, Yaacov Bourla

&

Chaim Solomon

Steve Alten thrillers:

MEG series

MEG: A Novel Of Deep Terror
The Trench
MEG: Primal Waters
MEG: Hell's Aquarium
MEG: Night Stalkers (forthcoming)

DOMAIN 2012 doomsday series

DOMAIN
RESURRECTION
PHOBOS (forthcoming)

GOLIATH

The LOCH

The SHELL GAME

Grim Reaper: End of Days and all Steve Alten novels are part of ***Adopt-An-Author***, a free secondary school reading program (grades 7 thru 12) that entices even the most reluctant teen readers to read. AAA offers free curriculum materials, tests, projects, classroom posters, and direct contact between our authors and students via e-mail, newsletters, classroom visits, and in-class calls.

For more information go to www.Adopt-An-Author.com

ACKNOWLEDGMENTS

It is with great pride and appreciation that I acknowledge those who contributed to the completion of GRIM REAPER: End of Days.

The concept for this series began five years ago during brainstorming sessions with my friend and fellow writer Nick Nunziata. After a three-day excursion in Manhattan, where we "walked in the shoes" of our characters, we pieced together a beat sheet that would eventually become a script. Although the screenplay was solid, I think we both instinctively knew there was a far deeper story to be told. Sixteen months later, I began penning the novel you are now reading, not realizing it would be a two-year journey, one I could not have completed without Nick's insights and creativity. *GRIM REAPER* remains our creation.

My heartfelt appreciation goes out to the great people at Variance Publishing: to my friend and owner Tim Schulte, his assistant Stanley Tremblay, and to my copy editors, Bob and Sara Schwager. My gratitude and appreciation to my editor, Lou Aronica at the Fiction Studio (laronica@fictionstudio.com) whose advice was spot-on; and to my literary agent, Danny Baror of Baror International, for his continued friendship and dedication. Thanks as well to his tireless assistant, Heather Baror.

Special thanks to Erik Hollander (www.HollanderDesign Lab.com) for his amazing cover art, and to artist John Toledo, who must have channeled the late great Gustave Dore in creating the original interior drawings. Thanks as well to publicist Lissy Peace at Lissy Peace and Associates, along with reader/editors Barbara Becker and Michael McLaughlin.

My extreme gratitude to two individuals who define the word "patriot." First, to attorney Barry Kissin, who continues to battle the windmills of injustice as he attempts to protect humanity by exposing a covert US biowarfare program that threatens us all. Second, to Captain Kevin Lasagna, an eighteen-year veteran whose experience training soldiers helped lend authenticity to the military passages included in the hero's journey. In Kevin's honor, and on behalf of all my fans in the military I offer this: The themes in this story may be interpreted as antiwar, but they are not anti-soldier. As such, I have not hesitated to bring up the darker side of issues that we need to bring into the light . . . for everyone's sake.

A very heartfelt thanks to my Kabbalah teachers, Eliyahu Jian, Yaacov Bourla, and Chaim Solomon, along with the entire Berg Family; Rav Philip S. Berg, his wife, Karen, and their sons Yehuda and Michael, who succeeded in mainstreaming a four-thousand-year-old ancient wisdom and whose books and teachings so profoundly influenced my life, my writing, and the characters in this book. Finally, to my soul mate, Kim, our children, and my parents, for their love and tolerance of the long hours involved in my writing career.

—Steve Alten
www.SteveAlten.com

AUTHOR'S NOTE

On May 5, 2009, at approximately 8:15 P.M. on a Tuesday night, I was vegging on the couch, recovering from a daylong writing session of *Grim Reaper,* resting up for a midnight edit. My six-year-old son was asleep in my bed; my fifteen-year-old daughter was at a neighbor's house being tutored.

I had been working on the novel you now hold in your hands for two long years, doing extensive research while coming to embrace a newfound sense of spirituality. With only two more weeks of writing anticipated, I felt excited to be in the home stretch of a book that contained a message I honestly believed could change people's lives.

What I had no way of knowing was that, within a span of minutes, reality would come crashing in, bringing me dangerously close to the very story I was writing.

Less than five miles away, my wife and soul mate had just entered a health-food store located in a strip mall close to our home. As she spoke to a clerk about her merchandise, two armed men wearing hoods and ski masks entered the store. One of the men aimed his gun at my wife's head . . .

Bad things happen to good people every day. Tragedies befall families. We search for meaning, we question God. Our faith is tested. Two years earlier, I had been diagnosed with Parkinson's disease at the age of forty-seven. No family history. I never blamed God; I simply thanked Him for not making it something far worse. There are so many people suffering in this world . . . how could I ever feel sorry for myself?

That night as I sat on the couch pondering my hero's fate, my wife was being held hostage, her arms and legs bound with duct tape as two men committed an act of evil that placed her life in their hands. After stealing her purse, jewelry, and the contents of the store safe, the armed robbers left. The police arrived. My wife called me, sobbing hysterically. Thankfully, no one in the store was hurt.

It was a bad night, but of course it could have been far worse.

This book is about good and evil, the choices we make, and why we are here. It draws wisdom from a two-thousand-year-old text that literally decodes the Old Testament, providing scientific explanations about existence and spirituality without the burden of religious dogma. My wife had involved me in these studies a year earlier, setting me off on my own spiritual journey. The information revealed to me in books and lectures provided answers to questions about life and death that were as simple as they were astounding, yet so clear that I instinctively knew it to be true. It also became clear to me that *Grim Reaper* was intended to be something far more than just a thriller. And yet, had the events of that fateful Tuesday night turned out differently, you might not be reading this book.

I'd like to think differently. I'd like to believe that my faith would remain unshaken had my wife been murdered and that, eventually, I would have finished the book in the light it was intended. Then again, I could just as easily have grown angry and torched the manuscript in a fit of rage, having learned nothing from my studies, or my own hero's journey through Hell.

Thankfully, my wife came out of it all right, and I was spared the test of grief. After a brief respite, *Grim Reaper* was completed—my own spiritual journey having taken on a new sense of purpose.

How should I interpret the events of May 5, 2009? Did God intervene? Did my wife's faith keep her safe? Were we simply lucky? Was the incident intended as a reward or punishment for some past deed? I have learned that cause and effect is made deliberately confusing to ensure free will; otherwise, we'd all be animals performing for our master.

But, who knows—perhaps one day the man who held a gun to my soul mate's head will pick up this novel and garner the spiritual tools he needs to transform his own life.

That would be nice.

Either way, I'm grateful to have you reading the book. I sincerely hope it brings Light and understanding into your life, as writing it has done for me.

–Steve Alten, Ed.D.

GRIM REAPER

STEVE ALTEN

"The earth was also corrupted before God and the earth was full of violence. God looked upon the earth and saw it was corrupt, for all flesh had corrupted their ways upon the earth. And God said to Noah, 'The end of all flesh is come before Me for the earth is filled with violence because of them. And behold, I will destroy them with the earth.'"

—Genesis

"The hottest places in Hell are reserved for those who, in times of great moral crisis, maintain their neutrality."

—Dante Alighieri, *Dante's Inferno*

PROLOGUE

TIGRIS-EUPHRATES VALLEY

(ANCIENT IRAQ)

His left arm had been hurting since he had awoken. It began as a dull pain, birthed deep within the shoulder he habitually slept on every night, his right arm always reserved for cradling his wife. But as he pressed his palms against the thick wall of cedar in the bowels of a swaying darkness, his left biceps began to throb.

The surly old man ignored it, but then he ignored most things. It was easier with age. Not so with youth. Pride had railed against the indiscretions of the masses; the more he had spoken out, the more he was beaten. Still, there were worse things than physical pain. Words cut deeper than any wound.

The Voice had beckoned in his misery. It had promised a soul mate. Children. A covenant was struck. The outcast was no longer lonely.

Surrounded by darkness and evil, the righteous man had cleaved to the nourishing Light. When the stain of corruption spread, he moved his family into the wilderness. But the Voice grew weary of the wickedness and sexual immoralities. And when the Voice told him of his task, he committed himself and his sons without question.

He could never ignore the Voice.

But as the years turned to decades and the scorn of the men of renown plotted against his household, the man's certainty waned, not because he didn't trust the Voice, but because he grew to despise the defiled ones whose ego-driven sins had so overwhelmingly changed the course of his own life, forecasting the End of Days.

Time and task stole his youth. His sons labored with him, married, and started their own families. He toiled on, forgoing comfort for devotion. Middle age bled into terminal weariness. As old age nestled within his bones, the memory of his covenant waned and his patience with the Voice gradually darkened to tolerance and at times resentment. What he never realized was that he was being tested, that his lack of compassion for the wicked had tainted his own soul, forever sealing his enemies' fate . . . and his own.

It began in the grayness of a heavy winter's morning. Icy rain. Unrelenting. After two days, the rivers overflowed. After a fortnight, the valley submerged.

The deluge made servants of the affluent and anchors of their gold. The suddenly homeless fled to higher ground. They demanded access into his vessel, but the old man said no. As the days passed, they offered to share their ill-gotten wealth. When the sea rose to meet the horizon, they pleaded.

The old man still refused. After a lifetime of humiliation and suffering, it was far too late for any reconciliation.

They threatened his sanctuary with fire, sealing their own fate. The mountainside erupted. The molten earth set the waters to boil. In the dark confines of his sanctuary, he listened to the tortured cries of the condemned . . . his satisfaction overcome by guilt. Taxed with the burden, he anointed himself the true victim; in doing so, he mentally excused himself from any accountability associated with the chaos, thereby discounting his own inaction and any transformation he might have had to bear.

Time passed. The Earth was baptized. He busied himself with daily worship. Maintained the livestock. His soul remained restless and tainted.

The candle flickered as it approached, its light partially veiled by the particles of barnyard dust churning in the air. His soul mate's face appeared, her inflection chiding. "And why is my husband hiding in the stables?"

He struggled to ignore the burning sensation radiating down his left forearm into his fingers. "Lower your voice, he might hear you."

"Who might hear me? The Blessed One?"

"The Angel of Death. Come closer . . . mind the flame. Press your ear to the cedar, then tell me if he is near."

Apprehensive but curious, she knelt by the wall and listened.

The middle deck was at water level, the boat rolling gently beneath them, and she could hear the sea beating against the vessel's creaking hull. For a long moment she waited, the heat within the suffocating enclosure causing her to perspire.

And then she felt it . . . a cold presence that filtered into her frail bones, obliterating the warmth. The animals sensed it, too. The horses grew agitated. The cattle herded themselves into an adjoining pen.

Then, more terrifying—a faint scratching sound—the supernal being's metal scythe testing the wood.

Unnerved, the old woman leapt to her feet, dropping the candle in the process. Flame met hay, the conflagration rising from the sparks like a hellish demon.

Stripping off his robe, the old man attempted to smother the beast, his feeble efforts only causing it to multiply.

Regaining her composure, his wife hurried to a trough, dipped a clay pot in the water, then doused the fire into submission. Steam rose from the ash, dispersing through the hold. Woodsmoke weighted the air.

The elderly woman embraced her naked husband in the darkness, their rapid pulses beating in sync. "Why is death stalking us?"

"Blood pressure's dropping, sixty over forty. Hurry up with that brachial artery, I need to administer Dobutrex before we lose him."

The old man babbled, confused by the strange voices suddenly sharing his head.

His wife grabbed him by the shoulders, shaking him back into the moment. "Why is death stalking us?"

He pushed her hand from his throbbing left shoulder, the pain magnifying in its intensity. "Man's negativity has summoned the Angel of

Darkness . . . he stalks the earth unbridled. Fear not, for as long as we remain hidden from sight, he cannot harm us."

"Your arm . . . is something wrong?"

"You sure this was an IED? Look at the skin hanging below the remains of his elbow; the flesh has melted."

The old man pulled away from his wife and moaned, his left arm suddenly radiating in scorching heat.

"Artery's closed, start the Dobutrex. Okay, where's the damn bone saw?"

"I think Rosen was using it to carve his brisket."

"What is it?"

He cries out in agony, the blood rushing from his weathered face. "The flesh . . . it's dripping off the bone!"

"How's his BP?"

"Ninety over sixty."

"Did you burn your arm in the fire?"

"No. It began hurting before the roosters arose to rant at the day."

"Tell me what to do. How can I help?"

"Fetch me a cutting tool."

"You're scaring me. Let me find our son—"

"No time . . . ahh!"

"Let's get another unit of blood in him before we take the arm. Nurse, be an angel and hold up that X-ray. I want to amputate right here, just below the insertion on the biceps tendon."

The surly old man collapsed. His wife knelt beside him in the swaying darkness, the scratching sounds growing louder. "Speak to me! Please, my love . . . wake up!"

"Doctor, he's awake."

The soldier opened his eyes to bright lights and masked strangers wrapped in surgical gowns. The pain was blinding, his left arm ravaged meat, the agony competing with the pounding ache in his damaged skull.

The anesthetic washed cool his nerve endings. The panic smothered, he closed his eyes, drowning in sleep.

From across the Baghdad surgical suite, the Grim Reaper stared at the soiled American soldier like an old friend . . . waiting.

PART 1

DARKNESS

"Evil does not exist, or at least it does not exist unto itself. Evil is simply the absence of God. It is just like darkness and cold, a word that man has created to describe the absence of heat. God did not create evil. Evil is the result of what happens when man does not have God's love present in his heart. It's like the cold that comes when there is no heat or the darkness that comes when there is no light."

– Albert Einstein

JULY

FORT DETRICK, MARYLAND

7:12 A.M.

Somewhere in the cul-de-sac, the grayness of morning is violated by the hydraulics of a garbage truck. A dog responds from a screened-in patio. A school bus negotiates the loop with an emissions-belching growl, transporting campers to the local YMCA.

In the house with no kids at the end of the block, the woman with the candy-apple red hair snores softly against a down pillow. Her subconscious refuses to be disturbed by the awakening neighborhood. Her bladder tingles, still she lingers in sleep.

Mary Klipot clings to the dream the way a non-swimmer clings to a capsized boat in tempest seas.

In her dream, the emptiness is gone. In her dream, her father is not a nameless John, and her drug-addicted mother feels the remorse of abandonment. In her dream, there is a home and a warm bed. Chocolate chip cookies and good night kisses that do not taste of tobacco. The air is lilac-sweet and the walls a cheery white. There are private bathrooms and showers and teachers who are not nuns. There is no soundproof room on Wednesday and Saturday mornings, no leather straps and holy water splashes, and certainly no Father Santaromita.

In her dream, Mary is not special.

Special Mary. The orphan with the high I.Q. Smart, yet dangerous. Satan is the tiny voice in your head that says torch the cat, it'll be fun. Jump off the ledge, you can survive. God is missing in these moments. The brakes on a runaway truck. The doctor with the cold stethoscope gives it a name—temporal lobe epilepsy, and offers a prescription.

Father Santaromita knows better. The weekly exorcisms last until her eighth birthday.

She takes the medication. The bridled I.Q. pays dividends. Parochial-school honors. A college scholarship. Degrees in microbiology from Emory and Johns Hopkins. The future looks golden.

Of course, there are "other" challenges. Parties and coeds. Beer and drugs. The introverted redhead with the steely hazel eyes might be trailer-trash cute, but she doesn't put out. Special Mary is branded Virgin Mary. Abstinence labels her an outcast. *Come on, Mary. Only the good die young.* Mary dies a hundred deaths. She works two jobs so she can afford her own apartment.

Isolation is easier.

Straight A's open doors, lab work offers salvation. Mary has talent. The Defense Department sets up an interview. Fort Detrick needs her. Good pay and government benefits. The research is challenging. After a few years, she'll be assigned to a Level-4 containment lab where she can work with some of the most dangerous biological substances on the planet.

The little voice agrees. Mary takes the job. The career shall define a life less lived.

In time, the dreams change.

The discovery had been unearthed in Montpellier. The archaeological team in charge of the dig required the services of a microbiologist experienced in working with exotic agents.

Montpellier is located six miles from the Mediterranean Sea. It is a town steeped in history and tradition, haunted by a nightmare shared by the entire Eurasian continent.

The archaeological dig was a mass grave—a communal pit that dated back to 1348. Six-and-a-half centuries had stripped away organs and flesh, leaving behind an entanglement of bones. Three thousand men, women, and children. The bodies had been discarded in haste by their tortured loved ones whose grief was rendered secondary to their own terrifying fear.

Plague: the Black Death.

The Great Mortality.

Three hundred people a day had perished in London. Six hundred a day in Venice. It had ravaged Montpellier, killing off 90 percent of the townspeople. In only a few short years, the Black Death had reduced the continent's population from 80 million people to 30 million—all in an era where transportation was limited to horse and foot.

How had it killed so effectively? How had it spread so fast?

In charge of the excavation was Didier Raoult, a professor of medicine at the Mediterranean University in Marseilles. Raoult discovered that pulp tissue found inside the remains of plague victims' teeth, preserved in many of the unearthed skulls, could yield DNA evidence that would, for the first time, unlock the mystery.

Mary set to work. The culprit was *Yersinia pestis*—bubonic plague. A pestilence delivered from Hell. Extreme pain. High fever, chills, and welts. Followed by swelling of the bulbous—black golf-ball-sized protrusions that appeared on the victims' necks and groins. In due course, the infected internal organs failed, often bleeding out.

A thirteenth-century nursery rhyme provided vivid clues as to how quickly the Black Death had spread: *Ring around the rosie, a pocket full of posies, at-shoo, at-shoo, we all fall down.* One sneeze, and plague infected a household, eventually the entire village, wiping out its unsuspecting prey within days.

Impressed with her work, Didier Raoult presented Mary with a parting gift—a copy of a recently discovered unpublished memoir, written during the Great Plague by the Pope's personal surgeon, Guy de Chauliac. Translated from its original French, the diary detailed the Great Mortality's near eradication of the human species during the years 1346 through 1348.

Mary returned to Fort Detrick with de Chauliac's journal and samples of the 666-year-old killer. The Department of Defense was intrigued. The DoD claimed they wanted protection for American soldiers in case of a biological attack. Thirty-one-year-old Mary Louise Klipot was promoted and placed in charge of the new project, dubbed Scythe.

Within a year, the CIA took over funding and Scythe disappeared off the books.

Mary awakens before the alarm sounds. Her belly gurgles. Her blood pressure drops. She barely makes it to the toilet in time.

Mary has been sick for a week. Andrew assured her it was just the flu. Andrew Bradosky was her lab tech. Thirty-nine. Boyishly charming and easy on the eyes. She had selected him from a pool of workers not because he was qualified but because she could read him. Even his attempts to foster a social relationship outside the lab were calculated toward promotion. The trip to Cancún last April was a welcome diversion, granted only after he acknowledged her rules of celibacy. Mary was saving herself for marriage. Andrew had no interest in marriage, but he did make good eye candy.

Mary dresses quickly. Cotton scrubs simplified her wardrobe choices. Loose-fitting clothing made for better choices in a BSL-4 suite and the environmental suit she wore for hours at a time.

Toast and jam were all her upset stomach could tolerate. This morning she would see the department physician. Not that she wanted to go. But she was sick, and standard operating procedure when working with exotic agents required routine checkups. Driving to work, she assured herself that it was probably just the flu. *Andrew could be right. Even a broken clock is right twice a day.*

She hated waiting. *Why were patients always relegated to antiseptic exam rooms with paper-lined cushioned tables and old issues of* Golf Digest*? And these exam gowns . . . had she ever worn one that actually fit? Did she have to be reminded that she needed to lose weight?* She vowed to hit the gym after work, then quickly dismissed the notion. She had far too much work to do, and Andrew as usual was behind on his duties. She considered bringing in a new technician, but worried about the innuendo.

The door opened and Roy Katzin entered, the physician's expression too upbeat to conceal bad news. “So. We’ve run the gamut of tests using the most sophisticated machines taxpayer money can buy, and we think we’ve nailed down the source of your symptoms.”

“I already know, it’s the flu. Dr. Gagnon had it a few weeks ago and—”

“Mary, it’s not the flu. You’re pregnant.”

"All sickness comes from anger."

—Eliyahu Jian

AUGUST

MANHATTAN, NEW YORK

The dashboard clock that had clung to 7:56 A.M. had somehow leapfrogged to 8:03 A.M. in the blink of time it had taken the intense brunette driving the Dodge minivan to negotiate her way across a minefield of moving traffic on the southbound lanes of the Major Deegan Expressway.

Now officially late, she managed to wedge herself in the right lane behind the carbon-monoxide-spewing ass end of a Greyhound bus. The gods of rush hour mocked her, vehicle after vehicle passing her on the left. Engaging the only available tool in her arsenal, she struck the steering wheel with both palms, the long blast of horn intended to rattle the nerves of the steel cow grazing in front of her.

Instead, the hold music on the hands-free cell phone animated into a Zen-like male voice bearing a rhythmically sweet Hindu accent that greeted her with, "Good morning. Thank you for holding. May I ask who I am speaking to?"

"Leigh Nelson."

"Thank you Mrs. Nelson. For security purposes, may I have your mother's maiden name?"

"Deem."

8:06 A.M.

"Thank you for that information. And how may I help you today?"

"How may you help me? Your freakin' bank put a freakin' hold on my freakin' husband's last deposit, causing eight of my checks to bounce, for which you then charged me $35 per check, severely overdrafting my account, and now I'm freaking out!"

"I am sorry this happened."

"No you're not."

8:11 A.M.

"I see your husband's check was deposited on the fourth."

She inches over to the right shoulder beyond the carbon-stained, vision-impairing Greyhound bus. The FDR South exit ramp remained a hundred yards ahead, the narrow shoulder lane all that separated her trapped vehicle from liberating freedom. She contemplated the opportunity like *Cool Hand Luke* working on a chain gang.

Shakin' it here, boss.

She accelerated through the opening, only to be cut off by a black Lexus whose driver shared the same idea. Brakes! Horn! Middle finger!

"The check will clear on Tuesday."

"Tuesday's bullshit. Since when do you put a week's hold on a General Motors deposit?"

"I am sorry for the inconvenience. Unfortunately, this is a new bank policy on all out-of-state checks."

"Listen to me. My husband just lost his job. His unemployment won't kick in for another four weeks. At least refund the bounced-check fees."

"Again, I am sorry, but I cannot change bank policy."

Now Luke, seems to me what we got here is a failure to communicate.

"I'm sorry, too. I'm sorry the government bailed your asses out with $800 billion of our tax money!"

"Would you like to speak to my supervisor?"

"Sure! Which part of freakin' India does he live in?"

9:17 A.M.

The Dodge minivan crawled past construction traffic on East 25th Street. Turned into the staff lot of the Veterans Administration hospital. Parked in a spot at an angle sure to annoy the owner of the car on the right.

The brunette wrenched the rearview mirror sideways. Rushed mascara through the lashes of her gray-blue eyes. Dabbed makeup on her pug nose. Smeared a fresh coat of a neutral lipstick over her thick lips. Stole a quick glance at the clock, then grabbed her leather briefcase from the toddler's car seat and hustled out of the minivan to the emergency entrance, praying she will not cross paths with the hospital administrator.

Double doors slid open, greeting her with cooled air tainted with the scent of the sick. The waiting area was standing room only. Coughs and crutches and crying infants diverted by *The Today Show*, broadcast on wall-mounted flat screens, secured to cinder block by steel cable.

She looked away, moving past admittance desks and attitudes. Halfway down the main corridor, she paused to slip on her white lab coat, attracting the attention of a tall Indian man in his early forties. He fought to catch his breath. "Please . . . how do I get to ICU?"

His torn expression quelled her urge to vent, his appearance assuring her he is not the bank employee she spoke with earlier. *Perspiration-stained dress shirt. Bow tie. Right pant leg coiffed with a rubber band. An academic visiting a sick colleague. Probably rode over from campus on his bicycle.* "Follow the corridor to the left. Take the elevators up to the seventh floor."

"Thank you."

"Dr. Nelson!"

Jonathan Clark's voice caused her to jump.

"Late again? Let me guess . . . traffic backup in New Jersey? No wait, today's Monday. Mondays are child-rearing conflicts."

"I don't have child-rearing conflicts, sir. I have two adorable children, the younger is autistic. This morning she decided to paint the cat with oatmeal. Doug's interviewing for a job, my babysitter called out sick from Wildwood and—"

"Dr. Nelson, you *are* familiar with my philosophy regarding excuses. There's never been a successful person who needed one, and—?"

Her blood pressure ticked up a notch. "There's never been a failure who lacked one."

"I'm docking you half a day's pay. Now get to work, and don't forget—we have a staff meeting at six."

Pick your battles, Luke. "Yes, boss."

Leigh Nelson escaped down the hall to her office. Tossed her briefcase on top of a file cabinet and collapsed into the creaky wooden chair perpetually teetering on its off-center base, her blood pressure set on broil.

Mondays at the VA were mental bear traps. Mondays made her yearn for her tomboy days back on her grandfather's pig farm in Parkersburg, West Virginia.

It had been a challenging summer. The Veterans Administration's New York Harbor Healthcare System consisted of three campuses—in Brooklyn, Queens, and her own Manhattan East Side. In an attempt to save what amounted to pocket change, Congress had decided they could only afford two prosthetic treatment centers. This despite two ongoing wars and yet another surge. A million dollars per fighting soldier, pennies to treat his wounds. Had Washington gone insane? Were these people living in the real world?

Certainly not in her world.

Longer hours, same pay. Soldier on, Nelson. Suck it up and repeat the mantra: *Be glad you still have a job.*

Leigh Nelson hated Mondays.

Twenty minutes, a dozen e-mails, and half a leftover donut later, and she was ready to sift through the patient files stacked on her desk. She was barely through the second folder when Geoff Payne entered her office.

"Morning, Pouty Lips. Heard you got caught on the last train to Clarksville."

"I'm busy, Geoff. State your business."

The director of admissions handed her a personnel file. "New arrival from Germany. Patrick Shepherd, sergeant, United States Marines, age thirty-four. Another IED amputee, only this poor schmuck actually picked the device up in his hand when it went off. Complete removal of the left arm just below the biceps insertion. Add to that bruising and swelling at the base of his brain, a collapsed left lung, three broken ribs, and a dislocated collarbone. He's still suffering from bouts of vertigo, headaches, and severe memory lapses."

"Post-traumatic stress?"

"Bad as it gets. His psychosocial diagnosis is in the file. He's not responding to anti-depression meds, and he's refused counseling. His doctors in Germany had him on round-the-clock suicide watch."

Leigh opened the folder. She glanced at the PTSD evaluation, then read the patient's military history aloud. "Four deployments: Al-Qaim, Haditha, Fallujah, and Ramadi, plus a stint at Abu Ghraib. Christ, this one took a tour of Hell. Has he been fitted for a prosthetic?"

"Not yet. Read his personal history, you'll find it especially interesting."

She scanned the paragraph. "Really? He played professional baseball?"

"Pitched for the Red Sox."

"Well, then, take your time ordering the prosthetic."

Geoff smiled. "We got off lucky. This kid would have been a Yankee killer. First year up, he's a rookie sensation, eight months later he's in Iraq."

"He was that good?"

"He was a star in the making. I remember reading about him in *Sports Illustrated.* Boston drafted him as a low-round pick in '98, no one gave him a shot at sticking around. Three years later, he's dominating hitters in Single A. The Sox lost one of their starters, and suddenly the kid's pitching in the majors."

"He jumped from Single A to the majors in one season? Damn."

"The rookie had ice water in his veins. Fans nicknamed him the Boston Strangler. First game up he pitches a two-hitter against the Yanks, that made him a cult hero with Red Sox Nation. Second game he goes nine innings and gives up one unearned run before the Sox lost the game in the tenth. His rematch with the Yankees was penciled in for mid-September, only 9/11 happened. By the time the season resumed, he was gone."

"What do you mean, gone?"

"He flaked out. Left the Sox and enlisted in the Marine Corps . . . crazy schmuck."

"The bio says he's married with a daughter. Where's his family now?"

"She left him. He won't talk about it, but a few of the vets remember hearing rumors. They say his wife took the kid and split after he enlisted. She was probably pissed off, who could blame her. Instead of being married to a future multimillionaire and sports celebrity, she's stuck raising her little girl alone, surviving on an enlisted man's pay grade. Sad really, but we see it all the time. Relationships and deployments have never made for a good marriage."

"Wait . . . he hasn't seen his family since the war began?"

"Again, he won't talk about it. Maybe it's for the best. After all this guy's been through, I wouldn't want to be sleeping next to him when he starts dreaming about combat. Remember what Stansbury did to his old lady?"

"God, don't remind me. Where's the sergeant now?"

"Finishing up his physical. Want to meet him?"

"Assign him to Ward 27, I'll catch up with him later."

INTENSIVE CARE UNIT
SEVENTH FLOOR

The room smelled. Bedpans and ammonia. Disease and death. A way station to the grave.

Pankaj Patel stood by the foot of the ICU bed, staring at the elderly man's face. Cancer and chemotherapy had combined to drain the life force from his mentor's physical being. His face was pale and gaunt. Skin hung from his bones. The eye sockets were brown and sunken.

"Jerrod, I am so sorry. I was in India with my family. I came as soon as I heard."

Jerrod Mahurin opened his eyes, the sight of his protégé stirring him into consciousness. "No . . . not there! Stand by my side, Pankaj . . . quickly."

Patel moved to the left side of the professor's bed. "What is it? Did you see something?"

The elderly man closed his eyes, gathering his last reserves of strength. "The Angel of Death waits for my soul at the foot of the bed. You were too close. Very dangerous."

Unnerved, Patel turned to look back at the empty space. "You saw him? The Angel of Death?"

"No time." Jerrod reached out to his protégé with his left hand, the pale flesh baby soft, marked by a minefield of telltale bruises from a dozen IV drips. "You've been an exceptional student, my son, but there is far more to this sliver of physicality we call life. Everything you see is but an illusion, our journey a test, and we are failing miserably. The imbalance is tipping the scales to favor evil over good, darkness over the Light. Politics, greed, the capitalism of warfare. And yet everything we have stood against are merely symptoms. What drives a man to act immorally? To rape a woman? Sodomize a child? How can one human being commit murder, or order the deaths of tens of thousands . . . even millions of innocent people without a single spark of conscience? To find the real answers, you need to focus on the root cause of the disease."

The elderly man closed his eyes, pausing to swallow a lump of mucus. "There is a direct cause-and-effect relationship in play, a relationship between the negative force and the levels of violence and greed that have once more risen to plague humankind. Man continues to be seduced by the immediate gratification of his ego, moving us farther away from God's Light. Mankind's collective actions have summoned the Angel of Death, and with it, the End of Days."

The blood beneath Patel's skin vasodilated, leaving goose bumps. "The End of Days? The conflict in the Middle East . . . will it lead to World War III? A nuclear holocaust? Jerrod?"

The dying man reopened his eyes. "Symptoms," he coughed. The smell lingered.

Searching an untouched breakfast tray, Patel spooned an ice chip, placing it in his teacher's mouth. "Perhaps you should rest."

"In a moment." Jerrod Mahurin swallowed the offering, watching his protégé through the open slits of his feverish eyes. "The End of Days is a supernal event, Pankaj, orchestrated by the Creator Himself. Mankind . . . is moving away from God's Light. The Creator will not allow the physical world to be eradicated by those drawing strength from the darkness. As with

Sodom and Gomorrah, as with the Great Flood, He will wipe out humanity before the wicked destroy His creation, and the terminating event, whatever it may be, shall happen soon."

"My God." Patel's thoughts turned to his wife, Manisha, and their daughter, Dawn.

"This is important. After I pass on, a man of great wisdom will seek you out. I've selected you."

"Selected me? For what?"

"My replacement. A secret society . . . nine men hoping to bring balance."

"Nine men? What am I required to do?"

A diseased breath wheezed softly from Jerrod Mahurin's mouth like a deflating bellows, the smell stale and harsh.

Pankaj Patel recoiled. "Jerrod, these men . . . can they prevent the End of Days? Jerrod?" Reaching for another ice chip, the pupil placed it gingerly on his teacher's tongue.

Water dribbled from the open slit of the elderly man's mouth.

A moment passed, the silence broken by the steady beep of the flatlining cardiac monitor.

Dr. Jerrod Mahurin, Europe's foremost authority on psychopathic behavior, was dead.

WARD 27

Leigh Nelson entered Ward 27, one of a dozen areas her colleagues referred to as a "fishbowl of suffering." Here, everything was on display, the carnage, the emotional wreckage, the ugly side of warfare that no one outside the hospital wanted to be reminded of.

Although there were only fourteen amputees treated during the entire first Gulf War, the second Bush administration's invasion was a far different story. Tens of thousands of American soldiers had lost limbs since the 2003 occupation, their long-term care overwhelming an already overburdened health-care system, their anguish purposely kept from the public eye. And still the war raged on.

It takes a special breed of health-care professional to work day after day in a combat amputee ward. Bombs leave the human body ravaged by burn marks and shrapnel wounds. The pain can be excruciating, the surgeries seemingly endless. Depression runs rampant. Many wounded vets are in their twenties, some in their teens. Coping with the life-altering loss of a limb can be devastating on the victim, his family, and the caregiver.

As bad as it was during the day, it was always far worse at night.

Leigh stopped by the first bed on her right, occupied by Justin Freitas. The corpsman, barely nineteen, had lost both eyes and hands ten weeks earlier while attempting to defuse a bomb.

"Hey, Dr. Nelson. How'd I know it was you?"

"You smelled my perfume."

"I did! I smelled your perfume. Hey, Doc, I dropped the remote to the television, can you hand it to me?"

"Justin, we talked about this yesterday."

"Doc, I think maybe you're the one that's blind. I have hands, I can feel them."

"No, baby doll. It's the nerve endings, they're confusing your brain."

"Doc, I can feel them!"

"I know." Nelson fought tears. "We're going to get you new hands, Justin. A few more surgeries, and—"

"No . . . no more surgery. I don't want any more surgery! I don't want pincers! I want my hands! How can I hold my little girl without hands? How can I touch my wife?"

The anger ignited like a flashpoint. Dr. Nelson barely had time to signal for help before she was forced to wrestle with her patient, fighting to prevent him from bashing the stubs of his bandaged forearms against the aluminum bed rails.

An orderly rushed over, helping her to pin Justin Freitas's arms down with Velcro strips long enough for her to inject a sedative into his IV drip, delivering him into an anaesthetized delirium.

Stalling to catch her breath, Dr. Nelson made notes on his chart. Sixteen more amputees lay in wait in this ward. The first ward of eight.

Every ward had its gatekeeper, a combat veteran who knew the pulse of his fellow soldiers. In Ward 27 it was Master Sergeant Rocky Allen Trett. Wounded by a rocket-propelled grenade eight months earlier, the double-leg amputee was sitting up in bed, waiting to greet her.

"Morning, Pouty Lips, you're late. The little one giving you a rough time at home?"

"What's the term you like to use? It's been . . . challenging. You seem in good spirits."

"Mona came by with the kids."

"Okay, don't tell me . . . the boys are Dustin and Logan, your daughter is Molly."

"Megan. Blue eyes, just like yours. Great kids. Can't wait to go home. Listen, I know I promised not to ask—"

"I called our prosthetist again this morning. He promised me no later than mid-September."

"Mid-September." Rocky struggled to hide his disappointment. After a few moments he regained his composure, pointing across the aisle. "Keep an eye on Swickle. He was bawling his eyes out earlier. Wife handed him divorce papers for breakfast. Says she can't deal with having a gimp for a husband."

"Lovely. Rocky, what about the new guy . . . Shepherd?"

Rocky shook his head. "Forget the prosthetist; that boy needs a shrink."

"Baby doll, we all need a shrink." She kissed him on the forehead, returned his smile, then proceeded to bed station 17, one of several areas that had been curtained off for privacy. "Sergeant Shepherd, my name is Dr. Nelson, and I'm your—"

She pulled back the curtain.

The bed was empty.

The Manhattan sky was awash in blue. A steady breeze coming from the East River kept the scent of soot to a minimum. Rows of industrial air conditioners hummed nearby, the mechanical groan of their rotating fans reverberating the roof's asphalt turf. The sound of traffic joined in the serenade seven stories below, the horn frequency increasing ever so slightly as lunch hour rapidly approached.

The VA hospital's helopad was empty, the medevac chopper on a run.

The lanky man in the gray sweatpants and white tee shirt walked barefoot along the eight-inch-wide concrete ledge surrounding the rooftop helopad. Long brown hair flopped with the breeze, his features and faraway look reminiscent of those of Jim Morrison, the late lead singer of the Doors. The soldier shared the artist's restless soul, imprisoned in a tomb of flesh.

His left hand felt like he had dipped his arm elbow deep in lava. The pain was excruciating, driving him to the edge of madness. *There's no arm there, you asshole. It's phantom pain . . . just like your existence.*

Patrick Ryan Shepherd closed his eyes, the one-armed man beckoning the sounds and scents of the urban jungle to flow into the hole in his memory—

—flushing out images from a long-lost past . . .

***The breeze is** steady, the sky awash in blue. The stickball bat is gripped firmly in the boy's balled-up fists.*

Patrick is eleven years old, the youngest kid in the game. Brooklyn is made up of ethnically divided neighborhoods, and this area of Bensonhurst is predominantly Italian.

Patrick is Irish, the runt of the litter.

An outsider pretending he belongs.

It is Saturday. Saturday's have a different feel than Sundays. Sundays are more somber. Sundays are dress pants and church. Young Patrick hates church, but his grandmother makes him go.

Sandra Kay Shepherd is disabled, having fallen from a ladder at work. The sixty-one-year-old is also an insulin-dependent diabetic. Twelve years earlier, Sandra's second husband walked out on Patrick's grandmother with no explanation.

Patrick's mother died of breast cancer when he was seven. Patrick's father is in jail, serving the fourth year of a twenty-five-year sentence for DUI manslaughter.

Two outs, the bases are loaded, only there are no bases. First and third are parked cars. Second base is a manhole cover. Home plate is a pizza box.

Young Patrick lives for these moments. In these moments, he is no longer the runt. He is no longer different. In these moments, Patrick can be the hero.

Michael Pasquale is on the mound pitching. The thirteen-year-old has already been embarrassed twice by the younger mick. The Italian throws the first pitch at Patrick's head.

Patrick is ready. He steps back and wallops the rubber pimple ball with the broomstick, the base hit whizzing past the pitcher's left ear. The bounding shot skids beneath several parked cars before disappearing from sight.

"Sewer ball! Ground rule double. Go fetch, German Shepherd."

"Don't you mean Irish Shepherd?"

Patrick moans as the older boys escort him to the concrete crevasse. The rules of stickball are simple: He who hits it retrieves it.

Two boys lift the manhole cover, unleashing a vomit-inducing smell. The liquid muck is five feet down, and Gary Doroshow, who normally brings the metal rake, is away with his parents at Coney Island.

"Down you go, Shepherd."

"Are you sure it went down there? I can't even see it."

"You calling me a liar?"

"Get your mick ass down in that hole."

Patrick descends, rung by rung, the collar of his tee shirt pulled high over his nose against the overpowering stench of liquid shit.

The blue sky suddenly disappears, the manhole cover clunking in place.

"Hey!"

The muffled sound of laughter causes Patrick's heart to race.

"Hey! Let me out!" He presses his shoulder to the cast-iron cover, unable to budge it beneath Michael Pasquale's weight. To his right is a sliver of opening between the curb and street. He tries to squeeze out, only to be met by kicking sneakers.

"Let me out! Help! Grandma, help!"

He gags, then vomits his breakfast into the muck.

Sweat pours from his face. He feels dizzy. "Let me out, let me out!"

Panic sets in, he can't breathe. Adrenaline turns his shoulders into battering rams, and he attacks the manhole cover, the force of his blows momentarily knocking Michael Pasquale off kilter. The resistance is quickly doubled by the weight of a second boy.

He feels faint. He feels small and scared. Cancer has stolen his mother, alcohol his father. Sport is the glue that has held him together, his athletic prowess leveling life's playing field. As the laughter grows and the last ounce of dignity leaves his body, he loosens his grip on the metal ladder rung, intent on filling his emptiness with the muck's drowning embrace.

Then he hears a girl's voice, firm and demanding. Backed by an older male presence.

The sneakers move off.

The manhole cover is lifted.

Patrick Shepherd looks up into the blue August sky at his angel.

She appears to be his age, only far more mature. Wavy blond hair, long and silky. Green eyes peer down at him below the bangs. "Well? You gonna stay down there all day?"

Patrick climbs out of the sewer and into the light, helped out by a man in shirtsleeves and a maroon tie. His gray wool sport coat is flung over one shoulder. "No offense, son, but you need to find yourself some new friends."

"They're not . . . my friends." Patrick coughs, trying to disguise the sob.

"By the way, that was a nice hit . . . the way you kept your wrists back. Try to lay off the pitches out of the strike zone."

"That's as good as they pitch me. If it's over the plate, I can take it deep, only we lose too many balls. Really though, I'm a pitcher, only they don't like me to pitch either–".

"–'cause you're so good, huh?" The girl smirks.

"What's your name, son?"

"Patrick Ryan Shepherd."

"Well, Patrick Ryan Shepherd, we're just on our way home from synagogue, then we're headed over to Roosevelt High to watch the baseball team scrimmage. Why don't you grab your glove and meet us there. Maybe I'll let you toss batting practice."

"Batting practice? Wait . . . are you the new baseball coach?"

"Morrie Segal. This is my daughter—"

"—no, don't get near me, you stink. Go home and shower, Shep."

"Shep?"

"That's your new nickname. Dad lets me name all the ballplayers. Now go, before I change your name to Stinky Pete."

Coach Segal winks, then leads his daughter away.

The sky is awash in blue, the August day glorious—

—the day life changed for Patrick Shepherd . . . the day he fell in love.

The man with no left arm opened his eyes. The phantom pain had subsided, replaced by something far worse.

It had been eleven years since he last kissed the only woman he has ever loved, eleven long years since he held her in his arms, or watched her play with their toddler daughter. The absence wrenched his heart, the organ a dam about to burst, releasing a swollen river of frustration and anger.

Patrick Shepherd loathed his existence. Every thought was poison, every decision of the last eleven years cursed. By day he suffered the humiliation of a victim, at night he became the villain, his actions in battles past replayed in heart-wrenching, skull-rattling, nerve-shattering nightmares of human violence, the reality of which no horror movie could ever capture on film. And yet, as much as he despised himself, Patrick hated God even more, for it was his accursed Maker, his eternal guardian of indifference, that arrived like a thief in the night and excised the memory of Shep's family from his brain, leaving in its place an empty hole. Try as he might, Patrick could not fill the void, and the frustration he felt—the sheer anger—is far too much for one man to bear.

His bare toes gripped the concrete ledge. A strange sense of calmness washed over his being like a soothing tide. Patrick looked up one last time at the clear blue August sky. Unleashed a primordial, guttural scream, announcing his death, and—

No.

He froze, balancing precariously on one foot. The whispered voice was male and familiar. Sizzling through his skull like a tuning fork. Patrick Shepherd whipped his head around, startled. "Who said that?"

The empty helopad mocked him. Then the rooftop exit burst open, the stairwell releasing a dark-haired beauty. Her white physician's coat flapped in the wind. "Sergeant Shepherd?"

"Don't call me that. Don't ever call me that!"

"I'm sorry." Dr. Nelson approached cautiously. "Is it okay if I call you Patrick?"

"Who are you?"

"Leigh Nelson. I'm your doctor."

"Are you a cardiologist?"

The reply catches her off guard. "Do you need one?" She saw the tears. The anguish on his face. "Look, I have a basic rule: If you're going to kill yourself, at least wait until Wednesday."

Shepherd's expression changed, his anger diffusing into confusion. "Why Wednesday?"

"Wednesday's hump day. By hump day, you can see your way clear to Friday, then you've got the weekend, and who wants to off themselves on a weekend. Not with the way the Yankees are playing."

Patrick's mouth twitched a half smile. "I'm supposed to hate the Yankees."

"That must have been quite a problem, a Brooklyn son pitching for the Red Sox. No wonder you want to jump. Anyway, you can call me Dr. Nelson or Leigh, whichever you prefer. What should I call you?"

Patrick took in the pretty brunette, his emptiness momentarily quelled by her beauty. "Shep. My friends call me Shep."

"Well, Shep, I was just about to grab a coffee and a donut. I'm thinking chocolate cream-filled, it's been a helluva Monday. Why don't you join me? We can talk."

Patrick Shepherd contemplated his existence. Emotionally spent, he expelled an exasperated breath and stepped down from the ledge. "I don't drink coffee, the caffeine gives me headaches."

"I'm sure we can find something you'll like." Hooking her arm around his, she led her newest patient back inside the hospital.

"What is absurd and monstrous about war is that men who have no personal quarrel should be trained to murder one another in cold blood."

—Aldous Huxley

SEPTEMBER

SENATE JUDICIARY COMMITTEE

HART SENATE OFFICE BUILDING

2:11 P.M.

"Please state your name and occupation for the record."

The wiry fifty-seven-year-old man smoothed his brown goatee, then spoke into the microphone, his Brooklyn accent heavy. "My name is Barry Kissin. I am an attorney currently living and practicing law in Frederick, Maryland, the home of Fort Detrick."

Chairman Robert Gibbons, the Democratic senator from Maryland leaned into his microphone to address the witness. "Mr. Kissin, could you briefly describe the nature of your work as it pertains to today's hearing."

"Over the last decade, I have been investigating US biowarfare activities, specifically as it pertains to the FBI's blatant cover-up regarding the anthrax letter attacks on two members of Congress as well as the media in September and October of 2001."

"Cover-up? Mr. Kissin, are you suggesting the FBI has willfully misled this committee?"

"Senator, the evidence is overwhelming. Case in point: At a prior committee hearing, held on September 17, 2008, Congressman Nadler specifically pointed out to the FBI and attending members that there are only two facilities in the world, let alone the United States, that have the equipment and personnel necessary to produce the dry silica-coated anthrax powder found in the envelopes of Senators Daschle and Leahy back in 2001. These facilities are the United States Army's Proving Ground in Dugway, Utah, and the Battelle Memorial Institute in West Jefferson, Ohio, a private CIA contractor. Despite numerous requests, the FBI still refuses to include these facilities in their investigation."

"Mr. Kissin, the Ames strain of anthrax was discovered in a dead cow in Texas back in 1981. The FBI's primary suspect, the late Bruce Ivins, experimented with the Ames strain as a potential bioweapon while he worked in a biosafety-3 lab located in Fort Detrick."

"Correct. But Bruce Ivins sent the strain to Battelle, where the anthrax was converted from Fort Detrick's wet slurry form into the powdered weaponized form found in the letters addressed to the two senators."

"In your opinion, Mr. Kissin, what was the motivation behind this alleged FBI cover-up?"

"The anthrax letters had 'Death to America,' 'Death to Israel,' and 'Allah is Great' printed in them, a crude propaganda attempt to make the public believe the letters were sent from Muslim terrorists following the events of 9/11. The Bush administration used this fear card to ram the Patriot Act through Congress, even though the evidence overwhelmingly proves that the military-grade anthrax came from labs run by our own intelligence agencies. The Amerithrax investigation metamorphosed into an FBI cover-up soon after the *New York Times* and *Baltimore Sun* reported that the Ames strain in the letters had been weaponized, meaning the anthrax had to have come from either Dugway Proving Ground or Battelle. From that point on, the FBI stonewalled, phasing out any reference to weaponization, referring to the anthrax spores as merely dried. This allowed the FBI to paint immunologist Bruce Ivins as a rogue operator in order to divert attention away from Battelle and Dugway. Ivins's reported suicide in 2008 was a convenient way to wrap things up and close the books on this case before the evidence trail could be traced back to the US intelligence community and Battelle's private labs. The cold harsh reality, Senator, is that the United States has embarked on a program of secret research into biological weapons that violates the global treaty banning such weapons, and threatens the lives of every citizen on this planet. These programs were begun under the Clinton administration without the president's knowledge, then embraced during the Bush administration and the tenure of CIA Director George Tenet, who was looking for ways to quote-unquote 'break the back of biological terrorism.' As a result, we now have a series of covert and extremely dangerous bioweapons research programs that are being controlled for profit by our own military intelligence."

"Can you elaborate more in regards to these secret research programs?"

"Yes, sir. As explained by the science editor of the *New York Times* in his book, *Germs,* in 1997 the CIA funded a covert project called Clear Vision, a program which focused on developing weapon systems that could effectively deliver lab-harvested biowarfare germs. President Clinton was never told about the program; in fact, only a handful of officials knew the program even existed, most of them associated with the military-intelligence industry. A second program, Project Jefferson, run by the DIA at Dugway, is focused on genetically engineering anthrax. Battelle was contracted to modify this anthrax into a weapons-grade form. The anthrax letters sent to Senators Daschle and Leahy contained two grams of this weaponized anthrax, each envelope holding over a trillion live spores per gram, more than 2 million times the average dose necessary to kill a person. It should be noted that Daschle and Leahy were the two Democrats who stood in the way of the Patriot Act being passed."

A murmur buzzed through the Senate chambers.

"Mr. Kissin, in your opinion, how involved is Fort Detrick in this . . . scandal?"

"Senator, that's not an easy question to answer. Fort Detrick serves many masters, including Homeland Security and the National Cancer Institute. I happen to know that there are many scientists at Fort Detrick who take the international treaty banning bioweapons very seriously. The problem is not Fort Detrick itself; the problem is the military-industrial complex and their insane goal to replace détente with full weapons spectrum dominance. And let's not discount the variable of profit in those plans. What is both terrifying and criminal is the fact that the new 10-billion-dollar lab expansion at Fort Detrick is being secured and managed at a sizeable profit by Battelle, the very organization responsible for weaponizing the anthrax attacks in the first place."

"Tell us more about Battelle. I know they're a private corporation—"

"—a private corporation that operates in conjunction with the military-intelligence-industrial complex. Battelle maintains a national-security division that offers the services of engineers, chemists, microbiologists, and aerosol scientists that are supported by state-of-the-art laboratories that conduct research in the fields of bioaerosol science and technology. Battelle's Pharmaceutical division, Battelle-Pharma, has developed a new electrohydrodynamic aerosol that delivers more than 80 percent of a drug into the lungs in an isokinetic cloud of uniformly sized particles, compared to 20 percent efficiency among competitors. To reiterate, the spores used in the anthrax letters were coated with a polyglass which tightly bound the hydrophilic silica to each particle. Bruce Ivins had zero access to this type of advanced technology at Fort Detrick. In short, Senator Gibbons, this is what we mean when we use the term weaponization. It's the necessary postproduction that allows a bioterror weapon to be used on a large population, be it on pamphlets dropped from airplanes or some other means of delivering a toxin to an enemy."

"The chair recognizes the Republican senator from Ohio."

Kimberly Helms offered a pert smile. "Thank you, Mr. Chairman. Mr. Kissin, with all due respect, I have a serious problem with your 'conspiracy theories' being made part of the public record. You just testified under oath that the FBI has been involved in a massive cover-up regarding the attempted murder of two US senators, the attacks originating from a covert bioweapons program run by our own intelligence agencies without congressional oversight or even the president's knowledge. In the process of attempting to frighten the American public watching these proceedings, you managed to smear the good name of the Battelle Corporation, a company that has never been a target of the Amerithrax investigation. As far as I'm concerned—"

"Everything I stated under oath is true, Senator Helms. Battelle worked on Project Clear Vision, Battelle was contracted to genetically modify the anthrax used in the 2001 attacks, and Battelle is now being paid to manage the biowarfare labs at Fort Detrick. What you refer to as conspiracy theory is conspiracy fact. More important, as a result of this insane black ops program, small unmonitored labs across the United States, funded by $100 billion in taxpayer money, are devising, as we speak, species-threatening agents for which there is neither a vaccine nor cure. And if that doesn't frighten you, Senator Helms, then perhaps we need to check you for a pulse!"

Ernest Lozano exited the Senate building into a budding September maelstrom. Thunder rumbled in the distance. The western sky had taken on a bizarre appearance—the cloud's low-hanging ceiling undulating like a forty-foot sea, the distant horizon over Washington, DC, appearing lime green.

Lozano descended one concrete stair at a time, each weight-bearing step causing his two artificial knees to buckle. Reaching the sidewalk, he limped toward a line of black limousines parked bumper to bumper along two city blocks.

There were many entry points into the lucrative military intelligence–private industrial complex, but the two most effective remained politics and the military. Lozano's career had been swept along by the latter, his years spent in Army Intelligence introducing him to gun runners, drug warlords, mercenaries, and despotic dictators—all part of a moving current navigated by clandestine factions within the CIA and other intel organizations. It was an arena that suffered no fools nor sense of morality, its operators using fear and fraud to create new niches within the global marketplace.

What few Americans understood was that the "war on terror" was big business, and big business had to be protected at all costs—costs defined in terms of swaying the legislation in power, be it through charitable contributions, political favors, or campaign contributions. It was the military-industrial complex that ruled the roost, and the new game in town was biowarfare. Unlike weapon systems, biowarfare monies could be tucked out of sight, budgeted under everything from Homeland Security to the National Cancer Institute, or farmed out to private companies like Battelle.

Of course, there were also practical military applications to consider.

To Ernest Lozano and the "Pentagon piranhas" he did business with, biological warfare was the wave of the future. Oil refineries and natural-gas pipelines were vital commodities that had to be protected; without them, populations would starve, economies would collapse. Tanks and soldiers were profitable, but their resources were limited to the availability of steel and flesh. A biological weapon was clean, quick, and indiscriminating in its lethality. Plus, there were plenty of residual profits to be made by allies in the pharmaceutical industry when it came time to mass-produce a cure. The swine flu "epidemic" had been a trial run—a resounding financial success.

Lozano walked to the last limousine. He verified the license plate, then signaled to the female driver, a short-haired woman in her forties, her black turtleneck sweater barely concealing a bodybuilder's physique and her 9mm sidearm.

Like Lozano, Sheridan Ernstmeyer was former CIA. Unlike Lozano, Sheridan had chosen combat over cash, joining the Joint Special Operations Command. The JSOC was an independent wing of Special Ops, exempt from any congressional or departmental oversight. Established after 9/11, the unit had been used as an assassination ring to eliminate perceived enemies of the United States, both home and abroad.

Sheridan unlocked the doors, allowing Lozano to climb inside the limo.

Alone in back was a spry seventy-three-year-old man. Silky white hair yielded to a receding hairline, magnifying the gray-blue slightly upturned eyes—an effect resulting from a recent face-lift.

Known around Washington circles as a "ruthless intellect," Bertrand DeBorn had established his tough-guy image during the late seventies, when he and two of his fellow foreign policy advisors in the Carter administration were reported missing on a three-day hunting trip in the Alaskan wilderness. A search-and-rescue mission had been deployed for more than a week when DeBorn was reportedly found by loggers, "delirious, dehydrated, and suffering from frostbite," thirteen miles southwest of his hunting lodge. Rumors of a "savage bear attack" were kept purposely vague, the only verifiable injuries coming from the frostbite that had cost DeBorn two toes on each of his feet.

The remains of his dovish-leaning colleagues were never found.

Old European blood ran through the National Security Advisor's veins. As a young man, DeBorn's paternal grandfather had survived Stalin's Great Revolution by trekking from Siberia to Warsaw. Once in Poland, he pretended to toe the Communist Party line rather than face a firing squad. DeBorn's father, Vasiyl, had been far more vocal about his hatred toward totalitarianism. Working covertly as a Cold War correspondent, Vasiyl smuggled letters out of Poland that detailed torture at the hands of the communist regime.

When he was eleven, Bertrand had witnessed his father's arrest by the secret police. Vasiyl DeBorn was tortured in prison over the next six months before being executed.

Bertrand dedicated the rest of his life to fighting the Communist Manifesto. His anti-Soviet views would play to a large audience in Washington during the 1970s and '80s. A hawkish Democrat, DeBorn was one of the architects of a plan to dethrone the Shah of Iran in order to strengthen Islamic Fundamentalism. By arming the Mujahadeen, DeBorn hoped the Afghani freedom fighters could give the communists their own debilitating version of Vietnam. They did far more, forcing the communists out of Afghanistan to a rousing defeat. That his plan indirectly gave rise to the birth of al-Qaeda never bothered DeBorn, who considered it a small price to pay for the collapse of the Soviet Union.

A decade later, the Bush/Cheney White House would use al-Qaeda to justify their own "war on terror," a decision that infuriated DeBorn, who saw Prime Minister Vladimir Putin as the real enemy of democracy. Working behind the scenes, DeBorn helped seal the deal with Polish Foreign Minister Radek Sikorski to deploy a U.S. missile interceptor system in Poland, a strategic move designed to incite officials in Moscow. Years later, he would team with Vice President Cheney to convince Georgian President Mikheil Saakashvili to attack the South Ossetian rebels during the 2008 Summer Olympics in China, an action designed to unleash a very public counterattack by Russia.

A founding member of both the Trilateral Commission and the Council on Foreign Relations, Bertrand DeBorn was a man on a mission to change the world, the cost be damned. The Washington power broker had backed Eric Kogelo's candidacy in the last presidential election, serving as a military advisor, offering the voting public the assurances they needed that the junior senator could handle the war on terror while bringing a conclusion to the ongoing wars in Iraq and Afghanistan. Having spent many long hours conversing with the candidate, DeBorn saw in Kogelo a conservative in liberal's clothing who could inspire like John F. Kennedy yet whose foreign views could be manipulated, aligning certain global variables necessary to bring about a new paradigm sought by both neoconservatives and hawkish Democrats for decades: a New World Order.

Novus Ordo Mundi: one government overseeing one united global economy serviced by a single monetary system. One language: English. One unified code of laws policed by one integrated military force shining its light of justice on every terrorist organization and third-world dictatorship cowering in the shadows of global apathy. To conspiracy wackos, the NWO represented an Orwellian nightmare, but to the world's richest and most influential movers and shakers, it was the only future that made any sense. Like it or not, the era of cheap oil that moved the global economy was quickly drawing to a close, bringing a forecast of famine and recession. Change was necessary to prevent anarchy and ensure the market's survival . . . a survival of the fittest. Like an unkempt forest, populations had to be pruned to prevent a potential blaze. Left to the tree huggers and liberal extremists, everything would end up burning to the ground—taking civilization with it.

And nothing effected change like war. DeBorn was an experienced hand in the game, having influenced Ayatollah Khomeni to rise against the Shah of Iran by using Iranian students to take over the American embassy, thereby strengthening a Muslim resolve that would be needed to challenge the Soviets. Reagan and the first President Bush had used DeBorn's war strategy to pit Iran against Iraq. More recently, Bush II and Cheney had created their own "war on terror" as an excuse to take over Iraqi oil reserves and secure a natural-gas pipeline across Afghanistan.

Now Bertrand DeBorn and his "commission" would instigate a completely new war—this one designed to spawn their New World Order. Iran, Syria, and Lebanon would be toppled first, followed eventually by Saudi Arabia. Any nation that refused to participate would simply be subdued or eliminated, their resources confiscated, all the while boosting the profit margins of key Western companies heavily invested in warfare. The only downside to ongoing combat operations was its drain on America's middle class, but then the middle class had no future in a New World Economy. As anticipated, higher gas prices had succeeded in further segregating the masses into the haves and have-nots, making society easier to manage. One either staked a claim at the banquet table or was relegated to servicing the needs of the upper class—that was "Law of the Jungle" economics.

Ernest Lozano climbed in the backseat of the limo, waiting to be acknowledged.

Bertrand DeBorn continued reading his *New York Times*, never bothering to look up. "How bad?"

"Bad. Kissin outed Battelle."

"Battelle will rebound," said DeBorn, turning to the op ed page. "They'll discover the cure to the next pandemic and the stock will split. What is needed now is the pandemic. You saw this morning's SAT images?"

"Six Russian-made Topol-M SS-27 mobile ICBMs, each missile having a seven-thousand-kilometer strike range."

"Eleven thousand kilometers, and it was a dog and pony show, orchestrated in part by Iran's biggest oil recipient, the Chinese. The clock is ticking, Mr. Lozano. We need a suitable biological solution."

"Yeah, well anthrax is out. And since Battelle is out, it has to be something coming out of Fort Detrick." Lozano searched his BlackBerry files. "West Nile virus, Venezuelan equine encephalitis, SARS, tuberculosis, typhus . . ."

DeBorn folded the newspaper, clearly perturbed. "No, no. These are all BSL-3 toxins. I need a BSL-4, something that strikes the masses with the fear of Marburg or Ebola but carries the weaponization component of the

Ames strain."

Lozano continued searching his files. "Lassa fever is Level-4, so is Crimean-Congo hemorrhagic fever. Wait a moment, here's something new . . . Project Scythe. It's a BSL-4 contaminant, with a small R & D team attached, headed by an unknown, a microbiologist named Mary Klipot."

"Scythe . . . I like the sound of that. What's the bacilli history?"

"*Yersinia pestis*—bubonic plague."

DeBorn smiled. The Black Death was a true pandemic. In only a few short years, it wiped out more than half the population of Europe and Asia. "What did this Klipot woman find?"

"Looks like they found the living virus."

"Who else has access to Scythe?"

"Besides command, just her lab assistant, another level-four geek named Andrew Bradosky."

"Get to him." DeBorn laid his head back.

"What's your timetable? No disrespect, but after today, we may not be the only buyer seeking product. I need to know the extent of my resources—"

The National Security Advisor grabbed Ernest Lozano by his left wrist, his icy blue glare causing the former commando to freeze. "Things are in play, my friend. Big things. The world is going to change. So you spend what you need to spend and eliminate anyone who stands in our way. I expect to be in Tehran, pumping crude, in eighteen months. As such, I want Scythe weaponized no later than early spring. That, Mr. Lozano, is *your* timetable."

SEPTEMBER 11
VA MEDICAL CENTER
MANHATTAN, NEW YORK
7:13 A.M.

The one armed man with the Jim Morrison looks and faraway eyes tossed ragged in his sleep, his mind caught in a hurricane of recycled memories . . .

"Where you from, Rook?"

"Brooklyn." The twenty-three-year-old sporting the fresh crew cut and

standard-issue Army tee shirt and briefs avoids the medical officer's face, his eyes glued to the series of vaccinations the dark-haired physician is preparing.

"Greenwich Village, we're practically neighbors. Got a name, Brooklyn?"

"Patrick Shepherd."

"David Kantor. I'm CO of the medical party you're assigned to. We play a lot of pickup games during downtime. You play hoops?"

"A little."

"Yeah, you look like an athlete. Got a decent team, but most of my surgeons are ninety-day BOGers. We could use you."

"BOGers?"

"Boots on the Ground. Surgeons rotate in every ninety days. Okay, this first shot is for anthrax. It'll hurt a little, and by a little I mean it'll feel like I injected a golf ball made of lava into your deltoid. Any preferences?"

"Yeah, don't do it. Wait, Doc, not that arm, do my left shoulder, I'm a righty."

David Kantor injects the elixir into his deltoid, the fire igniting thirty seconds later.

"Mutha F'er—"

"It'll cool down, but you'll feel that knot for about two weeks. This next shot is the bitch: Smallpox. Believe it or not, George Washington was the first one to inoculate his troops against the disease. Forward thinker, the general. Of course, when I say inoculate, I'm talking about sticking a fork into an infected soldier's pox, then stabbing the person to be vaccinated a few dozen times with the pus. Plenty of Washington's men died in the process, but the numbers were far better than the disease. The British were the first to use smallpox as a biological. Right arm or left?"

"Left."

"You sure? I have to jab you fifteen times."

"Just stick me . . . ahh!" Patrick winces, counting each injection out loud.

"They teach you some basic Arabic?"

"What's your name? Drop your weapon. Do you need medical assistance? I'll never remember it."

"You'll pick it up. Of course, they never teach you what the acceptable

responses are." Dr. Kantor finishes bandaging the area. "Okay, Brooklyn, this is important: You need to keep this area covered with a bandage for a month. Screw up, and you'll get pox pustules that will itch like hell. Plus we may have to vaccinate you again. So don't screw up. You all packed?"

"Yes, sir."

"Make sure you have extra socks and tee shirts, plus batteries for your flashlights and cleaning kits for your weapons. Buy some Sharpies, too. Anything that doesn't have a name on it walks away. Get a spool of the five-fifty paracord. It's light and strong, makes a good clothesline for drying your laundry. And don't forget duct tape. It fixes damn near everything, plus you'll need it to tape down the straps on your rucksack. Telltale noises get soldiers shot. How are you handling the Kevlar body armor?"

"Stuff's heavy."

"Forty-five pounds with the ceramic rifle plates. Plus your Advanced Combat helmet. Plus your ECWCS—seven layers of tactical pouches, pockets, and vests holding enough equipment to outfit a Boy Scout troop hell-bent on destruction. It's a lot of gear, but you'll be glad you have it. Wouldn't want to get your arm blown off . . ."

Leigh Nelson entered Ward 27, the physician heading straight for Master Sergeant Trett. "What happened, Rocky? What spooked him?"

The double-leg amputee sat up in bed. "I don't know. He had the usual nightmares, then started freaking out about an hour ago."

"Suicide threats?"

"No, not since that first day. This was different. Don't forget what day it is."

"September 11 . . ."

Rocky nodded. "There's a lot of us who enlisted because of that day. I'm guessing your boy was one of them."

"Thanks, baby doll." She left him, heading for the ward bathroom.

There were fist-sized holes in the drywall. One of the three community sinks had been torn from the wall, a mirror shattered. Two male orderlies had wrestled Patrick Shepherd to the ground. A nurse struggled to inject him with a sedative.

"Stick him already!"

"Hold him steady."

"Wait!" Leigh Nelson positioned herself so that her patient could see her face. "Shep! Shep, open your eyes and look at me."

Patrick Shepherd opened his eyes. He stopped struggling. "Leigh?"

The nurse jabbed the hypodermic needle into the left cheek of Shepherd's buttocks. The one-arm amputee's body went limp.

Dr. Nelson was livid. "Nurse Mennella, I told you to wait."

"Wait for what? This man is a walking billboard for post-traumatic stress. He shouldn't be in the VA, he should be in a sanitarium."

"She's right, Doc," added one of the orderlies, palpating a fresh welt over his left eyebrow. "The guy's a bull. From now on, I'm carrying a Taser."

"He is still a veteran. Try to remember that." Leigh Nelson gazed down at her inert patient, the knuckles of his right hand bleeding from punching the walls. "Put him back in his bed and use the restraints. Keep him sedated for the rest of the day. And nurse, the next time you take it upon yourself to ignore my instructions, you'll find yourself on bedpan duty for a week."

The nurse capped the hypodermic needle, waiting until Nelson was out of earshot. "Big deal. You want to pay me $45 an hour to clean bedpans, do it."

The injured orderly helped his associate lift the sedated patient off the floor. "You did the right thing, Veronica. The doc's just having a bad day."

"No, that's not it." She grabbed Patrick's right wrist, checking his pulse. "Nelson likes him."

COLUMBIA UNIVERSITY
501 SCHERMERHORN HALL
MORNINGSIDE, NEW YORK
9:58 A.M.

Founded in 1754 as King's College by the Church of England, Columbia University was a private Ivy League school that occupied six city blocks in Morningside Heights, a neighborhood situated between Manhattan's Upper

West Side and Harlem.

Professor Pankaj Patel exited Schermerhorn Hall, accompanied by a female graduate student representing the Columbia Science Review. "I do not have a lot of time. Where do you want to do this?"

"Over here." She led him to a park bench. Aimed the palm-sized camcorder, framing Patel's face in her monitor. "This is Lisa Lewis for the CSR, and I'm with Professor Pankaj Patel. Professor, you've written a new book, *Macrosocial Evil and the Corruption of America.* Maybe you can begin by telling our bloggers what macrosocial evil is."

The balding forty-three-year-old intellectual cleared his throat, unsure of whether to look at the girl or the camera. "Macrosocial evil refers to a branch of psychology which examines the pathological factors that are found among deviant individuals who, through the manipulation of wealth, political affiliations, and other affluent associations, prey on what they consider the moral weakness of society in order to rise to power."

"In your book, you call these people psychopaths with power."

"Correct. A psychopath, by definition, is an individual who engages in abnormal activity while lacking all sense of guilt. Imagine living your entire life having no conscience . . . no feelings of remorse or shame, no sense of concern for others. When it comes to morality, you're essentially without a soul, ruled by a sense of entitlement. Are you concerned about being different? Not at all. In fact, you consider it an asset, a strength—you are a wolf among sheep, acting while others hesitate. Sure, as a child, you were punished for microwaving the pet hamster or feeding firecrackers to the local duck population, but being a devious sort, you learned how to blend in, to appear 'normal,' all the while using your sociopathic tendencies to charm and manipulate your peers. For you, society's laws have no meaning, you are governed by the Law of the Jungle . . . if you want something, you take it. And if you happen to be born into the right family, the right social class, well then, the sky's the limit."

"What about political figures? You've actually named names on both sides of the political spectrum, including a certain former vice president. Are you worried about being sued?"

"What I worry about is a world run by members of the military-industrial complex who believe they have the right to kill innocent people in order to achieve their objectives."

"The book is called *Macrosocial Evil and the Corruption of America,* the author is Columbia's own Professor Pankaj Patel, and I am Lisa Lewis for CSR online." The reporter powered off the camera. "Thank you, Professor."

"That was a good interview. Did you enjoy my book?"

"Actually, I only read the inside flap. But I'm sure it's a great read."

He sighed, watching her leave. Crossing Amsterdam Avenue, he headed straight for the blue lunch truck parked along the curb. "Yes, I'd like a turkey sandwich on wheat, lettuce and tomato—"

"—and a bottled water, got it." The proprietor handed him his usual brown bag lunch, then swiped his debit card.

Making up for lost time, Patel ate as he walked, heading for Low Memorial Library. *An hour of research, then an hour at the gym before my last class. I should call Manisha again. September 11 is always a difficult day for her and—*

"Professor Patel, a quick question please?"

He turned, expecting to see the reporter, startled to find an Asian beauty in her twenties. Dressed in a black suit and chauffeur's hat.

"How many letters are there in God's name?"

The jolt of adrenaline seemed to electrify the pores of his skin. "Forty-two."

She smiled. "Come with me, please."

Suddenly feeling numb, he followed her across the street to an awaiting stretch limousine, his legs trembling beneath him. She opened the rear passenger-side door. "Please."

Unsure, he looked inside.

The car was empty.

"Where are we going?"

"Someplace close. You will not miss your next class."

He hesitated, then climbed in back, feeling like Alice entering the rabbit's hole.

The limousine turned right on 116th Street, then made another right on

Broadway. Heading north, they entered Hamilton Heights, a neighborhood of grad students and ethnic professionals, named after Alexander Hamilton, one of America's founding fathers.

The driver parked curbside at 135th Street, then exited the vehicle, opening the door for the nervous college professor. She handed Patel a magnetic entry key, then pointed to a seven-story building across the street. "Suite 7-C."

Unsure, Patel took the key and headed for the apartment building.

The doorman greeted him with a smile, as if he'd been expected. He nodded, crossing the marble-laden lobby to the elevators, using the magnetic card to summon a car.

Suite 7-C was on the top floor. Patel stepped out onto plush gray carpeting, the corridor empty. Locating the doubled oak door of Suite 7-C, he again used the keycard and gained entry.

The condo had an empty elegance hinting at Asian design. Polished bamboo floors led to floor-to-ceiling bay windows and a balcony overlooking the Hudson River. The living room was sparsely decorated—a white leather wraparound sofa, a flat-screen television, and a glass kitchen table. The high-priced apartment appeared to be unlived in.

"Hello? Is anyone here?"

Welcome.

The voice resonated in his brain, causing Patel to jump. He looked around, his scalp tingling, the thinning black hairs along the back of his neck standing on end.

Follow my utterance.

Taken aback, yet sensing he was in no danger, Patel walked past the living area to a short alcove and the master bedroom. The door was open, the king-size bed made up but empty. Hesitant, he peeked inside the master bathroom.

The whirlpool tub was rectangular, sized to hold two adults. It was filled with water.

Come closer.

Unnerved, Pankaj stepped forward until he was looming over the tub.

The small Asian man was underwater, lying faceup along the bottom. A white loincloth barely covered his groin, the color nearly blending with his pinkish ivory flesh, as hairless and shiny as the porcelain. The man's ankles and wrists were held down by Velcro-covered weights, his eyes fixed open, revealing opaque pupils.

The body appeared lifeless. The smile was serene.

Patel fought the urge to flee. As he watched, the left side of the man's bare chest jumped, the double cardiac beat releasing a ripple of blood that pulsated through his veins.

Incredible. How long has he been underwater?

Just over an hour.

Patel gasped a breath. "How are you—" Closing his eyes, he restated the question, this time saying it only in his thoughts. *How are you able to communicate with me telepathically?*

Through extensive study and the discipline acquired through time, I have been able to access the full extent of my brain. I sense you are uncomfortable. Please wait for me in the outer room. I shall only be a moment.

Pankaj backed out of the bathroom, closing the door behind him. He paused a brief second, long enough to hear a bizarre humming sound.

The professor double-timed it into the living room, certain that the Asian man had just levitated out of the tub.

He appeared ten minutes later, dressed in a gray Columbia University sweat suit, white socks, and Adidas sneakers. "Less unnerving?"

"Yes."

Moving to the refrigerator, the Asian man removed two bottles of water, the green label adorned in a ten-pointed figure, branded PINCHAS WATER. He handed one to Patel, then sat across from him on the couch.

Patel stared at the man's skin, which appeared to be entirely composed of keratin, the fibrous protein substance found—

"—in fingernails. Yes, my skin is slightly different than yours, Professor. Those who have come to know me have endeared me with the name, 'the Elder.' I know you have many questions. Before I provide you with the answers, let us begin with a simple deduction. Why are you here?"

"My teacher, Jerrod Mahurin. Before he died, he told me a man of great wisdom would seek me out. Are you that man?"

"Let us hope. What else did he tell you?"

"That I was to replace him in some sort of secret society . . . nine men hoping to bring balance to the world."

"Again, let us hope." The Asian man took a sip of water, then closed his opaque eyes, his face as serene as a pond on a windless day. "Little is known about the Society of the Nine Unknown Men. Our history traces back more than twenty-two centuries, to the year 265 B.C. and our founder, Emperor Asoka, the ruler of India and the grandson of Chandragupta, a warring leader who used violence to unify his nation. Asoka's first taste of battle came when his army laid siege upon the region of Kalinga, his men slaughtering one hundred thousand foreign combatants. It is said the sight of the massacre mortified the Emperor, the senselessness of the bloodshed causing him to forever renounce war."

Patel interrupted, excited. "I learned about Asoka when I studied back in India. The Emperor converted to Buddhism, adopting the *Conquest of Dharma*—principles of a right life. He preached respect toward all religions. The practice of positive virtues."

The Elder nodded. "Asoka's transformation spread peace throughout his empire, as well as Tibet, Nepal, Mongolia, and China. It was a sea change for the Mauryan dynasty, but for its last ruling emperor it was not enough. While Buddhism offered the prospect of enlightenment, what Asoka desired was the knowledge of existence: How did man come to be? How could man become one with the Creator? What was man's true purpose in this world? Why did man seem to have a propensity to commit violence and acts of evil? Most of all, Asoka wanted to know what was really out there, beyond the physical world . . . beyond death?

"To find these answers, Asoka secretly recruited nine of Asia's most renowned wise men—the greatest sages, scientists, and thinkers in the land. The Society of the Nine Unknown Men was tasked with seeking the truth about existence. Each member was responsible for recording his assigned body of information in a sacred text so that the acquired knowledge could be passed on to an apprentice worthy of safeguarding the information.

"Emperor Asoka died in 238 B.C., having never obtained the answers he coveted. His leadership would be missed; over the next three centuries India would suffer a series of invasions, falling under the spell of foreign rulers. But the quest of the Nine would go on.

"In A.D. 174, a man named Gelut Panim, a blood descendant of Emperor Asoka and one of the appointed lineage of the Nine, heard a strange tale about a man in the Holy Land who could walk on water and heal the sick. Seeking this man's wisdom, the Tibetan traveled to the city of Jerusalem, only to learn he had arrived too late, that the holy man, known as Rabbi John ben Joseph, had been tortured to death by the Romans."

"You are speaking of Jesus."

"Correct. Panim learned that much of Jesus's teaching came from his study of Kabbalah, an ancient wisdom that had been passed down from God to Abraham the Patriarch, who encoded it in the Book of Formation. Moses acquired the knowledge at Mount Sinai, only the Israelites were not ready for it—its energy remained buried in the original tablets. For the next fourteen centuries the Jewish sages kept the ancient wisdom hidden, encoded in the Torah's original Aramaic.

"The Romans had strictly forbidden the study of Torah within Jerusalem. After skinning alive the great Kabbalist, Rabbi Akiva, alive, the Romans went after his remaining students. One man, Rabbi Shimon bar Yohai, managed to escape to northern Israel with his son. The two holy men remained in Galilee, hidden in a mountain cave. They spent the next thirteen years decoding the ancient wisdom, which they eventually transcribed into the Zohar, the book of splendor.

"It was about this time that Panim found his way to the Sea of Galilee and the city of Tiberius, where he learned Rabbi Shimon had just come down from the mountain. When he finally found the Rabbi, he offered the man a small fortune to share his acquired wisdom, but the teacher refused. Realizing he had insulted the holy man, Panim dismissed his entourage, donated his gold and camels to the poor, then denied himself food until the Kabbalist would reconsider. For the next eight days he followed the Rabbi around until he collapsed, close to death. Impressed by the Asian's newfound sense of humility, the teacher brought Panim back to his home and fed him, instructing his new student to meet him in a cave on the next full moon, where he was teaching the ancient wisdom to Rabbi Akiva's surviving sages.

"Though the Zohar's knowledge was intended for all of God's children, mankind simply wasn't ready to comprehend concepts involving the Big Bang or atoms, let alone the true purpose of man's existence in the physical universe. And so the Zohar remained hidden until the 13th century.

"Gelut Panim returned to Asia decades later, a changed man. Convening the Society of the Nine in Tibet, he divided the ancient wisdom into sacred texts, assigning a field of study to each member. The ninth text dealt with the mystical, its teachings defying the laws of physics, tapping into the higher realms to enable mind over matter. So powerful and dangerous was this last subject that Gelut Panim felt it best to safeguard this sacred book of wisdom himself.

"And so the Nine ventured forth, spreading their teachings where they felt the knowledge might do the most good. Plato and Pythagoras called the ancient wisdom '*Prisca Theologia.*' Aristotle, Galileo, and Copernicus all served time as members of the Nine, along with Alexandre Yersin, the eighteenth-century French-Swiss bacteriologist who received knowledge from the book of microbiology in order to develop a cure for the bubonic plague. Isaac Newton acquired his own personal copy of the Zohar, relying on it as a scientific reference. Albert Einstein used the ancient wisdom to advance his Theory of Relativity.

"The Society of the Nine Unknown Men had hoped to use the ancient wisdom to maintain the balance between good—the Creator's Light—and evil, which is the darkness brought on by man's ego. According to the ancient wisdom, when the scales of humanity are finally swayed toward the Light, then fulfillment and immortality shall be had by all. But when negativity outweighs the positive forces, then the Angel of Death shall again walk freely upon the Earth at a time known as the End of Days. According to the Zohar, this epoch of human existence began in the Age of Aquarius on the twenty-third day of Elul, in the Hebrew year of 5760, ushered in by 'a great tall city, its many towers collapsed by flames, the sound of which shall awaken the entire world.' The Gregorian calendar date: September 11, 2001."

Patel felt his blood pressure rising. "September 11 was not a supernal event, it was a false-flag conspiracy, involving lunatics hell-bent on rewriting the map of the Middle East."

The Elder smiled with his eyes. "That you believe this does not make it so. As brilliant as you are, you remain stuck in the one percent of existence we call *Malchut*, the physical world of chaos and pain, war and pestilence, dying and fear. In your latest book, you blame September 11 on the psychopath, sweeping their enablers into a big tent labeled macrosocial evil."

"I *am* a psychologist. Understanding the root causes of evil is what psychology is all about."

"And yet nothing changes. Murder and genocide go on, despite the advent of drugs and overflowing prisons. Perhaps you are looking at the roots of the wrong tree?"

Willing himself to remain calm, the professor took a deep breath, then exhaled, flashing a false smile. "Go on, I'm listening."

"No, you are hearing with your ego. You have formulated a judgment without having heard one utterance. You remain deceived by your five senses, which, in turn, are being manipulated by the opponent . . . the Satan." The Elder pronounced the word: *Sa-tahn*, emphasizing separation between the two syllables.

Patel felt his patience waning. "With all due respect, I did not come here to be lectured by the Buddhist version of David Blaine. From what my teacher implied, your society could help root out corruption by identifying it to the masses—"

"—while seeking justice?"

"Two wars, a trillion dollars, a million innocent lives stolen. What's wrong with a little justice?"

"Justice will happen for each of us when we leave this realm. What you seek is driven by the ego . . . the self. You cannot experience justice and true happiness—the pursuit of justice will make you miserable."

This must be a test . . . he's testing me.

Life is a test, Professor Patel. Pain and suffering, chaos and evil all exist to test us.

Patel ground his teeth. "I hate that you can hear my thoughts."

"That is your ego speaking. The answers you seek are out there, only they have been purposely hidden from us."

"Why? Why must all the answers be hidden?"

"Because we asked the Creator to hide them."

"I don't understand."

"You will in time. For now, there are more immediate concerns. As I mentioned, when a critical mass realizes that we are all brothers and sisters, then the world will be transformed, and we shall receive immortality. The pendulum, however, swings both ways. There are times when the negative consciousness of humanity becomes so widespread that darkness affects every element of the physical world. When the desire to hate outweighs love, and war trumps peace, the Creator affects a general cleansing. The last time this happened on a global scale was during the time of Noah. We believe another supernal event may be coming soon, perhaps on the winter solstice—"

"—December 21, the day of the dead." Pankaj Patel swallowed hard. "My wife, Manisha, she is a necromancer—one who communicates with anguished souls. Manisha has told me things, describing warnings from the spiritual world about the End of Days."

"But you refused to listen. You harbored doubts."

"Regrettably, I am a man of ego."

"It is never too late to change."

"I shall try to change. As for the Nine . . . replacing my teacher, I regret I am not yet worthy of this honor."

The Elder nods. "I remember the day I first met your mentor. It was in Communist China shortly after he was arrested and tortured by the dark forces he would spend a lifetime attempting to shed his light of knowledge upon. He was more than a brother to me, he was a trusted friend. And like the rest of us, he made mistakes.

"There is a saying: 'May you live in interesting times.' Some interpret this as a blessing, others a curse. I prefer to see it as an opportunity for great change. Noah lived in interesting times—a time of great evil and selfishness where man's darkest, most barbaric traits reigned supreme. The Creator made a covenant between Himself and this righteous man, only then did He wipe the wicked from the face of the Earth. Abraham, too, made his covenant, and Sodom and Gomorrah were destroyed. The same with Moses. In each generation of evil, a righteous man has been selected and tested, each challenge intended to strengthen the chosen one's sense of spirituality and certainty, each covenant made between man and the Creator leading to the destruction of evil. Thousands of years have passed, the cycle repeated many times, culminating in this, the End of Days. If there is to be salvation this time around, it can only be found within the Light. Fail, and darkness shall rule the earth, leading to global annihilation and the death of more than six billion people."

The seniormost member of the Nine stood, the professor following suit.

"Pankaj Patel, do you swear upon your soul and all that is holy to safeguard the body of knowledge about to be entrusted in your care?"

"Upon my soul, I swear it."

"Do you swear to uphold and honor the secrecy and sanctity of the Society of the Nine Unknown Men under penalty of torture and death?"

"Upon my soul, I swear it."

"Do you swear to add to the body of knowledge for which you have been sworn to safeguard, and in due time recruit a qualified successor?"

"Upon my soul, I swear it."

The Asian monk stepped forward and placed his keratin-flesh palms upon Pankaj Patel's head. "I need to establish a connection with your biorhythm, linking your DNA with ours. In this way, you will know your brothers when your paths cross, and the dark forces can never penetrate our inner circle. You may feel a slight electrical discharge."

The professor jumped as a surge of energy raced down his spinal cord, then distally throughout his anatomy by way of his nerve endings.

"Pankaj Patel, I welcome you into the Society of the Nine Unknown Men. From this day until your last, you shall be known among your brethren only as Number Seven. May the Creator sanctify your acceptance with His blessings and keep you and yours in the Light."

"Thank you, Elder, for this honor. What is my first assignment?"

Gelut Panim, blood descendant of Emperor Asoka, student of Rabbi Shimon bar Yohai, turned to face the swiftly moving waters of the Hudson River. "I need you to be my eyes and ears in Manhattan. I need your wife to be our barometer in the supernal realm. There is a storm approaching, my friend. The Angel of Death has been summoned—

—and for reasons that remain unknown, it has targeted your family."

"Since I entered politics, I have chiefly had men's views confided to me privately. Some of the biggest men in the U.S., in the field of commerce and manufacturing, are afraid of somebody, are afraid of something. They know that there is a power somewhere so organized, so subtle, so watchful, so interlocked, so complete, and so pervasive that they had better not speak above their breath when they speak in condemnation of it."

—President Woodrow Wilson

"I never would have agreed to the formulation of the Central Intelligence Agency back in '47 if I had known it would become the American Gestapo."

—President Harry S. Truman

OCTOBER

VA MEDICAL CENTER

MANHATTAN, NEW YORK

4:22 *P.M.*

"Yes, he's suffering from stress-related paranoia, but this is way beyond the usual post-traumatic disorder. The inner rage, the feelings of emptiness, most of all his unstable self-image . . . this is textbook borderline personality disorder."

Dr. Mindy Murphy closed Patrick Shepherd's folder, handing it to Dr. Nelson. "Bottom line, Leigh, this one's dangerous. Pass him on to Bellevue and let them deal with it."

"Pass him on? Mindy, this man sacrificed everything . . . his family, his career—now you want to lock him up in a padded cell?"

"It doesn't have to be like that. There are new approaches for BPD. Dialectical behavior therapy has shown real promise."

"Good! You can treat him right here."

"Leigh—"

"Mindy, you're the best psychologist in the system."

"I'm the only psychologist in the system. Two of my associates quit last spring, a third took early retirement. My workload went from seventy-five patients to three hundred. I'm no longer practicing psychology, Leigh, these monthly meetings are nothing more than triage. Face facts, the system's underfunded and overwhelmed, and sometimes soldiers fall through the cracks. You can't save everybody."

"This one needs to be saved."

"Why?"

"Because he does."

Dr. Murphy sighed. "Okay. You want to play Florence Nightingale, go for it, but don't say I didn't warn you."

"Just tell me what to do."

"For starters, don't try to change him right now. Accept him as he is but don't coddle. If he tries to hurt himself again or contemplates suicide, let him know he's inconveniencing you, even jeopardizing your career. Have you measured him for a prosthetic arm?"

"Last week."

"Was he receptive?"

"No, but I bribed him with a DVD copy of *Bull Durham.* I'm being told there's a six-month backlog on prosthetics."

"It used to be worse. But getting him a new arm is potentially a good thing, it'll give him something to focus his mind on. If nothing else, it could help alter his self-image. The biggest challenge you're facing right now is finding a way to reignite his pilot light, to get him to desire something, to set a goal, to feel useful again. He's in decent physical shape, why don't you put him to work in the wards. Helping others is a great way to get someone to feel needed again."

"Good idea." Leigh Nelson scribbled herself a note. "What about his family?"

"What about yours? Shouldn't you be home with the husband and kids?"

"Mindy, his wife deserted him, and he has a daughter he hasn't seen in eleven years. Should I facilitate a reunion or not?"

"Go slow. There are a lot of anger issues there, feelings of abandonment. What makes you so sure you can even find them?"

"The two of them grew up in Brooklyn, they were childhood sweethearts.

She might still have relatives living over there."

Dr. Murphy shook her head. "You're married with kids, you work sixty-hour weeks, but somehow you have time to search for one of your patient's estranged wife's family who may or may not live somewhere in Brooklyn. Leigh, what are you doing?"

"I'm trying to save a lost soul, Mindy. Isn't that worth a little time out of my day? A little sacrifice?"

"Denial, Anger, Bargaining, Depression, and Acceptance: The five stages of grief."

"You think Shep's experiencing them?"

The former gymnast stood, tossing Patrick Shepherd's file onto a stack of fifty. "No, Leigh, I was talking about you."

FREDERICK, MARYLAND
4:59 P.M.

Andrew Bradosky turned north on US 15, the four-cylinder car lacking the power of his new Mustang. He had debated all morning about whether to waste another fifty dollars on a rental car. In the end, caution had outweighed frugality. Besides, what was fifty dollars when a big payday was coming down the pike.

Tonight's meeting would be the third in the last five weeks with the black ops officer. Andrew suspected Ernest Lozano was either CIA or DIA, maybe even Homeland Security. In the end, it didn't matter, as long as the deposits kept arriving every two weeks into his offshore account.

The Hampton Inn was on the right. Andrew turned into the driveway and parked, then headed for the lobby, the Baltimore Orioles baseball cap tucked low over his eyes. He kept his head down as he moved past the registration desk and bar, then took the elevator up to the third floor.

Andrew Bradosky was thirty-six when he began working at Fort Detrick following a two-year stint at Battelle's facility in Ohio. To his fellow employees he was a fun-loving guy, always good for a beer after work or the occasional male-bonding weekend in Vegas. His supervisors generally liked him, until time and activity revealed his work ethic to be less than stellar. To his closest friends, Andy remained the consummate bullshit artist, which was why they loved him. While he could charm the underpants off the hot chick with the frosty attitude, most of his peers agreed the terminal bachelor lacked the substance to progress from one-night stands to more meaningful relationships. In fact, Andrew preferred things that way. In small doses, women were sport; the trouble began when they started to nest, something that was clearly not in his best interest.

What Andrew Bradosky *was* really interested in was a better-paying job. Perhaps that was the reason he had maneuvered himself into the life of Mary Klipot. Had he met her in a bar or at a social gathering, she would never have progressed beyond small talk, but at Fort Detrick, the microbiologist had an intellectual flare that made her pseudoattractive. Andrew dubbed this the "Tony Soprano effect." In real life, a fat, balding middle-aged man like the HBO character could never get the kind of pussy he got on the show, but being a mob boss gave him a certain flare that attracted beautiful, albeit problematic women.

Mary Klipot's intellect and job title empowered her in the same manner. The fact that she was a loner working in-charge of a BSL-4 lab only made getting to know her that much more enticing.

The first day he had introduced himself at lunch was beyond awkward.

During the second lunch encounter, she had walked away.

For the next two weeks, she had avoided him by eating lunch in her lab. Ever the opportunist, Andrew learned that Mary worked out in the campus gym every other morning. Playing it cool, he began showing up to pump iron, never acknowledging her presence until the third workout. A few hellos led to small talk, enough to set the introverted redhead at ease.

His diligence paid off a month later when Mary selected him as a lab tech for Project Scythe.

Andrew stepped off the hotel elevator, following arrowed signs to room 310. He knocked twice, then once, then twice more.

The door swung open, Ernest Lozano beckoning him in. He pointed to the bed, reserving the desk chair for himself. "So how are things at work?"

"We're progressing nicely."

"I didn't summon you for a weather report. When will the agent be weaponized?"

"You said spring. We're on target. March or April, for sure."

Andrew never saw the stiletto until its point was inches away from his right eye. The lanky agent's powerful upper body leaned over him, pushing him back on the mattress, his face so close, the lab technician could smell a whiff of Alfredo sauce mixed in with the Aqua Velva aftershave. "We've paid you fifty thousand. For fifty grand I want assurances, not best guesses."

Andrew forced a nervous grin. "Easy big fella. We're on track, at least we were until Mary found out she was pregnant. Things got sort of complicated, but we're working it out, I swear."

Lozano backed off the bed. "Is it yours?"

Andrew sat up, wiping beads of sweat from his forehead. "That's where it gets complicated. Mary's a strict Catholic girl. Last April, we went to Cancún together and sort of got toasted doing shots of tequila."

"So you busted her."

"Yeah, but she doesn't remember anything about it, and all things considered, I figured it'd be best if I left it that way. But now that she's pregnant . . ."

"You told her?"

"I tried. She's convinced it was an immaculate conception. You gotta understand what I'm dealing with here. When it comes to biowarfare and genetically altering viruses, Mary Klipot's as brilliant as they come. Stuff like sex and emotional bonding and normal-relationship crap, she's like a functional retard. I mean, there's some seriously dark shit floating around in this chick's head . . . spooky shit. So hell yeah, if she wants to believe she's carrying Jesus's kid, who am I to tell her otherwise. As long as you keep paying me, I'll play father Joseph to her mother Mary, but the moment Scythe is ready for deployment, I'm outta there."

Lozano crossed the room, returning to the desk chair. "When is she due?"

"Third week in January, though she's convinced the doctor's lying. She swears baby Jesus will be born on Christmas Day."

"You need to stabilize the situation."

"How?"

"Propose marriage. Move in together. Tell her you want to be the baby's surrogate father. Don't do anything to rock the boat. Meanwhile, tie in the Scythe deadline with the baby's birth. Push her to finish as soon as possible, so she can take a long maternity leave."

"That could backfire. Scythe's supervisor, Lydia Gagnon, is already talking about bringing in another microbiologist or two. Mary agreed we need to keep things as proprietary as possible, especially after all those sanctions."

"What sanctions?"

"Don't bullshit a bullshitter, friend. You and your CIA pals started offing microbiologists at a steady clip right after 9/11. Six Israeli dudes shot down on two different airliners, that cell biologist at the University of Miami . . . the Soviet defector who had his head smashed in with a hammer. Mary knew Set Van Nguyen, and she went to grad school with Tanya Holzmayer. Tanya was shot dead when she answered the door for a pizza-delivery boy. Guyang Huang was shot in the head while jogging in a park in Foster City. Nineteen dead scientists in the first four months following 9/11, another seventy-one while Bush and Cheney were still in office. Bodies found in suitcases, two in freezers, a half dozen in car accidents. No arrests, everything kept out of the news and swept conveniently under the carpet. All of these eggheads had two things in common: Each worked for facilities that performed black ops biomedical research for the CIA, and they were all considered frontline scientists who would be selected to stop a global pandemic, should one ever break out."

Andrew got up off the bed, his feeble act of defiance building into a rehearsed speech. "You wanna use Scythe to wipe out a bunch of towel-heads, go for it, but here are my terms: First, forget the hundred grand, that was a down payment. I want two million deposited into my Credit Suisse account, fifty grand a week from now through March, with the balance due the week we turn over Scythe. Second, as insurance against pizza-delivery boys carrying guns and hammers, I've instructed attorneys in several different states to deliver the details of Scythe and our little arrangement to certain members of the foreign press in the event something should happen to me."

Lozano's expression caused Andrew's cockiness to crawl back up his sphincter. "Deliver Scythe by March 1, and you might just live to spend your money. Fail, and you'll join the Virgin Mary and Baby Jesus in an unmarked grave."

VA MEDICAL CENTER
MANHATTAN, NEW YORK
11:22 P.M.

***The East River** glistens olive green as they head south across the bridge for Brooklyn.*

"Your fastball had nice movement, your breaking ball froze their right-handed batters. But the college ranks and minor leagues are full of losing pitchers with great stuff. We need to start working on your mental game."

Coach Segal is driving the van, one of two school vehicles transporting Roosevelt High's varsity baseball team home from a 3-to-1 playoff victory in the district quarterfinals. Patrick Shepherd is up front in the passenger seat. The sixteen-year-old junior is today's winning pitcher. Squeezed in between Patrick and his baseball coach is Morrie Segal's daughter. Shep's classmate and best friend is resting her head against his left shoulder, her eyes closed—

—her right hand snaking its way playfully beneath the baseball glove and warm-up jacket resting on his left thigh, her touch sending jolts of electricity through his groin.

". . . your front shoulder and head were locked onto your target throughout your stride, and you kept your shoulder and hips closed, ready to uncoil, just like we worked on. You had perfect symmetry today, Patrick, but form will only you carry you so far. Sandy Koufax said many pitchers master the physical aspects of baseball, but most never become big winners because they fail to develop the mental part of their game. Sure, you thrive in the pressure situations—I love that

about you. But games can be won and lost with two outs and no men on base. You gave up a meaningless home run to a backup catcher hitting .225 because you didn't feel challenged. Mentally, you had already ended the inning. As a result, you rushed a curveball that never broke instead of delivering it smooth and easy."

Her bare right thigh is pressed against the back of his left hand. Her tan flesh is silky smooth. He attempts to inch his hand beneath her leg, only to jam his finger painfully against the buckle of her seat belt.

She closes her eyes, stifling a giggle.

"Every pitch counts. You need to play mind games. Challenge yourself so that you attack every hitter. Steve Carlton would visualize the lanes of each pitch before he threw, as if the batter weren't even there. Focus on the catcher's sign. Take a moment to visualize the successful flight of the pitch. Inhale slowly as you visualize, smell the fear in the batter's sweat."

Strands of the girl's long blond hair lay on his left shoulder. He inhales the scent of jasmine shampoo, her pheromones an aphrodisiac to his senses.

"You make a bad pitch . . . let it go. Walk off the mound. Get your anger under control by breathing. Remember, breathing is affected by what and how you think. Clear the negativity. Visualize success. Retake the mound only when you've regained control of your emotions."

The tips of her fingers inch closer to his groin, the girl now in full control of his body. What had begun as an innocent game of chicken has turned into something far more exciting, and he's unsure of what to do next. Sitting upright and at attention, he's afraid to breathe as she casually inches her hand closer to his genitals, the fabric of his uniform stretching . . .

"—ice the shoulder as soon as you get home, the last thing we need is swelling."

Her fingernails work the inside part of his plate—teasing him before retreating high and outside. Completely under her spell, he exhales and closes his eyes as she moves in again.

"I know pitching again on two days' rest is asking a lot, but if we can get you on the mound again Friday, then you've got a week to rest before the finals. Are you sore? How do you feel?"

"Baby, I feel great."

Patrick Shepherd sat up in bed. Eyes wide. Heart pounding. Tee shirt matted to his back and neck in perspiration. Anxiety builds. He searched the darkness. Focused on the glowing red EXIT sign. A temporary lifeline.

Reaching to the bedside table on his right, he searched inside the top drawer for the envelope. Inside was the partially burnt Polaroid. Taken before his first deployment, the picture was shot inside Fenway Park just after he had been called up from the minors. In the photo, his wife was holding their two-year-old daughter while Patrick, wearing his Red Sox baseball uniform, was leaning in from behind, embracing them in his arms.

A sudden rush of phantom pain. Shep squeezed his eyes shut, the crushing, bone-stabbing sensations causing every muscle to quiver.

Breathe! Regain control of your emotions.

He forced slow, deliberate breaths. The agony tapered off to a more tolerable level.

He sank back against the pillow. Attempted to sift through the shards of memory that always seemed to accompany the bout . . . the memory of the accident, the last day of his final deployment.

Gray sky. Warm metal in his left hand. A blinding light. The skull-rattling blast obliterating all sound, the sensation of his liquefying skin submerging him in blackness.

Shep opened his eyes. He shook loose the horror. Returned his attention to the Polaroid.

The explosive had been doubly cruel; not only had it robbed him of his left arm while gouging a hole in his memory, it had stolen the lasting images on the photo, singeing his wife's head. Try as he might, Patrick could not lock down her face, his mind's eye catching only fleeting, frustrating glimpses.

For wounded vets, the psychological scars associated with losing a limb run deep, often leading to bouts of depression. For Patrick Shepherd, the burden is nothing compared to the empty feeling of being separated from a wife and child whose presence he registers in his heart but whose faces he can no longer remember. The loss remains a constant assault on Shep's identity.

In waking hours, it could be overwhelming; during sleep, it fostered intense nightmares.

His doctors in Germany had given him a choice as to which stateside VA hospital he wished to be sent, and the choice was simple. From that day forth, he had imagined himself lying in bed, or perhaps engaging in therapy when his soul mate and daughter—now a teen—entered to reclaim him.

Through the partitioned curtain surrounding his bed, he listened to the snores and catcalls of his fellow war vets, his eyes glazing over with tears as he locked his gaze upon the glowing red EXIT sign, feeling as alone as a human being can possibly feel.

"The force of a correction is equal and opposite
to the deception that preceded."
—"The Daily Reckoning"

NOVEMBER

TEPITO FLEA MARKET

TEPITO, MEXICO

5:39 P.M.

Situated on the outskirts of Mexico City's historic downtown, the town of Tepito was located in the borough of Delegaciôn Cuauhtéemoc, an area composed of three neighborhoods—Tepito, Lagunilla, and Peralvillo. Together, they made up one of the largest flea markets in all Latin America. Lagunilla and Peralvillo are bohemian markets, selling everything from tee shirts to antiques and jewelry. Tepito, also known as the "Barrio Bravo" (tough neighborhood), was strictly black market.

Tepito's history dated back to the Aztec Empire, which established the area as part of its slave trade. When the people were forbidden to sell their goods in Tlatelolco, the Tepiteños set up their own market—a place where thieves could move their stolen goods.

Today, the neighborhood was ravaged with crime, policed by more than fifty gangs, and ruled by drug cartels. Enter the market, and you would find fake designer clothes, stolen cameras, and stall after stall of pirated CDs and DVDs. Used electronics were sold as new, cookware and other goods bore unbeatable prices, having "fallen off the truck." Lose your passport, and you could probably buy it back in Tepito for $5,000. Need phony documents or a gun while visiting Mexico? Tepito was your destination.

The people of Tepito were very religious. There were altars erected on almost every corner, dominated by the presence of *La Santa Muerte*—Saint Death.

No one knew for certain how this female Grim Reaper came into being. Historians traced her origins to Mictlantecuhtli, an Aztec death goddess whose skeleton was said to belong to the Virgin Mary. Condemned by the Roman Catholic Church, the cult of *Sante Muerte* remained underground until 2001. From one altar in Tepito rose twenty, the "skinny girl's" growing congregation demonstrating that the power of prayer was not limited to those who chose to live life without sin.

To gangbangers and members of Mexico's drug cartels, "*Santisima Muerte*" was a spiritual figure whose presence provided psychological strength. Prisoners prayed to her for protection against other inmates. Mexico's poor, sick, and oppressed sought the salvation she offered, free of judgment.

Others prayed to the female Grim Reaper to strike their enemies dead.

The taxi motored north along the Avenue Paseo de la Reforma, the driver glancing every few minutes at his female passenger in the rearview mirror. *Gold cross, no other jewels. Plain purse, no designer wear. Still, an American, and pregnant at that. The wedding ring is probably in the purse.*

He flashed a false smile. "*Senorita*, you have been to the Mercado de Tepito before?"

The woman continued staring out the window, absentmindedly palpating her swollen abdomen with her right palm, her left hand twirling a strand of silky red hair.

"I love you Mary. I want to be there when you have our baby. I want us to be a family. Marry me, Mary, and make me the happiest guy in the world."

If Andrew Bradosky's proposal was a blessing from heaven, then the two-carat engagement ring was the icing on the cake. Her head in the clouds, all Mary could think about was making arrangements for a December wedding.

Andrew had other plans. "Mary, darling, a December wedding . . . it's too soon. We'd have to rush out invitations, secure a banquet room, there are a million details. June is better for a wedding. The baby will be born, you'll have your figure back. Plus, I can hire a wedding planner while you focus on finishing Scythe."

Andrew's sentimentality touched her to the core. And he was right. How could she possibly prepare for the best day of her life while her mind remained absorbed in untangling the genetic secrets of the Black Death? And so she threw herself into her work, intent on finishing the weaponization of Scythe a full week before Baby Jesus's birth. After the blessed event, she'd take a six-month leave of absence, giving her time to bond with her child and plan out her wedding. She could not recall being so happy, feeling so alive.

Three weeks later, she began having doubts.

The cost of her diamond ring was beyond Andrew's means, but she had dismissed it as an emotional buy. His new suits and plasma television were justified by his decision to sell his condo and move into Mary's farmhouse, a recent investment in a down real-estate market. Then there was his new Mustang convertible. He had shrugged the purchase off a month earlier, explaining that his lease was expiring and he had gotten a good deal. When she decided to contact the salesman, another red flag popped up—he had paid cash for the new car.

Where was the sudden influx of money coming from? Could she risk allowing Baby Jesus to be raised under the same roof with a man she wasn't sure she could trust?

Mary had met Rosario Martinez at the gym, the two women sometimes working out together. Her curiosity was piqued by the female Grim Reaper tattoos that covered the Mexican woman's arms and back, one of which bore a six-inch scar across her left scapula.

"Saint Death watches over me. When I was younger, I was arrested for selling cocaine. The judge sentenced me to seven years' hard time at Almoloya de Juárez, a maximum-security prison. My cellmate had painted the skinny girl on our cell wall. Many of the inmates had *Santa Muerte* tattoos. My cellmate told me the skinny girl watched over her flock, especially the women. One day, two gangbangers jumped me in the shower. One hit me in the throat, another stabbed me in the back, the blade slicing through my tattoo of *Santa Muerte*. I woke up in the hospital, having been in a coma for two weeks. My doctor said it was a miracle I survived. But I knew Saint Death had saved me, you see, I saw her in my dreams. She was standing over me, wearing a red satin dress, her hair as dark as midnight. I promised that if she saved me I would make something of myself when I left prison. And I did. I owe my life to her."

"I'd rather be dead than worship Satan."

"This is not Satan worship. I go to the same church and believe in the same God as you. But all of us are going to die, and I want my death to be sweet, not bitter. I've done things in my life I'm not proud of. Saint Death forgave my sins, now she takes care of me. One day you may need protection. One day you may wonder about your man's intentions. There is a place in Mexico called Tepito. On the first of each month is a holy day, dedicated to the 'skinny girl.' Thousands of people go there to ask her blessings for the coming month. Go there, ask for her help. If you wish for money, she will grant you prosperity. If you are in danger, she will protect you from those who wish you harm. If you fear your man will leave you, pray to her, and she will punish him should his eye ever wander."

It was dark by the time the taxi exited the Avenue Paseo de la Reforma thoroughfare onto Calle Matamorosa, one of the local roads into Tepito. The traffic was congested. The crowd spilled over the sidewalk into the streets. A local startled her by banging on her window. He held up a baggy of marijuana. Despite her objections, he continued to barter until the taxi moved on.

The driver stared at her in the rearview mirror. "Tepito can be a dangerous place, *Señorita*. Tell me what you seek, and I can take you where you need to go."

She unfolded the paper given to her by her Mexican acquaintance, then read the address. "Twelve Alfareria Street."

The driver's eyes widened. "You are here to see the skinny girl?" He crossed himself, then surged through an opening in the traffic, vanquishing all prior thoughts.

He drove another half mile before pulling over. "The crowd is too large, *Señorita*, they've shut down Alfareria Street. You'll have to walk from here."

She paid the driver, then grabbed her tote bag and stepped out into a swarm of brown people, all moving toward one destination. Many locals were carrying Saint Death dolls, the four-foot skeleton figurines dolled up in long wigs and color-coded robes—white for protection, red for passion, gold for money, and black for bringing harm to another.

Somewhere up ahead, a mariachi band played.

Number 12 Alfareria Street was a brown brick apartment building with white trim, located across the street from a run-down laundromat. A small storefront featured a six-foot window display that had been converted into a shrine. Situated behind the glass was a life-size figure of *La Santa Muerte*—Saint Death, dressed in a bridal gown.

Mary followed a procession line, pushing in closer. The path leading to the shrine was adorned with fresh flowers, the ground made luminous from the flames of several hundred burning candles. Worshippers bearing color-coded candles knelt before the shrine, then rubbed themselves with the wax offerings before lighting them. Everyone brought gifts. Cigarettes and alcohol. Candies and apples. One of the owners of the shop placed the lit end of a cigar into his mouth and blew clouds of smoke out the other end at the doll, filling the shrine.

Mary moved closer, sensing the crowd staring at her. She assumed it was because she was an American. Then she heard the whispers, catching a few recognizable words in Spanish.

Pelirrojo? Rojo is red . . . they're staring at my hair.

She waited for a Hispanic family to finish their prayer, then knelt before the window, looking up at the female Grim Reaper manikin. The doll's long wavy hair was scarlet, the color matching her own.

From her bag she removed a stack of hundred-dollar bills, then turned to a short heavyset Mexican woman, her dark hair marked by a white "skunk's tail." "I have a request for the Saint. How do I go about asking it?"

"Come with me, *Señorita*." Enriqueto Romero led Mary through her store to a supply room out back. "You are American, yes?"

"Yes."

"Then you have traveled a long way to be here on this holiest of holies. The color of your hair is shared this evening by the skinny one, this is no coincidence. You are about to embark on a very special journey, am I right?"

"The man in my life, I need to know if he really desires me. I've been abandoned before—"

"—and you do not wish to be abandoned again. The most Holy Death can help in these regards. For this you must purchase a statue. The statue comes with a string knotted seven times. Cover the string with your beloved's semen, place it around the skinny girl's neck within its notch, then recite the ejaculatory prayer for nine consecutive nights. The Saint will make clear the intentions in your man's heart."

"And if he is lying to me?

"Then the Saint will be waiting for him . . . in Hell."

176 JOHNSON STREET
BROOKLYN, NEW YORK
8:12 P.M.

Built in 1929, the eight-story, sixty-four-thousand-square-foot building had originally been a toy factory, the company's big seller being the first electric football game. Today, the Toy Factory Lofts featured eleven-foot ceilings and wall-to-wall eight-foot-high windows.

Doug Nelson begrudgingly followed his wife and the building manager down the fourth-floor hallway to the last door on the right. "Kind of unusual for a landlord to hold an apartment open this long for a soldier."

Joe Eddy Brown, known to the occupants of the Lofts as "the Brown-Man," fumbled to find the right key. "Most of these apartments are condos. Mr. Shepherd bought his outright back in 2001."

"What about his ex-wife? She ever come around?"

Brown paused before inserting the pass key in the lock, running a weathered palm over his cleanly shaved head. "Haven't seen the missus around here for a while. Damn shame, she was easy on the eyes. Oh, well, you know what I always say, better to have loved and lost than never loved at all."

"Actually, Tennyson said that," Doug said. "And the man spent most of his life penniless and ended up in a sanitarium."

Leigh shot her husband a chastising look.

The loft was small, composed of a six-hundred-square-foot living area, a bathroom, and several large storage closets. A modern kitchen faced a view of the Williamsburg Bridge. The queen-size bed was located in one corner of the room, the mattress on the floor, the blankets and sheets unmade. There were no photos or artwork on the walls, no decorations of any kind . . . as if the owner occupied the dwelling but never called it home.

"I know what you're thinking—there's not much to look at. Mr. Shepherd, he pretty much spent his days walking the streets. He'd come home late at night, oftentimes drunk. Found him on the stoop passed out on more than one occasion. We don't tolerate that sort of behavior in Brown Town, but him being a war hero, I sort of let it slide. If he's intending to move back—"

"Mr. Shepherd has no memory that this place even exists," Leigh clarifies. "I'm only here because I found the address in his military file."

"And I'm only here because my wife dragged me here on a Saturday night." Doug met his wife's glare with his own.

"Ten minutes, Doug. Stop being so selfish."

"I'm being selfish?" He searches a magazine rack. Grabs an old issue of *Sports Illustrated.* "Let me know when you're ready to leave. I'll be in the bathroom."

"I'm sorry, Mr. Brown. Where's that closet you mentioned on the phone?"

Leigh followed the building manager to a mirrored wall. Brown tapped it with two fingers, releasing the magnetic clasp. He pulled open the door, revealing a walk-in storage area.

There were a few collared shirts on hangers and a navy suit. The rest of Patrick Shepherd's wardrobe was set in piles of dirty laundry. A whiff of alcohol-soaked denim, marinated with body odor before being aged, gravitated up from the polished wood floor.

The stacks of cardboard boxes appeared more enticing.

"Mr. Brown, I need a few minutes to go through my patient's belongings."

"Just pull the door closed when you leave. I'll come back later to lock the dead bolt."

"Thank you." She waited until he left before rummaging through the first few boxes. Baseball gear. Grass-stained cleats and jerseys. Bundles of never-worn tee shirts with the words, BOSTON STRANGLER printed across the chest. She sorted through three more boxes, then found the foot locker buried beneath a pile of jackets.

Going down on one knee, she popped open the steel clasps and raised the lid.

Aged air, musky and filled with discarded memories escaped from the long-sealed container. She removed a woman's hooded pink Rutgers University sweatshirt, then two toddler outfits, one a Yankees uniform, the larger one a Red Sox shirt. The three college textbooks, all dealing with European literature, were marked up and highlighted, the curvy penmanship clearly a woman's handwriting. She searched in vain for a name, then saw the framed photo, the picture taken outside a college dormitory.

The girl was barely twenty, blond, and model-gorgeous, her long hair wavy and bowed. Her boyfriend was hugging her from behind. Boyishly handsome, he wore a cocky smile. Leigh stared at the image of Patrick Shepherd in his youth. *Look at you. You had the world by the balls, and you walked away . . . just so you could crawl through hell.*

"Leigh? You need to see this."

Picture in hand, she joined her husband in the bathroom.

Doug pointed to the medicine cabinet. "I'd say your boy has some serious demons."

The handwritten note, yellowed with age, is taped to the mirror.

Shep:

The voice telling you to kill yourself is Satan. Suicide is a mortal sin. For your family's sake, suck it up and accept your punishment. Live today for them.

He's worse than I thought . . . She opened the medicine cabinet, its narrow shelves filled with expired prescriptions. "Amoxapine. Thorazine, Haldol. Trifluoperazine, Triavil, Moban. There's enough antidepressants and tranquilizers here to medicate the entire building."

"Looks like he was suicidal long before he lost his arm. Bet you dinner he keeps a loaded gun beneath his pillow." Doug left the bathroom and walked over to the bed, tossing the goose-down pillows aside. "What's this?"

Leigh joins him. "Did you find a weapon?"

"Not exactly." He held up the leather-bound book.

Dante's Inferno.

Doug headed west on 34th Street, guiding the Range Rover into one of the three lanes heading to New Jersey via the Lincoln Tunnel. "You want to know why I'm mad? It's because you spend more time with your soldier pal than you do with your own family."

"That's not true."

"Why him, Leigh? What's so special about this vet? Is it because he played baseball?"

"No."

"Then what?"

"I don't know." She stared out the window, consciously trying not to breathe the carbon-monoxide fumes as their vehicle raced through the brightly lit tunnel. "At first, I was just afraid that he'd try to kill himself again. Then, when I saw how much he missed his wife, I was afraid he'd try to get back together with her too soon."

"Thomas Stansbury again? Leigh, we've been through this a million times.

He had a night terror. It was out of your control."

"He strangled his wife, then he killed himself. I'm the one who released him."

Night reappeared, the tunnel delivering them into New Jersey. Doug remained silent, contemplating a course of action. "Invite him over for dinner."

"Who? Shep? What for?"

"At some point you're going to have to discharge him, right? Why not ease his transition with a little normalcy? We'll make him a home-cooked meal, he can play with the kids. Maybe you can even invite your sister over."

"My sister?"

"Why not? I'm not suggesting you make this a blind date, I just think it would be good for him. Plus, you know how lonely Bridgett has been lately."

"She's going through a rough divorce."

"Exactly my point."

"No, it would be too weird. Plus, Shep might be offended. He's still head over heels in love with his wife."

"So just call it dinner and see what happens."

"Okay. I can do that."

"Now answer my original question: Why Shepherd?"

Leaning over, the brunette laid her head on her husband's shoulder. "Have you ever met someone who just seemed so needy, so lost, yet at the same time had a personality you couldn't help but gravitate to. This will sound strange, but being around Shep, it's like hanging around with an old soul who's lost on an important journey, and it's my job to help him as much as I can before he moves on. Does that make any sense?"

"Old soul or new, guys like Shepherd who fought in combat have a tendency to want to self-destruct. I know you're his doctor, Leigh, but some people just don't want to be saved."

"In the councils of government, we must guard against the acquisition of unwarranted influence, whether sought or unsought, by the military-industrial complex. The potential for the disastrous rise of misplaced power exists and will persist."

—President Dwight D. Eisenhower

DECEMBER

VA HOSPITAL

NEW YORK CITY

3:37 P.M.

The funny thing was, he had never liked running. Not in high school when Coach Segal had required it of all his pitchers. Not at Rutgers, when his fiancée was in training for the field hockey team and insisted he join her on those four-mile jaunts around the university golf course. And certainly not when he pitched in the minors.

So why did he like it now?

The Beatles' "Help!" blasted over the classic rock radio station as the treadmill's built-in odometer approached the two-mile mark.

He liked it because the challenge made him feel alive again, and any feeling that was different from his usual doom and gloom was a good thing. He liked it because it made him feel less self-destructive, something Dr. Nelson attributed to 'happy endorphins' being released in his brain. Most of all, Patrick Shepherd liked to run because running gave his thoughts greater clarity, helping him to remember things. Like that his fiancée forced him to run the golf course back at Rutgers. Like that she, too, was a scholarship athlete. Like . . .

The song changed. He has not heard the tune in more than a decade, its lyrics prying open yet another sealed memory, the words, sung by the late Jim

Morrison, tearing open the fissure in his heart: *"Before you slip into unconsciousness, I'd like to have another kiss. Another flashing chance at bliss, another kiss, another kiss . . ."*

The one-arm runner stumbled, his right hand briefly grabbing the support bar before his legs rolled out from under him, and the treadmill spit him out onto the rubber matting.

"The days are bright and filled with pain, enclose me in your gentle rain. The time you ran was too insane, we'll meet again, we'll meet again . . ."

Patrick rolled over. Nose bleeding, feeling woozy, he leaned against the wall to listen to the rest of *The Doors'* song . . . the painted cinder block identical to the walls in his fiancée's old college dorm room.

***He's sitting on** the floor, leaning back against the dormitory wall. " The Crystal Ship" is playing on the tape deck, the blond coed in the muddied field hockey uniform staring at him from the bed, her hazel green eyes tinged blue with tears.*

"Are you sure?"

"Don't ask me again. If you ask me again, Patrick, I'm going to shove the dipstick up your ass, then we'll see if you're pregnant."

"Okay, okay. Let's not panic just yet. How far along are you?"

"I don't know. Maybe a month or two."

"Shouldn't you know?"

"Shouldn't you, Mister 'We Should Be Safe, You Won't Be Ovulating for Another Eight Days.' *God, my father's going to kill me when he finds out."*

"Here's an idea—let's not tell him. We take you to the clinic, they do whatever they do, and we get you on the pill."

She throws one of her field hockey shin pads at his face, hitting him squarely in the nose, drawing blood. "First, abortions cost money, something neither one of us has right now. Second, there's a baby growing in my belly . . . our baby. I thought maybe you'd react differently. I thought I was your soul mate?"

"You are. But what about our plans? You wanted to go to grad school, and I still have two more years of eligibility to improve my stock before the amateur draft."

"I can still finish school."

"They'll rescind your scholarship."

"I'll redshirt a year."

"Okay, sure. But seriously . . . are you really ready to have a kid?"

"I don't know." She covers her face, weeping uncontrollably.

Patrick's dumbfounded, he has never seen her like this. Reaching for her wrist, he guides her down on the tile floor next to him, holding her in his lap as if she were a little girl.

"The Crystal Ship" ends, mockingly yielding to the opening lyrics of "You Can't Always Get What You Want". And in that singular moment of clarity everything changes for Patrick Ryan Shepherd, the solution suddenly clear, as if his adolescence has just passed the baton of youth into adulthood.

"Okay, here's another option: You stay in school while I enter next month's draft. I won't hire an agent, so I'll still maintain my amateur status. If I'm drafted, we use the signing bonus to pay for diapers. If I'm not, I finish my junior year and work nights to pay for the kid's expenses. How's that sound?"

She stops crying, her face streaked with tears and sweat from the afternoon practice. "You'd really do that?"

"On one condition . . . marry me."

"**. . . that was** *The Doors*. This is your station for Classic Rock, the time now is 3:45. Coming up after the break we'll be playing the *Beach Boys*—"

The radio is turned off. "Shep, are you okay?"

Patrick glanced up at Dr. Nelson, his nostrils streaked with blood. "I never liked running."

"I told you not to run so fast, your gait is off-balance. You'll feel a lot more in control when your prosthetic arm arrives."

"What year will that be?"

"Honestly, I wish I knew. Are you still okay about tonight?"

"You sure this isn't a blind date?"

"It's just dinner. But you'll like my sister, she's a firecracker." Leigh opened the leather briefcase hanging from her shoulder strap. "Shep, I have something that belongs to you. I'm going to show it to you because I think it may help you to remember your wife's name, only I don't want you to get upset. Do you think you can handle it?"

"What is it?"

"You tell me." She removes the leather-bound book from her brief.

Shep jolts upright, staring at the object from his past. "*Dante's Inferno.* My wife bought it for me while we were at Rutgers. It was her favorite. Where did you get it?"

"From your apartment in Brooklyn."

"I have an apartment in Brooklyn?"

"Yes. But you haven't been there since before your last deployment. Shep, tell me about the book. What can you remember? Why was it so important that you kept it under your pillow?"

Shep's expression darkened. "It meant something to me because it meant something to her."

"But you still can't remember her name?"

He shook his head. "It's there, it's so close."

"She wrote a message to you on the title page. Take a look, see if it helps."

With a trembling hand, Patrick opened the front cover to read the first page:

For the sacrifice you are making for our family.
From your soul mate, eternal love always.

Patrick closed his eyes, hugging the book to his chest. "Beatrice. My wife's name is Beatrice."

OVAL OFFICE, WHITE HOUSE
WASHINGTON, DC

President Eric Kogelo looked up from his desk as one of his senior advisors entered the Oval Office for their scheduled meeting. "Have a seat, I'll be right with you." Kogelo continued multitasking, listening to his chief of staff on the telephone while he text messaged the first lady.

The older man with the silky white hair and upturned eyes glanced around the Oval Office, concealing his contempt.

The seat of power. Office of the most powerful man on the planet. And the public still believed it. America was like a chessboard, the president its king, a mere figurehead, capable of incremental moves barely greater than a pawn. No, the real power was not the pieces on the chessboard, it was the unseen players moving the pieces. The CIA maintained editorial influence over every major network, radio station, and print medium in the country. The insurance and pharmaceutical companies ran the medical industry while Big Oil monopolized the energy sector. But it was the military-industrial complex that ran the world, a dark queen whose tentacles reached into almost every politician's pocketbook and across Wall Street, pulling the purse strings that instigated revolutions, terrorist acts, and ultimately started wars.

He glanced across the room at the oil painting of JFK. *Eisenhower had warned Kennedy against the unchecked rise of the CIA and its military-industrial complex. JFK was determined to break up the intelligence agency and "scatter its pieces to the wind." A month later, the president was assassinated, firmly establishing who was really in-charge. Democracy had run its course, freedom merely a convenient illusion, intended only to keep the masses in check.*

President Kogelo placed his BlackBerry in his jacket pocket, turning his attention to his guest. "My apologies. Last-minute details before I leave for New York."

"Any of these details concern me?"

Kogelo leaned back in his chair. "The secretary of defense will be resigning in three hours."

"That's official?"

"He left me no choice. The last thing I need now is a member of my administration tossing verbal grenades at the negotiation table."

"For what it's worth, his remarks last week were justified. The Russians would not have sold Tehran ICBMs without China's approval."

"Maybe so. But this fire needs to be put out, not doused with gasoline."

"You are offering me the position?"

"You've got the experience, plus you have allies on both sides of the aisle. With everything that's going on in the Persian Gulf, we could use a quick confirmation. What do you say?"

National Security Advisor Bertrand DeBorn offered a Cheshire cat smile. "Mr. President, it would be my honor."

HOBOKEN, NEW JERSEY
5:18 P.M.

"**So Shepherd, did** you know Hoboken was the site of the very first baseball game?"

Patrick focused on the Jackson-Pollack-inspired motif of spaghetti on his dinner plate, still too unnerved by his surroundings to make eye contact with Leigh Nelson's husband or her younger, less refined sister, Bridgett.

"Elysian Field, 1846. The Knickerbockers versus the New York Nine. We've always been big baseball fans. Bridgett loves baseball, don't you, Bridge?"

"Hockey." Bridgett Deem chased a mouthful of broccoli with what little remained of her third glass of wine. "At least I used to." She turned to Patrick. "My ex . . . he used to get season tickets to the Rangers for me and my girlfriend. Later, I found out he only wanted me gone so he could *schtup* his secretary in our apartment while I was at the game."

Leigh rolled her eyes. "Bridge, do we really have to go there?"

"That reminds me of a joke," stampeded Doug, his segue accompanied by a boyish grin. "Shepherd, have you ever heard the one about the wife who was pissed off at her husband for not buying her a gift on her birthday? The husband says, 'Why should I waste more money on you? Last year I bought you a grave site, and you still haven't used it."

Patrick coughed, concealing a smile.

Leigh punched her husband on the shoulder. "Everything's a joke to you, isn't it?"

"Hey, I'm just trying to lighten things up. Bridgett's cool with it, aren't you Bridge?"

"Sure, Doug. I already knew men were insensitive scumbags, thanks for the contribution." She turned to Shep. "Barry used to tell me I was his soul mate. For a while, I actually believed him. Ten years, you think you know someone, but the moment your back is turned they run off—"

Patrick's heart convulsed in his chest as if stabbed by a stiletto. His eyes squeezed shut.

The blood drained from Leigh's face. "Bridgett, help me with the dishes."

"I haven't finished eating."

His left arm announces its return. The limb bathed in lava. Flesh melts down his forearm. His fingers drop off, covered in acid. A rubber mallet pounds the back of his skull. His body spasms. Breathe, asshole!

The back door plowed open, unleashing the Nelson's seven-year-old son, Parker, the boy's presence diverting intrusive eyes from his internal struggle.

"Mommy, you're home! I missed you."

"I missed you, too. How was the science museum?"

"Good. Autumn got in trouble again." The boy's head swiveled to face the stranger. Striking blue eyes focused on Patrick's empty left sleeve. "Mommy, where's his arm?"

From the hot darkness behind his squeezed eyes amid the dripping flesh and clenching heart, a voice whispered desperately into Patrick's brain. *Get out!*

"Honey, it's all right. This is Patrick—"

"Bathroom!" He was on his feet so quickly it startled the boy. He hugged his mother.

His father pointed until he could find the words. "Hall. On the left."

Patrick moved through purple spots of light in gelled air beneath muscles barely his to control. Half-blind, he entered the bathroom and sealed himself within the porcelain sanctuary. Blotches of perspiration had soaked his clothes. The pale man with the long, matted brown hair returned his distant glare in the mirror. Muted rants from the kitchen violated the small voice in his head as manic eyes searched for a taped note that was not there.

Thoughts pulled away to eavesdrop on the blathering Hispanic woman.

"Go on, Autumn! Tell your father what you did."

"Leave me alone!"

"I will leave you alone if you ever run away from me like that again!"

"Sophia, please."

The screaming child twisted free of the woman, knocking over Patrick's plate of spaghetti. She evaded her father's grasp and escaped down the hallway, screaming bloody murder as she stomped up the stairs to her room.

"Autumn, come back here! Doug?"

"Not me, Leigh. She needs her mother."

"I cannot control her, Mrs. Nelson," the au pair blustered. "She refuses to keep her seat belt buckled, she runs away when I speak to her. She is too hyper a child for someone my age to handle."

"It's getting late, I should probably go." Bridgett squeezed her sister's shoulder, suddenly grateful her marriage terminated without children. "Dinner was delicious, I'll call you tomorrow." She lowered her voice. "Did you want me, you know, to drop Patrick off at the hospital?"

"Patrick!" Leigh handed Parker to her husband and hustled down the hallway to the sealed bathroom door. "Shep, you okay?" No answer. Her heart skipped a beat. "Shep? Damn it, Shep, open the door!"

She twisted the knob. Surprised to find it unlocked, she stole a breath and pushed her way in, readying herself to scream CALL 9-1-1, all the while cursing her career choice and the self-indulgence and ignorance that has led to—

—empty.

She checked the window. Sealed and locked. *He's still in your home. Find him fast before . . .*

Exiting the bathroom, she took the stairs two at a time. Frantic, she searched Parker's room, then her master bedroom and bath. She checked the walk-in closet. Under the king-size bed. Nothing but her daughter's stuffed animal.

A kernel of thought blossomed into a parent's worst nightmare. "Autumn . . ."

Mother bear raced across the hall into her cub's bedroom. The Dora the Explorer lamp on the child's desk illuminated the two inert figures entwined on the bed.

Doug joined her in silence.

Patrick's head was propped by pillows. His eyes were closed. Curled up on the one-armed man's chest was the Nelson's daughter.

Two troubled souls. Comforted in sleep.

FREDERICK, MARYLAND
10:05 P.M.

The farmhouse sat on twelve acres in rural Frederick County. Built in 1887, the home was structurally sound, its former residents having buttressed the foundation, replaced the roof, and renovated the stone-face exterior. There still remained much work to be done—the rotting barn was an eyesore in desperate need of demolition—but the new owner, in her final trimester of pregnancy, has had little time for anything other than work and readying the nursery for her unborn child.

Mary Louise Klipot had purchased the home on a short sale when the bank had foreclosed on the previous owners. The location was ideal—isolated yet close to several shopping malls and only a twenty-minute drive to Fort Detrick.

Andrew Bradosky had moved in two weeks after proposing.

"**. . . with Bertrand DeBorn** accepting the responsibilities of acting secretary of defense on this, the eve of a global summit. Joining us now is FOX news political analyst, Evan Davidson. Evan, in your opinion, what impact will President Kogelo's eleventh-hour decision to dismiss his secretary of defense have on tomorrow's summit?"

Mary entered the living room from the kitchen, carrying a steaming mug of hot chocolate in each hand. She passed a cup to Andrew, who was kneeling by the fireplace, adding another log to the dying embers. "Darling, see if this is hot enough."

He sipped several swallows of the hot beverage, wiping whipped cream from his upper lip. "Mmm, that's good. Mary, can we finish our conversation?"

Mary half sat, half collapsed in the cushioned rocking chair, her lower back aching.

"I told you, Scythe should be ready by March, April the latest."

"April?" Jabbing at the embers with a poker, Andrew ignited the log, then sat on the fireplace stoop facing her. "Mary, timing is everything. By April, we could be involved in a full-scale invasion. The last thing we want is the CIA deciding they can replace us—"

"Andy, in case you forgot, the baby's due in a few weeks."

"The doctor said January."

"The doctor's wrong. Besides, I'm taking off at least six months to nurse."

"Six months? Mary, come on, the future of the free world's at stake!"

"Don't be such a drama queen. Anyway, I was just kidding. Scythe's way ahead of schedule. Now finish your hot chocolate so you can rub my feet."

"Geez, you had me scared." Relieved, he drained the mug, wiping his mouth with the back of his sleeve. "But cereal . . . surreally . . . surr . . ." Andrew dropped to his knees, the numbness in his lips creeping up his legs. "Wha . . . huh–?"

"No worries, darling, the paralysis probably won't affect your breathing . . . assuming I measured the dosage correctly. You did say you weighed 182? Oh, dear . . . I forgot about your asthma. Is it getting hard to breathe?"

Mary sipped her hot chocolate, wincing slightly as Andrew Bradosky's forehead struck the maple wood floor.

PART 2

END OF DAYS

Lost Diary: Guy de Chauliac

The following entry has been excerpted from a recently discovered unpublished memoir, written by surgeon Guy de Chauliac during the Great Plague: 1346–1348.
(translated from its original French)

Diary Entry: December 20, 1347

(recorded in Avignon, France)

Death advances upon the world.

For a year now, its shadow has moved west from China across the Asian continent. It has infiltrated Persia through the Mongolian trade routes and infected the Mediterranean seaports. Villagers fleeing the Great Mortality report tales of horror one-noxious breath and another is felled, one touch of infected blood and sickness takes an entire family to the grave. God's wrath is nowhere and everywhere at once, and there seems no escape.

Word of a spreading sickness reached Europe after the Mongolian army lay siege on Caffa (translator's note: Present-day Feodosiya, a Black Sea port in south Russia). The invaders must have brought the sickness with them, for on the dawn of victory they became so ill they were forced to retreat over the Eurasian steppe . . . but not before they poisoned Caffa with the remains of their dead, tossing the infected bodies over the city's fortifications.

As the chief physician to Pope Clement VI, I have been tasked with tracking the plague's advancement. Caffa is a major seaport. Based on our most recent reports, I have surmised that sometime in the late spring of this year, sailors infected with plague left Caffa aboard Genoese merchant ships, bound for the Mediterranean Sea and Europe. Mariners practice *costeggiare*, a method of sailing that keeps them in perpetual sight of the coastline. Stops would be frequent, allowing the sickness to spread from port to port. One of the infected Genoese ships apparently reached Constantinople sometime last summer. Like Caffa, the Great Mortality spread quickly through the city. A personal contact, a Venetian physician I trained with at the University of Bologna, sent word to the Holy See that the streets in Constantinople were littered with the dead and dying. His letter describes high fever, a coughing of blood, and a stench that reeks of death. Welts soon appear, red at first, then swelling to black, some as large as a ripe apple. With each new dawn, the physician found another dozen infected, by sunset he buried another family member or neighbor until the despair and fear became so overwhelming that he had to flee Constantinople altogether. His description of a surviving father being too afraid to bury his own child brought tears.

By late summer, the papacy learned that the pestilence had advanced as far south as Persia, Egypt, and the Levant, and as far north as Poland, Bulgaria, Cyprus, Greece, and Romania. While these reports cannot be verified, all of us live in fear of Death's impending arrival.

On 14 November, the Pope summoned me to his chambers to inform me that plague had struck Sicily. The Holy See's contact, a Franciscan friar named Michele da Piazza, claimed the sickness arrived on European shores a week after twelve Genoese galleys made port early in October. Belowdecks were found dozens of dead crewmen—all infected. Those still alive entered Messina, spreading the sickness to everyone they came in contact with before they, too, died. The friar reported black boils on the necks and groins of the inflicted, along with the coughing of blood and fever, usually followed by violent, incessant vomiting. Within days of being infected, every victim had died.

My own dread is compounded by anger. Despite the approaching Death, the Holy See remains more occupied by its ongoing feud with the King of England, who seeks to rule the Iberian Peninsula one French coastal city at a time; as well as Clement's ongoing quarrel with Rome, from which the papacy was removed several Popes past.

It is inarguable that the greed of an elite few has kept Europe cast in decades of endless war. Corruption has taken the Church, and the people have lost trust. Bouts of famine continue to ravage the countryside, a result of decades of failing crops due to incessantly harsh weather conditions that began when I was but a child.

Many say we are cursed, suffering God's wrath. I say our corruption, greed, and hatred for our fellowman, spewed through religious dogma, has paved the way for our own self-destruction.

Decadence now rules the Palais des Papes, war the papal states. Roving bands of *condottieri* attack Europe's villages, while the fortified cities have become cesspools of neglect. Influenced by politics, the Holy See has ruled it a sin to bathe, its orthodoxy backed by a conservative medical faculty of Paris, their determination made not on scientific fact but by their desire to remain in conflict with the more liberal traditions of Rome and Greece, who consider personal hygiene a cardinal virtue.

There is nothing virtuous about living in Avignon, where the commoner shares a bedchamber with his livestock. Each day, animals are slaughtered in the public streets by butchers, the blood and feces left to feed the flies and rodents. Rats are everywhere, their scourge feasting in the filth of Avignon and Paris and every city under the influence of the Holy See, overwhelming the homes of peasants in the countryside.

It is amid this stench of corruption that the Black Death approaches our once-great city.

May God have mercy on our souls.

—Guigo

Editor's Note:

Guy de Chauliac, also known as Guido de Cauliaco, was attending physician to five Popes during the late thirteenth century and is regarded as the most important surgical writer of the Middle Ages. His major work, *Inventarium sive Chirurgia Magna* (*The Inventory of Medicine*), remained the principal didactic text on surgery until the eighteenth century.

"Well, I just got into town about an hour ago . . .
Took a look around, see which way the wind blow
Where the little girls in their Hollywood bungalows
Are you a lucky little lady in the city of light,
Or just another lost angel . . . city of night
City of night, city of night, city of night . . ."
—The Doors, "L.A. Woman"

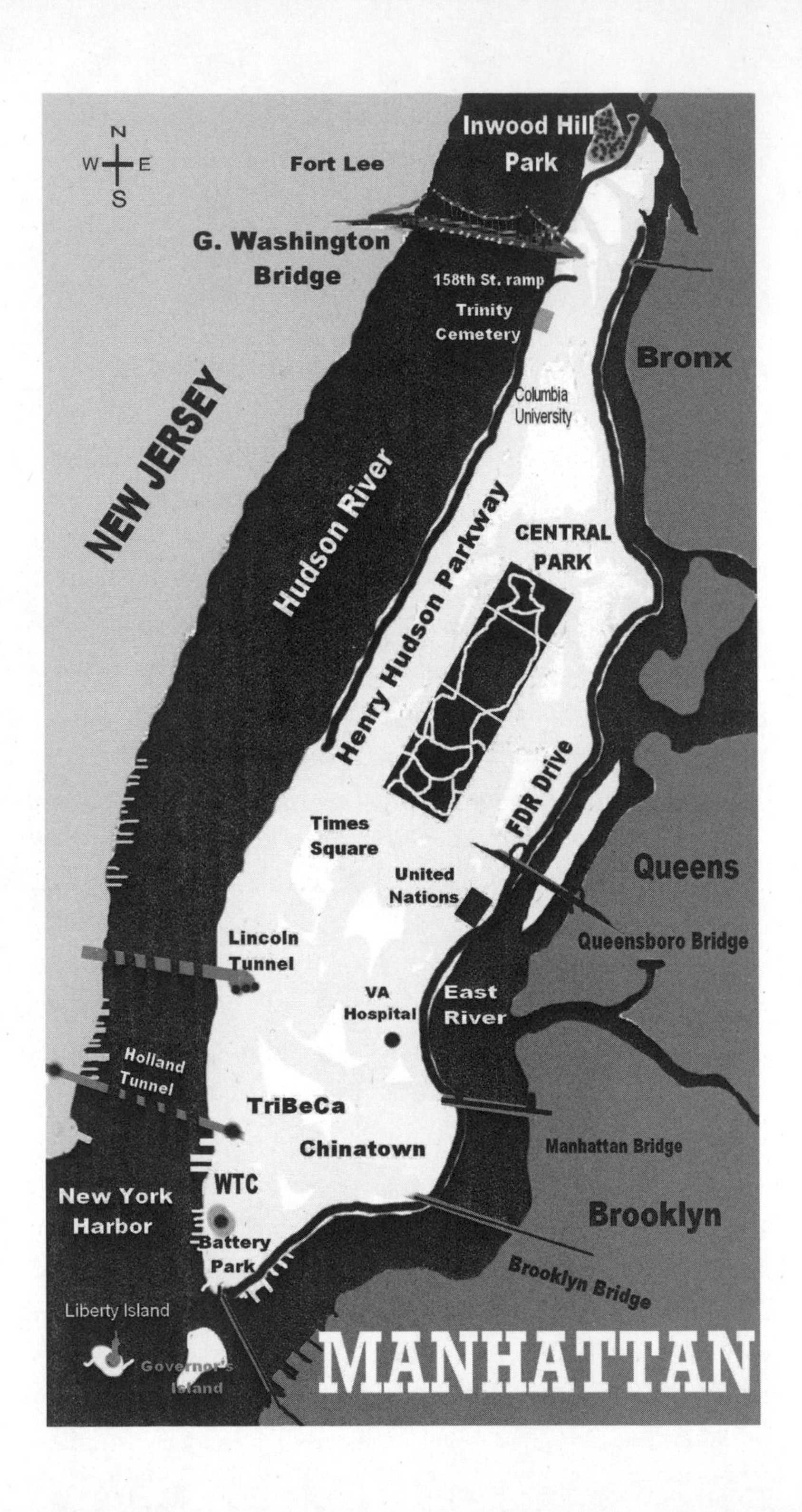
N
W
E
S
Fort Lee
Inwood Hill Park
G. Washington Bridge
158th St. ramp
Trinity Cemetery
Bronx
NEW JERSEY
Columbia University
Hudson River
Henry Hudson Parkway
CENTRAL PARK
FDR Drive
Times Square
United Nations
Queens
Queensboro Bridge
Lincoln Tunnel
VA Hospital
East River
Holland Tunnel
TriBeCa
Chinatown
Manhattan Bridge
WTC
New York Harbor
Battery Park
Brooklyn
Brooklyn Bridge
Liberty Island
Governor's Island
MANHATTAN

DECEMBER 20

NEW YORK CITY

8:19 A.M.

(23 HOURS, 44 MINUTES BEFORE THE PROPHESIED END OF DAYS)

Manhattan: an island Mecca, surrounded by water.

The Harlem River rolled south past the Bronx, widening into the East River—whitecapped behind a fierce four-knot current. The Statue of Liberty beckoned to travelers across New York Harbor. Farther north, the waterway became the mighty Hudson, the river separating the Big Apple from the northeastern shoreline of New Jersey.

Urban waters, frigid and gray. Eye candy to Realtors and sightseers. Ignored on a daily basis by commuters, nature's barrier neutered by a dozen bridges and tunnels.

Not today.

A winter sun splashed Manhattan's skyline in fleeting shimmers of gold. Endless construction slowed traffic to a crawl. Tempers flared. Ten thousand new text messages launched into cyberspace. Steam rose from grates. Islands of heat drew the homeless like moths to a flame. Their indignity ignored by waves of pedestrians. Like the rivers.

Cold bit at exposed earlobes, sniffling noses. Last night's snow, already trampled into slush. Christmas trees. Festive lights. The scent of hot Danish and cinnamon.

Thursday before Christmas. The approaching holiday energized Manhattan's returning workforce. Human sardines packed subways and trains. Half a million vehicles turned highways into rush-hour parking lots. Deal makers and hustlers. Shoppers and sellers. Lawyers and layman and parents escorting children to school. Fueled on caffeine and dreams and survival instincts honed after years in the urban jungle. Two million visitors entered Manhattan every day. Add to that figure another 1.7 million residents—all sharing twenty-eight square miles of island.

One hundred thousand human beings occupying every frozen city block. Good and bad, old and young; men, women, and children, representing every age group and nationality on the planet. A slice of humanity, poised on a precipice too large to comprehend, their indifference to the world's plight soiling any innocence, their deniability culpable.

No snowflake in an avalanche ever feels responsible.

Commuters inched their way west across the congested Queensboro Bridge—rats preparing to enter the maze. Ignore the drivers whose vehicles bear tri-state tags. Focus instead on the white Honda Civic with the Virginia license plate. The car was a rental, the driver an academic who had always preferred the suburbs to the temptations of big-city life. Yet here she was, having driven all night just to be in Manhattan on this chilly Thursday morning at this precise moment in human history. A virgin to New York, one might expect a case of rush-hour jitters. But the smile on Mary Louise Klipot's angular face was serene, the thirty-eight-year-old cranberry-apple redhead exuding a calm that only came through inner peace. Hazel eyes, void of makeup and rimmed red from lack of sleep, glanced at the gridlocked drivers to her left. Troubled faces all, she told herself, bearing the constant fear that came from uncertainty.

Mary Klipot was neither afraid nor uncertain. She was in a place beyond worry, beyond the human stain. Faith was a wellspring that drove her convictions, and it ran deep, for she was traveling along a road paved by the Almighty Himself—

—and she was traveling with His child.

Of course, Andrew had tried to convince her otherwise, her fiancé insisting that *he* was her unborn child's father. His argument held no sway, coerced by his clear intent to sell Scythe to the military, or to the intelligence community, or to some other rogue black ops group vested in its own geopolitical perversions. Did he think the microbiologist a fool? Baby Jesus *his*? When had this supposed "act of copulation" taken place? Why couldn't she remember it?

Having forced the Devil to show his hand, her "betrothed" had spewed a tale of desperation, claiming that they had slept together back in March while vacationing in Cancún. Frustrated sexually, Andrew admitted having slipped a little something into Mary's rum and cola, unleashing her libido's bursting dam. It had been a wild night of passion and lust—that Mary had no recollection of the event having more to do with her not wanting to remember than the benign chemical concoction he had used on her.

The poisonous lie had cost Andrew dearly. Having bound her fiancé to the old barn's center post, she poured acid over his wrists and handcuffs, clear up to his elbows. He had screamed until he passed out, the dilapidated structure's heavy interior walls dampened the sound, the nearest neighbor more than half a mile away.

Resecuring him to the structure's center post, she had waited patiently for him to awaken. Finally, she had prodded him with the business end of the 12 gauge.

"Darling Andrew, open your eyes. Mama has something for you."

The blast had splattered brains and blood and skull shrapnel across the entire back wall and rafters, the heavy jolt spraining her right shoulder, causing Baby Jesus to kick for ten straight minutes. She had rested in the manger until he calmed, then she cleansed the barn with fire, sending her fiancé on his one-way journey to oblivion. Mary had remained behind long enough to convince the local firefighters to allow the ancient structure to burn itself out, then she treated herself to a lobster dinner at the Benito Grill before heading off to her bio lab at Fort Detrick to pack.

The news came on the radio, beckoning her attention.

. . . world leaders clearly divided on how to deal with Iran, arriving in New York for an emergency session of the UN Security Council. Iran's Supreme Leader is scheduled to address the Security Council in General Assembly Hall at 9:15 this morning. President Kogelo's address is tentatively scheduled for 10:30, followed by China's General Secretary later this afternoon. Meanwhile, the US aircraft carrier, Theodore Roosevelt *is expected to join the USS* Ronald Reagan *battle group already in the Persian Gulf—a direct response to the sale of Russian-made ICBMs to Iran on August 9. Now back to more music on WABC New York."*

Mary powered off the radio, her heart beating faster as she exited the Queensboro Bridge to FDR Drive South—the United Nations complex situated somewhere up ahead. Today she would teach the elitists a lesson. Today they would fully comprehend the meaning of Matthew 5:5. "Blessed are the meek for they shall inherit the earth."

She glanced at the pile of blankets laid neatly on the passenger-side floor, fighting the urge to pull aside the wool camouflage and gaze upon the hidden object—a metal briefcase containing her key to the Pearly Gates. *In God's time, Mary. The Lord will be with you when you need Him. Don't anticipate the pain. Focus only on the present . . .*

VA MEDICAL CENTER
MANHATTAN, NEW YORK

Lost in the past, Patrick Shepherd dreamed . . .

They are moving down the streets of Baghdad, David Kantor on his right, Eric Lasagna on his left. Three Pied Pipers, followed by a dozen Iraqi children begging for handouts.

David pauses, allowing the young horde to circle his fellow soldiers. "Either of you two ever see Moby Dick*?"*

"I have," answers Lasagna. "Gregory Peck as Ahab. Classic."

"Remember when Ahab told his men to watch the birds, that the birds would tell them when Moby Dick was getting ready to breach? The locals are your birds. They usually sense when trouble is going to happen, so if you see them vacate the street, be ready. The kids are great, just be careful. Fanatics sometimes strap

bombs to them, forcing them to approach our troops."

A bright-eyed, dark-haired seven-year-old girl smiles at Shep, clearly flirting. Reaching into his knapsack, he removes an MRE, the presence of the recognizable portable meal generating excitement. "Okay, let's see what Uncle Sam has given us today. Anyone interested in two-day-old beef ravioli? No? Can't say I blame you. Wait, what's this? M&Ms!"

The children jump and wave and call out in Farsi.

Shep distributes three boxes worth of the chocolate candies so that each child gets an equal share, saving the last double portion for the smiling seven-year-old girl.

She consumes the handful in one palm sized mouthful, chocolate saliva oozing from her grinning lips. Shep watches her, lost in her big brown eyes—windows to a soul that has witnessed so much pain yet can still lose itself in innocence.

His new friend beams a muddy chocolate smile. She blows him a kiss and runs off—

—her exit ending his momentary reprieve in the eye of the storm, returning him to war.

MORNINGSIDE HEIGHTS
UPPER WEST SIDE, MANHATTAN
8:36 A.M.

The Cathedral of St. John the Divine, situated on thirteen acres just south of Columbia University's main campus, was the largest cathedral in the world. Built on a promontory overlooking the Hudson River, the Romanesque-Byzantine structure was designed in 1887, yet still remained unfinished.

Pankaj Patel paused on Amsterdam Avenue to gaze at the illustrious House of God. The cathedral was decorated in holiday lights, yet Patel felt anything but festive. It has been more than three months since the professor of psychiatry was accepted into the Society of the Nine Unknown Men, and the stress associated with the clandestine encounter with the Elder still weighed on his mind.

He stared at the cathedral's Fountain of Peace, its surrounding lawn carpeted white with snow, encircled by bronze animal figures. The detailed carvings depicted the epic struggle of good versus evil—the archangel Michael decapitating Satan, whose horned head hung to one side. *One more day until the winter solstice . . . the day of the dead. If the End of Days is really upon us . . .*

"Dad, come on! I'm going to be late for our holiday party."

His attention turned to his ten-year-old daughter, Dawn. The girl's long onyx hair, separated into braids, hung over her winter coat, her dark angelic eyes exuding a combination of anxiety and impatience. "I'm sorry. Was I lost in space again?"

"Totally." Tugging him by his wrist, she led him toward the entrance of the Cathedral School, a kindergarten-through-eighth-grade elementary school for children of all faiths. "Remember, I'm staying after school for band practice. See you at dinner."

"Wait!" Catching up with her on the frost-covered lawn, he bent down on one knee. "You know I love you. You are God's gift to your mother and me, our little angel."

"Dad"—she touched his cheek with her wool-covered fingers—"now your knee's all wet."

With a heavy heart, he watched his only child hustle to join the other children converging upon the school entrance. Brushing at the wet stain on his right pant leg, he continued up Amsterdam Avenue to Columbia University's East Campus.

LOWER EAST SIDE, MANHATTAN
8:44 A.M.

Mary Klipot's arms trembled as she gripped the steering wheel, her white-knuckled hands clenching the rosary beads. The bumper-to-bumper traffic on First Avenue had not budged in ten minutes, and the police presence along the adjacent United Nations Plaza was everywhere.

Her eyes darted from the digital clock on the dashboard to her rearview mirror. She stared at the four-foot-tall skeleton doll buckled into the backseat, the figure dressed in a bridal gown and wearing a red wig that matched her own hair. "*Santa Muerte,* I'm running out of time. Guide me, Angel. Show me the way."

Moments passed. Then the two lanes on her left miraculously surged forward. She swerved over from her right lane, skidded briefly on a patch of ice, then turned onto East 45th Street, in desperate search of a parking space.

The traffic crawled west, crossing Second Avenue. The parking garages were all full, the snow-piled curbs off-limits. The digital clock advanced to 8:54 A.M. She slapped her palms in frustration on the steering wheel, shattering the rosary beads in the process.

This is no good. You're heading too far west.

The baby kicked in her belly as she turned right on Third Avenue, then right again on 46th Street. Having looped around the block, she was once more heading east in the direction of the United Nations Plaza. She crossed over Second Avenue, her pulse pounding in her temples. *Don't get stuck on First Avenue again or you'll be late.* She glanced up at the rearview mirror. "Please skinny girl, help me find a place to park."

The alley on her left was so narrow she nearly passed it. Nestled between two high-rise buildings, it was an alcove reserved only for deliveries. She turned down the path, following it sixty feet until it dead-ended at a steel trash bin.

Cloaked in shadows, allowing for privacy while still within walking distance of the UN—perfect! "Thank you, *Santa Muerte.* Bless you, my Angel."

The NO PARKING—VIOLATORS TOWED signs were posted everywhere, but she would only be ten minutes, fifteen at the most, and besides, God had led her here, He would never abandon her now. She parked in front of the immense brown trash bin, turning off the car's engine.

It was time.

Mary pulled away the wool blankets stacked on the passenger-side floor, revealing the metallic attaché case. A biohazard warning label adorned its smooth surface, the USAMRIID logo embellished with a silver scythe.

She pulled the attaché case onto her lap. Turned her attention to its combination lock. Maneuvered the seven digits to 1266621 then flicked open the twin latches.

The steel locks popped open—

—tripped a microcircuit that sent a remote electronic signal to a secured receiver located 245 miles to the south.

US ARMY MEDICAL RESEARCH INSTITUTE OF INFECTIOUS DISEASES (USAMRIID)
FORT DETRICK-FREDERICK, MARYLAND
8:56 A.M.

The biodefense laboratories located at USAMRIID were the largest and best equipped of the three facilities in the United States designated to handle highly hazardous microbes. Expanded in 2008, Fort Detrick's campus now included the National Biodefense Analysis & Countermeasures Center (NBACC), a billion-dollar, 160,000-square-foot complex operated under the auspices of the Department of Homeland Security. The new facility housed approximately sixty thousand square feet of Bio-Safety Level-4 labs, designed to allow researchers to work with the most dangerous germs known in existence.

Dr. Lydia Gagnon's office was located in Building 1425 on the National Interagency Biodefense Campus (NIBC), one of the original facilities still in use. The pathologist from Ontario finished her second Pepsi of the morning, allowed herself one more minute before she had to leave for her nine o'clock staff meeting. She was in the middle of reading a personal e-mail from her sister when the Internet screen abruptly shut down.

ATTENTION: LEVEL-4 BIOHAZARD BREACH

The warning flashed over and over, the encrypted message prompting her to enter her security code. She typed in the seven-digit identification number and read, her blue eyes widening in fear behind her prescription glasses. After thirty seconds, she grabbed her office phone and dialed a three-digit extension.

"This is Gagnon in the NIBC. We have a Level-4 biohazard breach—repeat, we have a Level-4 biohazard breach. I want two A.I.T.s on the helo-deck ready to deploy in six minutes. Tell Colonel Zwawa I'm on my way up!"

LOWER EAST SIDE, MANHATTAN
8:56 A.M.

Mary Klipot opened the metal case, revealing molded foam compartments. There were three items secured inside: An inhaler designed to fit over the nose and mouth, an aerosol injector attachment, and a three-ounce glass vial containing a clear liquid, its capped top sealed with an orange biohazard sticker.

Methodical now, she removed the empty aerosol injector. Unscrewed its top. Placed it in one of the molded compartments so it stood upright. Carefully, she removed the glass vial. Peeled away the decal. Gently poured a single fluid ounce into the bottom of the empty aerosol dispenser.

A breath to calm her nerves. Then she reached into her jacket pocket and withdrew a Plexiglas test tube containing a chalky gray substance. A genetic modifier: The X factor of her labors. She unscrewed the cap, which doubled as the handle to a tiny internal measuring scoop the size of a head of a tack. She filled the scoop with the gray powder. Tapped off the excess. Added the scoop to the clear liquid in the aerosol dispenser, then capped the test tube and placed it in an open foam compartment. Replaced the aerosol dispenser's lid and gave the sealed ingredients a dozen delicate shakes. Satisfied, she attached the dispenser to the inhaler, then laid the device on the foam padding.

She checked the clock: 8:59 A.M.

From her purse she removed the envelope containing the forged United Nations identification card. Mary glanced at her photo, now assigned the name: Dr. Bogdana Petrova, Russian embassy. Dr. Petrova had been a microbiologist. Mary had met her at an international convention seven years ago in Brussels. Bogdana's remains had turned up six weeks later in a trash bin in Moscow, her death blamed on an Internet date gone bad.

We'll get them back for what they did to you, Dana. For what they did to all our colleagues.

She slipped the shoestring attached to the fake identification card over her head, then picked up the inhaler. Her heart pounded, her hand trembled. *This is it, Mary, this is why you were chosen. Scythe can't hurt the baby, you've already inoculated the placenta, but it must be properly inseminated to summon the Rapture.*

Staring at the red-wigged Grim Reaper doll in the rearview mirror, she recited the ninth passage from the nine-day cycle of prayers to *Santisima Muerte*, taken from the novena booklet she received in Mexico two months earlier. "Blessed Protector Death: By the virtues that God gave you, I ask that you free me from all evil, danger, and sickness, and that instead, you give me luck, health, happiness, and money, that you give me friends and freedom from my enemies, also making Jesus, the father of my child, come before me, humble as a sheep, keeping His promises and always being loving and submissive. Amen."

She pressed the inhaler over her nose and mouth. Squeezing the trigger, she inhaled the pungent elixir deep into her lungs.

The deed over, she laid her head back. Her heart beat wildly. Her eyelids fluttered. Her body quivered with adrenaline.

The internal voice, suppressed by the meds, now urged her haste.

She exited the car, slammed the door, and locked it before remembering the telltale metal attaché case. Clicking the keyless entry, she opened the door and grabbed the case, stomping her feet in the slush-covered street to keep her full bladder under control in the twenty-seven-degree chill.

She looked around, desperate. The dumpster beckoned. She tossed the attaché case inside and hurried off. The case popped open as it landed inside the empty steel bin with a loud crash.

She hustled out of the alley. Turned left, headed east on 46th Street.

Bubonic Mary quickened her pace as the infectious combination of toxins quickly seeped through her bloodstream.

VA MEDICAL CENTER
MANHATTAN, NEW YORK
9:03 A.M.

Leigh Nelson sat behind her desk, sipping the microwave-heated cup of coffee. Thursday morning, no reprimands. Her coat remained on, her bones still chilled from the four-block walk. *Thirty degrees out, ten with the windchill, and they have to pick today to start construction on the staff parking lot.*

Opening her laptop, she logged onto the Internet and checked her e-mail, progressively deleting the obvious spam. She stopped at the subject line: LOST PERSON INQUIRY and clicked on the e-mail.

Dr. Nelson:

Thank you for your inquiry regarding the whereabouts of BEATRICE SHEPHERD, age 30–38, ONE CHILD (female) age 14–16. TOP 5 Search States Requested: NY. NJ. CT. MA. PA. The following positive matches were found:
Manhattan, New York: Ms. Beatrice Shepherd
Vineland, New Jersey: Mrs. Beatrice Shepherd
See also: Mrs. B. Shepherd (NY - 4)
Mrs. B. Shepherd (NJ - 1)
Mrs. B. Shepherd (MA - 6)
Mrs. B. Shepherd (PA - 14)
To provide you with the highest-quality results, we suggest our LEVEL 2 Detective Service. Fee: $149.95.

Nelson's eyes locked onto the Manhattan match. She clicked on the link:

Shepherd, Beatrice—201 West Thames Street, Battery Park City, NY. Daughter: Karen (age unknown).
Phone: (212) 798-0847 (new listing)
Marital Status: Married (separated)
Click for MAP:

She printed the information. Checked the time. Cursing under her breath, she grabbed her clipboard and headed out, ten minutes late for her morning rounds.

The sound of catcalls and hollering could be heard clear down the hall. Leigh Nelson quickened her pace into a jog, bursting through the double doors of Ward 27.

The veterans were chanting from their beds. Those with hands were clenching fistfuls of money, those without were just as animated. At the center of the spectacle was Alex Steven Timmer, a US Marine Corps veteran. The single-leg amputee was balancing on his right leg and left prosthetic, a baseball bat cocked over his right shoulder. The breakfast tray by his feet served as home plate, a mattress leaning against the bathroom door was the backstop. An aluminum bedpan tied around the mattress was the strike zone, one baseball already caught in its well.

On the other side of the ward, standing in the center aisle sixty feet away, was Patrick Shepherd. Strangely imposing. A baseball gripped loosely in his right paw.

"What the hell is going on in here? This is a hospital ward, not Yankee Stadium!"

The men grew quiet. Shep looked away.

Master Sergeant Rocky Trett addressed the angry woman from his bed. "Timmer played college baseball for the Miami Hurricanes. Claims he hit .379 in the College World Series and that Shep couldn't strike him out on his best day. Naturally, we felt a wager was in order."

"Come on, Pouty Lips, give us two more pitches so we can finish the bet!"

"Yeah!" The men started cheering again.

Alex Timmer nodded at the brunette. "Two more pitches, Doc. Let us settle this like men."

"Two more pitches! Two more pitches! Two more pitches!"

"Enough!" She looked around, measuring her patients' needs against the reality of losing her job. "Two more pitches. Then I want everything back to normal."

The men cheered wildly as she walked down the center aisle to speak with

Patrick. "Can you even throw a baseball with only one arm? Won't you lose your balance?"

"I'm okay. Sort of been practicing in the basement."

She glanced over her shoulder at Timmer. "He looks like he can hit. Can you get him out without breaking anything?"

Shep offered a wry smile.

"Strangler! Strangler! Strangler!"

"Two pitches." She took cover behind the nurses' station alongside Amanda Gregory. The nurse offered a shrug. "Could be worse. At least they're not thinking about the war."

Alex Timmer pointed his bat at Shep, Babe Ruth style. "Bring it, hotshot. Right over the plate."

Shep turned away, adjusting his grip on the ball, using his upper thigh as leverage. Unable to maintain his balance in a full windup, he had to pitch from the stretch. He set himself, then, ignoring the batter, focused his eyes on the target. His left leg kicked, driving his knee up to his chest before extending forward into a powerful stride that simultaneously unfurled his right arm, a slingshot that hurled a spinning white blur through the air down the center aisle past the flummoxed batter a full second before he completed his awkward uppercut of a swing, the two-seam fastball denting the bedpan at its center point.

Strike two.

The men went crazy. Money was exchanged, a few tempers flared—the batter's among them. "One more, Shepherd, give me one more fastball. You'd better duck, this one's coming back up the middle."

Shep retrieved the last ball from one of the veterans. He set a slightly different grip on the seams, his expression rivaling the best poker faces in Vegas.

Nothing changed. Not the speed of the delivery or the angle of his arm or the release—just the grip. The white Taser flew past a sea of steel beds en route to the makeshift plate and the awaiting batter before the baseball suddenly nosedived into a breaking slider that slipped ten inches beneath Alex Timmer's whirling lumber—his swing rendered so violently off kilter that it corkscrewed the one-legged veteran 360 degrees. Ash wood met prosthetic leg, the device shattering into shards of aluminum and steel, landing Timmer hard on his buttocks. He howled as a slice of metal punctured his left butt cheek.

Silence stole across the crowd. Dr. Nelson stood by the nurses' station, her complexion as pale as her lab coat.

"Damn it, Shepherd! I waited eight months for this leg! Eight months! Now what am I supposed to do?"

Shep shrugged. "Next time, bunt."

The men whooped and hollered with laughter.

Grabbing the closest walker, the one-legged man pulled himself off the linoleum floor and limped up the aisle, intent on assaulting the one-armed man. Dr. Nelson remained frozen in place, watching dumbfounded as her interns hurried to intervene.

Her pager reverberated in her pocket. She fumbled for the instrument. Read the text message:

THE VIPS HAVE ARRIVED.

UNITED NATIONS PLAZA
9:06 A.M.

Her leap of faith was waning, replaced by a sense of dread. Heaviness weighed in her lungs. Nausea rose in her stomach. A dull pain took root in her temples, the headache made worse by the incessant ringing of bells. The Christmas sound grew louder as she approached the crossroad of 46th Street and First Avenue, the United Nations Plaza looming into view.

Heath Shelby stopped ringing the bell. Pulling off one glove, he scratched his face beneath the annoying Santa Claus beard. A freelance writer, Shelby also did voice-over for local radio spots. He had been a volunteer with the Salvation Army for two years—one of his wife Jennifer's requirements when she agreed to uproot their family from Arkansas.

Heath had no problem with charity work. The Salvation Army provided emergency services and hot meals to the less fortunate, along with gifts to children on Christmas. What he hated was wearing the cumbersome fat suit and the itchy white beard and the imitation-leather Santa boots that offered little to no insulation against the frozen sidewalk. He had been standing on the corner with his donation pot and bell since seven o'clock this morning. His feet and lower back ached. Worse, his throat was getting sore. With three new radio spots set up for next week, the last thing he needed now was a cold.

Screw this. Toss a twenty in the bucket and call it a day. Better yet, catch a cab down to Battery Park and work on the boat. A few more hours of repairs and she should be seaworthy. Can't wait to see Collin's face . . . kid hasn't been fishing since we left Possum Grape. Pick up another case of fiberglass resin before you head over and—

Ignoring the flashing DO NOT WALK sign, the pregnant redhead stepped off the curb and into traffic. A horn blared. The taxi skidded—

—Heath grabbed the woman by her elbow, dragging her out of harm's way. "You okay?"

Mary looked up at Santa Claus, dumbfounded. "I can't be late."

"Late's better than dead. You gotta watch the signs. Are you sure you're all right? You look kind of pale."

Mary nodded. Coughing violently, she rooted through her coat pocket, tossed loose change and lint into Santa's bucket. The light turned green again, and she followed a fresh wave of pedestrians across the First Avenue intersection.

Looming ahead, rising from what had once been the north lawn, was the new United Nations Conference Building, still partially under construction. On its right was the Secretariat Building, its gleaming green glass and marble facade towering thirty-eight stories, its lower floors connecting it with the old Conference Building, the South Annex, the library . . . and her target—the General Assembly Building.

Mary stared at the curved rectangular structure and its central-roof dome. *Just like in my dreams.* She followed the sidewalk to the plaza, shocked to see the size of the awaiting flock.

A thousand protesters infested the Dag Hammarskjöld eighteen-acre plaza. Tea baggers. Picket signs. Chants over bullhorns. Encouraged by a dozen film crews recording everything for the *News at Noon.* So dense was this sea of humanity that Mary could barely gauge her surroundings. She was aiming for the General Assembly Building and its barricade of policemen in riot gear when white specks of light impeded her vision, churning the nausea mustering in her gut.

Must hurry now, before the bacilli enter my liver and spleen.

She cloaked her mouth and nose with her wool scarf, guarding her protruding belly with her free arm as she pushed through the crowd. Unseen elbows collided with her shoulders and skull. The gray winter sky disappeared behind a wall of humanity that jostled her to the cold pavement and swallowed her whole. On hands and knees, she emerged at the barricade, her cries for assistance silenced by the overwhelming decibel level of the crowd. Desperate, she regained her feet, shoving her identification badge at the row of helmets and body armor forming the gauntlet.

Mucus thickened in her lungs. A fit of coughs took her as the crowd surged at her back and she went down again, pushed beneath the wood obstruction.

A police officer dragged her to her feet, his brass tag identifying him as BECK. He was shouting to her, pulling her on his side of the barricade, and suddenly she could see again.

"Go!" He pointed to the entrance.

Mary waved her thanks and hurried to the next security checkpoint, the pathogen raging through her body.

USAMRIID MEDEVAC UNITS ALPHA & DELTA
187 MILES SOUTHWEST OF MANHATTAN
9:07 A.M.

The two Sikorsky UH-60Q Blackhawk helicopters soared over rural Maryland, their airspeeds approaching 150 knots. Each Aeromedical Isolation

Team (A.I.T.) was equipped with a portable biohazard containment laboratory and mobile patient transportation isolator. The flight crew included an Army physician, a nurse, and three medics. The other members of these rapid response teams were Special Ops officers trained to deal with lethal contagious diseases, biological weapons, and patient isolation—the latter often the determining factor in whether a local population lived or died.

In charge of the two chopper response teams were Captains Jay and Jesse Zwawa, both men younger brothers of Colonel John Zwawa, USAMRIID's commanding officer. Jay Zwawa, the Alpha Team field commander, was an Army veteran who had served three years in Iraq. Known in his barracks as "Z" or the "Polish Pimp Dog," Jay stood six feet four inches and weighed an imposing 260 pounds. Covered in tattoos, the former Army sniper was a certified Gatling gun operator and diesel engine mechanic, and had earned a reputation as a practical jokester. When riled, however, Z had been known to knock out with one punch anyone who challenged him.

Younger brother Jesse was smaller than his two older brothers but was considered the smartest of the three Zwawa boys, at least by their sister, Christine. The two A.I.T. commanders were situated in the cargo hold of the lead chopper, assisting one another into their Racal suits—orange polyvinyl chloride protective garments possessing sealed hoods and self-powered breathing systems. The Zwawa siblings knew their destination but had not been briefed on the nature of the mission. Whatever older brother John had in mind, the colonel was taking no chances. The two crews flying into Manhattan were heavily armed, with orders that allowed them to supersede the police department, fire and rescue, and all branches of local government.

9:11 A.M.

The detail of armed guards stood at attention in front of the door to the General Assembly Hall, where the Security Council was meeting to accommodate all those who wished to attend. Mary rocked back on her heels, waiting while her forged identification card was scrutinized by a UN security officer. His partner searched her purse.

"Thank you, Dr. Petrova. Arms up, please, I need to pat you down for weapons." He hesitated to touch her swollen belly."

"It's okay, he likes you." She took the police officer's hand and pressed it to her stomach in time to feel the baby kick.

"Wow, that's . . . that's amazing." He turned to his partner. "She's cleared, let her through." The officer handed her back the laminated card, never questioning her phony Russian accent or the fact that she was pale and sweating profusely, her perspiration giving off a soured musk.

The auditorium was buzzing, its capacity crowd waiting to hear from Iran's Supreme Leader. Mary weaved down one of the main aisles. Through watering eyes, she gazed at the stage. A mural of a phoenix rising from the battlefield served as the backdrop to a specially installed horseshoe configuration of chairs, all surrounding a rectangular table reserved for the fifteen members of the Security Council.

I am the phoenix rising . . .

The chamber spun. Mary shook her head, fighting to maintain control. *Inseminate the carriers.* She coughed phlegm into each palm. Innocently touched a French delegate as she squeezed past his table. Infested England and Denmark with a sneeze. Coughed in the direction of Brazil and Bulgaria. Cut back across another aisle and headed for a table of Arabs in dark business suits. A placard identified them as Iraqis.

Onstage, the Iranian mullah took his place at the podium, his words simultaneously translated into dozens of languages via headphones. "Excellencies, I come to you today in the hopes of averting a conflict that will lead to another war. I plead my case to the General Assembly, knowing that the Security Council has been corrupted by the occupiers of Afghanistan and Iraq . . ."

Mary tapped the shoulder of an Iraqi delegate heading for his seat. "Please? Where is the Iranian delegation?"

The dead-man-walking glanced at her swollen belly. Pointed to an empty table.

A wave of panic sent her pulse to race. *The meek shall inherit the earth, not the mullahs.* She hustled out of the chamber, returning to the security desk.

"Please, I am late to meet with the Iranian delegation. Where can I find them?"

The woman at the desk scanned her clipboard. "Room 415." She pointed down the hall. "Take the elevator up to the fourth floor."

"*Spasibo!*" Mary hurried down the corridor, coughing up a thick wad of phlegm into her hand. She checked it for blood, wiped it off on her jacket, then pressed the UP button and waited, her internal clock ticking.

VA MEDICAL CENTER
EAST SIDE, MANHATTAN
9:13 A.M.

Leigh Nelson led her V.I.P., his two guests, and their security detail down the hallway to Ward 27, praying all signs of the early-morning baseball wager had been removed.

Bertrand DeBorn's visit to the VA hospital was far more than just a photo op. While President Kogelo was scheduled to address the United Nations later this morning, hoping to quell hawkish demands for an Iranian invasion, the new secretary of defense was seeding a privately funded covert campaign designed to recruit a new generation of young Americans to the military.

Two prolonged wars required altering the public's perception of combat. Working in conjunction with one of New York's biggest advertising firms, DeBorn intended to present America's wounded veteran as the nation's new elite—a true patriot whose financial needs were met, his health care guaranteed, his family's future bright. Slap the Stars and Stripes on it, and even a turd could be sold as smelling sweet . . . provided the chosen poster boy fit the image.

DeBorn caught up to the female physician and grabbed the petite brunette by her elbow, the back of his hand pressing against her right breast in the process. "No more paraplegics or cancer patients, Doctor. The ideal candidate must be good-looking and middle-class, preferably Caucasian, God-fearing, and Christian. As for the wounds, they can be visible without the gross-out factor. No head wounds or missing eyes."

Leigh ground her teeth, brushing aside the secretary of defense's lingering hand. "I was told to show you our wounded vets. Whom you select for your recruitment campaign is up to you."

Sheridan Ernstmeyer joined in on the conversation. "What about mental clarity?"

DeBorn weighed the question. "I don't know. Colonel, you're the expert. What do you think?"

Lieutenant Colonel Philip Argenti, an ordained minister, was the highest-ranking man of the cloth in the Armed Forces and DeBorn's handpicked selection to lead the military's new recruitment campaign. Toting a Bible in one hand and a rifle in the other, Argenti aimed to target families still reeling from the recession as well as military stalwarts—apple-pie-eating, flag-bearing rural Southern folk who still viewed service in the military as the ultimate definition of patriotism. "Mental clarity is certainly desired, but not entirely necessary, Mister Secretary. We'll keep everything to sound bites and tweets."

Applause and catcalls greeted Leigh Nelson as she led DeBorn's group into Ward 27. Embarrassed, she casually kicked aside the dented bedpan from earlier, hoping the men have calmed since her last visit. "Thank you, fellas, you do a West Virginia girl proud. Just remember, my granddaddy taught me how to castrate hogs when I was a little girl, so don't cross the line. I brought a very special visitor with me. How 'bout a warm welcome for our new secretary of defense, Bertrand DeBorn."

Ignoring the lack of response, the spry white-haired man moved quickly down the center aisle, nodding politely, pressing on as he mentally inventtoried each wounded combat veteran. *Hispanic . . . Hispanic . . . Black . . . he's white, but the wrong look. Quadriplegic, no good. This one looks white, but he's way too skinny, probably on drugs . . .* DeBorn kept his entourage moving, his frustration mounting like an obsessed breeder seeking a hunting dog in a kennel filled with poodles and dachshunds, until Sheridan Ernstmeyer grabbed his arm, the former CIA assassin motioning toward the last bed on their left. The curtain was partially pulled around, but not enough to cloak the disabled soldier—an African-American in his late thirties, probably an officer, paralyzed from the waist down.

"Wrong . . . look, Sherry."

"Not him, Bert. The orderly."

The man dressed in a white tee shirt and scrubs was Caucasian and in his early thirties, his long, dark hair pulled into a ponytail. The jaw was dimpled, his six-foot-four, two-hundred-pound frame chiseled like an athlete. The orderly was changing out his patient's bedding, rolling him on his side with his right hand, using his opposite shoulder as leverage, maneuvering him easily . . . despite the fact that he had no left arm.

"Dr. Nelson, that orderly . . . is he a veteran?"

"You mean Shep?"

"Shep?"

"Patrick Shepherd. Yes, sir, he served four tours in Iraq. But I don't think—"

"He's perfect. Exactly what we're looking for. Colonel Argenti?"

"Strapping young man, obviously an athlete. And working so diligently to aid his fellow soldiers. He's outstanding, Mr. Secretary. Well done."

Sheridan shot the minister a look.

Leigh attempted to pull DeBorn aside. "Sir, there are a few things you need to know about the sergeant–"

"Mission accomplished, Doctor. Have the sergeant meet us in your office in ten minutes. Ms. Ernstmeyer, see to it that Dr. Nelson e-mails us his personnel file." He checked his watch. *Still a few hours before the meeting.* "Colonel, join me outside, I'm in need of a cigarette."

9:26 A.M.

"**. . . yet it is** not an Iranian armada positioned in the Persian Gulf, nor is it Hezbollah who has established military bases in Iraq and in Afghanistan. It is the Great Satan who is responsible for this conflict . . . I can smell his sulfurous presence in this building even now. To him I offer this warning: The Muslim world will not allow you to invade the National Islamic Republic of Iran and steal our oil as you did to our brothers in Iraq. We shall fight—"

The security officer lowered the volume of the Iranian leader's speech on his video screen as he inspected Mary Klipot's identification. Satisfied, he pressed a button beneath his desk, buzzing into Conference Room 415. "You've got a visitor. Russian embassy."

Mary gritted her teeth, struggling to control the lung spasms urging her to cough.

A metallic *click* as the door to Room 415 unlocked and opened, revealing an Iranian security guard. "Speak."

"I am to deliver a message from Prime Minister Putin's office to the Supreme Leader's attaché."

"Your identification."

She held it up for him to read. The Iranian shut the door.

Mary Klipot's skin was hot and clammy, her fever rising past 101.5 degrees. She coughed bile into her scarf. Tasting the blood, she wiped it with her right palm, allowing the mucus to remain on her skin.

The security officer seated outside the door cringed. "That's a nasty cough. Keep it away from me."

The door reopened. "You have two minutes."

Mary entered the conference room, the guard motioning her to remain by the door. Two dozen men, some in business attire, others in traditional robes, were watching the Supreme Leader's speech on closed-circuit flat-screen monitors located throughout the suite.

Her heart raced as she spotted Iran's president speaking with a mullah on the other side of the room.

A man in a business suit approached, escorted by two large Arabs wearing security earpieces. "I am the Supreme Leader's attaché. Deliver your message."

Mary's eyes watered with fever. Her limbs quivered. Her dress and pantyhose were laced with sweat. Her chest constricted, sending her convulsing in a fit of coughs. "Prime Minister Putin wishes . . . (cough) the Supreme Leader to contact him . . . (cough) one hour after President Kogelo's speech."

The man's eyes narrowed. He reached for Mary's identification card to examine the photo—

—Mary cupping his hand in her moist palms. "С Рождеством . . . и с Новым Годом!"

The man pulled his hand free. He rattled off something in Arabic, causing the two guards to escort her roughly to the door.

Mary exited to the corridor. Hurried to catch an elevator. She managed to slip inside the closing doors, held open for her by a Mexican delegate in his late forties. The man instinctively moved to the rear of the car as he inhaled a whiff of Mary's burgeoning body odor.

A wicked smile twitched across the pregnant woman's face as her feverish mind translated the Russian phrase she had offered the Iranian: *Merry Christmas . . . and a happy New Year!*

The migraine struck the moment she stepped out of the elevator. Squiggly purple lines impeded her vision. A sudden rush of nausea sent her scurrying into the women's bathroom. She had barely made it to an empty stall when the bloody excrement burst from her insides, scorching her throat. For several moments she heaved the remaining contents of her stomach into the toilet, her entire body shaking as she hugged the cold porcelain to her contorting belly.

The nausea passed, leaving her weak and trembling. Dragging herself to her feet, she staggered out of the stall to a row of sinks, her reflection in the mirror startling.

She was ghostly pale, almost gray. Her eyes were sunken and red. Veins traced a faint blue latticework across her forehead. A red splotch the size of a walnut appeared above the lymph node along her neck. *Scythe's entered phase 2. Get back to the car. Use the vaccine—*

"Miss? Are you all right?"

The short, slightly stocky Caucasian woman wearing a food-services badge was staring at her, aghast.

"Morning sickness." Mary rinsed out her mouth, pushing the damp strands of hair away from her forehead. She left the bathroom. Exited the building.

The cool air kept her from fainting. She inhaled the December chill into her defiled lungs. Found her way past the police barricade and pushed through the crowd of protesters, every cough dousing the faceless multitude with specks of tainted blood.

Clearing the horde, she waited at First Avenue for the DO NOT WALK sign to change, clutching the traffic light pole for support, her mind racing. *Delirious yet victorious, a true warrior of Christ.* Her feverish eyes gazed at the black tow truck turning north on First Avenue—

—hauling her white Honda Civic!

"No . . . no!" Bloody excrement gurgled in her throat. She half staggered, half ran across the four-lane intersection.

Horns blared, brakes screeched, pedestrians screamed.

A crowd gathered around Mary Klipot's body, sprawled across First Avenue.

"Officials are trying to get to the bottom of how vaccine manufacturer Baxter International Inc. made 'experimental virus material' based on a human flu strain but contaminated with the H5N1 avian flu virus and then distributed it to an Austrian company (Avir Green Hills Biotechnology). Accidental release of a mixture of live H5N1 and H3N2 viruses could have resulted in dire consequences. If someone exposed to the mixture had been co-infected with H5N1 and H3N2, the person could have served as an incubator for a hybrid virus able to transmit easily to and among people. That mixing process, called reassortment, *is one of two ways pandemic viruses are created."*

—Canadian Press, February 27, 2009

DECEMBER 20

EAST 46TH STREET

TUDOR CITY, MANHATTAN

9:33 A.M.

(22 HOURS, 30 MINUTES BEFORE THE PROPHESIED END OF DAYS)

Thirty-four minutes have passed since Mary Klipot had disposed of the steel attaché case in the trash bin. Twenty-four minutes since the first black rat had arrived.

Rattus rattus. No one really knew how many of the rodents inhabited the Big Apple, estimates varied from 250,000 to upward of 7 million. Agile creatures, a rat could balance on its hind legs, climb ladders, leap three feet straight into the air, or scurry up a sheer wall. It could squeeze through a hole as narrow as a quarter, survive a sixty-foot plunge, or swim up a drainage pipe clear into a toilet. Though nocturnal, a rat could hunt both day and night. The name "rat" translated into "gnawing animal" and for good reason: So strong were its teeth and jaw that a rat could chew through brick and mortar, even reinforced concrete.

A rat's life spanned two to three years, consisting mostly of eating and breeding. Females averaged more than twenty sex acts a day from the time they reached three months old. Litters ranged from six to twelve pups, with a single female bearing four to six litters in its lifetime. Male rats had been known to mate with a female until it died of exhaustion . . . and then continued on well after her passing.

Intelligent animals, rats thrived in the city's endless banquets of refuse, their olfactory sense capable of detecting food anywhere within their territory. New York's black rat population had long lost its fear of man, and the pungent scent coming from within the dumpster was alluring.

MORNINGSIDE HEIGHTS, MANHATTAN

9:38 A.M.

Francesca Minos exited *Minos Pizzeria*, balancing a stack of cardboard soup bowls on her bulging abdomen. A week overdue with her first child, the twenty-five-year-old would rather have been lying in bed with her swollen feet propped on pillows than greeting yet another chilly New York morning in her sweat suit and overcoat . . . but Paolo had not missed a breakfast line in two years and, pregnant or not, she needed to help her husband.

Reaching into the steaming aluminum pot, she grabbed a wooden ladle and deposited a clump of oatmeal in a disposable bowl, leaving it on the table for the next person in line. Already the morning gathering extended down Amsterdam Avenue, with more homeless on the way . . . her devout soul mate determined to feed each and every one of them.

A platoon of vacant eyes and expressionless faces filed past her in silence. *Society's forgotten souls. Had temptation led them astray, or had they simply given up?* Many were drug addicts and alcoholics, no doubt, but others had fallen on hard times and simply had nowhere else to go. At least 30 percent were veterans of the Iraq War, half of those disabled.

Francesca filled another bowl, her fear turning to anger. There were almost a hundred thousand homeless in New York City alone. As bad as she felt for them, Francesca was more worried for her own family. Like most businesses, the pizzeria was struggling, and soon they, too, would have another mouth to feed. Were the homeless even appreciative of the free meal they were receiving? Or had the generosity of strangers simply been absorbed as part of their daily ritual? With each passing day, the line separating the

Minoses from their impoverished brethren grew slimmer . . . what would happen when they were finally forced to stop tithing altogether? Would the homeless understand? Would they thank their hosts for their past generosity and wish them well, or would they turn violent, smashing the pizzeria's windows, demanding their entitlement.

The thought made Francesca shudder.

His container empty, Paolo wiped his palms on his oatmeal-splattered chef's apron, then headed back inside for another refill.

"Paolo . . . wait."

The dark, curly-haired Italian paused, smiling at his expectant wife. "Yes, my angel? What does your heart wish of me?"

What do I wish? My back aches from hoisting this kicking bowling ball twenty-four/seven, my feet are killing me, and my hemorrhoids are falling out of my ass like nobody's business. What I wish is that you'd quit bleeding our household savings on these losers, or at least hit the damn lottery so you could take me away from all this!

She glanced again at the procession of street people, their worn shoes soaking wet from the pools of slush. Beaten into submission, they were living out their days in survival mode. And yet, at one time, each life had held hope and potential.

Like her unborn child . . .

"Francesca?"

Parting a strand of dark hair from her eyes, she returned her husband's loving smile. "Mind the stove, sweetheart, it's very hot."

Two blocks south of *Minos Pizzeria* and one block east of Riverside Park stood the Manhasset, an eleven-story century-old redbrick building. Condominiums were priced at over half a million dollars for a one-bedroom—washer and dryer not included.

The west-facing apartment on the Manhasset's tenth floor was dark now, the heavy drapes closed, their bottoms pressed to the bay windows by textbooks to prevent even a sliver of gray morning light from penetrating the room. Only a solitary flame illuminated the proceedings, the candle situated on the floor to the Hindu woman's back.

The necromancer closed her eyes. Dressed in her traditional white tunic, she wore no jewelry—save for the crystal dangling from a gold chain around her neck. Attuned to the vibrations of the supernal, the crystal was her canary in the coal mine, a device that alerted her to the desire of her spiritual companion to communicate.

Studying the art of necromancy in Nepal was no different than learning how to play a musical instrument—for some it was merely a hobby, for others a passion that might lead to mastery, assuming one possessed the talent. When it came to seeking communication with the spirits of the dead, Manisha Pande possessed the bloodlines of the gifted. Born in a Himalayan village, she shared a maternal lineage with necromancers that dated back to ancient Persia. By the Middle Ages the practice had reached Europe, where it was corrupted by self-proclaimed magicians and sorcerers—condemned by the Catholic Church as an agency for evil spirits. In Nepal, however, a talented practitioner could still earn a good living from the trade.

Despite her innate skills, Manisha grew up believing she had another calling. Her father, Bikash, and her paternal uncles were all physicians, and the teenage girl's desire to help others was strong. When she turned sixteen, Manisha pleaded with her father to allow her to move to India to live with one of her uncles so that she could study psychiatry, hoping to treat women who were victims of human trafficking. The trade was alarmingly robust in Nepal and throughout Asia, with thousands of women abducted and sold as sex slaves.

Manisha was surprised when her father agreed to support her plans. What she never knew was that Dr. Bikash Pande had been approached years earlier by a member of a secret society who had arranged for the physician's talented daughter to one day meet the prodigy of another family—the Patels, whose eldest son, Pankaj, was also immersed in the science of psychology, only as it applied to the genesis of evil.

Manisha Patel breathed in and out, waiting for her spiritual guide to appear.

Necromancy was an art form dependent upon developing relationships with the deceased. One could neither conjure nor command a spirit, they had to be a willing participant in the act. Having moved to New York with her family following the birth of her daughter (a year after the September 11 attacks), Manisha had been overwhelmed by the sudden deluge of supernal contacts willing to communicate. Over time, a special relationship had been forged between the necromancer and one of these restless spirits—a woman who had been aboard one of the hijacked planes that had struck the Twin Towers. Up until this morning, all communications between Manisha and her spiritual companion had been reserved for the twilight hours.

Not today. For the last two hours, Manisha Patel's crystal had been radiating like a tuning fork.

She had waited until Pankaj had left the apartment with Dawn. A close bond existed between her daughter and the dead woman's spirit, and the reverberations coming from the crystal this morning felt wrong. Normally, the presence of a spirit resembled the sensation of a well-played guitar string, its sweet strum reverberating in Manisha's heart, the Creator's infinite Light lifting her soul higher with every passing beat. But this morning's vibrations were distinctly out of tune. Manisha felt afraid, and the more she feared, the more horrifying the vibrations became. Suddenly she felt isolated and alone, unable to connect with anyone . . . as if trapped on her own island of self-doubt.

Manisha . . .

"Yes, I am here. Speak through me . . . tell me what is wrong."

You and your family must leave. Leave Manhattan . . . now!

FORT DETRICK-FREDERICK, MARYLAND
9:43 A.M.

Like his two younger brothers, Colonel John Zwawa was a physically imposing man. A veteran of two wars, the colonel had seen combat and been stationed in places as diverse as Egypt and Alaska. Approaching retirement, he was sixteen months into a four-year assignment as commanding officer at Fort Detrick. In charge . . . yet purposely kept out of the loop by the

Pentagon in regard to ongoing operations. Until this morning, the colonel's biggest worry had been making sure the base soda machines remained stocked.

As of today, the colonel would no longer play the role of caretaker. Lydia Gagnon's briefing had changed everything.

The microbiologist faced the remote cameras, her image appearing on secured monitors inside the Pentagon, White House, and aboard the two rapid-response-team helicopters racing to Manhattan. "The case that was removed from our Bio-Level 4 facility was part of a top secret project called Scythe. In short, Scythe is a self-administered biological weapon that allows an infected insurgent to rapidly spread bubonic plague throughout a military or hostile civilian population.

"Scythe is Black Death at its absolute worst, combining bubonic, pneumonic, and septicemic variants in a form that can be spread quickly across both animal and human populations. During the bubonic pandemic of 1347, the bacterium, *Yersinia pestis*, lived inside the stomach of its primary vector, the rat flea. Plague bacteria multiply quickly inside a flea, blocking off its foregut. This stimulates hunger and more biting. Each time the flea bites its host, it gags on undigested blood and plague bacilli, vomiting them into the wound. Infected fleas lived off their rat hosts, creating an epizootic spread that devastated Asia and Europe. While the most treatable, bubonic is in many ways the nastiest of the Scythe bacilli, leaving the victim looking and smelling like death. Symptoms include fever, chills, and painful swelling of the lymph glands, called buboes, which turn red then black. Historic bubonic also disrupts the nervous system, causing agitation and delirium. If left untreated, bubonic plague has a 60 percent mortality rate.

"Pneumonic plague is an advanced stage of bubonic. It occurs when the bacilli infect the victim's lungs, allowing it to be transmitted directly from human to human. The lungs become agitated, stimulating coughing and the spitting up of blood, followed by interminable vomiting. Inhale an infected person's breath or come in direct contact with their bodily fluids, and you contract plague. In colder temperatures, the expelled sputum can also freeze, allowing for greater range of transmission. Left untreated, the mortality rate among pneumonic plague victims is between 95 and 100 percent.

"The last variant—septicemic plague—is the most lethal of the lot. It occurs when bacilli move directly into the bloodstream, killing the victim within twelve to fifteen hours. Again, Scythe contains all three variants. It spreads rapidly, tortures its victims while eliciting fear, and kills within fifteen hours. Only our specifically harvested antibiotic can inoculate the public or cure an infected individual . . . assuming you can get to them in time."

"Tell us about the woman." Vice President Arthur M. Krawitz was seated next to Harriet Clausner. The president's secretary of state grimaced on the White House monitor.

"Her name is Mary Louise Klipot. We're e-mailing her photo and bio to everyone now, as well as to the FBI and New York police departments. Mary is the microbiologist who developed Scythe. She's the one who brought plague samples back from Europe.

"Mary is eight months pregnant. She is engaged to her lab technician, Andrew Bradosky, believed to be the father of her unborn child. Mary and Bradosky have both gone missing as of 2:11 A.M. this morning, when Mary left her BSL-4 lab. Security videotape reveals she was carrying a BSL variant transport case."

The vice president interrupted. "Dr. Gagnon, these attaché cases? Scythe was being readied for deployment, wasn't it?"

Lydia Gagnon looked away from the White House feed, hoping to avert a drawn-out debate. "We don't make policy decisions, Mr. Vice President, we simply follow orders. Our department has been following a 2001 directive to develop a system to subdue a hostile population. Those orders have never been rescinded."

"Who even knew the orders existed? I didn't, and I served on the Foreign Relations Committee for twenty-two years. This directive is not only illegal, Dr. Gagnon, it's genocide!"

"It's warfare, Mr. Vice President," Secretary Clausner interjected. "As I clearly stated in the last two PDBs, our military lacks the manpower to invade another country. Biological weapons offer us options."

"Wiping out 40 million Iranians is not an acceptable option, Secretary Clausner."

"Neither is allowing nuclear weapons to fall into the hands of terrorists."

"With all due respect, this isn't the time or place," Colonel Zwawa snapped. "Dr. Gagnon, where's the missing Scythe attaché case now?"

Using her laptop mouse, Dr. Gagnon clicked on a satellite map of New York City. A red circle zoomed in on 46th Street between First and Second Avenue. "It's in an alleyway located sixty meters west of the United Nations. Once our A.I.T.s are on the ground, Delta team will retrieve the attaché case while Alpha Team coordinates with Homeland Security and Albany's CDC to set up a secure perimeter around the plaza. We'll establish the UN Plaza as a temporary gray zone, at least until we can determine whether Scythe has been released. A.I.T.s are equipped with enough antibiotic to treat upward of fifty infected individuals, with more antidote being readied."

"Show us the worst-case scenario," Colonel Zwawa ordered.

Dr. Gagnon hesitated, then clicked her mouse on another link.

A black circle appeared over the UN Plaza and the southern tip of Manhattan. "Assuming the spread is limited to foot traffic during its first thirty to sixty minutes of insemination, we may be able to keep Scythe contained inside Lower Manhattan. If it gets off the island and is limited to vehicular traffic, hours two and three look like this—"

A second circle appeared, encompassing Connecticut, New York, the eastern half of Pennsylvania, and New Jersey.

"If, however, a human vector boards a train, or God help us, a commercial airliner, then Scythe could spread across the globe within twenty-four hours."

VA MEDICAL CENTER
EAST SIDE, MANHATTAN
9:51 A.M.

"What does he want with me?" Patrick Shepherd hustled to keep up with Leigh Nelson as she hurried through the congested hospital corridor, weaving her way around patients in bathrobes pushing IVs on wheeled stands.

"I'm sure he'll explain. Keep in mind, he is President Kogelo's new secretary of defense. Whatever he wants with you, I'd approach it as an honor."

Patrick followed his doctor into her office, the familiar sanctuary violated by the presence of the white-haired DeBorn, who had situated himself behind Dr. Nelson's desk.

The defense secretary dismissed his two Secret Service agents, allowing Leigh and Patrick to sit down. "Sergeant Shepherd, it's an honor. This is my personal assistant, Ms. Ernstmeyer, and this fine gentleman is Lieutenant Colonel Philip Argenti. The colonel will be your new CO."

"Why do I need a new commanding officer? I've already served my time."

DeBorn ignored him, squinting to read the file coming across his BlackBerry. "Sergeant Patrick Ryan Shepherd. Four tours of duty. Abu Gharib . . . Green Zone. Reassigned to the 101st Airborne Division. Says here you received some on-the-job training to be a chopper pilot."

"Blackhawks. Medevac choppers. I was wounded before I could test for my certification."

The secretary of defense scrolled down his screen. "What's this? Personnel file says you played professional baseball. That true?"

"Minor leagues, mostly."

"The sergeant also played for the Boston Red Sox."

Shep shot Dr. Nelson a look to kill.

"Really? Outfielder, I'd guess."

"Pitcher."

DeBorn looked up. "Not a southpaw, I hope?"

"Shepherd? Patrick Shepherd? Why does that name sound familiar?" Colonel Argenti tugged at his rusty gray hair, wracking his brain. "Wait . . . you're him! The kid they nicknamed the Boston Strangler. The rookie who no-hit the Yankees in his first start in the big leagues."

"Actually, it was a two-hitter, but—"

"You shut out Oakland your next start."

"Toronto."

"Toronto, right. I remember watching it on *Sports Center.* That one went extra innings, they pulled you in the ninth. That was crazy, they should have left you in." Argenti stood, pumping his fist excitedly at DeBorn. "Been a season ticket holder going on thirty years. I know my baseball, and this kid was a beast. His fastball was okay, a cutter in the low nineties, but it was his dirty deuce that was outright nasty."

DeBorn frowned. "Dirty deuce?"

"You know—the dirty yellow hammer . . . the yakker. Public enemy number two. A breaking ball, Bert! This kid had a breaking ball that was like hitting a lead shot put. Groundout after groundout, it drove hitters crazy." The priest leaned back against Dr. Nelson's desk, hovering over Patrick like an adoring fan. "You were a phenom, son, a nine day wonder. Whatever happened to you? You disappeared off the map like nobody's business."

"I enlisted . . . sir."

"Oh, right. Country first, but still. Crying shame about the arm. How'd you lose it?"

"I don't remember. They called it a traumatic amputation. Buddy of mine, medic named David Kantor, he found me . . . saved my life. D.K. said it was an IED. I must've picked it up, thinking it was a kid's toy. Woke up in the hospital six weeks later, couldn't remember a thing. Probably better that way."

"Ever think about pitching again?" Argenti smiled, offering encouragement. "That pitcher, Jeff Abbott, he managed pretty well with only one arm."

"Jim Abbott. And he was missing a right hand, he kept his glove on his wrist. All I have left is a stub where my left biceps used to be."

"That's enough baseball, Padre." DeBorn motioned for Argenti to return to his chair. "Sergeant, we need you for a new assignment, one that will help America combat our enemies overseas while keeping the homeland safe. Your job will be to help us recruit a new generation of fighting men and women. This is a great honor. You'll be traveling around the country, visiting high schools—"

"No."

The secretary of defense's complexion flushed red. "What did you say?"

"I won't do it. I can't. My wife's dead set against it. I couldn't do that to her again, no, sir."

"Where's your wife now? I'd like to have a word with her."

"She doesn't want to talk to you. She doesn't want to talk with me. She left me. Took my daughter and . . . well, she's gone."

"Then why do you care what—"

"She's in New York."

Everyone turned to Leigh Nelson, who squeezed her eyes shut, wishing she hadn't spoken.

The blood rushed from Patrick's face. "Doc, what are you saying? Did you speak to Bea?"

"Not yet. Her address was e-mailed to me this morning. I haven't had a chance to tell you. It's not a hundred percent, but everything sure fits her description."

Shep leaned back in the chair, his entire body quivering.

"There's a phone number. We can call and make sure. Shep? Shep, are you okay?"

The anxiety attack hit him like a tidal wave. Suddenly he couldn't breathe, couldn't see. White spots obscured his vision. Sweat burst from his pores in cold droplets as he slid onto the floor, his body convulsing.

Dr. Nelson yanked open her door, and shouted, "I need a nurse and an orderly!" She knelt by Shep, feeling for his pulse. Rapid and weak.

"What the hell's wrong with him? Is he having a heart attack?"

"Anxiety. Shep, honey, lie back and breathe. You're okay."

DeBorn glanced at Sheridan Ernstmeyer, who shrugged. "Anxiety? Are you saying he's having a panic attack? Good God, man up, Sergeant. You're a United States Marine!"

A nurse rushed in, followed by an intern pushing a wheelchair.

Dr. Nelson helped lift Shep into the chair. "Elevate his feet. Get a cold compress on his neck and give him a Xanax."

The intern wheeled Shep out of the office.

The white-haired secretary of defense stared down Leigh Nelson, his hawkish look meant to intimidate. "Where's the wife?"

"Like I said, she's in New York."

"The address, Dr. Nelson."

"Mr. Secretary, this is way beyond reuniting a broken family. Shep's unstable. His memory is fragmented, his brain is still affected by his injury. We deal with these things all the time. You can't keep redeploying GIs three and four times without tearing their families apart. Spouses relocate, sometimes because they find someone else, sometimes out of fear. The military no longer detoxes its returning vets properly, they go from combat to civilian life in a week. Some of these guys are walking time bombs, their minds still immersed in war. They can't enter their homes without doing a search of the premises, and they keep weapons by the bed. I've seen way too many cases of returning soldiers stabbing or shooting their loved ones while in the throes of a nightmare. I'm guessing that won't look too good on the new recruiting poster."

"I didn't ask you for a dissertation on warfare, Doctor. Now give me the wife's address."

She hesitated.

"With the economy still struggling, it must be nice to have a well-paying government salaried job. Of course, we could probably bring in two residents for what you're being paid."

Leigh's back stiffened. "Is that a threat, Mr. DeBorn?"

"Ms. Ernstmeyer, contact the Pentagon. Have them locate the sergeant's family."

"Wait. Just . . . wait." Reaching into her lab-coat pocket, Leigh retrieved the e-mail printout, reluctantly handed it to the secretary of defense.

DeBorn squinted as he read aloud. "Beatrice Shepherd. Battery Park, Manhattan."

"She's close by," Sheridan remarked. "Seems too coincidental. Maybe she's here because he's here."

"Find out."

"Whoa, slow down a minute," said Leigh, her ire drawn. "Shepherd's my patient. If anyone's going to approach his wife, it should be me."

"You're too close. Spouses who feel scorned by the military require a deft touch. This wife of his sounds like another bleeding-heart peace activist. Is she?"

"I wouldn't know."

"Women who place morality above family are the worst kind of hypocrites. Take that Cindy Sheehan. She loses her son, spends the next three years protesting the Armed Forces he risked his life to join, then she ends up deserting her family to pursue a political career. I suspect this Beatrice Shepherd is cut from the same cloth. Ms. Ernstmeyer knows how to handle their kind."

"Fine. Handle it. Now, if you'll excuse me, I have other patients to tend to."

"In a minute. I need you to fit the sergeant for a prosthetic arm."

"He was fitted three months ago. We've been told there's a four-to-six-month backlog."

"Colonel?"

"He'll have one by this afternoon."

Leigh Nelson felt like she was drowning. "With all due respect, slapping on hardware and forcing Shep to confront his wife won't even begin to address his psychological problems."

"Let us deal with his family, Doctor. You arrange for the psychiatric help."

Leigh balled her fists, her blood pressure soaring. "And where should I find this psychiatrist? Conjure him out of thin air? I've got 263 combat veterans in serious need of psychiatric care, a third of them on suicide watch. We're sharing two clinical psychologists between three VA hospitals and—"

"It's handled," interrupted Father Argenti. "By this afternoon, Patrick Shepherd will be speaking with the best shrink taxpayer money can buy."

Secretary DeBorn's eyebrows rose. "Any other challenges, Dr. Nelson?"

She sat back in her chair, defeated. "You want to hire your own specialist—fine by me, just keep it quiet. I don't want the other men in Shep's ward knowing about this. It's bad for morale. Shep won't go for it, either."

"Duly noted. Colonel, set up private sessions at the psychiatrist's office."

"That won't work. We had a situation last week. I took Shep out of the hospital as a first step to reorient him into civilian life. It didn't go well. You're better off doing sessions in the hospital."

"Then arrange for him to have his own room. Tell him it's a gift from the Pentagon." Secretary DeBorn stood, ending the meeting. "I'm due at the UN this afternoon, but I've got one more stop to make first. Colonel, you're in charge. Be sure the psychiatrist you hire knows Shepherd needs to be in Washington for January's State of the Union Address. That'll give him four weeks to get our boy in decent mental shape."

DeBorn headed for the door. Paused. "You like Shepherd, don't you, Doctor?"

"I care about all my patients."

"No. I see how you look at him. There's something there. Maybe a physical attraction?"

"Sir, I never—"

"Of course not. But it wouldn't hurt you to be there for the sergeant . . . you know, to ease his mind when his wife officially terminates their relationship."

Leigh Nelson snapped, "Not that it's any of your business, but I happen to be happily married with two beautiful children. And you can forget about Shep. Whatever happened between him and Bea, whatever fallout they may have had, he loves his wife and daughter intensely and would say or do just about anything to get them back."

DeBorn nodded. "That's exactly what I'm counting on."

UNITED NATIONS PLAZA
10:14 A.M.

The suddenness of the assault had blindsided the protesters. The combatants—three hundred members of New York's highly trained Emergency Service Unit (ESU), all wearing hooded gas masks and Homeland Security apparel, had stormed the plaza in one expedient, overwhelming wave. Working in teams, the troops had quickly subdued the crowd, binding their wrists behind their backs using trifold, single-use restraints before laying them out in organized rows along the cold concrete expanse.

Having taken out the mob, they turned on the media.

With little regard for camera equipment or Constitutional rights, the assault team physically herded the stunned reporters and their television crews to another section of the plaza, where they, too, were placed in restraints.

"This is America! You can't restrain the press!"

"Hey, asshole, ever hear of the First Amendment?"

What the members of the media never saw was that the police officers who had been forming a gauntlet against the protesters were also being sequestered, their weapons tagged and confiscated. After being told by health officials that their actions were merely a minor precaution against a possible swine flu outbreak, the law-enforcement detail was led inside a triage center, one of four mobile Army tents now occupying the plaza. Isolated in small, plastic-curtained compartments, the unnerved police officers were reassured that everything was fine, even as medical teams in white Racal suits moved from one cop to the next, performing a thorough physical examination.

"He's clean. Escort him to the observation tent."

"This one's fine."

"This one's running a slight fever."

"My kids have the flu . . . it's nothing."

"Treatment tent. Run full blood and hair analysis, then start him on antibiotics."

"Doctor, you'd better take a look at this one."

Officer Gary Beck was seated on the linoleum floor, his riot gear by his side. He was sweating profusely, his complexion a pasty gray . . . and he was coughing up blood.

"Isolation tent, STAT! Alert Captain Zwawa. I want full blood and hair analysis in ten minutes, followed by—"

The officer dropped to all fours and retched.

"Seal the compartment!"

"Triage-3 to base. We need a mobile isolation unit and a cleanup detail, STAT."

VA MEDICAL CENTER
EAST SIDE, MANHATTAN
10:21 A.M.

Leigh Nelson led her semiconscious patient inside the private room on the sixth floor. "Not too shabby, huh? Partial view of Manhattan, private bathroom—"

She watched Patrick Shepherd stumble in a Xanax-induced stupor around the room. He looked beneath the bed and between the mattresses. He searched inside the bed-table drawers and the closet . . . even behind the toilet.

"Baby doll, it's safe. And it's all yours. Now be a good boy and lie down, you're making me a nervous wreck."

The warm numbness was spreading, calming the waves of anxiety, weakening his resolve. He sat down on the bed, his body sinking into liquid lead. "Leigh, listen to me . . . are you listening?"

"Yes, baby doll, I'm listening."

"Do you know what true love is?"

"Tell me."

He looked up at her, his dilated eyes swimming in tears. "Boundless emptiness."

Leigh swallowed the lump forming in her throat. "Shep, you need to talk with somebody . . . someone who can help you cope with what you're feeling. DeBorn's sending over a specialist. Before you speak with Bea, I think it's important you talk with him."

"Why? So he can tell me to move on? To let her go?"

"No, sweetie. So you can get some clarity. Put your life in perspective."

He motioned to the box of personal belongings sitting on the desk. "Bea's book . . . get it for me."

She sorted through the cardboard container, retrieving the copy of *Dante's Inferno*.

"Read the opening canto . . . the first few lines."

She opened the book to the *Divine Comedy*'s first stanza and read aloud:

"About halfway through the course of my pathetic life, I woke up and found myself in a stupor in some dark place. I'm not sure how I ended up there, I guess I had taken . . . a few wrong turns." She glanced at Patrick. "Is this supposed to be you?"

He pointed to a framed painting of a beach house, the tropical scene providing the only color in the room. "That was supposed to be me." He closed his eyes, fading fast. "Now this is all I have to show for my pathetic life . . . trapped in purgatory. Hell awaits."

"I don't believe in Hell."

"That's because you've never been there. I have." He lay back on the bed. "Been there four times. Every time I close my eyes to sleep, it drags me back again. It soils you. It stains the soul. I won't let it stain my family." His words began to slur. "DeBorn . . . Tell him no. Tell him ta go fuh . . ."

The eyeballs flitted beneath the lids, his larynx rumbling into a soothing snore.

***The beach house** is open and airy, the A-frame living room's ceiling paneled in wood.* Fifteen-foot-high *bay windows reveal a deck and pool out back, and just beyond that the Atlantic Ocean.*

The Realtor opens the French doors, filling the house with a salty breeze and the soothing sound of crashing waves. "Atlantic Beach is a quaint little seaside village, you'll love it here. The house is Mediterranean, five bedrooms, six baths, plus the guest house. It's an absolute steal at $2.1 million."

Patrick turns to his better half. "So?"

The blonde-haired beauty balances their two-year-old daughter on her right hip. "Shep, we don't need all this."

"Who cares about need? I'm a big-league pitcher now."

"You pitched two games."

"But my agent says the endorsement deals he's working on will pay for three beach houses."

"It's so far from the city."

"Babe, this'll be our summer home. We'll still have our condo in the city."

"Boston or New York?"

"I dunno. Maybe both."

She shakes her head. "You're insane."

"No, no, your husband's right." The Realtor flashes a reassuring smile. "Real estate remains the best investment around, property values can only go up. There's no way you can go wrong."

"That's great to know." She switches the curly-haired toddler to her other hip. "Can my husband and I have a moment to talk in private?"

"Of course. But I have another buyer looking at the house in twenty minutes, so don't be too long." She heads out to the pool deck, leaving the door open so she can eavesdrop.

The blonde slams it shut.

Shep smiles defensively. "Husband. I love that."

"Let's be clear. We're not married yet, and we won't be if I catch you flirting with any more cheerleaders."

"They weren't cheerleaders, and I told you, I wasn't flirting. It was just a photo shoot for Hooters."

"Those twins had their hooters in your face when I walked in."

"It's my job, babe. Part of the new image. You know, the 'Boston Strangler.'"

The blonde sneers in disgust. "Who are you? Your ego's so out of control, I barely recognize you anymore."

"What are you talking about? This is what we wanted . . . we're living the dream."

"Your dream, not mine. I don't want to be married to some egomaniac, wondering whose bed he's sleeping in when he's not in mine."

"That's not fair. I've never cheated on you."

"No, but you're tempted. Face it, Shep, we've been together since we were kids. Tell me you're not the least bit curious about being with another woman, especially now, when they're practically throwing themselves at you."

He says nothing, unable to lie to her.

"Yeah, that's what I thought. So here's what we're going to do. I'm going back to Boston with our daughter while you decide if you'd rather get some strange from the Ooh-La-La twins or be tied down to a family. Better get it out of your system now. I don't want you waking up three or five or ten years from now,

thinking you made a mistake." Grabbing the baby's diaper bag, she heads for the door.

"Honey, wait—"

The blonde turns around, tears in her eyes. "Just remember, Patrick Shepherd, sometimes you don't really appreciate the things you have until you lose them."

Patrick moaned into his pillow, unable to shake himself loose from the drug-induced sleep.

UNITED NATIONS
GENERAL ASSEMBLY BUILDING
10:28 A.M.

A shaken Jeffrey Cook, head of the United Nations Department of Safety and Security (UNDSS) led the seven men dressed in Racal suits, full-face rebreathers, boots, and heavy gloves into the General Assembly Building's control room. "Can I have your attention please?"

A dozen pairs of eyes looked up from their security monitors.

"This is Captain Zwawa from the infectious disease lab in Fort Detrick. He needs our help with a possible security breach."

"Jesus, what's going on?"

"Is the air safe to breathe?"

"Are we under attack?"

"Stay calm." Jay Zwawa held up the copy of the USAMIRIID identity photos. "We need you to locate this man and woman. One or both may have entered one of the United Nations buildings as early as eight o'clock this morning. We need to know which buildings they entered, who they came in contact with, and whether they left the building."

Zwawa's team passed around copies of Mary Klipot and Andrew Bradosky's photo to each technician, along with a CD.

"The CD file contains the suspects' DNA markers. Run it through your surveillance system and search for a match. Start with the General Assembly Building before moving on to the rest of the UN complex."

"Who are they? Are we in any danger?"

"Shouldn't we be wearing protective suits, too?"

"The suits are a precaution for my frontliners. As long as you remain in this room, you'll be fine."

One of the techs looked worried. "I took a bathroom break about ten minutes ago."

"One of our medical staff will check you out."

"Medical staff? My God, is there a biological alert?"

"Easy. We're not even sure the suspects entered the UN complex."

The technicians inserted the CDs into their computer hard drives and cross-checked facial markers, using the morning surveillance tapes.

Jeffrey Cook pulled Captain Zwawa aside. "Your men are blocking the exits. You can't do that."

"It's a security precaution. No one leaves the UN complex without being checked."

"Checked for what?"

"You'll know if and when I decide to tell you. Let's hope it's not an issue."

"What about the diplomats? The heads of state? You can't tell these people they're not allowed to leave. They have diplomatic immunity."

"No one leaves unless they're medically cleared. Those orders are backed by the Pentagon and the White House."

"What about the president? Are you going to tell him he can't leave?"

"The president's here?"

"He's in the General Assembly Hall, addressing the Security Council as we speak."

"Got her!"

All heads turned to Cameron Hughes, a wheelchair-bound security technician. Jeffrey Cook hovered over the man's shoulder, staring at the frozen black-and-white partially blurred image on his monitor. The computer pixelized, sharpening its genetic markers until Mary Louise Klipot's face appeared ominously on-screen.

"Cam, where was this taken?"

"Main entrance. Aw hell, look at the time code . . . 9:11."

Sweat dripped from Captain Zwawa's face. He fought the urge to tear the stifling hood from his head. "Fast-forward the tape. Where does she go?"

The image jumped from one angle to the next, following Mary Klipot through several checkpoints until she entered the General Assembly Hall. They lost her inside the darkened auditorium.

"Get a security detail—"

"Sir, wait!" The image switched back to the corridor. "Look, she exited. See? She's speaking with security. Heading for the elevators."

The weight of time registered like extra gravity upon Jay Zwawa. He was an hour behind the eight ball, every minute of tape revealing another potentially infected victim, every second that went by allowing Scythe to spread throughout the United Nations complex.

"This is taking too long. Accelerate the tape, I need to know if she's still in the building. Cook, we'll need the names of every person she came in contact with, then I want the names of every person those people came in contact with."

"Are you crazy? You're talking hundreds, perhaps thousands of people. I don't have the manpower—"

"The woman we're after may have infected herself with a very contagious, very lethal form of bubonic plague. Every person she came within breathing distance of is a potential victim and carrier. Do your job, do it fast, and nobody leaves this room."

Zwawa removed a cell phone from his Racal suit's utility belt. He pressed a preprogrammed number with a gloved index finger, his other hand working the controls of the headset situated within his hood—

—switching from Fort Detrick's command post to his older brother's secured cell-phone number.

FORT DETRICK
FREDERICK, MARYLAND

The Fort Detrick Command Center had become the central hub for communication, linking the Oval Office, Pentagon, and assorted members of

Congress in an endless debate of babel. Tired of listening to the Joint Chiefs arguing with the vice president and his staff, Colonel John Zwawa was headed for the sanctuary of his office when his private cell phone reverberated silently in his back pants pocket. "Speak."

"Vicious, it's Delicious. Can you talk?"

"Stand by, Jay." The colonel closed his office door to speak with his brother. "How bad is it?"

"It's a major clusterfuck with tentacles. All those who were in the General Assembly Hall were infected. We're not sure how bad, but POTUS is in there right now, addressing the condemned."

"Hell, Jay Zee, get him out of there."

"Sure thing. Just tell me how to do that without causing widespread panic and losing containment."

The colonel's mind raced. "Bomb scare. I'll alert the Secret Service. Have your team standing by outside the chamber. Use the ESU guys to channel the delegates to their offices in the Secretariat Building, we'll lock them down from there. Once they're isolated, it'll be easier for the CDC teams to do a floor-to-floor triage."

"What about POTUS?"

"Assign him and his staff to a private floor away from the others. But Jay, nobody leaves the plaza until Scythe is contained, and I mean nobody. Is that clear?"

"POTUS's people may insist on getting him out of Dodge."

Colonel Zwawa glanced out his office window at the wall of monitors and its dozen talking heads. "That option is already being debated by the Pentagon assholes who got us into this mess. Fortunately, when it comes to containment, I'm in charge, so here are my orders, for your ears only: No one leaves the UN. If POTUS's people panic, your orders are to take out his Secret Service detail."

"Sweetheart, they don't call you Vicious for nothing."

"Whatever it takes, Jay Zee. We'll sort the bodies out at the trial. Where's Jesse?"

"In the alleyway, searching for the attaché case."

ALLEYWAY—EAST 46TH STREET
TUDOR CITY, MANHATTAN
10:42 A.M.

Jesse Zwawa and three members of Delta Team enter the alleyway. Rubber boots slogged through tire tracks crushed into patches of snow between pools of slush. Wind howled through the passage, muffled by their protective hoods. Orange Racal suits and rebreathers. Astronauts bound to Earth to fight an invisible prey. Three men carried field packs and reach poles, the oldest among them an emergency medical kit.

Dr. Arnie Kremer limped on a hip two weeks away from replacement surgery. He was too short for the assigned Racal suit, which bunched around his knees, making it difficult to walk. An hour ago, Kremer and his wife had been enjoying their breakfast at an all-you-can-eat buffet at the Tropicana Resort in Atlantic City. The beginning of a weeklong vacation—cut short by Uncle Sam. *Army Reserves: the gift that keeps on giving.*

The physician stumbled into the man in front of him. The team had abruptly stopped.

Captain Zwawa was fifty feet from the dumpster, a GPS in hand. The object they sought was in the trash bin but something was lying on the ground directly ahead. At first glance, the commander had assumed it to be a ragged pile of wet clothes—

—only now it was moving.

"Dr. Kremer, front and center."

Arnie Kremer joined the captain. The wet mass was obscured by the frenzied presence of a dozen or more rats, each the size of a football. Their black fur was slick with splattered blood. *Feasting . . . but on what?*

"Is that a dead dog?"

"Let's be sure." Zwawa extended his reach pole. Abused the mass as he flipped the heap over, his actions barely inconveniencing the rodents.

Both men jumped back. Kremer gagged inside his hooded mask.

It had been a maintenance worker. Rats had taken the right half of the man's face and both eyes. Two males fought over an optic nerve still protruding from a vacant eye socket like a strand of spaghetti. The rest dined on the remains of the man's stomach like a ravaging horde of puppies suckling from their mother's teats. Rodents were crawling over and inside the internal organs, causing the victim's bulging belly to undulate.

When a blood-drenched rat crawled out of the dead man's mouth, Zwawa lost it. Backing away, he wrenched his right arm free of the Racal suit's sleeve, ran his hand up his chest to the internally attached barf bag, then shoved it over his mouth a second before he regurgitated his breakfast.

The rest of Delta team hummed and clenched their teeth and tried their best not to listen to the sickening acoustics playing over their headphones.

Ryan Glinka, Delta Team's second-in-command, approached his commanding officer. "You okay, Captain?"

Zwawa nodded. Sealing the barf bag, he stowed it in an internal pocket, then turned to face his men. "Mr. Szeifert, I believe this is your area of expertise."

"Yes, sir." Gabor Szeifert stepped forward, but not too close. A veterinarian and epizootic specialist from Hungary, today's assignment marked his first actual field experience. "Something is not right. Rats normally don't feed like this. They appear to be stimulated."

"Shh! Listen." Ryan Glinka held up his hand for quiet.

Beyond the howling wind and the noise of a distant siren, they could hear rapid *thumps* coming from inside the steel bin. As they watched, a black rat scurried up the brown, rust-tinged metal and over the opening, leaping into the receptacle.

Dr. Kremer's skin crawled inside his protective suit.

Captain Zwawa attached a hook to his reach pole and handed it to Szeifert. "Retrieve the case, just be gentle."

Gabor approached the steel bin as more rats appeared, the rodents racing in and out of the trash receptacle at a frenetic pace. The Hungarian scientist leaned in closer to see over the edge of the open container. Looked inside—

"*Nem értem . . .*"

It was an orgy of dark bodies and flesh-tone tails, tearing and gnashing and scrambling atop one another in an effort to get at something buried beneath the moving pile. A kaleidoscope of the living and the dead, the wounded and the inflicted—all part of a churning rodent mass that moved like a synchronized black tide.

"Mr. Szeifert!"

"Sorry, sir. I said I don't understand. There are so many of them. We need to—"

A lone rat leapt onto Gabor's shoulder. The veterinarian attempted to swat the creature away as it furiously gnawed at his protective suit. Joined by two more, then another, then in threes and fours and far too many to count as the dumpster's open ledge became a launching point to the next buffet.

The animal specialist stumbled toward Dr. Kremer. Black rats swarmed across both men's shoulders, clinging to their backs and thighs, their clawed feet and sharp teeth tearing into the fleeing soldiers' Racal suits—

—instantaneously falling to the ground like bags of hair, their tiny legs writhing in spasms as Ryan Glinka gassed them into submission with a cylinder of compressed carbon dioxide.

Jesse Zwawa stepped over the gasping rodents, holding a CO2 grenade in his gloved hand. "Anyone hungry for ratatouille?" He pulled the pin, tossing the canister into the trash bin.

Boom!

Rat shrapnel blasted out of the container in all directions, the hollow metallic *gong* echoing in their ears as a swirling cloud of CO2 escaped above the damaged trash bin.

Dr. Kremer fought a gag reflex, forcing himself to wipe matted black hairs and bloody excrement from his faceplate. "That was a bit radical, don't you think?!"

"We need the attaché case. I'm guessing it's buried somewhere beneath the pile."

"If that's true, the rats could be vectors. I'll need live specimens to run toxicology exams."

"You want live rats, pull 'em off Gabor. You want fillet of rat, here's a whole dumpster filled with the sons of bitches." Walking around the back side of the steel bin, Jesse Zwawa leveraged his two-hundred-pound frame against the smoldering container—

—sending the Dumpster crashing forward, spilling its contents across the garbage-strewn tarmac.

Ryan Glinka extended his reach pole, sifting through the moist pile of rodent remains until he hooked the open attaché case.

The rats had chewed it beyond recognition. All that remained was a piece of its handle and a seventeen-inch section of bare metal dangling a bloodied hinge.

Glinka held the scrap metal in the air for his commanding officer. "I think we've got problems, sir. Captain?"

"Over here." Jesse Zwawa was on one knee, aiming his flashlight at the opening of a cracked drainage pipe situated along the brick facing of the adjacent building. His beam illuminated pairs of tiny, unblinking red eyes, the hovel of infected rodents staring back at him—

—waiting.

Lost Diary: Guy de Chauliac

The following entry has been excerpted from a recently discovered unpublished memoir, written by surgeon Guy de Chauliac during the Great Plague: 1346–1348.
(translated from its original French)

<u>Diary Entries: January 4, 1348</u>
(recorded in Avignon, France)

Death has arrived in Avignon.

We had heard reports for months . . . the horrors coming out of Sicily and Genoa, the warnings from the isles of Sardinia and Mallorca. There were rumors about Venice and Rome being infected, followed weeks later by panic coming from our fleeing neighbors to the east in Marseilles and Aix. Still we remained vigilant, terror-stricken yet convinced that God in His infinite mercy would spare the papal city and all its people.

Perhaps we were still not convinced. Perhaps we were simply waiting for a sign from the heavens—an earth tremor, a poisonous rain.

And yet none occurred. Instead, the plague that had brought the Mongolian Empire to its knees and death to every trade city along the Mediterranean and Black Seas came to Avignon one early winter's night as a whisper while we slept. By morning it was a stranger lying in an alleyway, by nightfall a fever blossoming in a dozen households.

On my recommendation, Pope Clement IV has ordered the gates of Avignon closed—

—only I fear it is far too late.

—*Guigo*

"The Criminal Investigation Division at Fort Meade has been investigating USAMRIID at Fort Detrick since early February. USAMRIID was shutting down most of its bio-research while it tried to match its inventory to its records, citing an 'overage' of biological select agents and toxins. Meade's CID, however, isn't concerned with overstock. Instead, agents are looking for what may have gone missing between 1987 and 2008."

—Katherine Heerbrandt, *Frederick News-Post*, April 22, 2009

DECEMBER 20

VA MEDICAL CENTER

EAST SIDE, MANHATTAN

10:44 A.M.

(21 HOURS, 19 MINUTES BEFORE THE PROPHESIED END OF DAYS)

The redheaded woman sitting up on the gurney in the back of the ambulance moaned in protest. Fever drew her into moments of blessed unconsciousness. Nausea spit her back out again. She vomited phlegm-laced bile across her blanket, and the action expelled her back into the swirling sea of reality. She forced open her eyes and scanned the vomit for blood. Scythe was progressing. Fueled by her genius.

Her head ached. Her hip throbbed where the cab had bounced her across 46th Street. Baby Jesus kicked in her belly. She suffered every bump and sharp turn *and that incessant siren*! The little voice screamed obscenities at her from the dark place in her mind that could no longer reason other than to recite the same alarmist mantra about ticking clocks and serums in the wheel hub in the trunk of her rental car and who's the genius now?

A lurching stop interrupted delirium. The siren silenced, yielding to a moment of quiet desperation. *Instruct your keepers before they put you under.* Before she could object, the gurney was launched backward into blinding gray skies and Arctic cold. Then she was mobile again. Up the ramp and moving through a corridor of fluorescent lights and controlled chaos. New faces wearing white lab coats and identification badges peered in on her world, refusing to listen.

"What have you got?"

"Taxi hit her. Late thirties, pregnant, appears to be well into her third trimester. Victim was conscious when we found her. Rapid pulse, high fever. Blood pressure's eighty over sixty. Looks like most of the impact was absorbed by the buttocks and backs of the legs."

"She looks pale. No open wounds? Loss of blood?"

"None that we could see, but she aspirated blood on the ride in. You're probably looking at an emergency C-section if there's any hope of saving the baby."

"Agreed. What's that stench?"

"I don't know. Maybe Russians don't like to bathe."

"How do you know she's Russian?"

"She was wearing this ID tag: Bogdana Petrova, Russian embassy."

"Get her to X-ray, we'll take it from here."

UNITED NATIONS
GENERAL ASSEMBLY BUILDING
10:46 A.M.

"**A bomb threat**?" The Secret Service agent stared suspiciously at the big man wearing the orange Racal suit. "Where's the bomb squad?"

"We are the bomb squad."

"Bullshit. Those are environmental suits."

"The threat was a biological device. And if there really is a bomb, and it goes off, we'll be protected. You, on the other hand, will basically be screwed. Now you either cue the president, or I'll do it myself and panic a thousand diplomats and their visiting heads of state.

Cursing aloud, the president's bodyguard and personal assassin walked briskly past the curtains and onto the raised stage to the podium, his head down.

". . . no one wants war, but we shall not shirk from it either if it means preventing the annihilation of one or more of our cities. Enriched uranium can be used in suitcase bombs as well as ballistic missiles. In the past, Iran has not hesitated to arm terrorist groups like Hezbollah and Hamas—groups that, in turn, would not hesitate to use a suitcase nuke against Israel or another sovereign nation. As such, any treaty—"

President Kogelo paused, the lanky leader of the free world listening intently as the Secret Service agent whispered into his ear.

"Mr. Secretary General, distinguished guests . . . I've just been told that the General Assembly has received a terrorist threat. Homeland Security has the situation under control, but as an extra precaution, we're being asked to postpone the rest of this morning's agenda while our munitions experts verify this chamber is secure. All diplomats and heads of state, including myself, are being asked to report to their nation's respective suites in the Secretariat Building and await further instructions."

The Secret Service agent took the president by the crook of his arm and led him off the stage as two dozen heavily armed Emergency Service Unit personnel, all wearing white Racal suits, entered the chamber from the rear doors and herded the shocked diplomats into the corridor.

EAST 22ND STREET & FIRST AVENUE
LOWER EAST SIDE, MANHATTAN
10:47 A.M.

Still another block to go, and Wendi Metz was exhausted.

The single mother of an eight-year-old boy, Wendi had been trying to lose fifteen pounds since she began computer dating back in October. Her exercise routine—walking from the UN Plaza, where she worked the breakfast shift, to the bus stop at East 23rd Street—had helped reduce her waistline two dress sizes in three months while saving on subway tokens. But this morning she felt drained, on the verge of passing out.

The inviting bus stop bench was within view, enticing her to continue walking. Every step was painful, the tightness shooting down her neck and spine into her lower back and legs and feet. The brisk winter breeze coming off the East River had been cooling her perspiration, but now that she has slowed her pace to a stagger, she could register the fever raging internally.

A gust of wind set her body to shivering.

She recalled for the umpteenth time the image of the pale woman throwing up in the bathroom and wondered if she might have caught something.

Her vision blurred, her eyes strained to gain contrast in the sudden brightness. She contemplated purchasing a yogurt from a nearby street vendor—*blood sugar's probably low*—until she spotted the X25 Bus weaving its way up First Avenue.

Get home. Take some cold and flu medicine, have a bowl of soup, then hustle to the diner before the lunch shift begins.

Flagging down the bus, Wendi Metz climbed aboard, joining the other seventeen passengers en route to Midtown East and Sutton Place.

UNITED NATIONS PLAZA
10:48 A.M.

The isolation tent was filling quickly. Those classified "infected" now numbered twenty-two, with a new patient added every six minutes. Most were either police officers or protesters who had been caught on the plaza grounds. Others had been working security inside the General Assembly Building when "Bubonic Mary" had taken her tour through the facility.

The first verifiable contact lay prone in a self-contained isolator, a lightweight stretcher surrounded by a demountable framework and transparent plastic. The bubble envelope was maintained by its own self-contained air-supply system, which created a negative pressure differential, preventing the escape of contaminated air. Eight plastic arm sleeves, four on each side, allowed medical personnel to reach inside the patient's containment area without breaching the isolator.

Officer Gary Beck was terrified. He knew he had been exposed to a hazardous biological substance. He knew because he could feel the toxin rippling through his body. The fever, coupled with anxiety, had caused his heart to race, his blood pressure to drop, his skin to crawl. The physicians in the white environmental suits had assured him that he would be okay, that the antidote being administered by an IV drip had reached him with ample time to spare. Beck had believed them, his panic losing its edge as the Valium, mixed with a clear elixir labeled SCY-ANTI, dripped into his veins.

Lying within the isolated bubble, Gary Beck thought about his wife, Kimberly, and his two children and gave thanks that they were in Doylestown, Pennsylvania, visiting his in-laws. He felt alone and definitely in the wrong place at the wrong time and willed himself to remain calm. *You're alive, you're okay. The experts are here to take care of you. Keep it together and cooperate, and you'll be home in your own bed before the wife gets back from her parents'.*

A woman in a white Racal suit approached, communicating by way of an internal intercom. "How are you feeling, Officer Beck?"

"Not good. I puked again, and everything still hurts. And my neck feels swollen, right here. It feels like something's growing."

"It's just a lymph node, try not to rub it. I'm going to take some more blood, okay?"

"Okay." Officer Beck closed his watering eyes, his limbs trembling as the nurse withdrew another syringe of his blood into an external collection tube.

Jay Zwawa felt like he was sinking in quicksand. He reread Dr. Kremer's medical report, then spotted his younger brother, Jesse emerging from an Army tent, and motioned him over.

"Two rodent extermination teams are on the way."

"You'd better read this. It's a toxicology report on the first wave of victims."

Jesse Zwawa scanned the report, his expression darkening behind the faceplate of his hooded suit. "That explains why—"

"Yeah."

"Then we're officially screwed."

"Pretty much. Jess, this stays between us and Dr. Kremer. If this gets out—"

"Have you told Zee?"

"I was about to make the call."

"Colonel, Alpha Team has an urgent transmission."

"Stand by." John Zwawa muted the cross conversations coming from the wall of video monitors. "Mr. Vice President, gentlemen and ladies, we have an update coming in from our ground team. Go ahead, Captain."

"Colonel, we've got a major situation. An analysis of the infected victims' blood reveals the bacilli don't match Scythe's DNA."

Dr. Lydia Gagnon grabbed the nearest microphone, her voice blaring over Jay Zwawa's headset. "What do you mean it's not a match? The stolen attaché case contained pure Scythe."

"Understood. But our antibiotics aren't working. None of the infected patients are improving. Somehow, the Klipot woman altered Scythe's DNA."

Suddenly light-headed, Colonel Zwawa found his way to a desk chair. "Captain, have Kremer upload all ground zero blood-work results directly to our Bio-4 labs. Dr. Gagnon, how soon can your labs produce an effective antibiotic? Dr. Gagnon!"

"How soon? I don't know, Colonel . . . a day? A year? Don't you see? It doesn't matter. Scythe kills within fifteen hours . . . it's spreading way too fast for my people to possibly break down its new genetic code, let alone find a cure. Anyone who contracted the plague is a walking corpse. That game is over, we lost. From this moment on, it's all about damage control. We have one shot at containing this thing before it becomes a worldwide pandemic . . . one small break. Manhattan's an island, technically it can be isolated. We have to shut down all access in and out of the city, and I mean right away!"

"She's right, Colonel," Jay Zwawa chimed in. "The UN's Head of Security just handed me a report on the potential list of people who made contact with the Klipot woman. At least a dozen have already left the UN complex. We lost perimeter containment thirty-three minutes ago."

Dr. Gagnon stood before the vice president's monitor, her voice trembling with fear. "Sir, we either isolate Manhattan right now and sacrifice two million people, or by tomorrow night the entire human race, save a few isolated third-world tribes, will become extinct."

10:51 A.M.

The island of Manhattan was separated from the boroughs of the Bronx and Queens by the Harlem River, from Brooklyn by the swiftly flowing East River, Staten Island and New Jersey to the south and west by the mighty Hudson. Linking this metropolis to its surrounding communities was more than six hundred miles of subway, two thousand miles of bus routes, eight bridges, four tunnel crossings, two major train systems, and dozens of ferries and helicopters. Now, the federal government wanted every entry point and exit route into and out of Manhattan shut down, and they were demanding it be done in less than fifteen minutes.

New York governor Daniel Cirilo II was en route to a skiing excursion in Vermont when he received the phone call from Vice President Krawitz. After being told to "stop asking questions and start issuing orders," the governor contacted the CEO of the Metropolitan Transportation Authority, a network that encompassed New York City's subways, buses, and railroads. Within minutes, all lines were shut down, the entire system placed under a Code-Red Terrorist Alert.

All incoming trains with scheduled stops at Grand Central Terminal and Penn Station were rerouted, all outgoing cars canceled until further notice. The FAA grounded all aerial vehicles leaving LaGuardia, JFK, and Newark International Airports. The Port Authority restricted all ferries and boats along both rivers. Homeland Security took over the Triborough Bridge and Tunnel Authority, dispatching orders to more than nine hundred officers posted at Manhattan's bridges and tunnel tollgates to shut down all vehicular and pedestrian traffic and turn away anyone attempting to enter or leave the island.

By 11:06 a.m. EST, every Manhattan highway bridge and tunnel was stifled in endless gridlock, the cacophony of a thousand blaring horns the harbinger of the chaos still to come.

VA MEDICAL CENTER
EAST SIDE, MANHATTAN
11:07 A.M.

***On a patch** of dirt and grass littered with spent bullet shells, in the shadow of a three-story building left in shards, a dozen young Iraqi children play soccer.*

Patrick Shepherd watches the game from the old church he and his fellow soldiers have been guarding during its renovation. The little girl he has come to know as "Bright Eyes" chases down the ball, only to be quickly overwhelmed by the pack. When the bodies clear, she is left on the ground crying, her right knee bleeding.

Patrick hurries to her. Squeezing through the circle of kids, he squats by her side to inspect the wound. "Don't cry, Bright Eyes, it's not too bad. Let's see if we can't clean it up."

Through brown eyes magnified with tears she watches the American soldier push aside his assault rifle and retrieve his medikit. He sprays the wound. Dabs it with gauze. Then fixes a clean bandage and wrap—

—earning himself a hug.

Patrick holds on to the child for a long moment, then releases her to her peers.

The game continues. He returns to the church—greeted by David Kantor. "That was nice."

"She's like me, a runt."

"She's a heartbreaker. Enjoying the downtime?"

"Not especially. I didn't enlist to guard a dilapidated church."

"This church happens to be a national landmark. Ever see the movie, The Exorcist?"

"No."

"The opening scene was of a desert church—this church. The scenes were filmed in Iraq before Saddam took over, back when the country made good money from the movie industry. Once we restore it—"

"I didn't enlist to restore old churches used in old movies." He removes his pistol from its holster, dismantles the gun, then uses an oily rag to wipe it free from sand.

"Why did you enlist?"

"To kill America's enemies. To prevent another 9/11."

"Saddam's regime wasn't responsible for 9/11."

"You know what I mean."

"What I know is that you've got some serious anger issues that won't be resolved with that gun you're cleaning."

"Ok, so why are you *here?"*

"I'm here because of an Iraqi translator I met in Kuwait back in 1991. He was assigned to our platoon as a translator. During a cultural awareness class, he told us he had been a soldier fighting for the national army against the Bathists when Saddam took over. With tears streaming down his face, he described fighting on the steps of the palace in Baghdad. He told us how he had been forced to flee his homeland or be executed. He had to leave his family behind, some of whom were hanged. He told us about how the Bathist soldiers raped and tortured women under Saddam, and how his family had lived in terror of their own government ever since. After the class, he and the other cultural trainers, mostly interpreters who volunteered to help us, walked around shaking our hands and thanking every soldier there for what we were doing. These men were risking their own lives and the lives of their families back home to help us, yet they were thanking us. They were tough grizzled old men—men who had seen fighting far worse than any of us had ever seen, and they were weeping as they recounted the events leading up to the time Saddam and his party had taken over Iraq. I grew to despise Saddam, and I hated the fact that our own government had helped manipulate the dictator into power, then had armed him to the teeth during the Iraq-Iran War. From these men and many others like them, we gained a deep respect for the Iraqi people and their culture. Like most of us, they just wanted to live out their lives in peace without being in constant fear of their own government. To answer your question, Sergeant, I came back here to right a wrong."

Reassembling his pistol, Shep slams the clip into place and chambers a round. "So did I, Captain. So did I."

Patrick Shepherd awakened with a start. Anxiety built as his eyes took in the strange surroundings. *DeBorn. Private room.*

He sat up in bed, his pounding heart demanding his brain remember something far more important. *My family . . . Nelson found my family!*

He swung his legs off the bed. *This was big. Unexpected and sobering. His wife and daughter were in Manhattan. A cab ride away. Would they see him? Could he handle it? What if his soul mate rejected him again? What if she had remarried? And his daughter . . . no longer the curly-haired toddler. Did she have a new daddy? Would she even want to meet him? What would Beatrice have told her about her real father?*

"Beatrice." He repeated the name aloud. It was definitely familiar, yet somehow still alien to him. "Beatrice Shepherd. Bea . . . trice. Bea Shepherd. Bea. Aunt Bea."

He slammed his palm to his right temple, frustrated to tears.

What about your daughter's name? First initial? Work the alphabet like the doctor in Germany taught you. A? Audrey? Anna? B? Beatrice . . . no. Barbara? Betsy? Bonnie? He paused. "Bonnie? Bonnie Shepherd? Something's there . . . ugh, but it's not fitting!"

He used the bathroom, his nostrils greeted by the usual "patient scent" that inhabited every hospital. "C? Connie? Carol? Maybe D? Diana? Danielle? Debby? Deanna? Dara? Find a book on baby names . . . oh, wait—the library's computer!"

After rinsing his hands, he hurried out of the private room, nearly running over a fit-looking man carrying a long cardboard box and a laptop computer. "You Sergeant Shepherd? Terry Stringer. I'm your occupational therapist."

"My who?"

"Your amputee tech. See? I've got your prosthetic arm. Real nice one, too. I'm here to attach it and train you how to use it. Your shirt . . . could you remove it?"

"Why? Oh, sorry." Patrick reentered his room with the therapist. Removed his shirt. "How does this thing work? How much strength will I have?"

"Well, you won't exactly be the bionic man, but with a little practice, you'll be fairly functional. Lightweight steel core, with a spongy flesh-like outer coat. This one's fabricated specifically for transhumeral amputees like yourself. It's actually a hybrid, one of the new prosthetic models the Defense Department's been working on to allow amputees to return to combat."

Shep backed away. "Get me an older one."

"An older one? Why would . . . oh, I see. Look, forget what I said. No one's sending you back." Stringer removed the flesh-colored device from the box, pulled off the protective plastic wrapping. "We slip it over your left shoulder like so, creating skin contact between the device's electrodes. This will amplify the voluntarily controlled muscles in your deltoid muscle and residual limb. The signals act as switches to move the electrical motors in the prosthetic's elbow, hand, and wrist. A little pinch . . . now we adjust the support straps. Okay, Sergeant, try moving your new arm."

Patrick raised the molded appendage but was unable to generate any movement in the arm itself. "It's not working."

"It'll take some getting used to. Let's practice using the simulator." Stringer opened his laptop, then connected a set of electrodes from the computer to several contact points located along Shep's new artificial limb. "Okay, the object is to generate a spike on the monitor by flexing the correct muscle in your deltoid and triceps. Go ahead, give it a try."

Patrick gritted his teeth and squeezed.

Nothing happened.

"Try this: Close your eyes. Now visualize the muscles connecting to the new limb in your mind. Relax and breathe."

Shep calmed himself. Tried again.

A tiny streak appeared on the monitor.

"Excellent. You just opened your pincers. Try it again, only this time keep your eyes open."

Shep focused, managing to flex the mechanical wrist, but was unable to consistently find the right combination to work the pincers.

"It's frustrating."

"It takes practice. Remember the phantom pain . . . how long it took your mind to accept the fact you had lost something so vital to your everyday existence? Over time you learned to adapt."

"I still get the phantom pain."

"It'll pass. Every amputee is different. The key is to retrain your brain in order to accept this new limb as your own."

Stringer worked with him another fifteen minutes, then gathered the trash and empty box. "I'll leave the computer with you so you can practice."

"I'm not sure I can do this."

"Sure you can. You're still an athlete—train like one. I used to wrestle in high school. My wrestling coach used to tell us fear is nothing more than false expectations appearing real, that the only limits are those we place upon ourselves by our own five senses. Look past what you perceive, Sergeant, and you'll change your perception."

TUDOR CITY, MANHATTAN
11:10 A.M.

***Xenopsylla cheopis*—the** rat flea—is a parasite specifically adapted to survive on the backs of rodents. Bloodsucking insects, the dozen or so fleas that had been living on the rat colony inhabiting the East 46th Street alley had become infected with plague the moment their four-legged hosts had entered the trash bin, launching an epizootic event in Lower Manhattan.

When it came to spreading plague, there was no greater vector than the rat flea. As bacteria proliferated in the insect's stomach, they impeded its throat, starving the tiny creature. Desperate for food, the infected flea attacked its host, biting the rodent over and over, causing the rat to become agitated and aggressive. The animal's increased pulse rate accelerated the toxin into its bloodstream, adding the rat as a plague vector even as its life ticked quickly away.

At first overly stimulated, then weak and dying, each infected rodent secreted a pungent aphrodisiac that lured another rat to host its plague-carrying fleas while setting off a cannibalistic chain reaction among the other members of the pack. Healthy rats devoured the weak, only to become infected themselves.

Having no use for a dead host, the infected fleas leapt upon the hides of the robust, creating thriving colonies of hundreds of biting, starving fleas that drove the rodents into a frenzy.

The infected swarm raced through Lower Manhattan's sewers like a frenetic army, moving southwest toward Chinatown and the Battery at a steady six miles an hour.

BATTERY PARK CITY, NEW YORK
11:13 A.M.

The two-bedroom apartment smelled of fresh paint and new carpets. The hallways were crammed with the last of the cardboard moving boxes.

Beatrice Shepherd poured herself a second cup of coffee and sat in her favorite chair in the alien living room, looking out the bay window at the New York skyline. Life was moving fast again. Her decision to sell her stake in the independent publishing company she had helped start up four years ago had been a difficult one. Of course, working for a major New York publishing house was far more prestigious, and there would be no more worries about making payroll. Still, she was not alone in the decision; there was her daughter. Did she want to come north with her? Was she willing to leave her friends in South Carolina to begin life anew in the Big Apple?

They had toured New York with a Realtor. The Upper West Side was her preference, but her daughter had liked Battery Park. A newer neighborhood. Tree-lined streets. Views of the water. Plus the building had a twenty-four-hour fitness club.

And so they had made the move—her daughter never suspecting that her mother had an ulterior motive for wanting them to be in New York.

ENGLEWOOD, NEW JERSEY

11:26 A.M.

The dark blue Lexus with the SUPPORT OUR TROOPS decal on the rear bumper turned into the southeast entrance of the JC Mall. Cars and SUVs and pickup trucks, their metal hides sooted brown from road salt and slush, monopolized every legal parking spot and every square foot of space not occupied by a mini-mountain of plowed snow. The driver of the Lexus selected a row and joined the game of "follow the shopper to their car" already in progress.

Last-minute bargain hunters. Long lines at registers. Screaming infants and young children playing hide-and-seek while their oblivious mothers carried on lengthy conversations with female cashiers as if they were long-lost cousins. Thermostats set on eighty-five degrees pumped out the kind of heat reserved for a greenhouse in stores lacking so much as a single folding chair.

Christmas week at the local mall. No place for men.

There was a time that Dr. David Kantor would have scanned the crowded parking lot, turned his car around, and left. Sent his assistant with a credit card and a list. Five military deployments in twelve years changes a man. Three Christmas holidays spent in Iraq, and suddenly the worst inconveniences become cherished memories. And so David circled the lot with the patience of Job. Sang along with an old *Temptations* song on the radio. Offered his expertly scoped-out soon-to-be-vacant parking space to a mother of four in a van. Happily.

The fifty-two-year-old physician and former Army medic no longer practiced medicine. The senior partner at Victory Wholesale Group had seen enough blood and guts and severed limbs and dying young men and women to last several lifetimes. The man who had enlisted in the reserves during the first Gulf War had no intention of going back to the endless second. Not even if they arrested him. Kantor had assured his wife, Leslie, that he already had a plan. The meniscus in his left knee was gone from playing pickup basketball. The anterior ligament hung by a thread. The former shooting guard at Princeton would pop the joint before he got on another transport plane.

The Kantor family was Jewish. David's four children had received their gifts last week during Chanukah. Today's shopping list was more business oriented. Knickknacks for vendors and a few special thank-you gifts for his managers. Plus a promised portable DVD player for Gavi, his thirteen-year-old daughter's reward for having earned straight As. David planned to visit one store and be out of the mall in twenty minutes.

War changed a man, but not everything.

He found another available spot next to a plowed mountain of snow and parked. As if on cue, his cell phone rang. He did not recognize the number. "Hello?"

"Captain Kantor?"

Mention of his military rank caused David's pulse to race. "Yes?"

"Sir, I'm calling from the Department of the Interior on behalf of the New Jersey National Guard. By order of the Adjutant General, you are ordered to report immediately to the—"

"Wait a second, now you just hold on! Don't tell me I'm being deployed again! I just got back from setting up a new medical unit eight months ago!"

"No, sir. This is a domestic matter. What is your present location?"

"You mean right now? Uh . . . Englewood."

"Stand by."

Beads of sweat drenched the back of his denim shirt. He flexed his left knee.

"Sir, you are to report immediately to the Fort Lee toll booth on the New Jersey side of the George Washington Bridge. On the south side of the road you will see the 42nd Infantry Division Support Command. All duties will be explained when you arrive, all questions answered. You are to power off your cell phone following our call. You are not to discuss this matter with anyone else, civilian or military . . . is that clear, Captain?"

"Yes, ma'am."

David hung up, then stared at the cell phone, unsure what had just happened.

GEORGE WASHINGTON BRIDGE
WASHINGTON HEIGHTS/UPPER MANHATTAN
11:34 A.M.

The George Washington Bridge was a two-level suspension bridge that fed vehicular traffic across the Hudson River, linking the island of Manhattan with northern New Jersey.

The taxicab inched its way north on Broadway through Upper Manhattan, stuck in a seemingly endless line of cars and buses, all waiting to turn left onto West 177th Street to access the George Washington Bridge. The driver cursed in Hindi, a language his three passengers all understood.

Manisha Patel was a bundle of nerves. Negative energy pulsated from the crystal dangling from her neck like the short-circuiting voltage from a single A battery. “Pankaj, why are we still not moving?”

Her husband, dealing with his own stress, continued to speed dial the cell phone number given to him months earlier by the Tibetan monk calling himself the Elder. “Manisha, please. The traffic will subside, we still have time.”

The driver pressed on his horn as another cab blocked the intersection. “Something must have happened . . . a terrible accident. Look, they are shutting down the I-95 access ramp.”

“Pankaj, do something.”

“What would you have me do? Part the traffic like Moses?”

Ten-year-old Dawn Patel was in the backseat, squeezed between her mother and father. “Please, no more fighting. If the bridge is closed, then find another way.”

“Our daughter is correct. Driver, turn us around. We’ll take the Lincoln Tunnel.”

GENERAL ASSEMBLY BUILDING
UNITED NATIONS
11:27 A.M.

Alpha Team commander Jay Zwawa stood in the moist heat of his cumbersome Racal suit in the evacuated chamber of the General Assembly Building and wondered if he were standing at ground zero for the end of the world. The bravado in him, instilled by a demanding father and an older brother in the military, said *not on my watch*. The intellect that graduated from West Point with honors pondered the Pandora's box pried open by the lunatics at the Pentagon and prayed for a miracle.

Members of the Centers for Disease Control, all wearing protective white Racal suits and working in teams of three, moved slowly through the aisles of the empty UN chamber. Each man was armed with a small racquet-shaped sensory device containing a nucleic-acid-based biochip designed to determine if toxic agents were present in the air.

While the CDC completed its work, two members of New York's bomb squad searched the chamber for the "threatened" explosive device, their presence necessary to sell the world on why the General Assembly Hall had to be abandoned. Distinguished by their fire-retardant jumpsuits and heavy Kevlar hooded jackets and rebreathers, the pair seemed as out of place as sports jackets and denim jeans at a black-tie event.

Jay Zwawa watched the men go about their business, wondering how long he could keep them on his wild-goose chase before accepting their "all clear," forcing him to alert the public about Scythe.

"Captain Zwawa, over here." Two of the CDC teams had stopped at the embassy table labeled IRAQ. "She was here all right, ribosomal sequences are a match. Everyone at this table was exposed to full-blown Scythe, probably every table on either side of this aisle from this point clear back to the exit doors."

"Make a list of every country situated along this row, I want their diplomatic offices checked first. Then begin a floor-to-floor, suite-to-suite triage of the entire Secretariat Building. Any contaminated offices are to be treated as isolation rooms, with armed guards posted outside. We've shut down the building's ventilation system, so you may want to offer blankets. Tell them we'll be announcing something soon. Until then, no one is to leave their office suites."

"How long do you think we can keep a thousand irate heads of state isolated under these circumstances?"

"It doesn't matter, Sergeant. My orders, and yours, are to get it done."

*"What difference does it make to the dead, the orphans,
and the homeless, whether the mad destruction is wrought under the name
totalitarianism, or the holy name of liberty or democracy?"*

—Mahatma Gandhi

*"Our society is run by insane people for insane objectives. I think we're being
run by maniacs for maniacal ends and I think I'm liable to be put
away as insane for expressing that. That's what's insane about it."*

—John Lennon

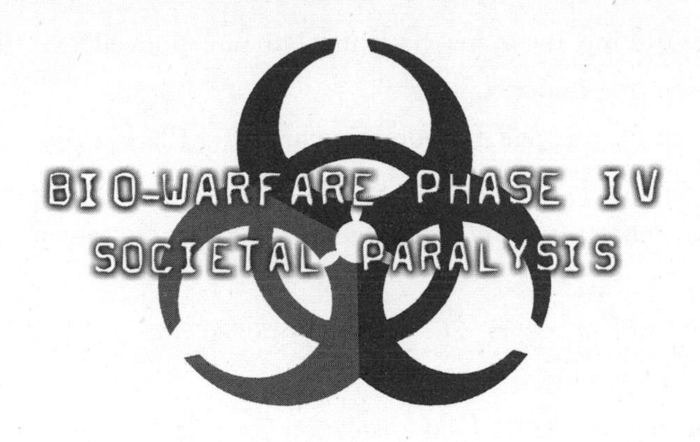

DECEMBER 20

VA MEDICAL CENTER

EAST SIDE, MANHATTAN

11:49 A.M.

(20 HOURS, 14 MINUTES BEFORE THE PROPHESIED END OF DAYS)

Dr. Jonathan Clark prided himself on being a man of intense self-discipline. Arising before dawn. Oatmeal for breakfast. Chicken salad at noon. Cardio workouts thrice a week for thirty minutes, followed by twenty minutes of weights. As the medical center's director, he remained the ultimate disciplinarian. The leader must set the pace. Staff were expected to arrive fifteen minutes early to all meetings, what Clark referred to as "Vince Lombardi time." Every duty had a checklist for success. In Jonathan Clark's book, rules saved lives and no one, save God, was exempt.

He would have both to thank should he live to see the end of this day.

The deathly pale Russian woman was in agony. She was running a high fever and coughing up blood. X-rays revealed a fractured pelvis. CAT scans showed no serious internal injuries. An emergency C-section was scheduled for 11:45. IVs had been administered, blood tests ordered.

By 11:15, the patient's delirium had turned violent. Screaming "The Devil exists!" she had carried on as if possessed. Orderlies were forced to strap her down. A nurse sedated her. She was moved to an isolation room to keep her from disturbing the other patients. No one noticed that the Russian woman was ranting in perfect English.

She was being prepped for surgery when Dr. Clark arrived at precisely 11:29 to make his 11:30 emergency-ward rounds. After reviewing the Russian woman's chart, he proceeded to don a protective gown, gloves, and mask.

"Sir, that's not necessary. She was only moved into isolation because she was raving like a lunatic."

"Isolation requires us to follow isolation protocols, I don't care if you're going inside just to change a light bulb. Now put on proper attire before I dock you a day's pay."

"Yes, sir."

"According to her chart, she works at the Russian embassy. Have the Russians been contacted?"

"We tried, sir. No answer. Apparently there's some kind of emergency going on at the UN."

Dr. Clark waited for the attending physician and nurse to complete dressing before leading them inside the negatively pressurized isolation room.

The woman's skin was hot to the touch, even through Dr. Clark's gloves. The flesh was so pale it appeared almost translucent, revealing a thin web of blue veins in her forehead, temples, and neck. Her breathing was shallow and erratic, her pupils dilated. The eye sockets were dark and sunken, appearing hollow. Her lips were white, drawn tight over the partially open mouth, which kicked up a blood-laced spittle with every panted breath.

The woman's ripe belly was exposed and swabbed. The unborn child inside was kicking and contorting violently within its mother's womb.

"Have you started her on antibiotics?"

"Cefuroxime. No effect."

Dr. Clark opened Mary's gown, exposing her smallish breasts. "What are these red marks?"

"We're not sure. At first we thought they were from the taxi's impact, she tumbled pretty hard when she hit the street. We're still waiting for the labs."

Dr. Clark palpated her abdomen, then worked his way down to her groin, feeling his way along the cotton panties . . . pausing at a bulge. Using a pair of blunt-nosed scissors, he cut loose the fabric, exposing a swollen purplish black rounded lump of flesh the size of a tangerine.

"Sir . . . I swear, that wasn't there before."

"This is a bubo, an infected lymph node. Who else besides the two of you have come in contact with this patient?"

"The orderlies. Hollis in Radiology."

"Plus the EMTs who brought her in."

"This room is officially quarantined. The two of you are to remain here while we set up an isolation ward and contact the CDC."

"Sir, I've had my TB shots."

"Me, too."

"This isn't tuberculosis, Nurse Coffman. It's bubonic plague."

There was a negative energy in the air. Though not as obvious as a shrill whistle or dentist's drill, its presence was palpable, and the occupants of Ward 19-C were clearly agitated. Those under sedation moaned in feverish sleep, their minds haunted, unable to escape the stain of war. The conscious among them clawed at their skin or joined in a chorus of F-bombs aimed at the nurses on duty. One man flung his soiled bedpan across the room, inciting a half dozen more responses.

The wounded soldiers in this ward and a dozen wards like it throughout the tri-state area were not missing limbs; nor were they suffering from bullet or shrapnel wounds. All of these veterans, ages twenty-one through thirty-seven, were dying of cancer.

Despite being outlawed, the United States Armed Forces had continued its blatant use of depleted uranium (DU) to create its munitions. A by-product of the uranium-enrichment process, DU shells were able to penetrate steel and were favored by military contractors because they were so cheap, the depleted uranium offered free to weapon manufacturers by the US government.

When fired, a DU shell burned on impact, releasing microscopic radioactive dust particles that traveled with the wind. Easily inhaled or ingested, depleted uranium was a toxic metal that weakened the immune system, could lead to acute respiratory conditions, renal and gastrointestinal illnesses . . . and cancer.

Staff Sergeant Kevin Quercio had spent two years in Basra as a crew member on a Bradley Fighting Vehicle that used 25mm DU rounds against enemy combatants in the town of Al-Samawah. For several months, Kevin and members of his crew had complained to their commanding officer about extreme discomfort, especially in the intestinal/rectal area. Medics dismissed the problem as hemorrhoids, but the pain only grew worse. After being passed from physician to physician, a reservist oncologist finally ordered X-rays . . . and discovered three cases of colon cancer, one case of leukemia, two men with Hodgkin's lymphoma and another soldier with a malignant brain tumor.

Kevin was shipped back to New York, where doctors cut into his rectum and burned the tumors off his liver, only to learn the cancer had already spread to both lungs. The twenty-six-year-old New York native woke to find himself with a colostomy bag and prognosis of incurable colon and lung cancer, the doctors giving him a year to live.

Compounding the news of his death sentence was Uncle Sam's declaration that cancer patients did not receive benefits like other wounded soldiers, the US government refusing to recognize the disease as a casualty of war. And so Kevin Quercio and thousands of American veterans like him lay in oncology wards in VA hospitals across the country waiting to die, deserted by the country they made the ultimate sacrifice to serve—everything kept out of the public consciousness so as not to disturb the ongoing war effort.

Only today, Kevin Quercio could not remain in bed. Today his psyche felt inflamed, his anger seethed. Grabbing the call button by his bed, he rang for the nurse, summoning instead the assistant director, who was making her rounds.

Patrick was alone in the elevator, flexing his new left arm. The disabled veteran's mind was in turmoil, the anticipation of being reunited with his wife and daughter after such a long separation causing great anxiety, the demands of the new secretary of defense unnerving him even more. *What if DeBorn plays hardball and won't allow me to see my family? What if he keeps them away, locking them up against their will just to get me to be his poster boy for a new recruitment surge?*

The elevator stopped at the seventh floor, the doors opening. Patrick Shepherd headed for Ward 19-C . . . the sounds and smells of chaos instantly transporting his wounded mind back to the trauma center at Ibn Sina.

"Blood pressure's dropping, sixty over forty. Hurry up with that brachial artery, I need to administer Dobutrex before we lose him."

"You sure this was an IED? Look at the skin hanging below the remains of his elbow, the flesh melted."

"Artery's closed, start the Dobutrex. Okay, where's the damn bone saw?"

"I think Rosen was using it to carve his brisket."

"How's his BP?"

"Ninety over sixty."

"Let's get another unit of blood in him before we take the arm. Nurse, be an angel and hold up that X-ray. I want to amputate right here, just below the insertion on the biceps tendon.

"Shep, it's David Kantor, can you hear me? Shep?"

"Shep!"

Patrick snapped out of it—Leigh Nelson was crying out for help! He raced through the ward to find Staff Sergeant Kevin Quercio holding the physician by the roots of her hair as he ripped the IV tube from his arm and attempted to strangle her with it.

"Let her go, Kevin."

The Italian-Irishman looked up . . . and froze. Manic rage washed into absolute terror. "No, not yet, Reaper. Please don't take me yet!"

Shep turned around, unsure to whom the soldier was speaking.

Kevin released Dr. Nelson and collapsed to his knees, tears streaming down his face. "Don't take me yet, please. I didn't want to kill those people. All I wanted was to serve my time and come home. Reaper, please."

The ward quieted.

"Kevin . . . it's me, Shep. It's okay."

"I was just following orders! I had no choice."

"Dude, it's cool."

"They lied to us. Please don't take me yet."

"Take you where? Kevin, where don't you want me to take you?"

Kevin wiped back tears, his chemo-weakened body trembling in terror. "Hell."

The orderlies burst into the room. One helped Leigh to her feet. Two escorted Kevin Quercio back to his bed.

Shep looked around. The other veterans—all cancer patients—were staring at him in fear. Several men crossed themselves.

Dr. Nelson pulled him aside, her body trembling. "Thanks, baby doll, you saved my scalp. You okay?"

"Are you?"

"Not really." Her lower lip quivered. "Sorry. It's been one of those days, you know? Oh my God, I didn't even notice the new arm. Wow, it looks great. Are you getting used to it?" Her pager interrupted them before he had a chance to reply. "Now what?" She glanced at the text message. "I've got to run . . . some kind of emergency."

"Leigh, my wife . . . you said you had an address."

Her expression fell. "I gave it to DeBorn, I'm sorry. But it's still in my e-mail. Go to the library and access it, my password is Virginia Fox. Wow, that's embarrassing." She kissed him quickly on the lips. "Thanks again, Shep. Gotta go."

She took two quick strides, then remembered something. "Colonel Argenti called. Your new therapist will be here this afternoon. Talk to him, Shep. Do it for Bea."

She waved, then hurried through the ward toward the elevators—

—unaware of the security team sealing the hospital exits.

UNITED NATIONS SECRETARIAT BUILDING
THIRTY-THIRD FLOOR
11:55 A.M.

President Eric Kogelo sat back in the easy chair and closed his eyes. Surrounded by a team of advisors, he was being assaulted by a nonstop torrent of cross fire that pushed the migraine deeper until it felt as if his eyeballs were being probed by an ice pick.

"—yes, Iran is threatening an attack, but with all due respect, Mr. President, our bigger concern right now is Scythe. The CDC guys confirm the Iranian delegation was contaminated—"

"—along with dozens of other delegates and hundreds of American citizens. So let's just table the finger-pointing."

"The woman infected herself with a Bio-Level 4 biological she cultivated in a CIA-financed lab in Fort Detrick. She specifically sought out the Iranian delegation. You want to see finger-pointing, wait until their Supreme Leader makes his next speech."

"That cannot be allowed to happen. Sir, I recommend we shut down all transmissions—"

The president massaged his temple, his mind searching for an island of tranquility in a stormy sea. In every great society there were opposing forces that preferred chaos over progress. Eric Kogelo had battled these forces at every step since the moment he took office, his administration attempting to negotiate a middle ground rather than upset the applecart. In doing so, he had disappointed progressives while still failing to convert Republicans, who preferred to polarize the country with fear rather than support meaningful change. Refusing to give in, Kogelo rallied his supporters and began making headway against an opposition led by the health-insurance industry, pharmaceutical companies, and the fossil-fuel monopoly. Still, the young president knew a bigger force remained cloaked in the shadow of war. Dealing with the military-industrial complex was a dangerous game.

Never had he imagined a day like today.

"Mr. President, Scythe isn't just an Iranian problem. For all we know everyone in that chamber could have been infected . . . including you, sir."

Heads turned to the chief of staff as if he had just cursed God.

Kogelo's press secretary attempted a rescue. "Sir, the mayor's scheduled to address the media in fifteen minutes . . . maybe you should be there?"

"He can't leave the complex. The moment he leaves, the other delegates will demand to leave, and we lose containment."

"Who says we even have containment? Have you looked outside lately? Those Army guys just added two more tents, and the entire plaza's surrounded by military vehicles."

"Exactly why we need to make a move now, before it's too late. Get an EVAC chopper on the roof. Let's get the president out of Manhattan."

"You mean get *you* out of Manhattan."

"Is that such a crime? I have a wife and kids. None of us are even infected."

"Are you so sure—"

"Enough!" Eric Kogelo stood, the pain in his head excruciating. "Instruct the mayor. Tell him to go public about isolating Manhattan, but he's to emphasize this is purely a precaution, more a response drill than an actual emergency. Reveal nothing to him about Scythe, the last thing we need right now is widespread panic. Where's the first lady?"

"En route to the White House from Chicago."

"Keep her there, make sure my family's safe. I need to lie down . . . an hour to think." The president headed for the bedroom, then turned, making eye contact with each of his advisors. All were fearful, yet none looked away . . . a good sign.

"We're in a tough fix, but let's not lose our composure and panic the herd. The last thing we want is to give our enemies the excuse they've been hammering for to take over Iran's oil reserves and jump-start their New World Order."

"Sir, Scythe was released just minutes before you were set to address the UN Is it possible—"

"That we have a Judas in the White House?" The president exhaled, pinching the bridge of his nose. "Trust no one outside this room."

CITY HALL PARK, LOWER MANHATTAN
12:04 P.M.

Born in Niagara Falls, raised in the Bronx, Mathew Kushner was a New Yorker in every sense of the word. After graduating from Syracuse University and New York Law School, Kushner joined his father's practice, specializing in immigration law. The attorney was less than a mile from his Lower Manhattan office on the morning of September 11, 2001, when the first hijacked commercial airliner violated New York's airspace and struck the World Trade Center.

Mayor Kushner stood on the top steps of City Hall before a podium riddled with microphones, fighting the urge to kick the lectern into the crowd. Once more his beloved city had been violated, Manhattan forcefully isolated without his input or approval. He was being fed half-truths from Washington while black military Hummers raced through the streets, and men in Racal suits stoked fear throughout Tudor City and the UN. It didn't take an immigration attorney to figure out that civil rights were being violated; nor did it take a psych major from Syracuse to know that Manhattan's blood pressure would continue to simmer until it led to an uprising that would make the Watts riots look like a tailgate party.

And in the end, that was why Mayor Kushner had relented in playing the dutiful role of press secretary, not because he believed the story but because he had to believe it . . . because sometimes the difference between civil obedience and civil destruction was the white lie of politics.

"Good afternoon. As most of you know by now, all bridges, tunnels, walkways, highways . . . basically all means of leaving or entering Manhattan, have been temporarily shut down. This order, which came directly from the White House, is a precautionary action that allows medical personal from the Centers for Disease Control to manage, maintain, and monitor a small outbreak of a flulike virus that was detected earlier today at the United Nations Plaza. For your own safety, and to allow gridlock conditions to ease, I am asking everyone in Manhattan, whether resident or guest, to remain indoors until the CDC officially gives us the all clear sign."

"Mayor Kushner–"

"Mr. Mayor!"

Ignoring the press, Mathew Kushner followed his aides back inside City Hall, preparing to unleash his fury at the first Kogelo administration staffer foolish enough to answer his phone call.

143 HOUSTON STREET
LOWER MANHATTAN
12:55 *P.M.*

Built in 1898, the Sunshine Cinema first housed the Houston Hippodrome motion-picture theater, then a Yiddish vaudeville house before being converted to a warehouse. Fifty years later, the Cinema was restored as a theater, featuring five state-of-the-art screens, stadium seating, Dolby Digital Surround EX sound and gourmet concessions, along with a Japanese rock garden and a bridge that offered breathtaking city views from its third-story glass annex.

Thirteen-year-old Gavi Kantor stood outside the box office with her two best friends, Shelby Morrison and Jamie Rumson. Having voted earlier to skip the last day of school before Christmas break, the three seventh graders were arguing over which matinee to see.

"How about *Sisters of the Traveling Pants-3*?"

"Are you gay, Jamie? Seriously. What about you, Gavi?"

"I don't care. I would have been fine watching Blu-Ray movies in Mrs. Jenkins's class."

"You mean, watching Blu-Ray movies with Shawn-Ray Dalinky."

"Shut up, Shelby."

"Don't even try to deny it. He's practically all over your Facebook page."

Shelby's cell phone rang. She checked the number. "Gavi, it's your mom! What should I do?"

"Don't answer it!"

"Hello? Oh, hi, Mrs. Kantor. No, I haven't seen Gavi . . . I mean, I missed her in second period. I, uh, had bad cramps and had to go to the nurse's office. Why? Is anything wrong?" The teenager's eyes widened. "For real? Okay, when I see her, I'll have her call." She hung up.

"What?"

"There's some kind of emergency going on. Your mom said they closed down the roads and trains."

"How do we get home?"

"As of now, we don't. We'll probably have to camp out in the gymnasium."

"Oh, yeah, baby. Gavi and Shawn-Ray Dalinky, snuggling together on the hardwood floor."

Jamie laughed.

Gavi worried. "We'd better get back to school."

Ignoring her friend, Shelby handed the woman working the box office her debit card. "Three for *Stranglehold.*"

"Shelby, what are you doing?"

"We're here, Gavi. Why should we rush back to school? Call your mom later and tell her your phone died."

"Forget it. I'm going back. Jamie?"

"I'm staying."

Gavi hesitated, then left, crossing Houston Street, heading for Chinatown.

"Gavi, don't go. Gavi!"

"Forget her, Jamie. I'm surprised she even came with us. Come on, you're buying the candy and popcorn."

GEORGE WASHINGTON BRIDGE
1:07 P.M.

The traffic on the New Jersey side of the bridge was backed up for miles. Center barriers had been removed, forcing drivers to make U-turns onto the eastbound lanes of Interstate 95, returning them to Fort Lee.

David Kantor held on to the bench seat in the back of the Army transport vehicle as it raced east across the now-empty upper deck of the George

Washington bridge, heading toward Manhattan. The suffocating breathing apparatus covering his face echoed each labored breath. The forty pounds of gear strapped to his back caused the muscles in his shoulders to ache. The tear-gas canisters clipped to his utility belt and the assault rifle loaded with rubber bullets scared the hell out of him. But not as much as what he saw out of the truck's open tailgate.

While an Army demolition team duct-taped munitions to suspension cables, a team in rebreathers and jumpsuits spray-painted the bridge's roadway and undercarriage, using long reach poles.

David knew what was mixed in with the paint, and that was what unnerved him. *This is insane. Something bad has happened.* He cursed himself for giving up his cell phone before calling his wife to see if Gavi ever made it home.

The military vehicle skidded to a halt. As the senior officer present, David instructed the ten National Guardsmen and three Army Reservists to line up behind the back of the vehicle.

"Captain Kantor?" The booming voice rattled the two-way radio inside David's hood. He turned to face an imposing bearded man, his physique bulging beneath a uniform marked UN.

"I am Commander Oyvind Herstad. My men are in charge of this outpost. You are the senior officer for the domestic force?"

"At the moment, yes."

"Your people will be used strictly to communicate; we will maintain the gauntlet."

"Gauntlet? What gauntlet?"

Commander Herstad led him around the truck.

At the end of the road where the bridge met Manhattan was an impediment of military Hummers positioned across all eight lanes of Interstate 95. Beyond the vehicles were coils of barbed wire, stretched across the upper-bridge roadway and the two pedestrian crossings, all backed by heavily armed soldiers in camouflage khaki uniforms, protective headgear, and hoods.

Beyond the gauntlet into Manhattan, pedestrian traffic was ensnared as far as the eye could see. Most civilians remained in their vehicles to stay warm.

Others milled about in packs, yelling at the soldiers, demanding answers. Several men waited their turns to defecate behind a steel bridge support, the public having designated it a makeshift bathroom. Farther to the east, David could see the 178th Street ramp, its bridge-bound lanes lined bumper to bumper with thousands of cars, buses, and trucks. Both upper and lower arteries remained blocked on the Manhattan side of the bridge.

"Why?"

"Manhattan is now under a strict quarantine. No one is permitted to enter or leave the city until further notice."

"What happened? Was there a terrorist attack?"

"Biological attack. Plague. Very contagious. Your men will take positions closest to the civilian walkways. Reason with the people. Keep them calm. The Freedom Force will maintain the quarantine."

"What the hell is the Freedom Force?"

"We're an international division. Professional soldiers."

"Since when does the United States use professional soldiers in domestic emergencies?"

"Field studies have shown that a domestic militia will hesitate to use the force necessary to combat their fellow citizens. The Freedom Force was created to address those situations. Our militia recruits from the Canadian Military Police, Royal Netherlands Brigade, and the Norwegian Armed Forces, among others."

"This is insane."

"This is the world in which we now live."

"We passed a demolition team working on the bridge. What are they doing?"

"Ensuring we do not lose the quarantine."

"You're planning to blow up the George Washington Bridge?"

"It is a fail-safe only. Rest assured, my men will maintain the gauntlet. Do your job and—" Herstad cocked his head and listened to commands coming over his earpiece. "Bring your men, quickly!"

David hurried back behind the truck. "Detail—with me!"

The soldiers formed two lines and fell in behind their commanding officer, double-timing it across the asphalt highway, heading for the commuter walkway located on the south side of the bridge, where a growing mob of several hundred people were threatening to push their way through the barricade, using spare tires and tire irons to attack the barbed wire. A dozen civilians were waving handguns.

"Let us through now, Comrade!"

"None of us are sick! Let us go!"

"My wife's in the car, she's going into labor."

Commander Herstad pulled David aside, handing him a bullhorn fitted with a plug-in attachment for his headgear. "Order them back, or they leave us no choice." The Norwegian fingered the trigger of his weapon. "These are not rubber bullets."

David approached the crowd. Men mostly. Driven by desperation. Fueled by fear and the need to save themselves and their loved ones. Outgunned, yet holding the numbers to win once organized. A hundred thousand cornered cats.

His heart pounded. "May I have your attention? My name is David Kantor, I'm a captain in the United States Army Reserve—"

"Let us through!"

"We can't do that right now."

"Then we'll do it for you!" A revolver was raised above the crowd.

A firing line of Freedom Force fighters raised their assault weapons in response.

The crowd cowered, even as more handguns appeared.

"Wait!" David stepped in front of the firing line.

The foreign militia never budged, their fingers remaining on their triggers.

"Where's the pregnant woman?" No reaction. "I'm a medic. If there's someone who needs medical assistance, let her through."

Heads turned. The crowd parted. A Hispanic couple in their early thirties approached the barbed wire. The woman was stooped over, supporting her swollen belly.

"What's your name?"

"Naomi . . . Naomi Gutierrez. My water broke. This is my fourth. It won't be long."

Commander Herstad pulled David aside. "What are you doing?"

"Negotiating."

"There is nothing to negotiate."

"We're negotiating for time, Commander. The 42nd IDSCOM hasn't arrived yet with their armored vehicles, and I'm laying odds your demolition team isn't quite ready to blow a gap through all fourteen lanes of a two-level suspension bridge. At the same time, I think we both know your men can't stop hundreds of vehicles crashing your gauntlet simultaneously. So here's the deal: You let the woman through. We set her up in the back of the truck with some blankets, and if need be, I help deliver her child. That buys us some time. In Iraq, we called that the human touch. But hey, I'm sure there's a field study lying around somewhere if you need to read it."

Herstad scanned the crowd, the mob having tripled in the last few minutes. "Lower your weapons. Allow the woman through. Just the woman."

David scanned his command. Located one of the female National Guardsmen. "What's your name, Corporal?"

"Sir, Collins, Stephanie, sir."

"At ease. Corporal Collins, I want you to escort Mrs. Gutierrez to the truck we just rode in on. Make her comfortable, but do not compromise your protective gear. Is that clear?"

"Sir, yes, sir."

David watched Herstad's men retract a small section of barbed wire, allowing the pregnant woman to pass through. Activating the bullhorn, he addressed the crowd once again. "The woman will be fine. Now please, for your own safety, go back to your vehicles and wait until the all clear sign is given."

The mob slowly dispersed.

The Freedom Force lowered their assault weapons.

David Kantor followed the two women to the military vehicle, his eyes focused on the demolition crew a hundred yards away—

–continuing to spray paint the underside of the bridge.

VA MEDICAL CENTER
EAST SIDE, MANHATTAN
1:32 P.M.

Leigh Nelson hustled to keep up with Dr. Clark, who was dictating orders to her even as he directed interns, relocating dozens of patients, who were organizing a ground-level isolation ward in the E.R. "We contacted the CDC in Albany. They're already at the UN Apparently the outbreak started there."

"Makes sense. The Russian woman's a delegate."

"We'll perform the C-section in the E.R., then return both mother and child to the third-floor isolation ward. The infant will remain in a self-contained unit. The mother is to remain restrained."

"Yes, sir."

"Are the antibiotics having any effect?"

"No, sir, not yet. Cold packs brought the fever down a little. Once the newborn's delivered, we'll start the mother on a morphine drip to deal with the pain."

"No, keep her lucid. The CDC wants us to get as much information from her as we can. Who she came in contact with, what buildings she entered . . . that's your job, Dr. Nelson. Find out everything. The CDC claims they'll be able to contain this thing, but I know bullshit when I smell it, especially with the feds shutting down the transit system. I ordered a dozen environmental suits brought over from inventory and sent Myers on a bleach run. Prepare for the worst, Leigh, it's going to be a long night."

The old man entered the emergency ward. His face was serene, contrasting with the chaos surrounding him. Bypassing the turmoil at the front desk, he strolled down a corridor lined with moaning patients in wheeled beds and confused interns seeking answers from frustrated nurses. Arriving at a row of elevators, he pushed the UP button.

The middle elevator arrived first, its doors opening—

—releasing a hospital administrator and three interns, all wearing gowns, gloves, and masks. They were pushing a gurney enveloped in a portable plastic isolation tent, its patient—a ghostly pale pregnant woman, her wrists and ankles bound to the bed rails by restraining straps.

"Sir, please step back."

Mary Louise Klipot opened her sunken eyes, staring aghast at the old man. He offered a simple wave hello before stepping onto the vacated elevator.

*"**Hey, Whitebread,** phone call. It's either your old lady or the whore you shacked up with last night."*

Patrick Shepherd grabs the pay-phone receiver. "Sorry, babe. Just one of my teammates messin' with you. How's your dad?"

"Not good. The cancer's moved into his lymph nodes. The doctor says . . . it won't be long."

Tears roll down his cheeks. "Okay. I'm coming home."

"Dad said no, and he meant it. He said if you leave the team now, you'll lose your spot in the rotation."

"I don't care."

"He does! Whenever the fever breaks, you're all he talks about. How's Shep? Did he pitch today? So . . . how is it going?"

Shep checks the hallway, making sure no one is listening. "Class A ball sucks. I'm surrounded by a bunch of eighteen-year-old Dominicans who can't speak a lick of English. These guys are crazy, like they were just let off the boat." He pinches away tears. "The truth is, I'm lonely. I miss you and the baby."

"We'll see you soon enough. How's the competition?"

"Raw. But a few guys . . . you can tell they're juicing."

"Don't even think about it."

"What if it's my only chance?"

"Patrick—"

"Babe, I'm a nineteenth-round draft pick signed for fifteen hundred bucks out of Rutgers. A few needles, and I bet I could add at least four miles an hour to my fastball."

"No steroids. Promise me, baby."

"Okay. I promise."

"When's your next start?"

"Wednesday night."

"Just remember what Dad taught you. Don't take the rubber until you visualize the pitch. When the first batter goes down flailing, no smile, no emotion, just the Iceman. Shep, are you even listening?"

"Sorry. I can't think straight. Knowing what's going on with your dad . . . not seeing you and the baby . . . it feels like I have a hole in my heart."

"Stop it. Stop whining! You are not a victim."

"He's not just my coach, he's the only father I've ever known."

"You said your good-byes three weeks ago. We all knew that. We all cried. If you want to honor him, utilize the lessons he spent a lifetime teaching you. And don't forget our deal. I'm not marrying you until you pitch in the majors."

"Okay, tough guy."

"You think I'm kidding?"

"We're soul mates. You can't leave your soul mate."

"A deal's a deal. Quit the team now, or start putting needles in your ass, and I'm gone in a New York minute. Me and your daughter."

"Why are you doing this?"

"Because Dad's too sick to slap you around himself. Because we agreed to a plan the day you found out I was pregnant. You need to succeed, Shep. Don't back down now. We're counting on you."

Patrick Shepherd sat up in bed, panting. His body was lathered in sweat, his mind once more struggling to identify his new surroundings.

"That must have been quite the dream."

Shep turned, startled.

The old man was leaning back in the desk chair, watching him. More aging hippie than senior citizen. A long mane of hair, silvery white, pulled back over a tan forehead into a six-inch ponytail. A matching mustache and trimmed beard framed his jaw line down to his Adam's apple. The eyes were blue, kind but inquisitive, obscured behind teardrop glasses, their lenses tinted burgundy. He was wearing faded blue jeans, brown hiking boots, and a thick gray wool sweater over a black tee shirt. Bearing a slight paunch, he resembled an elderly, healthy version of the late Grateful Dead singer, Jerry Garcia, had he lived to see his mid to late seventies.

"Who are you? What are you doing in my room?"

"A friend of yours sent me to speak with you. Something about your needing help. By the way, who's Trish?"

"Trish?"

"You yelled out her name."

"You mean Beatrice. Beatrice is . . . was my wife. DeBorn sent you, you're the shrink."

The old man smiled. "Not what you expected when you asked for help."

"You look more like a refugee from the sixties than a psychiatrist."

"How should a psychiatrist look?"

"I don't know. More brainy."

"This was the best I could do on short notice. Should I lose the beard?"

"Dude, I could care less what you look like. And just to set the record straight, DeBorn's not my friend; he's just using me for some new Army recruiting deal of his. You should know up-front I'm not doing it."

"Okay."

"Okay? Just like that?"

"Well, we could torture you, I suppose, but I've always been a proponent of free will."

"DeBorn's not going to pay you if I don't do as he says."

"Let's not concern ourselves with Mr. DeBorn. Besides, what's said between us stays between us, isn't that the rule?"

"It's more complicated than that. He can keep me from seeing my family." Shep slid off the bed and pulled the sweat-soaked tee shirt off with his right hand, carefully working it around his new prosthetic arm.

"Has he kept you from seeing them up until now?"

"Well . . . no."

"Then why haven't you seen them?"

"I guess I wasn't ready."

"But you're ready now?"

"Yes."

"Good. How long has it been since you last saw them?"

"Too long. Eleven years, give or take. It's hard to remember."

"Then why see them at all? Seems like you'd just be opening up old wounds." The psychiatrist picked up the leather-bound copy of *Dante's Inferno* lying on the desk. Casually flipped through the dog-eared pages.

"Old wounds? They're my family. I just found out they're here, in Manhattan."

"Don't you mean, your *estranged* family. Eleven years is a long time, give or take. As your shrink, I'd say it's time you moved on."

"You're not my shrink . . . and could you put that book down! Borrow it from the library if you want to read it so badly."

"Oh, I've read it." He turned the book over, reading the summary aloud. "*Dante's Inferno*, written by Dante Alighieri between 1308 and 1321, is widely considered one of the greatest and most revered works of world literature. Divided into three distinct parts—*Hell*, *Purgatory*, and *Heaven*—*Inferno* describes Dante's journey through Hell, depicted as nine circles of suffering. Allegorically, the *Divine Comedy* represents the journey of the soul toward God, with *Inferno* describing the recognition and rejection of sin—"

Patrick snatched the book from the old man. "I know what the story is about. I've read it so many times I've practically memorized it."

"And do you agree with the author's conclusions?"

"What conclusions?"

"That the wicked are condemned to an afterlife of misery without any hope of salvation."

"I was raised a Catholic. So yeah . . . I believe it." The question weighed on Patrick. "Just out of curiosity, what do you believe?"

"I believe that even in one's last instant of life redemption can still be achieved."

"You don't believe God punishes the sinner?"

"Every soul must be cleansed before it moves on, but punishment . . . what I prefer to call obstacles, are opportunities to gain access to the Light of God."

"You sound like some sort of New Wave guru. What religion are you?"

"Honestly, I'm not a big fan of religion."

"So you don't believe in God?"

"I didn't say that. I just don't believe the Creator intended spirituality to be an open competition. What about you? Do you believe in God?"

Patrick sneered. "I believe God fell asleep at the wheel long ago. As useless as teats on a bull. I have zero faith in Him. The guy's a bigger screwup than I am."

"You blame God for the loss of your arm?"

"I blame God for the world. Look at all the evil, all the needless suffering. Two wars going on, another one looming. People starving. Dying of cancer—"

"You're right. Screw God. If He was any kind of creator, he'd have cleaned up this mess eons ago. Lazy no-good bastard."

"Yeah . . . no, that's not what I meant. I mean, some of it's our fault, free will and all that."

"But you blame Him for your life."

"No. I blame Him for separating me from my family."

"Didn't you say they're in New York?"

"Yeah, but—"

"They lock you in at night?"

"No."

"So leave. Go find your wife and kid . . . or don't. But stop playing the victim."

The blood drained from Patrick's face. "What did you say?"

"I think you heard me."

"You think it's that easy?" Shep sat on the corner of the bed, the edginess returning. He fidgeted with the steel pincers, feeling uncomfortable in his own skin. "There are things, you know . . . in my head."

"Ah . . . the nightmares."

"You're a real man of genius. Yeah, the nightmares. And don't ask me about them either."

"You're the boss." The old man sat back, flipped through *Dante's Inferno.* "An interesting read. I enjoy books that deal with challenges of the human spirit."

"*Inferno* deals with justice. Punishment for the wicked."

"Back to God being asleep at the wheel?"

"I've been in combat. I've seen innocent people suffer. Why must there be so much hatred? So much senseless violence and greed . . . so much corruption. There's no justice in the world. That's why these things keep happening."

"You want justice or happiness?"

"Justice would give me happiness. If God's really out there, then why does He allow evil people to prosper while the good among us suffer?"

"Are you counting yourself among the good?"

"No."

"Are you suffering?"

"Yes."

"Congratulations, there's justice in the world. Be happy."

"Ugh! You just don't want to get it, do you?"

"I get it. You want God to strike every sinner down the moment they sin. But what good would that do? Ever watch how they train animals? When the animals complete a desired action, they get a treat. When they do something bad, they get shocked. Spirituality isn't about being conditioned, it's about free will and resisting the negative urges to react to temptation. It's about controlling the human ego . . . the true Satan. Satan is clever. He removes time from the equation of cause and effect, making it confusing to track rewards to good deeds and evil acts to punishments."

"Okay, but real justice still comes, right? Say I've done things . . . things justifiable in war, only maybe I'm no longer sure. Will I be punished?"

"Let's be clear: Sin is sin, there's no wartime exemption for killing or rape. As far as real justice—the fire and brimstone of Dante—no soul returns to the Light without being cleansed. For some, the cleansing process can be quite painful."

"You keep saying the Light."

"My apologies. By Light, I'm referring to the Light of the Creator. The infinite. Endless fulfillment."

"Like Heaven?"

"If you want to simplify it."

Shep pondered this. "What happens when evil surrounds you . . . when it seems to be everywhere all at once, when every choice is the wrong choice, and you can't escape it?"

"When wickedness achieves a critical mass, when it becomes widespread like a runaway plague so that it shuts off access to the Creator's Light, then even innocent souls are subject to destruction. In that case, a cleansing must take place, on a scale that transcends the depravity of the wicked. You remember the story of Noah? Of Sodom and Gomorrah? Ah, but I guess those cleansings took place before God fell asleep at the wheel."

Shep didn't reply, he was staring at the old man's left wrist. The sweater's sleeve had ridden up, revealing a number tattooed along the outside of his forearm. "You were in the Holocaust?"

"I was there."

"Then you know evil better than most."

"Yes."

Patrick's eyes teared up. "I know evil, too."

"Yes, son, I believe you do."

"I've done some terrible things."

"Things your wife would never approve of?"

"Yes."

"And now you want her back?"

"And my daughter. They both left me. I miss them so much."

"What makes you so certain your wife wants to see you again?"

"Because she's my soul mate."

The old man sighed "Those are powerful words, my friend. Do you even know what the term means? A soul mate is two halves of a single soul, divided by God."

"I never heard that before."

"It's part of an ancient wisdom, one that predates religion. The reunification of soul mates is a blessed event, but know this: Soul mates cannot be reunited until both parties complete their *tikkun* . . . their spiritual correction. And you, my friend, are far from ready."

The old man stood to leave.

"Whoa, Doc, wait a minute. I changed my mind. I do want your help. Tell me what I have to do to get my soul mate back, and I'll do it."

"Everything has a cause and effect. Fix the cause, and you'll fix the effect."

"What the hell does that mean? She left *me,* remember. You want me to apologize? Would that make it right again?"

"Take some time. Think about things. Decide what it is you want out of your life. When you're ready to stop playing the victim, come and see me."

The old man fished through his sweater pocket, extracting a business card. He handed it to Shep and left.

Patrick Shepherd stared at the card.

VIRGIL SHECHINAH
INWOOD HILL, NEW YORK

INWOOD HILL, NEW YORK
1:51 P.M.

Located at the very northern tip of the island, Inwood Hill was a Manhattan neighborhood unlike any other. There were no skyscrapers here. The Harlem River marked its northeastern border, High Bridge Park and Washington Heights situated directly to the south. Among its western landmarks were athletic fields belonging to Columbia University, nestled close to a heavily wooded mountain terrain that seemed a thousand miles from the Big Apple.

This was Inwood Hill Park, the only natural forest left in Manhattan. Climb its rocky summit, and one was rewarded with a magnificent view of the Hudson River. Explore its dense wood, and you might discover ancient caves once inhabited by the Lenape Indians long before the first Europeans arrived.

The Black Chevy Suburban entered Inwood Hill, made a U-turn at the intersection of Broadway and Dyckman Street, then parked.

Bertrand DeBorn exited the car. Slammed the rear door. Crossing the street, he walked to a new i-pay phone, verified that it was operational, then dialed a number on his cell phone.

"Yes?"

"It's me. Call me back at 212-433-4613." The secretary of defense hung up and waited. Snatched the pay-phone receiver on its first ring. "What happened?"

"Someone unleashed Scythe."

DeBorn's skin crawls. "Where? When?"

"The UN Plaza. About five hours ago."

"Five hours? Five hours is a lifetime. You have no idea how fast this biological can spread in a major metropolis. I need to get to the UN before they run out of vaccine—"

"Bert, Scythe was genetically altered. It's not responding to any of the harvested antibiotics."

A cold sweat broke out across the defense secretary's forehead.

"Homeland Security shut down access in and out of Manhattan. Where are you now?"

"North. Still on the island."

"Are you clean?"

"For the moment. I've been in a secure location, meeting with key council members."

"And?"

"They support the plan, all of which has just been rendered moot."

"Not necessarily. Think about it. If Scythe broke out in Tehran next month, no one could possibly blame–"

"Enough! You have no idea what you're even saying. If Scythe leaves Manhattan in its present form, we're all dead. All of us! Without a vaccine, Scythe is a runaway train. I need to get off this island quickly before I'm infected. Where's POTUS?"

"He's being held in quarantine at the UN. No one's allowed to leave."

"POTUS will be airlifted out, so will the others. They'll all be sent to Fort Detrick and held while a cure is found. I need to get to the UN, it's my only hope. Call me on my cell with any updates."

"Bert, it's not a secure line."

"No one's listening. Plague has infested Manhattan."

Lost Diary: Guy de Chauliac

The following entry has been excerpted from a recently discovered unpublished memoir, written by surgeon Guy de Chauliac during the Great Plague: 1346–1348.
(translated from its original French)

Diary Entries: January 17, 1348

(recorded in Avignon, France)

Plague has infested Avignon.

What began as a whisper in the night has blossomed into the wails of the dying and bereaved. And there seems no escape.

Within days of the first mortalities, the dead and dying had passed the death onto their caregivers and loved ones. Bells tolled each hour as the graves filled quickly. Terror consumed the living while Death's cold hand wound through the streets, sparing barely a soul from its invisible embrace. Neither parent nor child. Cardinal or prostitute.

Villagers collapsed in pubs and in pews.

Entire households were vanquished of the living.

Last rites were canceled, lest our remaining priests catch the scourge.

The sick were robbed while they lay dying in their beds, the thieves succumbing to the Great Mortality days later.

And oh how the body count did rise; dozens yielding to hundreds, hundreds to thousands. When the churchyards were filled, the Pope purchased a new cemetery. When it, too, was filled, massive graves were dug outside the city walls. When the grave diggers fell ill, rustics came down from the hills to claim a beggar's wealth—Avignon paying them a small ransom to cart off its dead each morning and afternoon, burying them by sunset. Piled atop one another, the deceased are wheeled to mass burial pits and laid out in neat rows by the hundreds. By nightfall, the top layer of the day's collection is covered by dirt, only to be decimated hours later by wild dogs and pigs that tear the toxic flesh from the bones, leaving the scraps to the rats.

Every night I bed to incessant weeping in the streets, with each new dawn I awaken to the sound of pull carts and my own fearful breaths as I check my vital signs. By midmorning the newly afflicted form lines at my door, coughing mothers cradling their crying infants, husbands their fallen wives. All seek aid I cannot give, and they are far too numerous to treat even if I knew of a cure. The Pope requires my services, and so I take my leave, tending to those I can upon my return from the palace if only so I might live to understand this sickness and one day find a cure.

When it comes to disease, I have been taught that it is the body out of balance that is prone to sickness. For so many to have perished would require a mighty imbalance . . . and one has come to light. Months earlier, a rare galactic phenomenon became evident in the night sky, bringing Mars, Jupiter, and Saturn into alignment. This cosmic imbalance has no doubt cast its toxic vapor upon the Earth, infecting mankind. The vapor may indeed be worse in the city, causing the rich among us to flee to their chateaus in the countryside.

I have begged Clement VI to leave Avignon, but the Pope refuses. Instead, he has allowed me to place fire pits in his personal chamber, the heat and flames perhaps capable of incinerating the toxic miasma vapor. So far it has proved effective in keeping the Pope free of the sickness—

—but the stench of evil lurks all around us and I fear the worst is yet to come.

—Guigo

"Seeing the swine flu virus spread within a raft of countries, the United Nations health agency today raised the international alert to Phase 5 on a six-point scale, signaling an imminent pandemic and urging all countries to intensify preparations."

—United Nations News Centre, April 29, 2009

"Disruption of life-as-usual could come from economic collapse, runaway climate change, war, peak oil, pandemic, or some unforeseen combination of these and other factors. What makes these prospects especially terrifying are potential human responses to them. We could see either societal breakdown—in which each person turns on others in a battle for dominance or survival—or fascism, in which people allow all-powerful leaders to run things out of fear of chaos."

—Sarah van Gelder, Executive Editor, *Yes Magazine*

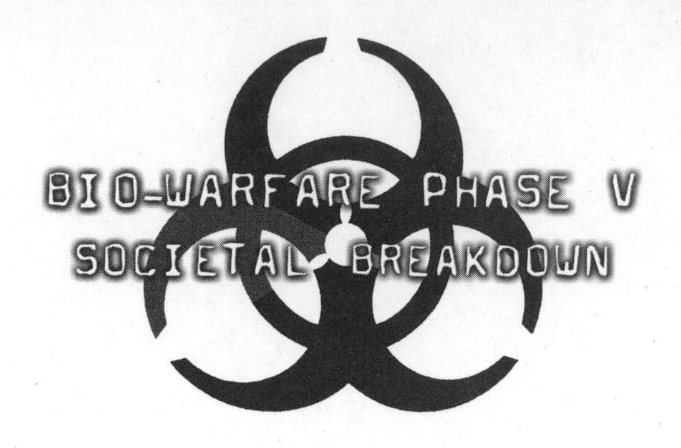

DECEMBER 20

SECRETARIAT BUILDING

UNITED NATIONS PLAZA

2:39 P.M.

(17 HOURS, 31 MINUTES BEFORE THE PROPHESIED END OF DAYS)

The thirty-nine-story Secretariat Building loomed high over the United Nations Plaza. Rectangular with a green glass facade, it was one of the more easily identified structures in New York. As part of the UN, the building was considered "international territory" and its delegates had never been subjected to the laws of New York or the United States—

—until today.

Heavily armed members of New York's Emergency Service Unit (ESU) were posted in the Secretariat lobby and on every floor. Electricity had been shut off to prevent the spread of Scythe through the ventilation systems, the cold temperatures adding insult to injury. Updates were delivered every hour, the stall tactic allowing six teams of CDC units to make their way floor by floor, office by office, performing triage on the UN's imprisoned diplomats.

The elevator was powered by a generator off the grid. Two ESU escorts and Dr. Roy Mohan rode in silence to the seventeenth floor. Mohan understood tragedy all too well. A drunk driver had stolen his wife and infant son six months ago. Now the physician put in sixty-hour workweeks at the Centers for Disease Control, using his job to blunt the pain. In the last four hours, he had examined more than seventy civilians and thirty-one police officers. What he had seen had churned up all the bad memories.

Scythe was a ruthless killer, designed to spread faster than any virus the microbiologist had ever worked on. Its effect was sinister. Almost supernatural. Within minutes of being infected, the new host was already infecting others. A kiss. A cough. A hug. A handshake. Sometimes simple proximity. As Scythe continued its lethal spread, the Secretariat Building had become an incubator of toxic bacilli.

"Doc, you ready?"

He nodded to the ESU officer. The three men exited the elevator. One of the officers tapped on the door of Suite 1701 with the butt end of his Taser. A plaque identified the tenants as the Democratic Republic of Congo.

After a moment, the door cracked open, revealing a cocoa-skinned male in his early twenties. Wrapped in a blanket. A bloody hand towel held over his nose and mouth. His dark, jaundiced eyes were wide in fear. "*Mai . . . poladó.*"

The security officer looks looked back at his partner. "Anybody speak African?"

"It's Lingala." Dr. Mohan reached into his backpack and extracted a bottled water.

The man grabbed it from him, draining it.

"Do you speak any English?"

"A little. Just what I learned at Tasok . . . the American school in Kinshasa. My name is Matthew Vincent Albert Hawkins. My parents work for the government. You will tell me what is killing us."

The first police officer answered "It's just a bad flu. We need to examine everyone in the suite, then we'll come back with medicine."

"You are a liar. This is not flu." Hawkins opened the suite door wider.

There were at least a dozen of them inside, mostly blacks, a few whites, including a Caucasian woman in her fifties. Their faces were covered by newspaper. Streaks of fresh blood were visible on the print.

"Fourteen dead. Five more in the adjoining office, alive but infected. I am a premed student, so you will not lie to me again. What is killing us?"

"Bubonic plague," Dr. Mohan replied. "A strain that spreads very quickly."

"Why have you not issued antibiotics?"

"Unfortunately, we haven't found any that are effective."

Hawkins teared up, his nostrils sniffling, his brow knitted in anger. Lowering the blanket, he tore open his dress shirt—revealing the tattoo of a lion over his heart, encircled by the words *Mwana ya Congo*. Above the tattoo, situated along his neck, was a swollen black bubo the size of an apple. "We deserve better. Yes?"

"Yes."

"My brother and sister . . . they are also thirsty."

Dr. Mohan handed him his backpack. "There's water and some supplies. Go with God."

Hawkins nodded. Closed the door.

VA MEDICAL CENTER
EAST SIDE, MANHATTAN
2:44 P.M.

Leigh Nelson hovered outside the portable plastic isolation tent. Directed her light into the half-open sunken eyes of the Russian woman. The pupils responded.

Beneath the feverish hot water within the ebb and flow of nausea in the endless sea of pain, Mary Klipot followed the light to the surface of consciousness.

"Dana, my name is Dr. Nelson. Can you understand English?"

"My baby?"

"Your child is safe. We had to perform an emergency C-section."

Baby Jesus is born! "I want to see my baby."

"Dana, listen to me. Your baby is fine, but you are very sick. We have to wait until you feel better. The antibiotics should take effect soon."

"Bring me my child." The words rasped in her throat, gurgled in blood.

"Dana, you're contagious."

"The child's protected. I inoculated him against Scythe."

"Scythe?"

"Bubonic plague. A new strain. Harvested in my lab."

The color drained from Leigh's face. "What lab?"

Mary coughed up blood, then licked the residue away, staining her lips. "Fort Detrick."

"You did this?"

"Known antibiotics won't stop it. The antidote . . . is in my car. In the spare-wheel hub."

"Where's your car?"

"It was towed this morning . . . near the UN. Bring me the antidote, and I'll show you how to use it."

USAMRIID
FORT DETRICK-FREDERICK, MARYLAND
2:53 P.M.

The real-time satellite map of Manhattan featured on the 140-inch projection screen was a hybrid, listing streets and identifying buildings. Red dots represented the verifiable number of infected individuals in a given neighborhood, the tallies quantified along the border of the image.

Most of the damage appeared in the Lower East Side along a four-square-block area encompassing the United Nations Plaza, where the numbers of infected were approaching two hundred.

Of greater concern to Colonel Zwawa's team were the growing number of cases being reported in other areas of Manhattan, including Lenox Hill, the Upper East Side, and Central and East Harlem, where Scythe had leapfrogged west to Lincoln Square and Manhattanville. Each locale had begun as a single case, only to blossom into a patch of red Xs as the infected individual had unknowingly spread plague to unsuspecting family members, friends, and, finally, medical workers.

Colonel Zwawa glanced at the wall clock. *Seven minutes until Mayor Kushner's next press conference and still no word from the president.*

As if reading his thoughts, a blank wall monitor activated, revealing President Eric Kogelo. Drained. His complexion a pasty gray. "My apologies. With the power out, we've had to deal with some technical challenges. Our conference monitors aren't working . . . is the vice president on the line?"

"Right here, Mr. President. I'm in the Situation Room with Secretary Clausner and the Joint Chiefs. I've asked Lieutenant General Folino from the National Guard and Admiral Ogren from the Coast Guard to join us. They've mobilized their forces to help secure Manhattan's bridges, tunnels, and waterways."

"Whose decision was it to mobilize the Freedom Force?"

The vice president offered an irritated frown. "You'd have to speak with Secretary Clausner about that, sir."

Harriet Clausner refused to cower. "It was my call, Mr. President. The director of Homeland Security called me personally while en route to New York and flatly stated that it would take him three hours to mobilize the Guard and have them in position to seal all of Manhattan's exits and entry points. We were given minutes. I contacted the Freedom Force. They sent a squadron from Jersey City. I did what I felt was necessary."

"Understood. Who's in charge of the foreign militia?"

"That would be me, Mr. President." A blue-eyed man appeared on-screen. Short-cropped blondish gray hair. His accent classic Sandhurst. "James O'Neill, British Armed Forces, Acting Commandant of the Freedom Force. Let me put your mind at ease, Mr. President. Dealing with civilian populations is our specialty. My units have served in Kosovo, Sierra Leone, Northern Ireland, as well as—"

"I'm not questioning your qualifications, Mr. O'Neill, only my secretary of state's decision to employ a private international militia in a domestic matter."

"With all due respect, sir, today's events are exactly why your predecessor funded our unit. When it comes to domestic challenges, the Freedom Force can mobilize quicker and more efficiently than the National Guard."

"We appreciate your service, but this is a delicate matter, and your presence could make matters worse. General Folino?"

"Here, sir."

"How quickly can we replace the Freedom Force with US troops?"

"We've mobilized the Third Infantry Division's First Brigade Combat Team; they're en route from their home post at Fort Stewart, Georgia. As for the Guard, we'd have to free up a division or two helping to reinforce levees along the Mississippi."

"Whatever it takes, General, I want the Freedom Force replaced. Colonel Zwawa, what's the situation at the UN?"

"Not good, sir. A.I.T. and CDC teams are being overwhelmed by the sheer number of the infected. We're preparing to pull out and relocate to Governor's Island."

"Wait . . . are you saying we've lost the United Nations?"

"Mr. President, we lost Manhattan hours ago."

"Manhattan? Dear Lord . . ."

"Sir, we expect to have a suitable facility set up on Governor's Island by seven o'clock this evening. We'll be bringing in choppers to evacuate your party as well as the surviving delegates. To reiterate, we have every Bio-4 lab facility in North America working on developing an effective antibiotic on this mutated version of the virus."

"Straight talk, Colonel. You're moving us to Governor's Island so you can keep us quarantined. Is that essentially it?"

"Quarantined, yes, but also you'll be more readily accessible so that we can quickly administer an effective antibiotic once we have it."

"But we've lost Manhattan?"

"Yes, sir. While we haven't received a single report of plague outside Manhattan, Scythe is spreading across the island, each infected area similar to a small brush fire capable of burning out of control."

"General Folino, can your troops maintain the quarantine?"

"For the moment. It's like herding cattle. A dozen cowboys on horses can do it, provided there's no stampede. Once these neighborhoods reach a saturation point, the herd will panic, and suddenly you've unwittingly organized a mob of several hundred thousand people. Our forces simply cannot maintain containment against those odds."

"What do you recommend?"

"Instruct the mayor to clear the streets. Order everyone indoors, then institute martial law. Civilians congregating in public places are Scythe's kindling, every riot a threat to overwhelm our containment."

"Admiral Willick?"

Steven Willick, Chairman of the Joint Chiefs of Staff, appeared on-screen. "I agree. As it stands now, our biggest concern is the hundred thousand commuters stuck in gridlocked traffic along Manhattan's bridges and tunnels. Panic that herd, and we're looking at a mass vehicular exodus that will overwhelm our gauntlets. Should that happen, we collapse the bridges. Then there are the Hudson, Harlem, and East River escape routes. We're patrolling shorelines along the Bronx and Queens, and we're treating Roosevelt Island as part of Manhattan. Two more Coast Guard cutters are en route to guard the waterways, along with a cargo plane loaded with our latest combat aerial drones. Right now, we need the mayor to buy us enough time to get our units into position."

"How much time do you need?"

"Two hours."

The president massaged his temples, closing his eyes to think. "Put me through to Mayor Kushner."

SUNSHINE CINEMA
LOWER MANHATTAN
2:47 P.M.

Shelby Morrison fed from the trough of popcorn perched in her lap. Her friend Jamie texted in the dark movie theater. "Brent Tripp just asked me out."

"The buzz cut from Georgia?"

"He's cute."

"Shh!" A heavyset woman two rows back scowled at them.

Shelby lowered her voice. "He's like a Boy Scout or something."

"Eagle Scout. So what? The guy's cool. He's like, going to be a filmmaker."

"Seriously?"

"Shh!"

"Oh shush yourself!" Shelby grabbed another handful of popcorn—screaming as she tucked both feet onto her seat. "Jamie, something just ran across my foot!"

"A dog?"

"I think it was a rat."

"Oh my God." Jamie Rumson pulled her feet up and looked down as a two-pound black rat scurried up her leg!

"Ahhh! Ahh!" Using the tub of popcorn, the horror-stricken teen swatted the creature into the next row as an army of black rats scurried along the floor and over the seats, sending waves of screaming patrons hurrying into the aisle.

"Run!" Shelby tried to walk across the seats, gave up, and stepped on a rodent's back, twisting her ankle. The houselights turned on, revealing the heavyset woman struggling up the main aisle ahead of them, rats leaping upon the back of her fur coat.

Jamie grabbed Shelby's hand, and they pushed through the crowd toward the screen for a sliver of daylight coming from the open exit door. Bodies pressed in from all sides. Wedged between a wall of human overcoats, they shuffled along blindly, grabbing for balance, praying not to fall. A cold blast of December followed gray daylight and they were in an alleyway, hurrying past a trash bin overstuffed with plastic garbage bags and a homeless man. He was writhing on his side, inebriated and ranting. A dozen rats swarmed over his ragged clothes, tearing into his flesh.

Screaming all the way through the alley, the teens followed the dispersing crowd across Houston Street, stopping traffic.

"Oh my God, oh my God . . . I'm going to be sick."

"Shelby, my leg is bleeding. I think it bit me."

"Seriously? Oh my God, Jamie, you are bleeding."

"Oh my God, am I going to die?"

"No, it's okay. People get bitten by rats all the time. We better wash it off or something before you get rabies. Come on."

CHINATOWN
2:51 P.M.

Manhattan's Chinatown was home to more than 160,000 people living and working in a maze of narrow streets crowded with vendors and greengrocers, fishmongers and jewelry shops and more than two hundred "authentic" Chinese restaurants. But there was more to Chinatown than dim sum and cheap perfume. An undercurrent of black-marketed goods flowed through this Asian ghetto, luring bargain hunters seeking illegal imitation designer sunglasses and handbags into storefront back rooms and alleys and basements.

Gavi Kantor had detoured to Mott Street in search of a Christmas present for her new beau, Shawn-Ray. The "spotter" took inventory of the Caucasian teen from one corner. Radioed his "tout" as she approached.

"Prada . . . Gucci . . . Coach. You want Prada? Gucci? I get you good deal."

"Actually, I'm looking for a watch. For my boyfriend."

"How much you got?"

"Forty dollars."

"Hmm. Seiko. Timex. Wait! How 'bout Rolex?"

"For forty bucks? Come on."

"Slightly used. Look brand-new. Work perfect. You like very much. Even have box. Come on, I show you."

With visions of an overwhelmed Shawn-Ray Dalinky floating in her head, the naïve thirteen-year-old chased her Pied Piper through a twisting alleyway and down a flight of steps leading into a redbrick building's basement corridor and the darkness that awaited . . .

TIMES SQUARE
BROADWAY & 45TH STREET
MIDTOWN MANHATTAN
3:02 P.M.

It was the heart of Manhattan: A brilliantly lit twelve-block Mecca of multiplexes and Broadway shows sandwiched between glass towers and computerized billboards. Now, a quarter of a million people paused amid gridlocked traffic to gaze up in silence at the multiple images of their mayor broadcast over half a dozen giant HD screens.

". . . in order to prevent the spread of the virus and allow health authorities to properly treat those infected, we are instituting a mandatory 5 P.M. curfew. Anyone remaining on the street after 5 P.M. will be subject to arrest. Those of you who are stranded on Manhattan's bridges and interstates will be transported by buses to Madison Square Garden for the night. This mandatory curfew will remain in effect until the Department of Health issues their all clear sign."

A collective moan took the crowd.

On the big screens, reporters shouted over one another to be heard. "Mr. Mayor, the United Nations is under quarantine. What about President Kogelo?"

"President Kogelo, his staff, and the rest of the United Nations delegates are under lockdown orders until the danger has passed. The president is asking all of us to take similar precautions."

"How lethal is this virus?"

"It's extremely contagious. Nobody said it was lethal."

"Come on, Mayor Kushner! There are teams of health workers dressed in environmental suits bagging bodies in the UN Plaza. It's all over YouTube! How can you stand here and tell us it's not lethal?"

In the crowded intersection, among a quarter of a million suddenly uneasy shoppers and tourists and businessmen, Santa Claus arrived on foot to spread a different kind of "holiday cheer."

Still in uniform, Heath Shelby staggered through the crowd. Feverish. His body ached. Strands of white hair from his wig stuck to the sweat beads lining his forehead and pasty complexion. Droplets of coughed-up blood stained the fake beard and mustache adhering to his face. Another wave of nausea built.

"Mr. Mayor, how can you stand here and tell us it's not lethal?"

Lethal? The Salvation Army volunteer looks up at the big screen mounted on the side of the truncated triangular building known as One Times Square. *The pregnant woman at the UN? She was sick.*

Heath Shelby's heart pounded with the rapid rhythm of a man who had just received a death sentence. He needed to flee . . . to get to a hospital, but he was surrounded by a sea of people, his very presence among the throng threatening their existence, the crowd's overwhelming numbers denying him the privacy to succumb to the hot bile rising from his gut.

Pushing bodies out of his way, he staggered to a trash can and retched.

"Mommy, look! Santa Claus is sick."

The mother shakes her head. "He's not really Santa, honey, he's just some hopeless drunk."

"No, Mommy, he's really sick. Look at all the blood."

The mother turned to look again. "My God . . . he's got the virus. He's infected!" Picking up her six-year-old, she pushed her way through the crowd, screaming, "He's sick! Get out of my way!"

Heads turned.

Realizing his secret was blown, Heath Shelby wiped his mouth and stumbled forward, forging a path through the urban forest of humanity—

—Scythe infecting a new crop of hosts with every step.

WEST 38TH STREET & TWELFTH AVENUE
MANHATTAN, NEW YORK
3:19 P.M.

The cab driver glanced up at his rearview mirror at the pretty brunette in the backseat wearing a mask over her face. "Traffic's not moving. The police station's six blocks away. Probably quicker if you walk."

Leigh Nelson paid the driver, then forced her way onto the crowded sidewalk. She paused to get her bearings, only to be jostled by tides of angry pedestrians sweeping past her in both directions, cell phones plastered to their ears, their conversations anything but private.

". . . then call the senator! I dropped twenty grand on his last campaign, he'd better find a way to get me off this godforsaken island!"

"Honey, I don't know when I'll be home, they've shut down everything. I guess I'll just sleep at the office."

The police depot was located en route to the Lincoln Tunnel, the busiest underground vehicular passage in the world. Located in midtown Manhattan, the three-tube passage and its six traffic lanes descended beneath the Hudson River bed, transporting over 120,000 vehicles a day to and from central New Jersey.

Leigh followed signs for I-495 West. Reaching Ninth Avenue she stopped, the scene ahead surreal.

Having been dammed at its mid-Manhattan toll booth, the Lincoln Tunnel had spawned a logjam of cars and buses that clogged the city streets as far as the eye could see. Many passengers had abandoned their vehicles to scream obscenities at armed Port Authority workers and police officers. Others congregated in small groups, discussing options for a revolution.

"What the hell are we supposed to do in Madison Square Garden?"

"Do you remember what happened to those people trapped in the New Orleans Superdome during Hurricane Katrina?"

"All I know is that I need to eat and use the bathroom. Lock the car and grab a kid. We're walking."

It took Leigh Nelson twenty minutes to negotiate the mile-and-a-half walk to the impound lot. The police station was chaotic, patrolmen and SWAT team members moving in and out, many wearing gas masks.

She pushed her way to the front desk. "My name is Dr. Nelson. It's very important I search one of the vehicles towed to this location early this morning."

"Sorry, Doctor. We're not releasing any vehicles until the city reopens."

"I don't want the vehicle, I just need to search it. There's medicine inside the trunk. My patient's dying."

She argued another ten minutes before relinquishing her credit card to pay the city impound fee.

The white Honda Civic with the Virginia license plate looked innocuous enough. Still, the sight of it sent chills down Leigh's spine. She watched as the police officer applied a tire iron to the trunk, popping open the lock and setting off the alarm.

Donning rubber gloves, she removed the spare tire, exposing a polished wood container the size of a cigar box. Unlatching its two hinges, Leigh opened the lid, revealing a dozen small vials of clear liquid, secured in styrofoam pockets. A typed note lay folded on top.

SCYTHE MK-36 Vaccine/Antidote.

INSTRUCTIONS: Take orally. One dose per patient.

WARNING: This antibiotic contains a powerful neuro-transmitter that crosses the brain-blood barrier. May cause hallucinogenic effects. Anger and reactive behavior exacerbate symptoms. Keep patient calm. Do not leave unsupervised for the first six to twelve hours.

Leigh removed her cell phone and pressed a preset number. "Dr. Clark, its Dr. Nelson. I have it!"

"You're certain it's the right vaccine?"

"I won't know for sure until we test it on a patient, but the woman was practically begging me for it."

"How soon until you can get back to the VA?"

"Give me an hour."

"Okay, I'll alert the CDC. Well done, Dr. Nelson. You may have just saved us from a pandemic."

Her heart pounding with adrenaline, Leigh removed her backpack and opened it, carefully positioning the case between her surgical gown and wool scarf. Adjusting the carbon-filter mask over her face, she headed for the impound lot's exit at a brisk jog.

CENTRAL PARK, MANHATTAN

3:42 P.M.

Situated at the very center of Manhattan, it was the most frequented city park in the United States. Two-point-six miles long and half a mile wide. A perfect rectangle of nature, yet completely man-made. Comprised of 136 acres of forest, 250 acres of lawns, and 150 acres of waterways, the largest being the 106-acre, billion-gallon Jacqueline Kennedy Onassis Reservoir. There were 58 miles of pedestrian paths, 4.5 miles of bridle paths, 6.5 miles of park drives, and 7 miles of benches. Twenty-one playgrounds. Thirty-six bridges and archways. The highest structure was a seventy-one-foot, 244-ton granite obelisk made in Egypt in 1500 B.C., the oldest was Central Park's most important natural feature—its underlying geology—a glaciated metamorphic schist bedrock that dated back 450 million years.

Thirty-six-year-old Marti Evans and her life partner, Tina Wilkins, followed the flow of humans moving south along West Drive. The winding pedestrian walkway took them past a boulder grotto, known as the Pool, where the women had first met. The grassy banks from that spring day eleven years ago were now blanketed in snow, the willows, laid bare by winter, bent over the lake's partially frozen surface.

Marti pushed the stroller holding their five-year-old daughter, Gabi. The lesbian couple resided in Des Moines, Iowa, but had decided to spend the Christmas holiday in New York. They had visited Radio City Music Hall earlier in the day and promised to show Gabi the giant Christmas tree in Rockefeller Center after dinner.

Now they just wanted to leave Manhattan alive.

The two women followed thousands of other frightened civilians, everyone moving to one rallying point advertised on a hastily printed flyer. They passed the reservoir on their left, the waterway so vast it covered ten city blocks. American Elms closed in on either side of the winding footpath, the bare branches creating an arching briar-patch effect overhead. Spindly fingers cast against the gray afternoon sky like a vision out of Sleepy Hollow.

Fifteen minutes later they arrived at the Great Lawn. Ahead, Belvedere Castle rose out of Vista Rock. The stone structure loomed above Delacorte Theater, where ten thousand people have gathered, with more on the way, their presence on the fifty-five-acre lawn turning the blanket of snow into slush.

A large vinyl banner on wires stretched high above the stage:

CITY OF N.Y. PRESENTS DISNEY ON ICE
DECEMBER 28—JANUARY 7

Volunteers had set up a microphone and PA system on the amphitheater stage. All eyes followed a Caucasian man in his sixties, sporting dark, slicked-back hair and a south Florida tan. He strode purposely across the stage and took the microphone.

"My name is Lawrence Hershman. I served as deputy assistant to the undersecretary of defense for policy during the second Bush administration. I'm here to tell you that all of us are being lied to, and unless we act soon, we're all probably going to die."

The restless crowd hushed one another to hear.

"What I'm about to tell you is confidential. For years now, the United States and other Western governments have been preparing to unleash a new pandemic that would be even more devastating than the Spanish Flu epidemic that wiped out 30 million people back in 1918. The pharmaceutical industry is in it up to their elbows, having been secretly awarded huge government contracts to mass-produce vaccines for genetically engineered hybrid viruses. These viruses, developed by lunatics over at the Defense Department, were designed to wipe out the populations of targeted hostile nations. One of these biological weapons was unleashed this morning at the UN. Somehow, the crazy bastards screwed up the vaccine and lost containment. The military's keeping everyone away, but the bodies of the dead are piling up faster than they know what to do with. In a city like Manhattan, the virus will spread like a wildfire."

Tina gripped Marti's hand, the two women shaken.

"There's only one chance to survive, and you need to act now, before they start shooting people in the streets: Cover your mouth, nose, and skin as best as you can, then find a way off the island. Take to the subway tunnels, swim if you have to . . . just get out of Manhattan before you end up in a body bag."

"Five to one, baby
One in five
No one here gets out alive, now
You get yours, baby
I'll get mine
Gonna make it, baby
If we try . . ."

—THE DOORS, "FIVE TO ONE"

DECEMBER 20

USAMRIID

FORT DETRICK-FREDERICK, MARYLAND

3:47 P.M.

(15 HOURS, 28 MINUTES BEFORE THE PROPHESIED END OF DAYS)

Colonel John Zwawa jumped as the cell phone reverberated in his back pocket. "Go ahead, Jay."

"We may have caught our first break. CDC just took a call from one of the local hospitals claiming they have a plague patient who says she has access to Scythe's vaccine. Her description fits the Klipot woman."

The colonel's heart raced. "Where's the vaccine now?"

"In the trunk of her rental car, being held at a police impound."

"What's the address?"

"It's moot, the administrator sent his assistant to retrieve it. She's on her way back as we speak."

"How far is the hospital from you?"

"It's East Side, but in this traffic it'll take me an hour, and I can't spare the detail. We're scheduled to bug out at 1900 hours."

"Okay, okay . . . we'll send in a retrieval team. Which hospital?"

"The VA on East 23rd Street."

UPPER EAST SIDE

3:45 P.M.

For the last two hours, the irate female driving the Black Chevy Suburban had been using her siren and police emergency light to force her way through and around bumper-to-bumper traffic. Inching her way south on Park Avenue, she approached a neoclassical four-story limestone building located on the northwest corner of East 68th Street.

Turning to the man slumped in the passenger seat, Sheridan Ernstmeyer violently roused Ernest Lozano from his catnap.

"What?"

"We're passing the CFR. Maybe we should hole up inside?"

"Maybe." Lozano leaned over the seat and gently nudged Bertrand DeBorn on the knee. "Sorry to wake you, sir. We're passing the Council's headquarters. Should we stop?"

"What the hell good would that do? You think the Council on Foreign Relations is immune to the Black Death?"

Sheridan smiled to herself.

"No, sir. I just thought—"

"If you had *thought,* you would have gotten to the Klipot woman instead of her flaky fiancé!" The reverberation in his pocket cuts him off. The secretary of defense rubbed sleep from his eyes and answered his cell phone. "Speak."

"Good news. Turns out there is a vaccine."

DeBorn's heart jump-started. "Who has it?"

"It's being delivered as we speak to the VA hospital. Inoculate yourself, then we'll airlift you out. Claim you were part of a DARPA medical team collecting blood samples for a new antibiotic. You'll play the hero . . . the press will eat it up."

"Well done. I'll phone as soon as I arrive."

"Just be careful out there. I'm watching the news. The natives are growing restless."

VA MEDICAL CENTER
EAST SIDE, MANHATTAN
3:49 P.M.

In the quiet emptiness of an antiseptic room that held neither memories nor a future, Patrick Shepherd stared at the painting of a beach house hanging from a yellowed wall and contemplated what his life should have been. *What was it the shrink said? Everything has a cause and effect. Fix the cause and you'll fix the effect. I went to war, and Beatrice left me. I'm back from war, and my family is in New York. After all these years, why now? Maybe she wants a divorce? Maybe it has nothing to do with me? How am I supposed to know?*

Reaching for the painting with his prosthetic arm, he attempted to grab its wooden frame with his pincers. Failed. Tried again and failed.

Seething with rage, he swept the steel arm sideways, knocking the painting from the wall. *Stop being a victim. Find Bea. Find out why she's here. One way or another, it's time to move on.*

BATTERY PARK CITY, MANHATTAN
3:51 P.M.

Beatrice Shepherd searched the last of the cardboard moving containers. Old manuscripts, bound in rubber bands. Sentimental, but her new apartment lacked the closet space. She tossed them into a trash box reserved for paper recyclables.

At the bottom of the container was a plastic file box. She hauled it out. Peeled away the sticky yellowed tape and opened it. Removed a stack of unopened letters. Found the picture frame. Wiping dust from the glass, she regarded the photograph of the bare-chested, strapping twenty-five-year-old in his Army desert fatigues.

Her eyes welled up in tears. For a long moment she stared at the photo, then set it on the bookshelf by the flat-screen television and wondered how she would explain her decision to her daughter.

Her eyes caught the muted news report on the TV. Locating the remote, she turned up the sound. Heard the words *pandemic* and *mandatory curfew* and grabbed her phone, speed dialing her daughter's cell-phone number. After four rings, it switched to voice mail. "It's mother. Call me as soon as you can."

The phone rang the moment she replaced the receiver. "Where are you?"

"Mrs. Shepherd?"

The older man's voice startled her. "Yes? Who is this?"

"Ma'am, you don't know me. I'm calling about your husband, Patrick. He's in New York, and he needs to see you."

HAMILTON HEIGHTS, NEW YORK
4:02 P.M.

The Tibetan monk sat in a lotus position on the polished bamboo floor before the open laptop. Microthin wires ran from the back of the computer and out the open door onto the seventh-floor balcony facing the Hudson River, connecting to a small satellite dish mounted on the brick facing.

The Elder meditated.

A Coast Guard cutter rolled south along the waterway and the monk could feel its twin engines gurgling thunder, the disturbance reverberating in his bones.

At precisely 4:08, Gelut Panim opened his eyes. He reached for the Japanese Kabuki mask by his right knee and slipped it in place over his face as the satellite uplink connected, the screen instantly splitting into three rows of three. Eight different ornamental masks stared back at him, including his own in the upper left-hand corner. Slot number seven remained blank.

The Society of the Nine Unknown Men convened what more than a few members feared would be their final transmission.

The Elder confirmed his brethren's biorhythms before he spoke. "My friends, the world is changing before our eyes. The first domino has been toppled."

"Scythe was never intended to be the first domino. The Klipot woman was a wild card."

"Yes, Number Four. But was she a wild card, or was it divine intervention? Either way, it altered the Illuminati's plan."

"I'd wait a few days before calling it divine intervention. By then, every person on this planet not wearing a loincloth may very well be dead."

"Perhaps, Number Two. But I sense something important is happening. That the Creator chose to intervene before the evil ones could ignite World War III is . . . encouraging."

"DeBorn and his enlightened brethren won't go quietly into the night," uttered Number Five, the accent distinctly French-Canadian. "They'll spin this as easily as Cheney convinced the American public that Saddam had to be brought down for 9/11. Next thing you know, the Klipot woman becomes a Muslim fanatic and a US-led coalition will be invading Iran. Russia and China will mobilize, and DeBorn will have his war."

"Number Four, where is DeBorn now?" Number Eight asked.

"My contacts confirm he is still in Manhattan."

The Elder nodded. "He must be dealt with before the end of this day."

"What about Number Seven?"

"He and his family are trapped in New York. Cell-phone transmissions are being blocked, but I can sense his presence."

"You will continue to use him as bait?" Number Three asked.

"If this is truly the End of Days, as we believe it to be, then the Creator has selected a righteous man to offer humanity a last chance at salvation. For reasons that remain unclear, Number Seven's family has been chosen to serve the cleansing process as a conduit, linking this righteous person with the supernal world. By monitoring Number Seven's biorhythms, I can determine if and when contact is established and offer my services to the righteous one, should he or she require it."

"What about Scythe?"

"My immune system can handle it."

"Seven isn't immune. He and his family could be dying as we speak."

"In fact, Number Six, I fully expect Seven and his family to be stricken before this night is over. And yes, there is a good chance they may perish, along with the rest of us."

Verbal responses were at odds with the eight unyielding expressions.

The Elder waited for silence. "Many people are going to die before the winter solstice dawn. What remains to be seen is whether our species survives the cleansing. Scythe is not the executioner, my friends, it is the test."

"What else can we do?"

The Kabuki mask remained placid. "Pray."

VA MEDICAL CENTER
EAST SIDE, MANHATTAN
4:18 P.M.

Leigh Nelson jogged down East 23rd Street, the VA campus in sight. She slowed as she reached First Avenue, shocked by the changes that had occurred over the last ninety minutes.

The ambulance parking lot had been converted into a triage zone. Hundreds of people formed a line that snaked from First Avenue all the way up to East 25th Street. Faces were concealed behind carbon-filter masks and scarves. Mothers rocked screaming infants in blankets. Husbands and wives. Friends and families and single workers. The silent killer's work made easy.

Medical personnel, dressed in gowns, masks, gloves, and yellow plastic ponchos performed quick examinations before segregating patients into tented waiting areas by the main entrance (suspected plague) and the staff parking lot (confirmed plague).

She spotted Dr. Clark as he hustled out of the emergency-room entrance, followed by two interns carrying blankets. "Children under twelve only. Make sure the cops know."

"Dr. Clark!"

He saw her. Signaled her to wait. Grabbing a clean poncho from a stack, he met her halfway across First Avenue and slipped the waterproof sheeting over her head.

"Sir, all these people—"

"If they weren't infected when they arrived, they're infected now. We're just stalling for time, shuffling them from one waiting area to another.

Where's the vaccine?"

"In my backpack."

"We moved the redheaded woman to the fourth floor to prevent her from seeing her newborn. Administer the vaccine and report back to me with the results."

They looked up as a Black Chevy Suburban, its siren wailing, pulled onto the sidewalk on 23rd Street.

"Secretary DeBorn? What's he doing back here?"

"I'll deal with him. You get that vaccine started."

"Yes, sir."

Patrick Shepherd entered the hospital library, surprised to find the media center deserted. He moved past shelves of donated books. Located the row of computer stations and situated himself at one of the terminals.

He typed in Dr. Nelson's e-mail address and password, accessed the Internet, and sorted through her old e-mail. He stopped at the subject line: LOST PERSON INQUIRY and clicked open the e-mail.

Dr. Nelson:

Thank you for your inquiry regarding the whereabouts of BEATRICE SHEPHERD, age 30–38, ONE CHILD (female) age 14–16. TOP 5 Search States Requested: NY. NJ. CT. MA. PA. The following positive matches were found:

Manhattan, New York: Ms. Beatrice Shepherd

Vineland, New Jersey: Mrs. Beatrice Shepherd

See also: Mrs. B. Shepherd (NY - 4)

Mrs. B. Shepherd (NJ - 1)

Mrs. B. Shepherd (MA - 6)

Mrs. B. Shepherd (PA - 14)

To provide you with the highest-quality results, we suggest our LEVEL 2 Detective Service. Fee: $149.95

He fumbled with the mouse. Clicked on the address link and printed the page. Hurried to another booth, this one containing an i-pay phone. He sat at the built-in desk and swiped the machine with a prepaid phone card:

CREDIT REMAINING: 17 MINUTES

He began to dial the Battery Park phone number, then crumpled beneath a wave of anxiety so unnerving it stole his breath. "What am I doing? What do I say? Hey, baby, it's Shep. So, I'm back. Wanna get together? Ugh!"

He slammed the phone back on its receiver in disgust.

Think it through, asshole. Remember what the shrink said . . . cause and effect. Try beginning with an apology. "Hey, uh, it's Shep. I'm sorry for leaving you and the baby and enlisting . . . ugh! This is all wrong, I need to write it out. Better yet—"

He left the booth and hustled to the information desk, searching through drawers until he found what he was looking for—a palm-size recording device used by amputees for dictating letters. Returning to the booth, he cleared his mind, then pressed RECORD.

"Bea . . . it's Shep. Remember me?" He stopped, erased, then started again. "Bea, it's Patrick. I'm back, honey. I'm in New York, at the VA hospital. Maybe it's fate we're both in Manhattan. Babe, I was wounded. I can't be whole again without you. You're my soul mate, Bea, I need to see you and our little girl . . . only I guess she's not so little anymore." He swallowed hard, the words catching in his throat. "I made a bad mistake. I was angry. I didn't think things through. Babe, I'm so lost without you. If there's any way you could find it in your heart to forgive me—"

He paused as the library door opened . . .

Mary Klipot lay on her back in the self-contained isolator, her wrists and ankles shackled to the bed rails. A plastic hood enveloped the bed, preventing the escape of contaminated air. The hood also sealed in the combined stench of her breath, her sweat, and the vomit staining her hospital gown. Despite the morphine drip, the pain and nausea she felt remained overpowering, pushing her delirium toward the brink of madness. She had become a mindless wretch, her thoughts consumed by the fever. Every breath was panted. Her eyes were rolled back in her head, her open mouth locked in a gnarled grimace. Her lips, white and curled back, exposed bloodstained yellow teeth.

The cool liquid washed through her bloodstream like a cleansing tide, soothing the rhythm of her breathing. Within minutes, it had drawn away the fever, bathing her irritated internal organs with blessed relief.

Mary's eyes rolled back into place, and she looked up.

Leigh Nelson hovered outside the isolation bed, holding the empty vial. "The vaccine—is it working?"

Mary attempted to speak, but her throat was still too parched, her coughs lubricated in bloody spittle.

Leigh adjusted Mary's mattress so she was sitting up at a forty-degree angle. Using one of the isolation tent's plastic sleeves, she passed through a bottle of water, positioning the straw in her patient's mouth.

Mary drank. "Bless you, sister."

"Who are you? What is Scythe?"

"Release my restraints, and I will tell you everything."

Positioning her free hand in an open sleeve, Leigh reached inside the tent and unbuckled the leather strap pinning Mary's right arm to the bed rail.

Mary flexed her arm, then freed her other wrist.

"Now tell me, what is Scythe?"

"A biological weapon . . . a genetically harvested pandemic. Part of a black ops biological program. The disease feeds on negative emotions, especially anger."

"Anger? How?"

"As the infected individual becomes more reactive, adrenaline and noradrenaline are released, affecting the heart rate, blood pressure, and the pancreas. The greater the anger, the faster the disease spreads throughout the body. The vaccine . . . did you bring both boxes?"

"No. I only found the one."

"Take me to the car, I'll show you where the second is hidden."

"First tell me who released Scythe in Manhattan?"

"God. He sent me as his vessel."

"God told you to unleash a man-made plague?"

"After He impregnated me with His child. Where is he? Bring me my baby!"

She's insane. Clark told you to keep her restrained. You need to put her under again and—

"The End of Days is upon us. Scythe is the deliverer, it will save us from the heretics. I have delivered the Messiah. Where is my son? Bring me the Christ Child!"

"Your child is being cared for in a specially designed incubator. Oh, by the way, the Christ Child . . . it's a girl."

"What? No . . . that can't be. You're lying!"

"I'm lying? Listen to me, you pathological murdering bitch. Your plague has killed thousands of innocent people, maybe tens of thousands, maybe millions before we can harvest your antidote."

"Wait . . . today's not the twenty-fifth."

"Are you even hearing me?"

Mary's expression darkened her voice crackled. "The child was supposed to be born on the twenty-fifth. You took him out too early!"

Leigh backed away, moving toward the nurses' station phone on the wall—

—when the room was suddenly overtaken by a deep *thrumming* sound, the disturbance growing louder until it reverberated the windowpane. Mary heard it, too, her eyes growing wide and intense, her pulse rate leaping on the heart monitor. "Satan. He has sent his minions to kill me. How did they find me so quickly?"

Leigh walked to the window, raised the shade. "Now what?"

Three black helicopters hovered overhead, releasing dozens of Special Ops commandoes, who rappelled several hundred feet to the street below. They were all heavily armed, dressed from their hooded heads to their boots in black uniforms, their faces masked behind air rebreathers.

What Mary Klipot saw was something entirely different—the Scythe vaccine had moved from her bloodstream into her brain, affecting her central nervous system while disrupting the release of serotonin, a neurotransmitter that modulated mood swings and sensory perception. The sight of the Special Ops commandoes had unleashed terrifying thoughts—flashbacks from Mary's earliest grand mal seizures. The images distorted her senses and sent her tattered mind on a hallucinogenic trip that filtered present-day events into nightmarish visions of Hell.

Black-winged demons flap past the fourth-floor window. Crimson eyes stare through her. Voices whisper sulfurous thoughts into her brain: "There is no escape, Mary Louise. Our claws shall tear the flesh from your bones. Your existence shall be blotted from the book of the living, your soul cast into the rivers of Hell, basking in Satan's light for all eternity."

"*Santisima Muerte,* Most Holy Death, I ask you with all my heart, chase these demons away!" Mary turns to her left—

—the female Grim Reaper materializing before her eyes. Purple satin robe. Candy-apple red wig.

"Santa Muerte!"

The Goddess of Death animates, her scythe cutting the air with a short chop, her skull protruding from its hood as its jaws bellow a silent command at the demons circling outside the window.

Hell's minions disappear.

Leigh's attention was drawn below to the commandoes, who were ordering everyone to the ground. A mother holding her sick child was too slow to react and was struck in the head by the butt end of a 5.56mm assault rifle. The attack sent Dr. Clark rushing across the ambulance parking lot. The commandoes in black opened fire.

Leigh screamed as she saw Dr. Clark's bullet-pummeled body dance, then spiral backward into a heap—

—the room abruptly spinning into blackness.

Mary Klipot straddled the unconscious physician. She dropped the aluminum bedpan, the sudden exertion causing her to stagger. "*Santa Muerte* . . . is it true? Is the child female?"

The hooded figure nods.

"The child . . . whose is it? Is it . . . God's?"

The female Grim Reaper's bony left hand motions to its cloth-covered loins.

"Oh, no . . . no!" Mary stumbled over the doctor and took her white lab coat. Then, wrenching open the window, she climbed out onto the fire escape, fleeing the scene.

Shep hid beneath the i-phone station's built-in desk, his paranoia on overdrive, his left eye tracking Bertrand DeBorn through a slit in the corner of the booth. The secretary of defense crossed the library. He entered the i-phone station next to Shep's and dialed a number.

"It's me. I'm back at the hospital . . . Yes, I made an appearance, now I need an extraction. Make it for three, my security team's coming, too."

Shep held up the recording device and taped Bertrand DeBorn's conversation.

"I don't give a damn what strings you have to pull. Scythe's already reached stage-six saturation levels, I'm in danger of being infected . . . No, I can't get to Kogelo, the roads are jammed, we were lucky to make it back to the hospital . . . No, you listen! I'm sitting in the middle of plague central, now you either find a way to extract me within the hour, or I'll leak everything I know about Amerithrax and Battelle on the six o'clock news . . . You're damn right I'll name names, beginning with your two FBI pals shredding files in West Jefferson."

The muscular contraction in Shep's left shoulder became a tremor. Try as he might, he could not maintain his balance on the slippery prosthetic elbow. Shifting his weight, he fell back, banging his head against one of the legs of the desk.

"Who's there?" DeBorn disconnected the call and peered over the shoulder-high cubby.

Patrick stood, revealing himself. "Amerithrax?" He stared at DeBorn, his mind piecing together the plot. "You crazy bastard. You're trying to initiate another war."

DeBorn backed out of his booth, reaching for his cell phone. "Every war serves a purpose, Sergeant. In this case, it preserves the American way of life while reducing the threat of communism. We're on the cusp of instituting real change in the world . . . you could have been a part of that. Instead, you've just become collateral damage."

DeBorn pressed an intercom button on his cell phone. "I need you."

Sheridan Ernstmeyer entered the library from the outer corridor.

"Agent Ernstmeyer, I just caught Sergeant Shepherd on the phone making a bomb threat to the United Nations. Under section 411, subsection B of the Patriot Act, I order you to arrest Sergeant Shepherd using extreme prejudice."

The former CIA assassin grinned. Removing the Glock .22 from her shoulder holster, she methodically screwed an AAC 40 Evolution suppressor to the end of her gun barrel.

Shep dived over the back of the i-phone booth, his steel arm shattering the glass partition as he scrambled on his hand and knees to reach the nearest row of bookcases.

Her silencer in place, Sheridan methodically moved through the stacks, stalking her quarry, her pulse barely over seventy.

Patrick Shepherd ran down one of the twelve parallel rows of eight-foot-high bookcases until he reached the back wall. Hiding behind the end of one stack, he ducked low and peered around the corner.

The female assassin had removed her shoes and was quietly moving from right to left along the opposite end of the bookcases, visually checking each row before moving on.

DeBorn's voice bellowed from the librarian's desk. "Come on out, Sergeant. We're not going to shoot you. You're a veteran . . . a hero. I'm sure whatever threat you made can be chalked up to post-traumatic stress."

The woman was three rows away. Two rows. The gun in her left hand aimed down each row before she showed herself.

She's a lefty.

The shard of memory replayed in his consciousness like an inescapable jingle.

Clear the negativity. Visualize success. Retake the mound only when you've regained control of your emotions.

Shep's breathing slowed, his mind clearing.

It's not about power, Shep, it's about cunning. With lefties, you have to use your change-up to keep them off-balance.

The female assassin was one row away.

Use your change-up. Set her up.

Shep removed his left shoe and positioned it on its side so the sole protruded slightly along the bottom edge of the bookcase to his left. Then he crawled to the end stack on his right. Peering between books, he waited for the woman to appear.

Sheridan Ernstmeyer peeked around the far end cap, looking down another empty aisle. She knew her target was pinned down, hiding behind one of the end caps. She searched the next row. *There!* Seeing the sliver of shoe, she slid along the tile floor in her stocking feet, moving silently down the aisle, her gun sight trained on the exposed left sole—

—unaware that Shep was quietly crawling up the previous aisle. Reaching the midway point, he pressed his right shoulder against one of the long case's vertical supports, driving his powerful legs.

The twenty-foot-long, eight-foot-high bookcase wobbled, threatening to topple over.

Books rained down on Sheridan Ernstmeyer's head. She instinctively leapt, sliding to the end of the row, where her eyes caught sight of the empty shoe. She looked up—

—as Shep's steel appendage slammed against the back of her skull. "Change-up. Strike three." He grabbed the woman's gun, retrieved his left shoe, then hurried up the next aisle to confront Bertrand DeBorn. He aimed the Glock at the secretary of defense's forehead.

The gray-blue upturned eyes showed no fear. "Think it through, Sergeant. Kill me, and you'll never find your family. That's right, I know where they are. Think you can reach them before my people? Maybe you can. Or maybe I've already sequestered them away."

"I taped you . . . your entire conversation. I'm going to play it on the six o'clock news."

DeBorn's expression changed. "You have nothing."

"I guess we'll see."

"A trade then—the tape for your family. Colonel Argenti spoke with your wife earlier today. After all these years, she still wants to see you. Don't blow it by doing something stupid."

Shep's right arm trembled. "He spoke with Bea?"

DeBorn's voice softened. "Put the gun down, Sergeant, and I'll take you to her."

His thoughts were fragmented, his mind unable to focus, unable to reason. He lowered the weapon—

—as the sound of gunfire exploded outside the library, shattering the outer glass doors.

Confused, Patrick pushed past DeBorn and ran, heading for the small alcove on the other side of the lobby. Hurrying past the librarian's office, he kicked open the fire door at the end of the corridor—

—finding himself in a concrete stairwell.

Leigh Nelson opened her eyes, dazed and a bit queasy. She sat up, the lump on the back of her head throbbing from where Mary Klipot had struck her with the bedpan. She looked around.

The redhead was gone.

She staggered to the swivel exam chair and her overcoat. Hidden beneath her jacket was the polished wood case containing the vials of vaccine, exactly where she had left it.

Leigh heard the gunfire and panicked. *They killed Clark, they'll kill me, too! Gotta get this vaccine to the CDC in New Jersey . . . but how?*

The thunder of the Special Ops helicopters diminished in the distance. *The medevac chopper. Find the pilot . . . where would he be? Maybe upstairs in the lounge.*

She cracked open the door to the isolation ward and looked down the corridor toward the nurses' station. Three female nurses were lying on the floor, their wrists bound in plastic cuffs, as two commandoes pinned a male nurse—John Voyda—against a wall.

"Where's the vaccine?"

The former collegiate football player glanced down the hall at Leigh and looked away quickly. "What vaccine? Nothing we tried works."

A commando lifted one of the nurses off her feet and pressed the barrel of his assault rifle beneath her neck. "Tell us where Dr. Nelson is, or this nurse dies."

"She left about an hour ago. I swear I haven't seen her since."

The other commando shook his head. "He's lying. Take her out and shoot her, see if that jars his memory."

Leigh darted from the room, sprinting for the stairwell.

"There she is! Freeze!"

She ducked low, yanked open the steel fire door, and raced up the steps to access the roof.

The two commandoes entered the stairwell, radioing ahead. "We've got her. Northern stairwell, heading for the roof."

A bullet whizzed past her ear, then something bit her in the left calf muscle, and she went down.

The two black-clad militiamen stood over her.

"Please don't kill me! I have two young children."

"Get the case."

One of the commandoes knelt to take the wooden kit from Leigh—

—the other screamed as a white-hot chunk of lead tore through the back of his left leg and exploded out his kneecap. " Sonuvabitch —"

Patrick aimed the Glock at the second commando. "Drop the gun and move away from the doc. Now!"

"You're making a big mistake, friend. You and me . . . we're on the same side."

"Shut up." Shep kneed the man in his groin. As the commando doubled up in agony, he smashed him in the back of the head with the butt end of the gun.

Leigh leapt to her feet and hugged Shep around the neck. "Come on, baby doll, we need to get to the roof." She grabbed the wooden case and limped up the stairwell.

Shep grabbed her arm, steadying her. "Doc, what's happening? Who are these guys?"

"One of my patients, a redheaded woman we had in isolation, she released a man-made plague at the UN. Manhattan's under quarantine. These assholes killed Dr. Clark. They're after the vaccine."

"So give it to them."

"DeBorn's people created this monster. You think I trust them with the only vaccine? We have to get this container to the CDC in New Jersey before this thing becomes a pandemic."

"Jersey? How?"

"The medevac chopper. Shep, you're a pilot, you can fly it!"

"No I can't."

"Yes you can!"

"No, I can't. Leigh, my family's in Battery Park, I need to find them before DeBorn kills them."

She reached the roof, too winded to ask about DeBorn. "We'll find your family. First fly me to Jersey."

"I can't—"

"Shep, listen to me. We need to harvest this vaccine. If we don't, Bea, your daughter, and two million New Yorkers will be dead by tomorrow morning. Now come on."

Leigh unbolted the roof fire door and pushed it open, greeted by a burst of frigid air. The wind swirled around them, the daylight fading fast. Bullets ricocheted inside the stairwell as a dozen more commandoes joined the hunt.

She slammed the door closed behind them. "Give me the gun. Take the vaccine and start the chopper. I'll hold them off."

He hesitated.

"Go!"

Patrick ran for the helopad and the Sikorsky S-76 Medevac helicopter. Climbing into the pilot's seat, he tucked the wooden box between the copilot's chair and the center console, then powered up the two five-hundred-kilowatt turboshafts.

Slowly, the four-blade main rotor came to life, gradually picking up speed.

Leigh cracked open the roof door, blindly squeezing off several rounds with the Glock in an attempt to slow the commandoes' stairwell assault. Slamming the door shut, she looked around—

—spotting the fire hose mounted along the outside of the brick wall.

Dropping the gun, she grabbed the hose's nozzle, dragged a twenty-foot length of the eight-hundred-pound test off its wheel, feeding it through the roof door's steel handle.

Shep's right hand gripped the cyclic control stick—a throttle used to steer the aircraft once the chopper was airborne. His feet were situated on the two rudder pedals on the floor, enabling him to control direction using the tail rotor.

Sweat beads poured down his face as he struggled to direct his prosthetic arm's pincers to open, allowing him to grip a horizontal control stick located on the floor alongside his left hip. The collective pitch controlled the angle of the main rotor's blades, enabling the chopper to ascend and descend. If he could not manipulate the stick, he could not take off. Worse, if he failed to coordinate the movements of his still-alien appendage with his other three working limbs once they were airborne, his actions could cause the chopper's blades to spin down more than fifteen percent from their normal velocity, transforming the airship into a seven-thousand-pound rock.

Come on . . . open!

The rotors had reached their required rpm for liftoff. He signaled to Leigh with his right hand, still unable to open the pincers.

Pulling up the slack on the fire hose, Leigh looped the nozzle back through its wheel, tying it off in a knot. She ran toward the waiting chopper as the commandoes reached the top of the stairwell. They attempted to open the roof door, but the hose held.

Leigh Nelson was twenty feet from the helicopter when the door was blasted open and she was struck from behind by a burst of gunfire. She went down. Bullets ricocheted off gravel. A few struck the helicopter. Unable to move and in agony, the thirty-seven-year-old physician and mother of two looked up at Shep, her cry of "go" lost beneath the roar of the spinning rotors.

The wave of adrenaline coursed through Patrick Shepherd like an electric shock. Commanding the prosthetic pincers to open, he gripped the collective pitch and lifted it away from the floorboard, launching the airship off the roof in a sudden, dizzying forward lurch.

The commandoes aimed their assault rifles—

—the medevac chopper barely clearing the roof before it plunged out of sight.

Special Ops Commander Bryant Pfeiffer signaled his team to cease fire. Crossing the asphalt helopad, he jogged to the west end of the roof and looked down. "Damn."

Three stories from the street, the helicopter's rotors had caught air. For a moment it remained suspended above the fleeing crowd, then it slowly headed west, following East 25th Street, remaining well below the Manhattan skyline.

Pfeiffer switched channels on his two-way radio. "Delta One—Delta Six. Suspect has escaped with the Scythe vaccine in a medevac chopper. Target is heading west above East 25th Street, approaching Park Avenue. Intercept at once—repeat, intercept at once."

The commander looked down at the disheveled figure of Leigh Nelson. The petite brunette was moaning, her battered body surrounded by a half dozen spent rubber bullets. "Gag her and bag her. I want her on the next transport to Governor's Island."

Swirling blades, threatened by lampposts and buildings. Metallic thunder echoed in his ears. Shep slowed his airspeed, matching the vehicular traffic moving thirty feet below his landing gear. He was afraid to risk a higher altitude, his pincers barely maintaining their grip on the collective pitch, and so he flew through a maze of skyscrapers, maneuvering west, then north, then west again. The blistering wind scattered pedestrians, the noise as deafening as a howitzer. He had passed midtown Manhattan above 40th Street when his pincers slipped. The chopper dropped precariously, the upper branches of elm trees in Bryant Park threatening his tail rotor.

Releasing the throttle, Shep lunged across his body with his right hand. Pushing the pincers down, he squeezed them into a locked position around the collective pitch and quickly raised the now-secure stick with his prosthetic arm.

The helicopter soared upward like an elevator past buildings and architectural spires. His right hand back on the throttle, Shep headed west, soaring high over Central Park, the Hudson River in sight, New Jersey only minutes away.

Land in Jersey just long enough to drop off the vaccine. Pocket a few vials for your family, then hightail it back to Manhattan. Bea lives in Battery Park. All I have to do is land this bucket of bolts on a nearby rooftop and—

The black airships appeared out of nowhere. Apaches. Flanking him from above. Two M230 machine guns swiveled into position beneath the military gunships, the menacing barrels aimed squarely at his cockpit. A house cat cornered by rottweilers.

"Easy, fellas, I'm on your side." He held up the vaccine kit.

The pilot in the Apache on his starboard side signaled him to land.

Shep offered a thumbs-up, stalling for time as he descended at a shallow angle, his chopper still heading west toward the Hudson River. *Don't let 'em force you down in Manhattan. Get out over the water.* He saw the George Washington Bridge to the north and headed for the landmark.

The air ripped apart behind two hundred 30mm rounds spit from the starboard Apache's turret, the bursts crossing his path, forcing him into a steeper descent. Heart thumping with the rotors, Shep eased down on the collective pitch, the medevac rattling dangerously as he fought to maintain control in the rough air over the Hudson shoreline.

Land, and they'll kill you or capture you. Either way, you'll never see your family again. Desperate, descending fast, he scanned the geography below, his eyes focusing on the George Washington Bridge . . .

"Easy, don't push, I need to turn her." Sliding his gloved fingers deeper along either side of Naomi Gutierrez's fully dilated vaginal opening, David Kantor gently maneuvered the unborn infant's tiny shoulders. "Okay, one more good push."

A moist blotch of matted black hair squeezed through the widening womb, the crown preceding a tiny head and scrunched face guided gently by a latex-covered palm, then suddenly, miraculously, emotionally, the entire squirming purplish pink eight-pound, ten-ounce body squeezed free of the opening, dangling two legs and trailing a twisting length of umbilical cord.

"Congratulations, it's a boy!" David's mask fogged up as he cradled the infant. Using a moistened towelette, he cleared the newborn's airway with his little finger. A gurgling wail turned into a baby's healthy cry, the infant's purple face flushing pink with the infusion of air. Stephanie Collins wrapped the newborn in a blanket, the teary-eyed corporal passing the baby to its weeping mother.

"*Gracias . . . gracias.*"

"*Mazel tov.*" David had turned his attention to the umbilical cord and emerging placenta—

—when the sound of gunfire erupted like the Fourth of July.

"Damn it." Quickly tying off the chord, he severed it with the blade of his pocketknife, then peeled off the bloodied rubber gloves. "Corporal, stay with the mother–"

"Sir . . . your hands!"

"Oh, yeah, right." David slipped on the environmental suit's gloves and jumped down from the back of the truck. Leaving his assault weapon, he ran toward the gauntlet . . . stopping halfway across the expanse of interstate, panting in his rebreather as all hell broke loose.

Cold, hungry, angry, and desperate with fear, the pedestrian mob positioned directly behind the razor wire and concrete barriers were shooting at the Freedom Force. The Freedom Force were tossing gas grenades . . . and the National Guardsmen were caught in the cross fire. Some crawled to cover. Others joined their countrymen and fired upon the foreign militia, and suddenly it was war, blood spilling and bodies falling, and that was it, there was no turning back, as drivers gunned their engines and honked their horns, signaling the launch of an all-out assault. The front rows of vehicles rammed the concrete barriers, only to be met by the lethal barrage of heavy artillery.

Cars exploded, igniting like gasoline-powered bombs, torching passengers whose fate had been determined hours earlier by their place in line.

The second wave of vehicles plowed into the back of the first, pushing the burning debris forward, driving it beyond the two-ton barriers into the bumpers of the Hummers, and all of a sudden it was a demolition derby, the gauntlet's survival measured in seconds.

Through the chaos, David spotted Colonel Herstad. The militia commander was lying on the roadway, covered in blood—

—yelling orders into his walkie-talkie.

David's eyes went wide. "No . . . no!" He sprinted back to the military vehicle. Climbing inside the cab, he gunned the engine, tossing his stunned passengers about as he raced the truck west over the George Washington Bridge.

The two Apaches herded the slowly descending medevac helicopter toward a patchwork of tennis courts located south of the bridge between the river and the Henry Hudson Parkway.

Now!

Shep plunged into a sudden steep descent, looping away from the two gunships and out over the water. Whitecaps sprayed his windshield as he leveled out, the choppy surface less than ten feet below his landing gear. Wind whipped at his cockpit as he soared west over the waterway—

—the Apaches cutting him off, forcing him to loop north on an intercept course with the undercarriage of the George Washington Bridge!

Shep dropped his altitude until his landing gear skimmed the lead blue water, guiding the chopper beneath the suspension bridge's lower deck. An echo of rotors rattled his eardrums, then he was out the other side—

BOOM . . . BOOM . . . BOOM!

Sound disappeared behind a hollow ring, the December air heated as suddenly as if the sun had swapped places with the moon, igniting blinding orange bursts of incinerating fireballs that mushroomed into the heavens. Steel girders basted with thermite-laced paint exploded into white-hot flames exceeding five thousand degrees, melting metal girders and support cables as if they were butter in a microwave. Thick belches of black smoke partially concealed a section of westbound Interstate 95 as the liquefying upper level collapsed upon the still-erupting lower deck, the entire midsection of the George Washington Bridge and its sixteen lanes of highway toppling into the

Hudson River—

—the avalanche of sizzling steel taking the two Apache helicopters with it!

Debris slammed into the sides and tail section of the fleeing medevac chopper like hail from a flaming meteor. The pedals beneath Shep's feet went limp as the tail rotor snapped into kindling, and the main rotor fought to catch air as he soared north over the Hudson like a fluttering pelican. Fighting to maintain altitude, Shep yanked back hard on the collective pitch, sending his chopper leaping into the overcast sky in a dizzying tailspin, the river disappearing below, replaced by a hillside covered in trees.

The angle of his rotors violated the rules of aerodynamics. With a sickening lurch, the medevac helicopter plunged landing gear first through the forest canopy, the snapping branches tearing great gashes through the plummeting airship. Rotors sheared, cockpit glass shattered, the unforgiving earth greeting him with a final, bone-rattling wallop that collapsed the interior compartment around him.

Chaos deadened into settling metallic ticks, then silence.

A cold, harsh wind whistled through the violated cabin.

Patrick Shepherd opened his eyes. Through the haze he could make out dark pillars, each a massive tree trunk. The roots were knotted with age, partially buried beneath a blanket of dead leaves and a patchwork of snow.

A downed sign leaned against his crippled landing gear. He struggled to bring the words into focus.

WELCOME TO INWOOD HILL PARK

He turned his head, sensing another presence lurking in the shadows. The lanky figure's head and body were cloaked in a dark robe. Hollowed eyes stared. Waiting.

The vision disappeared, absorbed within the blackness of unconsciousness.

PART 3

UPPER HELL

"There are nine circles in Hell, each corresponding to the seriousness of the sins of the damned souls, in the lowest of which is Satan himself, frozen forever in ice."

—Dante's Inferno

FIRST CIRCLE

LIMBO

"About halfway through the course of my pathetic life, I woke up and found myself in a stupor in some dark place. I'm not sure how I ended up there; I guess I had taken a few wrong turns."

—Dante's Inferno

DECEMBER 20

INWOOD HILL PARK

MANHATTAN

7:37 P.M.

(12 HOURS, 16 MINUTES BEFORE THE PROPHESIED END OF DAYS)

Darkness. Absolute. Impenetrable, save for a howl of wind, its biting cold convincing him he might be blind but he was not dead. He struggled to move. Something was pinning him down by his shoulders and waist and left arm. The claustrophobic suddenness of the situation triggered a hot flush of panic even as a strand of memory forced him to reason.

The medevac chopper . . .

His eyes widened. He craned his neck to see past a ceiling of black yielding to a patch of cloud-infested lunar light. The panic subsided. Replaced by a dawning recognition: He was strapped in his pilot's seat. He was in a dense forest. It was night.

Wind whistled through the vented acrylic glass, biting his flesh, the frigid air seeping bone deep. Unseen oaks, their creaking branches made brittle from winter's embrace, clawed against the shattered cockpit.

Shep's right hand explored until it located and unbuckled his shoulder harness. He attempted to stand, only to discover that his prosthetic arm was pinned between the crushed forward console and floor. He could not see the predicament, nor could he pull himself free.

Panic crested again like a wave. He tugged at the accursed appendage, his efforts succeeding only in separating the plastic flesh from its metal skeleton. He continued the battle, each thrust husking the false skin from the steel rod, inch by excruciating inch.

He stopped, sensing the animal. He smelled the raw musk of fur. His hair bristled against his wool sweater as he heard paws negotiate the forest floor. Adjusting to the darkness, his eyes focused on the evolving pattern of movement through the broken cockpit glass.

The wolf stepped out of the woods into the dull lunar gray. It was a male, dark and emaciated. Saliva gurgled within its throat, its quivering upper lip drawn back, revealing yellowed fangs and wisps of breath.

The predator crept closer, evaluating its trapped prey.

Shep's heart pounded in his chest as his right hand searched the cabin for anything he could use as a weapon. "Go on, git! Get out of here!"

The wolf growled louder, a thin web of saliva dripping from its exposed teeth.

Adrenaline pumping, Shep braced his legs against the crushed forward console and forcibly yanked his prosthetic arm free, bolts popping loose from his pincers as he sheared the molded flesh from the steel appendage.

The wolf approached the cabin. It peered inside, its ears suddenly perking. It listened, then retracted its head and dashed off effortlessly, consumed by the night.

Shep laid his head back, panting. Then he too heard it—a deep baritone rumbling of thunder overhead. Only not thunder. Spotlights cut swaths from above, the helicopters' search beams barely able to penetrate the dense forest canopy.

Move!

He climbed out from behind the console, tripping and falling over a cabin crushed topsy-turvy, kicking away remnants of glass from the shattered windshield. Overhead, the thunder of rotor blades violated the trees, the two shifting searchlights illuminating the forest floor. Shep looked up. Spotted the soldiers rappelling from their perches and ran.

The vaccine!

Retracing his steps, he hurried back to the medevac and ducked inside, his right hand searching the copilot's seat until he located the polished wood box. Turning again to flee, he sliced his forehead on an unseen shard of glass, droplets of blood dripping into his eyes.

The invaders punched through the forest canopy, the heavily armed commandoes forced to slow as they negotiated a jagged entanglement of upper tree limbs.

Shep found himself surrounded by woods and darkness without a discernible path.

"Hello? Anybody alive?"

He turned in the direction of the unseen man, his voice somehow familiar. Seeing the handheld flashlight, he hurried toward it. "Over here! Can you help me?"

The heavyset man stepped into the clearing, his unzipped leather coat revealing the white letters of the hooded navy Columbia University sweatshirt. White hair and ponytail. A matching beard . . .

"Virgil?"

"Sergeant Shepherd? Were you the one piloting that helicopter?"

"Yes! I was transporting plague vaccine when I was forced down." He looked up as dark bodies dropped into beacons of light revealing assault weapons. "They're after me. Can you get me out of here?"

"Take my hand." Virgil led him through the forest along an unseen path into a periphery cloaked in darkness.

GEORGE WASHINGTON BRIDGE
FORT LEE, NEW JERSEY
7:51 P.M.

The staging area had tripled in size, two more battalions of National Guardsmen having arrived with their heavy artillery. In the distance, black smoke continued to rise from the smoldering remains of what had been the center portion of the George Washington Bridge, the five-hundred-foot gap preventing anyone trapped in Manhattan from using its roadways to escape into New Jersey.

David Kantor had barely made it over the bridge before the interstate had collapsed in a ball of flames in his rearview mirror. Exhausted, growing angrier by the minute, he paced the medical tent, waiting for his commanding officer to return.

Colonel Don Hamilton entered. Fifty-nine, yet still active in the National Guard, Hamilton had been shanghaied from his auto dealership in Newark and tossed into the domestic emergency with a short briefing and a skeleton staff. For the first few hours, his mind kept drifting back to his Christmas week sale of hybrids, until the unexpected detonation of the George Washington Bridge had doused him in its sobering reality.

Hamilton handed the medic his cell phone. "All calls into Manhattan and the surrounding boroughs are being jammed, but you should be able to reach your wife in New Jersey on this line. Remember, no details about the operation."

David dialed his home number, the colonel remaining within listening distance. "Leslie, it's me."

"David! Where are you? I've been trying to reach you all day. Have you seen what's happening?"

"I was called to duty by the Guard. I'm close by. Les, did Gavi make it out?"

"No, but I managed to get through to her school. They're keeping everyone in the gymnasium overnight. David—"

"Don't panic. If she stays inside, she should be fine." He looked up at Colonel Hamilton, who was motioning for his phone. "Leslie, I have to go. I'll do what I can from my end."

"I love you."

"Love you, too." He hung up, handing the phone back to his CO."

"I'm sorry to hear about your daughter, Captain. My wife and I . . . we lost our son to leukemia when he was seven. Passed on our fifteenth wedding anniversary. There are no words." Hamilton turned to leave.

"Colonel, the Gutierrez woman . . . how's she doing?"

"Orders are orders, Captain. I'm sorry."

Adrenaline mixed with anger and fatigue. David grabbed Hamilton by his biceps hard enough to bruise, driving him backward into a table. "What do you mean you're sorry? She was fine!"

"Back off!" The colonel twisted free. "No one leaves Manhattan unless they're in a Racal suit or a body bag. Those are my orders."

"Bastards, you killed her! Not the baby, too?"

"War is hell, Captain. I'll say a prayer for your daughter."

GOVERNOR'S ISLAND, NEW YORK
7:58 P.M.

Governor's Island: 172 acres of prime real estate situated in New York Harbor. A mere half mile from the southern tip of Manhattan, Governor's Island had been a fortified outpost during the Revolutionary War and a strategic military base in the War of 1812. Over the century that followed, the island had been converted to a military prison before opening to visitors and boating excursions. For decades, investors had flirted with turning it into a gambling resort.

Tonight, the tourist attraction had been designated a gray zone.

Leggett Hall occupied the very center of Governor's Island. Large enough to house an entire regiment and once listed as the longest structure in the world, the building was hastily being refitted as a Level-4 isolation ward—a holding area for world leaders and diplomats desperately awaiting relocation back at the UN Plaza.

Captain Jay Zwawa walked through the enormous barracks, relieved at finally having shed his Racal suit after nearly twelve hours. His younger brother, Jesse, had remained at the United Nations to coordinate a scheduled midnight airlift—assuming the medical "way station" would ever be ready to receive its guests.

The man in-charge of converting the barracks was Joseph "Joey" Parker, a good ole Tennessee boy with the frame and disposition of an offensive tackle. Jay Zwawa located the medical engineer inspecting a ventilation duct while yelling at his foreman over a walkie-talkie.

"Listen to me, you dumb sumbitch, there are more holes in this barracks than a Vegas whorehouse. And this piece of Swiss cheese you call a ventilation system needs a total rehaul."

"Problems, Mr. Parker?"

The engineer snapped his cell phone shut, turning to confront Zwawa. "My constipated horse has problems. What we got here are life-and-death situations. For starters, we need to jack up the exhaust flow rate in this antiquated turd house, or we'll never reach a differential pressure strong enough to keep your virus from escaping with the next cool breeze. And don't ask me when we'll be finished. I've seen chicken coops that were less porous."

"Tell me what you need. More men? More equipment?"

"What I need is more time and a few dozen miracles. Whose brilliant idea was this anyway? You should be flying those ivory-tower assholes to a real Level-4 containment facility."

"We have our reasons, Mr. Parker. Now how soon?"

"How soon . . . how soon. Assuming I can get the new ventilation system online by nine o'clock . . . you might have one ward ready by two A.M."

"Our goal was midnight."

"And my goal was to keep all my hair, but that sure as hell didn't happen either." He snatched his cell phone on the first ring. "Susan Lynn, I gotta call you back."

Zwawa shot him a look.

"Lookie here, Captain, you flew me in to do a job, and I'll do it. My crew's working their asses off, the problem is your choice of facility. It's old, and even with the new internal sheeting in place, we're still leaking air everywhere. Lose air, and you lose the vacuum that keeps viruses from flowing out of a containment area. If that happens, you can kiss this whole prairie-shit island good-bye."

Jay Zwawa's cell phone vibrated. "Zwawa."

"Sir, the woman from the VA Hospital just arrived. We have her in Building 20."

"On my way." The captain turned to his engineer. "Two o'clock, Mr. Parker. A minute later, and your next job will be cleaning air-conditioning ducts in midtown Manhattan."

FORT TRYON PARK
INWOOD, MANHATTAN
8:22 P.M.

They had moved with purpose through the forest, Virgil using the tree trunks as cover against the soldier's night-vision glasses. Descending along paths unseen, the rocky elevation had dropped precariously, sending Shep tripping over knotted roots camouflaged by leaves and the heavily forested darkness.

In due time they had left the helicopters' searchlights behind and eventually the thunder of the choppers' blades. Emerging from the woods, Virgil led them to a clearing harboring a children's playground.

Shep coughed, the cold affecting his lungs. "Where are we?"

"Fort Tryon Park. What happened to your arm?"

"My arm?" Patrick inspected the damaged left appendage under the light of a park lamppost. From the elbow joint down, the prosthetic device had been stripped of its fake flesh. The pincers were gone, too, the distal end of the sharp metal forearm now bent into a sickle-shaped curve.

"Must've done that when I yanked it loose from beneath the console." Shep raised the deformed device, then cut downward, the sharp edge of the mangled appendage whistling through the crisp night air as if it were a blade. "Cuts like a scythe. Bet it would make a nasty weapon."

"Just the same, you'd better remove it before you slice open your own leg."

Shep reached beneath his sweater and attempted to unbuckle the harness. "It's jammed. And the sensors below my deltoid . . . they must have fused together. I can't budge it."

"Patrick, that wooden box . . . you said it contains a vaccine?"

"That's what Leigh . . . what Dr. Nelson said. The bastards shot her as I took off in the chopper. They came after me, too. I'm lucky to be alive."

"The night's still young. Open the case. Let's see what's inside."

Shep sat down on a park bench, placing the polished box on his lap. Releasing the two front clasps, he opened the lid. There were eleven vials of clear liquid secured inside the case, the twelfth foam compartment empty.

Virgil read a typed note that had been folded and tucked inside one of the styrofoam edges. "Warning: This antibiotic contains a powerful neurotransmitter that crosses the brain-blood barrier. May cause hallucinogenic effects. Anger and reactive behavior exacerbate symptoms. Keep patient calm. Do not leave unsupervised for the first six to twelve hours."

"Nelson wanted me to deliver this to the Center for Disease Control in New Jersey. I guess that's no longer an option."

"Patrick, people are dying in the streets by the tens of thousands."

"What should we do?"

"We? You're playing God on this one, not me."

"What's that supposed to mean?"

"It means you hold the power of life in your hand, and that, my friend, makes you God. So, Lord Patrick, who shall live this evening, and who shall die?"

"DeBorn . . . I forgot about him! Virgil, I have to find my family, they're in terrible danger."

"Patrick—"

"DeBorn tried to kill me, now he'll go after my family. I have to get to Battery Park before—"

"Patrick, I spoke with your soul mate."

The blood rushed from Shep's face. "You spoke with Bea? How? When?"

"This afternoon. After I visited you in the VA."

"What did she say? Did you tell her how much I miss her? Does she want to see me again?"

"She loves you, but she's afraid you may do something desperate. I told her you're lost and you're scared, and she prayed that I could help you find your way again. I promised her I would. I promised that I would bring you to her and to your daughter . . . when you're ready."

"I'm ready! I swear to God, Virgil—"

"Son, look around us; everything has changed. The Angel of Darkness feasts in Manhattan, the entire city is in a state of panic. We're in Inwood, at the very northern tip of the island, Battery Park its farthest point south. That's a good seven miles as the crow flies, double that on foot. There's no public transportation, and the roads are stifled with endless gridlock. We'd have to walk the entire way, and the streets are paved with death, entire neighborhoods stricken with plague."

"I don't care. I'd walk through Hell if it meant seeing my family again."

"All right, Dante. If it's a journey through Hell you seek, then I'll lead you there, only you'd better drain one of those vials first or you'll never make it out of here alive."

"Yeah . . . okay, that makes sense. You'd better take one, too."

"Me? I'm an old man, I've seen my better days. Besides, one of us needs to keep his faculties if we're to find your family."

"You take the vaccine then, I'll lead the way."

"A noble gesture, but it's not an option. I know the area. You'd get us lost in five minutes. Now do as I say, we're wasting precious time. Those soldiers want the vaccine, too, and I suspect they'll shoot first and ask questions later. But who am I to tell you."

"Okay, but I'm saving vaccine for you, just in case." Shep removed one of the containers. He pulled off the corked cap with his teeth and drained the vial of its clear liquid.

"How do you feel?"

"Good . . . excited. Like I finally have a sense of purpose."

"Better prepare yourself, son. What lies ahead . . . it can steal a man's soul."

Virgil set off, following a line of shrubs paralleling Riverside Drive, the tarmac path leading them toward the river and the Henry Hudson Parkway.

Lost Diary: Guy de Chauliac

The following entry has been excerpted from a recently discovered unpublished memoir, written by surgeon Guy de Chauliac during the Great Plague: 1346-1348.
(translated from its original French)

Diary Entry: March 2, 1348

(recorded in Avignon, France)

I am surrounded by death.

It encompasses every waking moment of my existence. It haunts every dream. That I remain free of plague at the moment of this diary entry may be God's will or a result of my precautions while treating the infected (translator's note: see Chirurgia magna). Either way, it is important only in that my continuance in this life might grant me the time needed to record the observations necessary so that others may fair better in finding a cure to this Great Mortality.

That I remain symptom-free is not to say I have not been affected. As personal physician to the last three Popes, I could have chosen to remain within the safer confines of the papal palace, spending my days monitoring His Eminence's bowel movements and analyzing stool samples. These tasks were acceptable before the arrival of plague, but not now. To expand the body of medical knowledge requires me to take risks. *Ignoti nulla curatio morbid*—do not attempt to cure what you do not understand. That I may succumb to the very malady I seek to cure is a fate I have entrusted to God, but in truth part of me would welcome an end to the mental anguish that has become nearly unbearable.

There are no words that adequately describe real human suffering, and I am only bearing witness to the deed. To comfort a weeping mother as she clutches her suffering infant is to witness grief; to assist the grieving parents with the child's burial is to share their sorrow; to beg the shattered husband to abandon his wife's infected corpse a day later is well beyond my medical training.

How does one console the tortured? How does one continue to pray to a Creator who blesses us with life, only to snatch it away so cruelly? How does one awaken each morning and will oneself to get out of bed when all that awaits is more of the same?

In my loneliest hours, my poisoned mind contemplates our existence and I see things with a clarity only Death can provide. Suffering has been with us far longer than plague, we of the unaffected simply had chosen to ignore it. The devastation of war . . . the cruelty of starvation . . . the evil unleashed by the regal and royal among us who believe themselves blessed by our Maker to wreak havoc upon the lives of others. As a physician, I have stood in the presence of both the mighty and the meek, I have borne witness to the beauty of life and its ugly cousin, callousness, and I know now that we are reaping what we have sown . . . that God is an angry parent, disappointed with his children, and we are paying His penance for our indiscretions.

My penance is to remain free of the infection while I treat the afflicted. In truth, I have tasted so much suffering that my heart has become numb, my veiled existence creating perpetual darkness—a darkness that awaits the light of the Angel of Death.

He watches me, this reaper of souls, for I have seen him lurking by the grave sites, his face shrouded by his hooded gown, his bony hand clutching his staff—a common sickle used by the farmer to slice through fields of wheat. That he senses me watching him I have no doubt, for he comes to me often in my dreams, his presence weighing cold on my soul.

I am not alone in my observations. Others speak of his presence, this merchant of death, greeting him with *la Danse Macabre.* When first witnessed, I thought the gesture to be one of hysterics . . . the infected mind of the survivor unable to cope with the sudden, painful loss of so many loved ones, but now I am not so sure. When there is nothing left to live for . . . when every breath is torturous and every heartbeat bitter, then the living welcome death with open arms and beg his merciful embrace.

One day soon, I, too, may beckon the Grim Reaper, but not now—not when my work remains unfinished. Until then I will carry on, recording my observations, attempting to find a way to curb the Great Mortality, if only to justify my own wretched existence to my Maker.

—***Guigo***

SECOND CIRCLE

LUST

"This way to the city of pain. Thru here ceaseless agony awaits. All lost souls must enter here. Justice inspired God to make this place. It was built with three tools: Omnipotence, Wisdom, and Love. When only eternal things were made. And it, too, shall remain immortal. Abandon all hope upon entering here."

—Dante's Inferno

DECEMBER 20

HENRY HUDSON PARKWAY SOUTH

INWOOD HILL, MANHATTAN

8:32 P.M.

(11 HOURS, 31 MINUTES BEFORE THE PROPHESIED END OF DAYS)

Patrick Shepherd followed Virgil through a clearing onto Riverside Drive. The deserted access road led them down to the southbound lanes of the Henry Hudson Parkway, an eleven-mile highway that ran along the west side of Manhattan, offering scenic views of the Hudson River.

Stretched out before them was a sea of vehicles, wedged bumper to bumper and door to door between the parkway's concrete dividers. The three northbound lanes were submerged beneath a blinding wall of stagnant headlights. The three southbound lanes merged into scarlet trails of taillights that paralleled the river before looping higher in the distance as it rounded an access ramp to reach the now-destroyed George Washington Bridge.

Nothing was moving. The urban chaos was eerily silent, violated only by an occasional gust of wind and a few engines still purring in neutral, burning their last gallons of fuel.

"Virgil . . . what happened here?"

The old man pressed his bearded face to a passenger window, peering inside a stalled SUV. "Plague."

Clutching the vaccine box, Shep moved from car to car, the scenes within each vehicle varying, the implications inarguable. Trapped together in endless gridlock, a diverse community of tens of thousands of strangers had mingled along the roadside to vocalize their grievances, discuss options, perhaps even to share a snack or beverage. As the sun had faded into dusk and their anger had turned to desperation, they had retreated back to their mobile shelters against the plunging temperatures, the infected among them condemning the rest.

Scythe had been swift and merciless, each vehicle serving as its private incubator, equipped with a recirculating ventilation system that ensured a saturation of toxic bacilli among its passengers.

The images were as gruesome as they were heart-wrenching: parents clutching their children in a final embrace. Grandparents wrapped in blankets. Pale complexions frozen in fear and anguish. Blue lips pasted with blood. Family pets and cargo spaces overloaded with personal belongings.

Human desperation. A highway of death.

Everything suddenly so familiar. Shep swooned, his vision swirling from the vaccine—

—as night became day, winter retreating into summer.

Patrick Shepherd's sweater evolves into body armor, the remnants of his bladelike prosthetic arm morphing into flesh, securing his M16A2 rifle.

The passenger vehicles on the Iraqi highway are charred, smoldering beneath the desert sun. The scent of scorched flesh mixes with gasoline. Black smoke drifting above orange flames. Body parts are everywhere, the car bombs having turned the public bazaar into a bloodbath. Date palms line the Shiite enclave, the thick tree trunks chewed apart with shrapnel from rocket-propelled grenades. Their shade wasted on twenty-one bullet-ridden corpses. The men, all local farmers, had been dragged from their homes by gunmen wearing Iraqi military uniforms before being shot.

Sergeant Shepherd searches the dead, his gun barrel trained to swivel toward anything that moves. He pivots to his left, the tip of his right index finger flirting with the M16's trigger, the crosshairs of his gun sight homing in on the Shiite woman. Cloaked in a traditional black burka, she weeps and babbles incoherently as she clutches the torn body of her dead son, wiping his blood on her charred face.

He moves on, as useless to the bereaved mother as is his English.

Paranoia fuels a body overweighed with equipment. Confusion fills a mind deprived of sleep. In the distance, he hears the cries of another female, only these screams are different, reflecting a present tense.

Separating from his men, he enters the charred police headquarters, ignoring the commands coming through his earpiece. The building, riddled with shrapnel, had been one of the targets of the Sunni insurgents' raid. He moves through the rubble-filled interior, his assault rifle drawn as he approaches the back room.

There are three of them . . . and the girl. She is in her early teens, her shirt torn open and bloodied, her lower body naked, stretched belly down across a desk.

The sadists are part of Iraq's patchwork security force, a renegade bunch long accused of protecting sectarian death squads. One man violates her doggy style, his trousers around his ankles, his fingers entwined in her onyx hair. His two companions, both heavily armed, await their turn like animals in heat.

Dark eyes and rifles greet him as he enters the den of iniquity.

A tense moment passes. The men grin nervously at the American, emboldened by their shared gender. "You wish a taste of this Sunni dog, yes?"

The voice in Shep's earpiece urges his retreat. ". . . not our battle, Sergeant. Leave the premises . . . now!"

His conscience, stained yet still functioning, says otherwise. His mind negotiates with his tongue to speak.

The girl cries out to him. The Farsi needs no translation.

Shep's pulse pounds in his ears. The injustice demands he take action, yet he knows his next move will set off a chain reaction that could end his own life and possibly the girl's.

His right hand quivers against the M16's magazine, his index finger sliding toward the trigger. The dark eyes watching him grow antsy.

"Sergeant Shepherd, report at once."

God, why am I here?

"Shepherd . . . now!"

He hesitates, then backs out of the building—

—day returning to night, the frigid December wind causing his sweat-laced body to shiver.

"Sergeant?"

He turned to Virgil, his eyes glassy with tears. "I didn't act. I should have killed them all."

"Killed whom? Whom should you have killed?"

"Soldiers. In Baladruz. They were raping a young girl. I stood by . . . I let it happen."

Virgil said nothing, weighing his response. "These men . . . they deserved to die?"

"Yes. No . . . I don't know. It's complicated . . . a Shiite village, there were bodies everywhere. The insurgents were Sunni, so was the girl, but there has to be rules. But there were no rules, no sides. One day you're fighting a Sunni, the next day a Shiite . . . all the while innocent people are dying . . . butchered like sheep. They look at you like it's your fault, you try not to think about it, but inside you know you're a part of it . . . maybe the cause of it . . . a million people dead since this whole thing began. Why am I here? They didn't attack us. They weren't a threat. Saddam . . . sure, he was an evil bastard, but were we so much better? Killing is killing, no matter who fires the bullet."

"Was there hatred in your heart on that day?"

"Hatred? I was numb. I found myself walking on a road covered in body parts, my boots drenched in the blood of children. Then something happened, I heard a scream. Instinct took over, I mean, what if it was my daughter they were raping? Hatred? Yeah, there was hatred. You should have seen their eyes . . . like wild animals, filled with lust. I should have stopped them. I should have blown their fucking heads off!"

"Three dead men for one dehumanized soul. One act of evil begetting another."

"Yeah . . . I mean, no. It's just . . . I was ashamed. It's like, by not acting, I became a part of it. I mean, what should I have done?"

"It's not for me to say. You could have taken action, perhaps you should have. Sometimes there are no clear answers, sometimes innocent people suffer. You told me you were deployed how many times? Four?"

"Yeah. This happened on my first deployment, my third week out."

"There are interesting parallels here. Life is a test, Patrick. Some souls, like soldiers, must be redeployed over and over, condemned to repeat their journey until their lessons on Earth are learned. The ancient wisdom I spoke about earlier calls this *tikkun,* the process of spiritual repair. It is said that a soul may travel to the *Malchut*—the physical world—up to four times to correct its misgiving. Perhaps the Creator was offering you an opportunity for transformation."

"Come on, Virgil. Are you saying God purposely had me witness an innocent girl being sodomized so I could learn some lesson? What possible lesson is worth all that?"

"That's for you to discover. The Creator operates on a level beyond our perception. Just remember that a single act of evil, like a drop of plague, can infect a million people, but so too can one good deed. What happened to the girl?"

"She died. Badly." Shep moved to the southbound lane's concrete barrier, his eyes drawn to the Hudson River. He paused, his blood running cold as he spotted the figure standing by the Amtrak train tracks sixty feet away.

"Oh . . . geez."

The blinking red train signal illuminated the gangly figure every twenty seconds. Dark hooded garment. Long staff, curved sickle. Shep could not see the Reaper's face, but he could sense the cold stillness of the being's presence.

"Virgil, we need to go . . . we need to get off this highway, now!"

"Calm yourself, Sergeant—"

Shep wheeled around to confront the old man. "Don't call me that anymore! It's Patrick or Shep, not Sergeant. I'm no longer in the military."

"Understood. Patrick, the vaccine . . . is it affecting your senses?"

"The vaccine?"

"It causes one to hallucinate. Are you hallucinating?"

"Yeah. Maybe." He searched for the Grim Reaper but saw only shadows. "There's too much death around us, Virgil, too much plague. Unless you intend to immunize yourself with the vaccine, we need to get you away from this highway of death. Look, there's a bunch of exit ramps just past the bridge. Are you up for a quick jog? Come on, I'll help you."

With his right arm, Patrick Shepherd swept the older man around his waist, hurrying him through the southbound lane's jigsaw puzzle of vehicles, the smoldering George Washington Bridge looming ahead.

GOVERNOR'S ISLAND, NEW YORK
BUILDING 20
8:43 P.M.

The cellar walls were gray cinder block, the floor concrete and damp.

Leigh Nelson lay curled in a fetal position on the bare mattress beneath an olive green wool Army blanket. Her body ached from the impact of the rubber bullets. Her stomach growled with hunger. The shackles around her ankles had rubbed the skin raw. Her mascara was smudged from crying. She missed her family. She wanted desperately to call her husband and ease his worry. Most of all, she tried to convince herself that her worst fears were unwarranted, that an outbreak of plague could never become a worldwide pandemic, and that her captors knew she was a physician—one of the good guys.

Try as she might, she was losing this psychological battle. After being shot, handcuffed, and strapped down in a portable isolation unit, she had been airlifted to Governor's Island, then stripped and doused with a green bactericide before being subjected to a ninety-minute medical exam. Blood tests confirmed she was plague-free, but the indignity she had felt from one MP's lust-filled eyes had unnerved her, fueling her resolve not to cooperate.

She heard the front door opening upstairs. Several people entered the building, their presence registering along the squeaking floorboards above her head. Crossing the expanse, they reached the cellar door.

Leigh sat up, wrapping the blanket around her shoulders as the men made their way down the basement stairwell.

The MP led the way, his commanding officer descending two steps behind him. He was a big man, his body language revealing fatigue.

"Ms. Nelson?"

"It's Dr. Nelson. Why am I being held like some prisoner of war? We're supposed to be on the same side."

"Is that why you allowed your friend to flee aboard the medevac chopper with the Scythe vaccine?"

"Your commandoes assaulted our hospital like we were a terrorist camp. You killed my boss!"

"We used rubber bullets."

"How the hell was I supposed to know that? Haven't we had enough shock and awe for one day? Why couldn't you have just introduced yourself properly? I would have gladly handed over the vaccine, along with the redheaded woman who created it. We could have worked together to save Manhattan."

"Manhattan can't be saved."

She felt light-headed. "What are you talking about? Of course it can be saved."

"The president can be saved. The diplomats at the UN under triage—most of them can be saved—*if* we locate the vaccine in time. Most important, the world can be saved from a global pandemic, assuming the quarantine holds up through morning. Everyone else on Manhattan . . ." He shook his head.

"Are you insane? There are two million people—"

"Three million, including the daily workforce, all sharing twenty-eight square miles of urban jungle, exposed to a highly contagious form of bubonic plague that kills its victims within fifteen hours. Even if we had the vaccine, we'd never be able to produce enough of it in time."

"My God . . ."

"Yeah."

"What are you going to do?"

"Everything I have to in order to keep this nightmare contained to Manhattan. We estimate upward of a quarter of a million people are already dead, half of them on the access routes leading out of the city. We've sealed the tunnels and blown the bridges, but as the remains of the dead become more visible and the people more desperate, we stand a far greater chance of a few creative individuals slipping through unnoticed. Your family . . . they live in New Jersey?"

"Hoboken."

"That's a short boat ride, or an hour's swim across the Hudson. Most of them won't make it, of course, but New Yorkers are a pretty resilient bunch, so maybe we lose Jersey, too."

"What is it you want?"

"I want that vaccine. Your pilot made it as far as Inwood Hill before he crash-landed in the park. Who is he? Where would he go?"

"Sergeant Patrick Shepherd, he's one of my patients."

Jay Zwawa typed the information on his BlackBerry. "He's a vet?"

"Yes. As of this morning, he's wearing a prosthetic for a left arm. His wife and daughter are living somewhere in Battery Park."

"What's her name?"

"Beatrice Shepherd."

"Sergeant."

"Yes, sir?"

"Release Dr. Nelson. She's coming with me."

BATTERY PARK
MANHATTAN
9:11 P.M.

Beatrice Shepherd exited the northern stairwell of the twenty-two-story apartment building, her mind in a state of panic over her daughter, who was still not home. She made it as far as the lobby entrance, then froze, remaining hidden in the shadows.

Death had taken Manhattan, rotting the Big Apple to its core. It lay spread-eagled on the curb beneath the building awning and bled on the sidewalk. It lurked in the driver's seat of a still-purring taxi. It infected a city block of buses and mobilized the living dead . . . desperate, frightened tourists with nowhere else to go.

Across the street, a father of three smashed a brick paver through the plate-glass door of a darkened pawnshop. A visitor from England seeking shelter for his family. The shotgun blast was blinding and lethal, the store owner, huddling in the dark, firing into the night.

Beatrice backed away from the lobby. God had given her a sign. Her daughter had a better chance of finding her way home than she did of locating her in this chaos.

She would remain in her apartment and pray.

158TH STREET RAMP
HENRY HUDSON PARKWAY SOUTH
9:47 P.M.

It had taken them twenty minutes to reach the George Washington Bridge's underpass, the closer they got, the louder the chaos. Screams and cries for help rang hollow in the frigid December air, interspersed with the staccato popping sounds of distant gunfire. Strange whirring noises echoed across the Hudson as unseen aerial drones soared overhead. Patrol boats passed in the darkness, their searchlights trained on the river, their engines growling. High above their heads on the Cross Bronx Expressway, bonfires turned the night into patches of glowing orange. Dozens of vehicles burned, illuminating silhouettes of a gathering mob.

The scent of the smoldering bridge remained overpowering.

Patrick and Virgil hurried past the bridge's eastern foundation, keeping low behind the Henry Hudson Parkway's central divider. Beyond the labyrinth of off-ramps connecting the ruptured expanse, they climbed over a four-foot concrete barrier to access the northbound lanes, then over a steel guardrail onto the 158th Street exit ramp. Deserted, the winding road was a steep and steady climb. The two men continued their trek, their breaths visible in the chilled air.

"Virgil, back at the hospital, you said everything has a cause and effect."

"Fix the cause, and you'll fix the effect."

"And how do you fix all this? People are dying by the thousands. DeBorn and his ilk are manipulating the world into another war. How can you fix so much evil?"

"A timeless question. Am I responding as a psychiatrist or as a spiritual counselor?"

"I don't care, I just need to know."

The old man continued walking, weighing his response. "I'm going to give you an answer, but you won't like it. Evil serves a purpose. It makes the choice of good possible. Without evil, there could be no transformation—transformation being the desire to change one's nature from the selfish to the selfless."

"What kind of esoteric bullshit is that? God, I actually thought you were tuned in. Is that what you'd tell a grieving mother whose kid was gunned down in the street?"

"No. It's the response I'm offering the soldier who pulled the trigger."

The road spun out from under him, a sudden vertigo that forced Patrick to his knees on the concrete ramp. His chest constricted. He fought to breathe. "Who . . . told . . . you? DeBorn?"

"Does it really matter?"

"The father was angry . . . he was running at me. The Farsi, I couldn't remember what to say, I was trained to react. I didn't want to kill him! I didn't have a choice."

"Do you honestly believe that?"

Shep shook his head. "I should have ended it right then . . . my life for the boy's father. Instead . . . oh, God!" The dam burst, raking his body in convulsions, his anguish flowing into a night already heavy in despair.

"Suicide is not transformation, Patrick. It's blasphemy." Virgil sat down next to Shep and placed an arm around his shoulder. "The incident, it happened how long ago?"

"Eight years, three months."

"And you anguish over these deaths to this day?"

"Yes."

"Then there is some justice. What is lacking is transformation."

"I don't understand."

"You asked me about evil, why God allows it to exist. The more important question is why does any of this exist? What is man's true purpose? What if I told you that everything that surrounds us—this ramp, this city, the planet—everything you refer to as the physical universe represents a mere one percent of existence, created for one purpose . . . as a challenge."

"A challenge for who? Man?"

"Man is just a vessel, designed to be fallible." Virgil winced. "My back is stiffening, help me up."

Shep slid his right arm around the older man's thick waist, assisting him to his feet. With a grunt, the old man continued walking up the long, winding highway off-ramp.

"Every being possesses a soul, Patrick, and every soul is a spark of the Creator's Light. God's Light is pure, intended for only one purpose—to give. The soul is pure, intended for only one purpose—to receive the Light's endless fulfillment. To receive the Light requires desire. To be more like the Creator, the soul desired to earn its endless fulfillment. That required a challenge. And here we are."

"That's your answer? *Here we are?*"

"There's more to it than that, and I'll tell you more when I think you are ready. For now, understand that man's ego taints the soul's desire to receive. Ego is the absence of Light. It leads to reactive behavior—violence, lust, greed, jealousy. The story you told me about the soldiers molesting that girl . . . it's an example of what happens when the Light of God is cut off from the soul, allowing the negative forces to run amok."

"You should have seen them. The look in their eyes . . . the anger."

"Anger is the most dangerous trait of the human ego. It allows one to be taken over by the darker forces. Like lust, anger is an animal response. It can only be corrected through selfless acts that expand one's vessel to receive more of God's Light."

"But people who have sinned . . . aren't they forbidden from accessing the Light?"

"Not at all. Transformation is available to everyone, no matter how evil the deed. Unlike man, the Creator feels unconditional love for all

His children."

"Wait. So Hitler can exterminate six million Jews, but as long as he asks for forgiveness, then everything's cool? Come on."

"Transformation has nothing to do with asking for forgiveness or saying ten Hail Marys, or fasting. Transformation is an act of selflessness. What you did in Iraq, you'll be judged for in *Gehenom.*"

"*Gehenom* is Hell, right?"

"It can be for some. Just remember, every act of kindness completed before your last breath can help ease the cleansing process after you move on."

"So how do I transform?"

"For starters, stop being a victim. You weren't created to be miserable. By wallowing in misery, you're veiling God's Light. Surely there must be something you desire?"

"Honestly, the only thing I desire is to see my family again."

"There's a reason you're apart, Patrick. You need to resolve the cause to overcome the effect. Until you can do that . . ." The wind picked up, bringing with it a driving rain. The old man glanced up at the heavens, then ahead, where the ramp ended at a highway underpass. "There's shelter up ahead."

The ramp had brought them to Manhattanville. Ahead lay 158th Street, the deserted road cresting before them, running through a massive arch belonging to a highway overpass. Someone had spray-painted graffiti on its concrete wall, the red letters still dripping:

Welcome to Hell.
Abandon all hope upon entering.

WELCOME TO HELL
ABANDON ALL HOPE
UPON ENTERING

THIRD CIRCLE

GLUTTONS

"Huge hailstones, dirty water, and black snow pour from the dismal air to putrefy the putrid slush that waits them below. And they too howl like dogs in the freezing storm, turning and turning from it as if they thought one naked side could keep the other warm."

—Dante's Inferno

DECEMBER 20

158TH STREET RAMP

MANHATTANVILLE, MANHATTAN

10:06 P.M.

(9 HOURS, 57 MINUTES BEFORE THE PROPHESIED END OF DAYS)

The rain became a driving sleet. Patrick and Virgil sought shelter beneath the concrete arch—the massive foundation supporting Riverside Drive. Situated within the underpass was a garage, part of a maintenance system run by New York's Department of Transportation.

Entering the garage revealed a vast cavernous substratum formed by the roadway overhead. Steel girders framed a ceiling five stories high. A gravel access road disappeared into the dark recess before them. The wind howled through the tunnel, causing Shep to shiver uncontrollably, his rain-soaked sweater all but useless against the December cold front.

A small windowed office lay dark and vacant on their left. Virgil tried the door. Finding it unlocked, he entered, returning a moment later carrying a black ski parka. "Put this on."

"Too small. I c-c-can't get it over the p-p-prosthetic."

Virgil stretched the jacket's left sleeve in front of him. "Use your prosthetic blade. Cut the left sleeve, so your appendage can slip through the hole."

With one downward swipe, Patrick slashed through the material at the elbow, sending goose down feathers flying.

Virgil held the altered garment for Patrick. Guiding the end of his deformed steel arm into the tailored left sleeve, Shep managed to work the alpine ski jacket over his shoulders, the old man helping him with the zipper. "Better?"

"Much better. Virgil, listen."

The wind had died down, allowing them to hear a woman's cry for help, the desperate plea echoing in the darkness.

"Come on!" Shoving the vaccine container inside his ski jacket, Patrick raced into the bowels of the underground structure, Virgil trailing behind.

The tunnel continued for several hundred yards, dead-ending where the ceiling tapered down to meet a concrete retaining wall and a descending stairwell, lit by a fading emergency light. Three rottweilers were bound by their leashes to the step's iron rail, preventing anyone from using the exit. The animals' chains had become entangled, pinning the vicious black-and-tan guard dogs side by side. Their lathered fangs remained out of reach of the woman.

She was in her late fifties, Caucasian and rotund. Stripped down to her underwear, she was standing chest deep in a pit of mud created by one of the drainage pipes, which had cracked open, depositing its refuse around the stairwell.

Seeing Patrick and Virgil, the woman immediately began to vent. "Well, it's about time, I've only been screaming for help for twenty minutes. First they stole my jewelry. Then they took my air mask, which cost me five thousand dollars. Then the little bastards stripped me down to my bra and panties and left me here to die."

The snarling dogs barked at Patrick as he approached the woman—

—their bodies morphing together in his mind's eye, melding into a single three-headed beast . . . Cerberus! The mythical hound of Hades rears on its hind legs, its multiple mouths snapping at Patrick, saliva flying from its lathering jowls.

Shep backed away, the surroundings spinning in his vision—

—the cement wall becoming a long, concrete-block corridor, barred steel doors

on either side. The prisoners huddle together on the floor at the end of the hall. The guards are laughing, barely restraining the three guard dogs. The rottweilers tug at their choker leashes, growling at the terrified, naked Iraqi prisoners.

The Intelligence Officer turns to Shep. "We call this 'fearing up' the detainees. The interrogators appreciate it. They say it helps loosen their lips."

"What did they do?"

"Who cares? Our job is to put the fear of Jesus in 'em for the Gitmo boys. That one, drag his fat ass over here."

Shep grabs the Iraqi by his elbow, separating the frightened man from the group.

The Intelligence Officer shoves the barrel of his sidearm in the man's ear. "Smitty, tell him to grab his ankles. Tell him if he let's go, I'll blow his brains out. Shepherd, when I tell you to, I want you to beat this Arab dog across his back with the rubber hose."

"Sir . . . I don't think I can."

"Think? Who asked you to think? I'm giving you an order, Sergeant."

"Shepherd, these orders come directly from the defense secretary's office. We do our jobs over here, and we prevent another 9/11 back home. Is that so hard to understand? Now pick up the fucking hose. Go on, Smitty—tell him!"

The private contractor from Titan Corporation issues commands in Farsi to his prisoner. Quivering in fear, the heavyset Iraqi bends over and grabs his ankles.

"Shepherd, now—beat his terrorist ass!"

Patrick hesitates then lashes the forty-one-year-old taxi driver and father of five across his hairy back with the rubber hose.

"What are you, a Muslim lover? Hit him, Sergeant! That's it! Beat him like a mule." The MI Officer winks at the private contractor as he removes the cigarette from his mouth and stubs it out in the detainee's left ear.

The Iraqi man howls in pain. Fearful of releasing his ankles and being shot, the prisoner falls forward, smashing his head against the unforgiving tile floor, knocking himself out.

The Intel Officer and private contractor break out in hysterics.

Shep backs away from the injured man, the dogs barking and snapping—

—one rottweiler suddenly gagged. Another followed suit, then the last—

all three animals choking at something lodged in their throats.

"Patrick, are you all right? Patrick–"

Shep shook the memory of Abu Ghraib from his vision until he was again standing in the underground maintenance shaft. Virgil was by his side, his right hand caked in mud.

The three dogs were gagging, their mouths filled with the muck.

The heavyset woman was on her feet. Wallowing past the dogs, she disappeared down the concrete stairwell, leaving a trail of sewage and mud.

Virgil looked at Shep, who appeared pale and shaken. "Another hallucination?"

"A bad memory."

"Tell me."

Patrick stared at the dogs, the scene still vivid in his mind's eye. "My second deployment . . . I was assigned to Abu Ghraib prison as a systems administrator—basically a glorified computer guy. The new guys got relegated to the night shift. That's where a lot of things happened."

"By 'things,' you mean torture?"

Shep nodded. "I was forced to participate. When I complained, I was told to shut my mouth and do my job. Things got worse when the spooks arrived from Guantanamo. Sick bastards. They'd use sleep deprivation . . . playing children's nursery rhymes nonstop around the clock, it drove the inmates insane. Sometimes they'd handcuff a prisoner in painful contortions and leave him like that for hours. I never saw it myself, but I heard about the water-boarding. A few times the spooks went too far and drowned the detainee. When that happened, they'd toss the dead man's remains in a body bag and order us to dump it somewhere during the night."

"But that's not what haunts your dreams."

Shep shook his head, his eyes misty. "There was an Iraqi flag officer, Hamid Zabar. To get him to talk, the spooks brought in his sixteen-year-old son. They tortured the officer's kid while he was forced to watch . . . while I was forced to watch."

Patrick regains his composure. "I was stationed there for six months. A few of us managed to leak the details back home. After a while, there was an inquiry. I was back in New York at the time and offered to testify, but they refused to bring me in. The whole investigation was a sham, designed to appease the media and the American public while placing the blame on a few 'bad apples,' all noncommissioned officers, even though our commander in chief had authorized the use of torture. Nothing about Rumsfeld, who had encouraged the worst of it, or his deputy henchman, Paul Wolfowitz, who saw it for himself, or Major General Geoffrey Miller, the man Rumsfeld sent over to turn Abu Ghraib into Gitmo East. None of the guilty were ever charged or disciplined, only schmucks like me, the ones who blew the whistle. For offering to testify, we were dropped a pay grade, then secretly placed on a 'permanent redeploy' list. Eight months later, I was back in Iraq."

"And the detainees?"

"That's the worst part. Most of these people were innocent bystanders, picked up on sweeps by the private-army guys or turned in for cash rewards by locals. A lot of them weren't even being tracked or registered, just held indefinitely."

"And you did nothing to stop it?"

"I told you, I reported it. What else was I supposed to do?"

"Hey, you two! You're late."

They turned, confronted by a man dressed head to toe in camouflage black fatigues, his face concealed behind a rebreather. He motioned down the concrete stairwell with his assault rifle. "Better move it, assholes. The barge'll be here any minute."

Grabbing the dogs' leashes, he pulled the animals aside, allowing Patrick and Virgil to make their way down the concrete stairwell into the dark recesses below.

PIER A
BATTERY PARK CITY
10:11 P.M.

Built in 1875, Pier A was a 285-foot-long, forty-five-foot-wide solid masonry dock that jutted into the Hudson River at the southwest end of the Financial

District at Battery Park Place. The pier supported an aging three-story structure, highlighted by green-and-white-painted arched windows and a Victorian clock tower located at its seaward end.

Hours earlier, the ferry docks adjacent to Pier A had been a beehive of activity. Tens of thousands had converged upon the waterfront park, mostly visitors, desperate to secure passage off the island. Kayaks were sold for $5,000 in cash, paddleboats exchanged for the keys to Jaguars and Mercedes Benzes. By sundown, any vessel that could float had been purchased, overloaded with civilians, and launched into the Hudson—

—each one intercepted within minutes and sunk by the Coast Guard, the surviving passengers forced to swim back to shore in frigid, limb-paralyzing water.

Few survived. The lucky ones had drowned.

The gate to Pier A's chain-link fence swung open and closed with each gust of wind, the Arctic blasts coming off the harbor rattling the scaffolding. There were lights on in the structure—a half dozen bare bulbs connected to a portable generator.

Beneath the lights, resting on its trailer, sat the 1982 Bayliner 2850 Contessa Sedan Bridge Cuddy Cruiser. The boat was ten feet long, its fiberglass hull trimmed in blue and cream. Large enough to hold eight passengers comfortably, the cruiser featured a galley equipped with an alcohol-and-electric stove and a head that housed a sink, shower, and Porta Potti. The aft berth slept three.

The cruiser was hooked up to a winch, perched over a retractable section of deck that allowed access to the water beneath the northwest section of the pier.

Heath Shelby had purchased the boat for $6,000 from one of the pier's managing partners. The engine seemed sound, but the hull was leaking from a collision that had occurred years earlier. The repairs had been improperly completed, making the vessel less than seaworthy. As part of the deal, the owner agreed to keep the vessel inside Pier A while its new owner completed the necessary repairs.

Heath Shelby lay on the dust-covered wood floor, his Santa Claus outfit serving as a blanket. He was burning with fever. Every few minutes, he coughed up a quarter-sized glob of bloodstained bile. A kiwi-sized tumor grew ripe beneath his left armpit.

Alone and terrified, Heath was more frightened of exposing his wife and son to plague. And so he had isolated himself here with the boat, praying he would survive the night.

His cell phone rang again. Through feverish eyes, he gazed at the caller ID, making sure it was not his wife. "Speak."

"Heath, is that you?"

"Paolo?"

"I just spoke with my sister, she's worried sick."

Heath sat up, delirious. "Jennie's sick?"

"No, I said she's worried sick. She says you won't answer your phone."

"Bad day at work."

"Bad day? Heath, Manhattan's been infected by plague; we have to get our families off the island."

Heath lay back down, fighting the urge to vomit. "How?"

"The boat we were working on for Collin. It can take us across the river. Did you fix the leak?"

"Yeah . . . no, I don't know. Paolo, I'm in the boathouse . . . I'm really sick. I don't want anyone else exposed to this thing. It's ripping my insides apart."

"What can I do?"

"Nothing. Just stay away. Tell my family to do the same."

"Heath, the plague is spreading everywhere, by dawn no one will be safe. Your family hasn't been infected yet, they can still be saved. Get the boat ready to motor across the Hudson. Francesca and I will meet Jenni and Collin in Battery Park as soon as we can. I'll make sure we get them to safety. When we get to Jersey, we'll find a way to help you."

"Too late for me. Take the boat, I'll finish the repairs and leave. Just do me one favor, Paolo. Tell Jenni I love her. Tell Collin his daddy is very proud of him."

"I . . . will. Hello? Heath, are you still there?"

Dropping the cell phone, Heath Shelby crawled to the nearest trash can and retched.

GOVERNOR'S ISLAND, NEW YORK
10:14 P.M.

Rising high above the northwestern shore of Governor's Island was the circular red sandstone fortification known as Castle William. Built in 1807 to protect New York City, the structure was two hundred feet in diameter, its walls forty feet high and eight feet thick.

Leigh Nelson followed Captain Zwawa past a large garden in the center of the castle. Entering the tower, they ascended a winding stairwell, emerging on a terrace overlooking New York Harbor. Battery Park and the Manhattan skyline loom a scant half mile across the waterway.

"Captain, please . . . I need to call my husband. I need to let him know I'm okay."

Jay Zwawa ignored her, his attention focused on the magnificent view of the Financial District, the skyline aglow with lights. "I'm a bit of a history buff. Did you know that, prior to the attacks of 9/11, the worst violence ever experienced in New York happened right here? It was July of 1863, during the Civil War. Rebel agents from the Confederacy incited riots that left two thousand dead and another eight thousand New Yorkers wounded. Governor's Island was attacked, but the militia drove the insurgents back."

"Captain . . . my phone call?"

"When we get the vaccine."

"I'm cooperating. You asked me to cooperate, and I have. What happens if your men can't find Shep?"

"Then your call isn't going to matter."

An aide joined them on the terrace. "Sorry to interrupt, sir. All cell-phone signals are now being jammed. We're ready to black out the island."

"Do it."

"Yes, sir." The aide disappeared down the stairwell.

Leigh Nelson looked aghast. "You're shutting down power?"

"Our objective is to contain three million people. By shutting off the power we darken the city, giving our thermal sensors a better view from above. We also want to encourage the populace to remain indoors."

"You're inducing more panic."

"Doctor, we passed panic five hours ago."

As they watched, the southern tip of Manhattan seemed to evaporate into the night. The rolling blackout continued through Battery Park and the Financial District . . . Chinatown and the Lower East Side . . . Tribeca, Little Italy, and SoHo. Continuing north, the wave of darkness worked its way through midtown and Central Park, blanketing the Upper East and West Side until the entire island of Manhattan—save for the glow of light from the vehicular traffic—was suffocated in velvety black.

The sound rose from the emptiness as one, reaching across land and sea like screams from a distant roller coaster–

–the sound of millions of condemned souls, crying out in the darkness for help.

BENEATH THE 158TH STREET OVERPASS
MANHATTANVILLE, MANHATTAN
10:31 P.M.

Through the darkness they descended, Patrick and Virgil, one man inoculated against plague yet debilitated by the emptiness in his heart, his older companion debilitated by age yet inoculated by a selfless sense of purpose. The two men held hands to keep from falling down a concrete stairwell illuminated only by the gunman's flashlight. Each unseen step brought them closer to dankness and disease, each breath rendered putrid by the stench of sewage that rose to greet them from below, the scratching sounds of rodent claws over cement setting their flesh to tingle.

Three levels became six, eight a dozen, until the stairwell finally ended, depositing them at the opening of an eight-foot-high concrete tunnel, the passage a foot deep in partially frozen mud and sewage. Footprints revealed the hundreds who had come before them.

The gunman barked orders for them to continue moving. Calf deep in filth, they negotiated the trail, the armed man driving them forward into the darkness.

Patrick's temper flared. The former Marine contemplated wheeling about with a vicious backhand of his damaged prosthetic, using the makeshift blade to slice open the gunman's throat.

As if reading his mind, Virgil maneuvered Shep in front, separating him from his intended target.

The passage continued east another hundred yards, releasing them on the banks of the Hudson River. The sleet had let up, the stars made visible in the night sky by the strange absence of city lights.

Patrick looked to the shoreline where a crowd of people were huddling in small groups. Moving closer, he could distinguish two clearly different sects. The elite were dressed in expensive parkas, their faces concealed behind high-tech gas masks and rebreathers, sized even for the few children among them. Their servants, the majority being foreign, were wearing secondhand outer garments, filtering the night air through cloth painting masks and scarves while they kept vigil over children's backpacks and overstuffed suitcases. A few were walking dogs on leashes.

A dozen masked gunmen herded the procession to a small pier. All eyes were on the river, where a massive garbage scow was slowly making its way south down the Hudson.

The barge docked. Patrick recognized its corporate logo, the vessel owned by the Lucchese family, a crime syndicate operating out of Brooklyn. A skeleton crew tied off the three-thousand-ton flattop. An African-American woman in her early forties climbed down from the pilothouse, dressed in a long black leather coat, matching boots, and dark camouflage pants. A gas mask was strapped to her face. A holstered .44 Magnum at her slender waist.

She approached Greg "Wonderboy" Mastroianni, a *capo* in the Lucchese crime family. "I'm Charon. The senator's aide arranged for us to off-load the suits at Governor's Island. We need to move. We've only got a twenty-minute window before the Coast Guard cutter returns."

"Load 'em . . . after they pony up the admission fee."

"You heard the man! Cash, jewels, gold—no one gets on board without paying up front."

A well-dressed man in his forties cut in front of an older couple, opening his attaché case. "Here's $26 million in bearer bonds. That should be more than enough to cover the eleven of us and our two au pairs."

Charon used her flashlight to exam the bonds. "Oil companies, huh? Works for me. Okay, old man, you're next. How many you bringing on board?"

The frail man with the silver hair and fur-lined aviator hat was in his late seventies. His wife balanced on a walker, assisted by two large bodyguards. "There are eighty or ninety of us. Half the money's already been transferred, you'll receive the other half when we arrive safely. My wife just had a hip replacement, make sure you find her someplace comfortable on board."

"This look like the *Queen Mary* to you? She can sit in garbage like everyone else."

The frail man's voice rasped venom. "How dare you! Do you have any idea who I am?"

Virgil pulled Shep aside. "We need to leave . . . now."

"What about the children? I still have ten vials of vaccine. If I save two for my family, that leaves me with—"

"Hide the box and say nothing. We'll cross paths with other souls more worthy of being saved."

"What if I give them a few vials to take to the health authorities in New Jersey. Dr. Nelson said—"

"Open your eyes, Patrick. These are society's gluttons, they have no desire to save anyone but themselves. Rich and powerful, they've lived their entire lives believing the world was left to them alone to control. Corruption veils them from the Light, greed binds them to Satan. Behind those masks are the faces of men who raped the retirement funds of hardworking families even as they pocketed tens of millions of dollars in bonuses. Even now, they attempt to use their ill-gotten fortunes to buy a passage to freedom, oblivious to the reality that their escape from Manhattan could potentially spread the plague to the rest of the world. Take a good look at them, son. See these gluttons for what they *really* are."

Patrick stared at the silver-haired old man, who had foolishly removed his gas mask to argue with the black woman. "Now you listen here. My ancestors were running this country back when yours were still running buck naked in the jungle. And you, my Sicilian friend, who do you think arranged this little excursion out of Manhattan? Your boss works for me, and so does the senator! Without me, you assholes wouldn't make it a hundred feet past this pier."

The Mafia *capo* shined his flashlight on the old man's identification, then unfolded a slip of paper and verified the name. "Ah, damn. Let him on."

"Get some of your thugs to assist my wife, then get us to Governor's Island, pronto. My private jet is waiting for us at LaGuardia. I need to be in London in eight hours."

The silver-haired man paused, as if sensing a presence. Slowly, he turned to face Patrick—

—his eyes nocturnal and glowing, like a cat's. His ears—pointed and bat-like. Thin lips retract to reveal rotting, pointy yellow teeth. The fingers narrow into talons. Though his posture remains decrepit, the frail old man seems wired with an inner strength. A living corpse, more reptilian than human. A creature of the night.

The servants cleave to him, their bodies encircled by swarms of wasps and hornets. The domestics' faces are swollen and bleeding from the stings, their mouths sealed permanently with a sewn-on hundred-dollar bill.

The silver-haired Nosferatu rasps at Shep, each word hissing like a snake. "Yessss? You wisssh sssomething?"

The black woman, Charon, hovers behind the vampire's right shoulder. She smiles seductively at Shep, her leather coat having morphed into a pair of giant wings. The gunmen surrounding her have devolved into Neanderthals, their bulging eyes behind the gas masks jaundice yellow.

Virgil dragged Shep back through the crowd, away from the hungry eyes burning with malice, out of earshot of the whispers cursing him in the darkness. They managed to clear the area without incident, moving south along a deserted shoreline dusted white with sleet and snow.

Patrick faced into the wind, the frigid air helping to clear the hellish vision from his brain. "The vaccine . . . the hallucinations seem so real."

"What did you see?"

"Demons and the damned. Bags of flesh without souls."

"What I see are people who have no love of God nor respect for other human beings. They may succeed in crossing this river, but the baggage they carry with them is chaos and darkness. They'll die unrepentant and pay for their sins with a currency measured by the suffering they've inflicted upon their fellowman."

Virgil and Patrick huddled by the river's edge, watching as the last group climbed aboard the barge, the rich using their luggage as chairs on the acre of garbage. After a few moments the twin engines throttled to life, the churning propellers gradually moving the flattop away from the pier, pushing the scow on its southerly course toward Governor's Island.

The sensation was one of weight, as if the Earth's gravitational pull had suddenly doubled around him, turning Patrick Shepherd's blood into liquid lead. In a dream state he turned to his left, his movements slow and surreal, the terror causing his lower intestines to clench.

The Angel of Death stood by the Hudson's lapping waves, its black wing-like garment tattered and heavy, the creature exuding an aged musk that permeates Patrick's lungs. The hood had reduced the profile to a long, thin nose and pointed chin, the flesh spackled over bone. The knobby right hand clutched the scythe by its wooden handle, the blade held upright, the metal tinged a bizarre asparagus green.

The Grim Reaper watched the barge as it passed . . . and grinned.

HUDSON RIVER/JOHN F. KENNEDY INTERNATIONAL AIRPORT
10:47 P.M.

The Reaper hovered three thousand feet above the Hudson River, its nocturnal eyes piercing the darkness as it hungrily searched for any humans attempting to escape Manhattan.

Thirty-six feet long, with a sixty-six-foot wingspan, the MQ-9 Reaper was a five-thousand-pound unmanned aerial drone designed to provide its operators with long-range intelligence, surveillance, and reconnaissance. Larger and more powerful than the MQ-1 Predator, the Reaper was classified as a Hunter-Killer, its reinforced chassis armed with AGM-114 Hellfire missiles, GBU-12 Paveway II laser-guided smart weapons, and GBU-38 Joint Direct Attack Munitions.

The "Reapers" had arrived at JFK International aboard a C-130 Hercules transport plane, accompanied by a dozen technicians, four two-man flight-control teams, a mobile trailer containing two advanced cockpit ground control stations, and Major Rosemarie Leipply, a former drone operator and the unit's commanding officer.

It took two people to fly a Reaper aerial drone—a pilot using real-time imagery provided by infrared sensors and a sensor operator who controlled the aircraft's cameras, sensors, and laser-guided munitions. Major Leipply's trainees were neither commandoes nor pilots, they were the future of military combat: Generation Xers—video-game wizards whose reflexes and hand-eye coordination made them exceptional candidates for operating remotely controlled drones, their lack of flying experience actually an asset.

Leipply's star pupil was Kyle Hanley, his military bio typical among her crew. Poor grades in school. Anger issues. Impregnated his girlfriend at seventeen. Stole a car. Enlisted in the Army as an alternative to a jail sentence. Lasted two weeks before going AWOL. Sent to military prison, where he demonstrated superior reflexes in a video game called World of Warcraft—bringing him to the attention of Major Rosemarie Leipply.

Kyle was stationed on Reaper-1 as the drone's sensor operator. Before him was an array of monitors featuring night-vision and thermal scanners, the latter able to distinguish a warm-blooded human from the icy waters of the Hudson. Kyle called out instructions over his headset to his pilot, Brent Foehl, a three-hundred-pound behemoth wearing an old Brian Dawkins Philadelphia Eagles football jersey. "Two more jet skis. Zooming in on Camera One. We've got two passengers each. Descend to three hundred feet."

"Roger that. Descending to three hundred feet, coming about on course one-eight-zero . . . that should put you right in their path."

"Munitions locked and loaded."

"Targets are splitting up."

"I see 'em. We'll take 'em north to south."

"Roger that. Range: fifty meters. Reducing speed to forty knots. Hit 'em, baby. Let 'em feel the rain."

The hail of white bullets across the dark screen cut a lethal broadside swath through the first Jet Ski, instantly killing forty-eight-year-old South Carolina native Cindy Grace and her husband, Sam before homing in on their in-laws. A sudden blast of white light momentarily blotted out Kyle's thermal imager as the second jet ski's gas tank exploded.

"Four more in the hole." Kyle leaned over and high-fived his pilot.

"Enough!" Major Leipply felt her insides quaking, her undigested rations threatening their return. "Those bogeys are not monsters on a video game or enemy combatants, they are human beings. American citizens!"

"We had to make a game of it, Major," retorted Brent Foehl. "You think we could do this if we actually thought about what we were doing?"

"We'll try to keep it on the down-low," Kyle promised, bowing his head.

"That would help, thank you." She glanced at the digital clock posted above their station. "Finish your shift, I'll check on your relief."

Kyle waited until Major Leipply left. "Those bogeys are not monsters on a video game . . . blow me, Major Hypocrite. Funny how you never had a problem with it when we were picking off locals in Pakistan."

"Amen, brother. Eddie baby, what's the score?"

Sensor operator Ed White leaned out from his station on Reaper-2. "Six minutes, assholes. We're still up by fourteen kills."

"Don't start spending your winnings yet, hotshot." Brent launched Reaper-1 into a steep climb before following the Hudson to the south. "Coming to course two-seven-zero. Let's see if anything's brewing down by the remains of the G.W."

Kyle leaned over to whisper to his pilot. "Yo, man, the Hudson's a no-fly zone until 2300 hours."

"So says you. I was told anyone escaping Manhattan could infect the rest of the world with plague. No one's going near the Harlem River for at least another half hour, and I ain't losin' this bet. I don't care if it's a rowboat, a scuba diver, or a bunch of whores on a dinghy . . . as far as I'm concerned, if it leaves, it bleeds."

"True that."

Brent altered the Reaper's course, banking to the southwest, keeping the drone four hundred feet above the Hudson River's eastern shoreline.

Kyle scanned the four screens mounted above his control console. As the drone passed the George Washington Bridge, a large wake appeared on his Synthetic Aperture Radar, a remote sensing device that used microwave electromagnetic energy to create two-dimensional images that pierced both dense cloud cover and the night.

"Got something, partner. Big-ass bow wake and two wave trails. Come to course two-three-three. Target is 3.7 kilometers south of the bridge, moving south at twelve knots. Way too big to be a cutter. Drop us to five hundred feet so I can get a thermal reading."

Brent homed in on the coordinates, reducing his airspeed as he maneuvered the Reaper on a steady descent. "Forget it, it's just a garbage scow."

"A garbage scow . . . loaded with people! Dude, check out the thermal imager. We hit the mother lode!"

Eric White climbed out from his station console to take a look. "You're out-of-bounds, girls. The Hudson's no-man's-land until 2300 hours."

"Ignore him, Kyle. What's your body count?"

Kyle scanned the data scrolling across his thermal scan. "Two hundred and twenty-eight people . . . along with seventeen dogs and a few hundred rats."

"Man your weapons, partner, it's time to toast vermin."

Kyle typed in commands on his monitor, his pulse racing. "Locking and loading one Hellfire missile. Been waiting all night to launch one of these babies."

"Twenty seconds. Hurt so good . . . c'mon baby, make it hurt so good. Here we go, sweetheart . . . Four . . . three . . . two—"

Kyle grinned. "Time to light the night."

HUDSON RIVER, MANHATTAN
10:54 P.M.

There was no telltale sound of engines, no warning, simply a white-hot blinding phosphorescent burst of energy that ignited night into day, followed by a thunderous explosion that unleashed a blast wave of heat across the river, expanding in all directions.

Patrick collapsed to his knees and covered his head. Purple blotches clouded his vision, his eardrums rang as he was consumed by a wave of intense heat—

—followed by a blistering hail of shrapnel. Scalding hunks of garbage sizzled as they struck the Hudson's tainted waters, charred lumps of human flesh plopping down on the melting snow around him like burnt marshmallow spewed from a roaring campfire. Not until the debris stopped sleeting did he dare raise his head to gaze at the sinking island of fire.

The flame's diminishing glow revealed another spectator standing to his left. The Grim Reaper tilted its robed head back, the creature's bony arms spreading its wing-like cloak wider, as if the supernal being were inhaling the souls of the incinerated passengers.

The Reaper turned slowly to face him. Death's once-vacant eye sockets were now filled with hundreds of fluttering eyes. The curved olive green blade of his scythe dripped fresh blood.

Shep's throat constricted in a vise. His muscles locked up.

A gust of foul wind cooled the soggy earth. A crack of purple lightning rippled across the spinning heavens.

Darkness reached for Patrick Shepherd, pulling him toward Hell . . .

Lost Diary: Guy de Chauliac

The following entry has been excerpted from a recently discovered unpublished memoir, written by surgeon Guy de Chauliac during the Great Plague: 1346–1348.
(translated from its original French)

Diary Entry: May 17, 1348

(recorded in Avignon, France)

The Angel of Death walks among the living, sent by God to destroy us. That these are the End of Days, I have no doubt, for I have borne witness to the very evil that has summoned the Reaper to oversee our demise.

To what evil do I speak? The murder of innocent children. The burning of thousands of victims at the stake. The inhuman slaughter of an entire sect of people.

The blasphemy of our actions is as audacious as our denial of the sin.

That I am recording these thoughts to paper endangers my being as much as my daily exposure to the pestilence itself, yet I am compelled to render the words, if only to save my own soul from the Hell that awaits.

History has not been kind to the Jew—a resilient yet despised people who have been abused and slaughtered since the time of the Pharaohs and through the subsequent rise and fall of the Roman Empire. During the seven centuries that followed, hatred demonized itself into a new kind of persecution—the pogrom. In what can only be described as an almost erotic form of massacre, Christian crusaders would raid Jewish communities in the middle of the night, dragging innocent men, women, and children from their homes by the hundreds. Family members were forced to watch the mutilation and burning of parents and siblings—acts so horrendous that some Jewish men chose to kill their own wives and children rather than see them face the horrors that awaited them outside.

Unable to travel freely or acquire land, Jews turned to the profession of money-lending, an act restricted by canon law to Christians. High interest rates brought more hatred upon the Jews, who were forced into alliances with kings, bishops, and governing councils for protection. In France, this hatred was manifested by the Parisians' infamous "Trial of the Talmud" in 1240, the mass expulsion of Jews in 1306, and the pogroms that followed the Great

Famine, an era that preceded the plague we now face.

It was around the time of the Great Famine, in the spring of 1320, that a band of shepherds, the *Pastoureaux*, assembled in southwest France along the banks of the Garonne River. Desperation breeds fear, fear manifests into hatred, and the Jews were easy targets. Recruiting more pagans and peasants, the shepherds marched to Toulouse, killing every Jew they could find. When the movement's leaders were captured, they were set free by the monks, who pronounced their escape "divine intervention."

The killing spree continued, the evil spreading like plague. When it was finally over, the *Pastoureaux* had wiped out over one-hundred Jewish communities in the south of France, Spain, and Catalonia, brutally murdering more than ten thousand innocent people.

Though the *Pastoureaux* were eventually arrested, the crops continued to fail and the populace to starve, bringing more hatred upon those who had acquired the financial means to survive. In 1321, a rumor spread about an alleged plot involving the use of lepers to poison the wells in southern France, an attempt to overthrow the crown. When word reached Philip V, the king ordered mass arrests. Lepers who confessed were burned at the stake, those who pleaded their innocence were tortured until they confessed, then they, too, were burned at the stake.

Naturally, the lepers' wealth was confiscated by the crown.

If the vast treasures accumulated by the lepers made them enticing targets, then so, too, did the wealth of the Jews. By Holy Week, conspiracy rumors had expanded to include the Jews as coplotters, and eventually the Muslims.

The killing began anew. In Toulon, one-hundred-and-sixty Jews were marched into a bonfire. In Vitry-le-Francois, another forty Jews slit their own throats before their Christian torturers could reach them.

On April 26, a cosmic event took place in France that sealed the Jews' fate. Over a four-hour period, the afternoon sun was blotted from the sky as if engorged in blood. (Editor's note: solar eclipse) Convinced the day of doom was upon them and that the Jews were to blame, another series of pogroms was unleashed, with every Jewish soul living in France either exterminated or imprisoned.

I was but a young man during the Great Famine, my early years spent on my parent's farm in Languendoc, pushing a plow. The violence that spread through southern France was appalling, still I turned a blind eye to it, for what else could I do, other than thank the Almighty that I wasn't born a Jew.

Then one day, as fate would have it, I witnessed a young noblewoman tossed from her horse. The wounds were severe, her left leg broken. I was able to stop the bleeding and set the bone so that it healed properly. Months later I was paid a visit by her father—a moneylender and Jew. In gratitude for saving his daughter's leg and perhaps her life, her father agreed to pay for my medical education. I immediately enrolled in Bologna, where I studied anatomy and surgery . . . my course in life having been significantly altered by an act of kindness, my indifference to the plight of the Jews and any oppressed people changed forever.

All of which brings us back to the plague.

It came as no surprise when blame for the Black Death was eventually assigned to the Jews. In point of fact, one of the reasons I have worked so feverishly to find the cause of the mortality was to forestall this inevitability.

Though expected, the ferocity of the attacks on the Jewish community has left me sickened and stunned.

Like the pogroms of the past, the first massacre occurred during Holy Week. On the night of Palm Sunday, April 13 past, the Christian locals in Toulon raided the Jewish quarter, dragging family members from their beds. Homes were torched, money and valuables stolen, the Jews butchered in the streets, their naked bodies dragged through the village.

From Toulon, the pogrom spread as fast as the plague. Massive bonfires exterminated entire Semitic villages. In some cases, Christians offered to spare Jewish infants by baptizing them, but their mothers refused to turn against their faith and leapt into the fire, clutching their children in their arms.

By Easter, a new "fear" was spread throughout France, this one stating that Jews had caused the plague by poisoning the wells and springs. Though similar to the stories of 1321, the rumor was given further validity when it was reported that authorities in Chillon, Switzerland, had tortured confessions from a few of their Jewish villagers, linking a local Jewish surgeon and his mother with creating the plague poison.

As I pen this entry, a terrible cycle of evil runs rampant throughout Europe. By blaming the outbreak of plague on the Jew, the populace has acquired a Satanic sense of empowerment. Instead of feeling helpless, they feel proactive, believing their village might be spared if every Jew in the region is butchered. That Jews are also dying of plague makes no difference to these angry mobs, for even if innocent, the death of a moneylender carries with it the added benefit of erasing the killers' debt.

Three hundred Jews were murdered just last week in Tarrega, dozens more in Barcelona. New tortures are being invented every day, the latest being the violent placement of a crown of thorns upon a Jew's head, the object then mashed into the skull using a blunt object until the prisoner is dead.

And so the pestilence has unleashed an orgy of not only death but immorality, our fears and hatred bringing forth the very worst attributes of mankind. My soul is sickened by the conduct of my own species, and I have voiced as much to Clement VI. In response, the Pope recently issued a papal bull stating that it cannot be true that the Jews are the cause of the pestilence, for the plague infects them as well.

Still, the slaughter goes on.

Meanwhile, the Pope has left the papal palace for his retreat in Etoile-sur Rhône with Cardinal Colonna, swearing to me that he will keep the chamber fires burning to cleanse the air.

I have refused Clement's invitation to escape to the countryside. As chief surgeon, my rightful place is in Avignon, but there is another reason I have turned down my Pope's request—

—I, too, have been stricken with the mortality.

—Guigo

FOURTH CIRCLE

AVARICE

"It was squandering and hoarding that have robbed them of the lovely world, and got them in this brawl. I will not waste choice words describing it! You see, my son, the short-lived mockery of all the wealth that is in Fortunes' keep, over which the human race is bickering; for all the gold that is or ever was beneath the moon won't buy a moment's rest for even one among these weary souls."

—*Dante's Inferno*

DECEMBER 20

HUDSON RIVER SHORELINE

NORTHERN MANHATTAN

11:04 P.M.

(8 HOURS, 59 MINUTES BEFORE THE PROPHESIED END OF DAYS)

Patrick Shepherd opened his eyes. The human sleet had passed. The cloud cover overhead yielding to blotches of starry sky.

"Are you all right, son? You fainted dead away."

He looked up at Virgil, the old man kneeling by his side. "What happened?"

"Something destroyed the barge, probably a military drone. The blast wave must have knocked you out."

"All those people—"

"They died as they lived . . . only for themselves."

Shep's memory came flooding back. "Virgil, I saw him. He was standing on the shoreline, just before the explosion."

"Saw who?"

"The Angel of Death, the Grim Reaper. He's been following me since the chopper crash!"

"Calm down—"

"It's not the vaccine, Virgil, I'm not hallucinating this! You have to believe me."

"I believe you."

Patrick saw the look in the old man's eyes. "You've seen him too, haven't you?"

"Not tonight, no. But the souls of the wicked call out to him. We need to hurry if we are to find your family. Can you walk?"

Patrick stood, feeling light-headed. He couldn't remember his last meal. He could barely remember his name. He looked around, unable to get his bearings.

The shoreline was littered with smoldering debris and the remains of the dead. Arms and legs and upper torsos and parts rendered unidentifiable. Scorched beyond recognition.

To the south, Manhattan's skyline was cloaked in darkness, the outlines of its buildings blotting the horizon like a towering alien mountain range. The neighborhood to the immediate east was aglow in sporadic patches of orange light, its elevation above the banks of the Hudson making it difficult to discern the source. To reenter the city they must again ascend the gauntlet of highway overpasses and exit ramps, a task that seemed impossible.

"Virgil, I don't think I have the energy to climb another exit ramp."

"I know a better way." Virgil handed him the polished wooden box. "Don't forget this, your loved ones will need it."

Gripping Patrick's right elbow, he led him back toward the Henry Hudson Parkway and a stretch of sidewalk that intersected with Riverside Drive West.

CHINATOWN
11:09 P.M.

Thumpa . . . thumpa . . . thumpa.

The rhythmic pounding was relentless, baiting her consciousness through the blackness like a fish to a bobbing worm.

Thumpa . . . thumpa . . . thumpa.

So annoying . . . just let me sleep.

Thumpa . . . thumpa . . . thumpa.

Gavi Kantor opened her eyes, the teen lost in a sea of delirium.

Bare bulb. Bare mattress. The heavy stench of sex. People talking gibberish.

Thumpa . . . thumpa . . . thumpa.

She stared like a fascinated kitten at the IV bag dangling high above her head, her dilated eyes tracing its plastic tubing down to her forearm even as her drugged mind fought to gain a foothold on reality. When it did, she could only manage a moan.

"Help. Somebody please . . . hello?"

The sound echoed in her brain, hollow and distorted. She attempted to sit up and was introduced to the restraining straps around her ankles and wrists.

And that was when the dream is shattered, her captivity rushing at her so fast its gravity drained the blood from her face, and she bellowed a hyperventilated, anxiety-induced scream, "Oh my God . . . oh my God . . . help! Help me!"

She cried and thrashed about until her captor showed herself.

The Mexican woman was in her fifties. The fatty deposits on the back of her arms quivered as she coldly injected the elixir into Gavi's IV bag and adjusted the drip. "Go back to sleep, *Chuleta.* We'll tend to you shortly."

The thumpa . . . thumpa . . . thumpa of the industrial washing machine faded into blackness as the thirteen-year-old sank back into the depths of unconsciousness.

GOVERNOR'S ISLAND, NEW YORK
11:17 P.M.

The MH-60G Pave Hawk soared over New York Harbor, its pilot having taken a circuitous route from New Jersey to avoid the Hudson River's no-fly zone. The medium-lift combat helicopter contained two GAU-2B machine guns mounted along its side windows and a pair of .50 caliber machine guns situated just inside the cabin's two sliding doors. A pilot, copilot, and flight engineer were stationed in the cockpit, eight heavily armed US Army Rangers in back . . . along with one exhausted and slightly intimidated Army Reserve medic.

David Kantor felt like a field-goal kicker among defensive lineman. His insides recoiled as the airship lurched into a dizzying turn and descent, landing with a bone-jarring thud. The Rangers methodically checked their gear and disembarked before the twin engines were switched off.

Alone in the cabin, David closed his eyes, gathering himself mentally. *Why am I here? There must be a reason.* Forcing his exhausted leg muscles back into action, he regained his feet and jumped down onto the frozen lawn.

An MP stood by a jeep, signaling him over. "Captain Kantor? Come with me, please."

David climbed in the vehicle, gripping the edge of his seat as they accelerated across the frost-covered lawn, then over a dry moat's one-lane bridge into the harbor fortress.

Fort Jay's ancient quadrangle had been turned into a twenty-first-century command post. Rows of generators and a seemingly endless entanglement of heavy-duty cables crisscrossed the compound, providing power to portable banks of computer consoles and satellite dishes. David was led into one of four brick barracks, the interior illuminated using portable lights, the heat provided by kerosene furnaces. At the center of the room was a seven-foot-by-ten-foot map of Manhattan, spread out over a Ping-Pong table.

The commanding officer was a large man wearing an orange Racal suit, the upper torso of which hung tied off around his waist. He was yelling over the phone, his voice hoarse. "No, you listen! There are no exceptions to a Level-4 quarantine, I don't give a rat's ass what arrangements the senator made." The man's complexion changed from red to purple. "I don't care if your V.I.P.'s the king of Siam! And if you ever try to end-run me again, I'll personally fly down to DC, toss you and the senator in an Apache helicopter, and drop both of your asses in the middle of Times Square, you got that, maggot!"

The CO slammed the receiver down. "Ker . . . rist."

The MP hesitated. "Excuse me, sir. I brought Captain Kantor as ordered."

The big man looked up. "Who?"

"David Kantor, sir. We flew him in from New Jersey. Dr. Nelson's patient–"

"The medic, right . . . sorry." The CO turned to David. "Jay Zwawa, welcome to purgatory. Did Colonel Hamilton brief you?"

"No, sir. Only to say my services were needed for something special."

"If by 'special' you mean saving the lives of our president and several hundred diplomats while preventing a global pandemic, then yeah, I'd say this was special." Zwawa dismissed the MP, then handed David a military file. "The man we're after managed to acquire the only known vaccine to a biological weapon that's already infected half the population of Manhattan, killing off a good four hundred thousand by our latest estimates. Turns out the most wanted man in the world is a friend of yours."

David opened the file and stared at a photo taken three years earlier at a security checkpoint in Iraq's American-controlled Green Zone. "Shep? You're after Shep?"

Zwawa signaled to another MP, who escorted a petite brunette across the room, her torso swallowed by an Army parka. "Dr. Leigh Nelson, Dr. David Kantor. Tell Kantor about your patient."

"Seven hours ago, Patrick escaped an unnecessarily violent military invasion of the VA hospital in Manhattan aboard a medevac chopper. He crash-landed with a box of plague vaccine in Inwood Hill Park. I strongly believe he's making his way south through Manhattan, heading for the Battery."

"Why? What's in the Battery?"

"His wife and daughter."

David laid the file down on the table, his mind racing. "Shep told you his family was in the Battery?"

"Actually, no. I managed to track them down earlier in the day."

"We're sending in an extraction team, Kantor, only we can't take a chance that your pal won't flip out and destroy the vaccine. Captain, are you listening?"

David looked up, weary. "You want me to join your extraction team to hunt down Shep."

"Basically, yes."

"And what if his wife and daughter are no longer in Manhattan? What if they've already left the city?"

"He thinks she's in the Battery, that's all that counts. We know he attempted to contact her earlier today. It's the vaccine we're after, not your friend."

David walked around the table to the southern tip of the map, glancing down at Battery Park City. *It's close to Gavi's school, no more than a few miles. Don't appear too anxious. Force him to strike a deal.*

"One condition . . . this is it for me. No more deployments, no more stopgaps or reservist action. I want signed discharge papers now, or I'm not going anywhere."

"Done. Dr. Nelson, why don't you grab our boy here a couple of sandwiches from the mess tent while we fit him for body armor."

FINANCIAL DISTRICT, MANHATTAN
11:22 P.M.

It began with a headache, a dull throb, followed by an annoying purple blind spot. The chills came next, a prelude to the fever. The lump removed any lingering doubts—a small reddish welt about the size of a quarter, growing over a gland, perhaps the neck or armpit, perhaps the groin. By hour two the welt became an annoying purple grape, swelling with blood and pus. The fever raged on, the eyes became glassy. The sweat was unusually thick, laced with a distinct stench. The complexion paled as the buboes blackened, ripening to the size of a small onion, unleashing the Black Death into the bloodstream.

Nausea took over. A gag reflex ignited the vomit—traces of the victim's final meal laced with blood. The teeth and lips were stained, but vanity meant nothing when everything hurt. The pain was bone-deep. The muscles ached. Internal organs were failing. Hour four arrived, and there was no relief in sight . . . except death.

The sensation originated in the toes and feet as an icy chill. The numbness rose slowly up the legs, then into the groin. The intestines shut down. The sphincter unclenched, releasing the bowels—one last indignity of the human condition. A reflexive twinge disrupted the victim's final breath as Death's cold hand claimed the heart.

The soul abandoned the body. It lingered, but only briefly, drawn to the Light and its warm, soothing sanctuary.

The plague, too, had abandoned the body, its DNA instructing it to seek another victim. It was all too easy. A touch of sweat, an unavoidable sneeze or cough, a noxious breath inhaled, a bloody towel tossed in the garbage. Care was a fleeting concern when one was overcome by grief. Isolation was impossible in a two-bedroom condo in a ten-story high-rise.

Horror was the realization that set in after the first family member passed, leaving behind a fleshy sack of infection that had to be disposed of, coldly and immediately.

A closet? The stench was too overwhelming. *The hallway?* What would the neighbors say?

Scythe in Manhattan was the *Titanic* sinking without a solitary lifeboat. There were no miracles to be had, only a steady dose of reality: Death was advancing—

—and there was no escape.

Shelby Morrison sat on the living-room floor nursing her fourth beer, staring at the scented candle burning on the coffee table. Her girlfriend's uncle was seated by the living-room window. Rich Goodman taught high-school chemistry. His wife, Laurie, was in the master bedroom with their two young children.

Jamie Rumson was in the guest room. Moaning and retching.

There was no doubt in Rich Goodman's mind that his niece was dying. The question that burned like a hot cinder in his brain was how many members of his family would she take with her.

The answer was all of them . . . unless he acted coldly and decisively. And that was the dilemma, for what was the cost of survival? *My soul . . . to save my family. Do it now before the debate is moot . . . the girlfriend first.*

Rich Goodman picked up the brass candlestick, blew out the candle—

—and whacked Shelby Morrison hard on the back of her head. The blow fractured her skull with a gut-wrenching *craaack*. The thirteen-year-old's forehead struck the kitchen table as it followed the body's deadweight onto the floor. Dark blood pooled like pancake syrup along the linoleum, a bone fragment causing the wound to spurt like a whale's blowhole, splattering Goodman's left cheek and sweater.

Goodman tore the garment from his body and doused his face with dishwasher liquid and water. He stepped over the girl to access the kitchen window. For an infuriating minute and a half he struggled to release the double catch before he worked each prong with two hands and managed to fling the frost-covered window open.

An arctic wind whipped through the apartment, blowing out the candles.

Goodman dragged Shelby's body off the floor, blood dripping everywhere. Making haste, he half tossed, half shoved her corpse headfirst out the window, her midsection balancing precariously over the ledge. Grabbing her ankles, he coldly flipped the girl out the open apartment window.

Ten floors. Thirty-two feet per second.

The body struck the sidewalk with a pulse-jumping *thud*.

Goodman backed away, trembling yet somehow feeling a sense of accomplishment. His shoes slip-slid in blood as his criminal mind, entering its adolescence, raced to catch up with the deed. *Clean the blood first! No, no . . . do that after you toss Jamie. Then clean, bleach, and fumigate. Gloves . . . you'll need gloves and a mask.*

Goodman rummaged beneath the kitchen sink until he located a pair of women's rubber gloves and a small stack of cloth filter masks last used when he painted the kitchen six years ago. Dousing the gloves in bleach, he headed for the guest room—

—ignoring the queasiness building in his gut and the fever rising in his bloodstream.

WASHINGTON HEIGHTS, MANHATTAN
12:03 A.M.

They had followed Riverside Drive for several miles, their silence heavy against the backdrop of wails and agonizing screams hurled into the night from the neighborhoods to the east.

The cacophony of human suffering unnerved Patrick. Shards of memory flashed across his mind's eye, each image harnessed to a specific emotion that had defined the moment.

Purgatory at Fort Drum. Endless training. Burning hatred. Like sulfur.

Deployment. Transport plane. Kuwait's desert heat. Annoyance as they were herded into tents like sheep.

First night. Air-raid sirens. Scuds. Fumbling with his gas mask. Two more alerts. No sleep, no food, just liquids. Body armor and mask and hundred-degree heat. Combat is a terminal sauna. Confusion as his body had shut down. Anxiety as the medics tore off his flak jacket to administer fluids.

Baghdad. The sound of air being torn as an AK-47 round zips close by. Welcome to the show, rookie. Bone-rattling 155mm shells. Ears ringing. Nostrils burning from white phosphorous and oil.

Blood flows from an injured comrade. He dies as Shep fumbles to wrap the gushing mortal chest wound in gauze. An Iraqi mother clutches her armless infant . . . a husband his butchered spouse . . . a child her lifeless mother. This is the war the politician can never allow his fellow countrymen to see, a reality that energizes demonstrations and forges peace.

For the rookie soldier, combat replaces hatred with doubt, patriotism with questions.

Home is a million miles away, combat an island of loneliness and fear and confusion—confusion over right versus wrong, good versus evil, morality redefining itself with every passing moment. Eventually the rules simplify—to get home you have to survive.

To survive, you have to kill.

The village is on the Euphrates River, the locals rural, most having never seen an American before. The man and his son are rushing toward Patrick, their intent as alien as the Farsi phrases they are shouting from their mouths. He motions for them to stop, but his mangled translations are ignored. The distance is closing, the threat of a hidden explosive imminent as he enters their kill zone.

His weapon spits out a round of hot lead. The father goes down.

The son, all of nine, kneels by his murdered parent in disbelief, reality slowly bleeding into cognizance . . . churning into rage. The Iraqi youth sprints toward the invader who has stolen his father and perhaps the rest of his family, all in the name of a cause he cannot possibly fathom.

Life is conceived in an instant and ends in an instant. The boy's proximity defines him as a threat. The rules of survival are simple.

Patrick shoots the boy, reuniting him with his father.

Time passes in a vacuum. It is like that for animals. Shep has devolved into a subhuman grunt, a tool of the military establishment, intended to be used but not interviewed by the press, seen but never given a voice. Day becomes night, the dreams of a better life gradually fading into nightmares that force accountability of the soul. The mind is placed on life support, just as the military always intended. Creativity is vanquished, along with the memory of his wife's face and the child he'll never hold again in his arms—a relationship stunted in its infancy.

The geography changes. The first tour is over. Two weeks in detox, pretending to be Patrick Shepherd, and now he's back in Boston—

—alone.

The town house is cold and empty. His wife and daughter are long gone. There is no note, but the soldier already knows the story: The misery he has sown he must now reap.

Reality comes crashing in, the pain ripping apart his heart. Somewhere the souls of a hundred thousand dead Iraqis are smiling as the real torture begins.

He self-medicates. His friends come by, but the Patrick Shepherd they once knew is dead. The Red Sox inquire, but the image of the nine-year-old boy intervenes. He sells the house and moves into a bad neighborhood, just to be left alone.

Uncle Sam finds him eight months later. He is missed in Hell.

Deployment number two begins . . .

"**Patrick, open your** eyes! Patrick, look at me . . . can you hear me?"

"Virgil?"

"You went into a stupor. You were hallucinating again, weren't you?"

Hot tears poured from his eyes.

"Patrick?"

"I can't . . . sorry. Let's just . . . let's keep moving."

"Son, you can't run away from your own head."

"No! You don't talk about this, you just . . . you deal. You just deal with it and move on."

"Only you haven't moved on. Your family's moved on, but not you."

Ignoring the old man, Shep continued walking south on Riverside Drive.

"Stop playing the victim, Patrick. Victims are like worms, they prefer to live out their lives under a rock. It's easier in the darkness."

"Maybe the darkness is what I deserve."

"Spoken like a true victim."

"Leave me alone, shrink."

"If that's what you wish, we can part ways here. Your soul mate was convinced you still had something positive to offer the world. I guess she was wrong."

The words cut deep. "She really said that?"

"It's the only reason I'm here."

Shep turned to face the old man, his vision blurred by the tears. "I killed a child. He was as close to me as I am to you, and I shot him . . . right after I shot his father." Shep wiped snot from his watering nostrils. "I'm not a victim, I'm a murderer. How do I cleanse that from my soul?"

"You begin by taking responsibility for your actions."

"Are you deaf, old man? Didn't you hear what I just said?"

"What I heard was a confession. Guilt and self-loathing will not help you, son. If you really want to change, if you want to bring the Light back into your life, then you have to take responsibility for your actions."

"How? By going to confession for the rest of my days? By talking to a shrink?"

"No. You take responsibility, not by exiling yourself in pain but by transforming from being the effect to the cause, by making a positive difference in other people's lives. Within you lies the force of giving, sharing, loving, caring, being generous. No matter what you've done, there is still good inside you. "

"You don't get it. Making a difference is why I enlisted. I sacrificed everything . . . my family, my career, fame and fortune, all to right a wrong . . . to protect my country!"

"A righteous man, surrounded by chaos, corrupted by his environment."

"Exactly."

"Perhaps you should have built an ark?"

"Yes. Wait . . . what? Did you say an ark?"

"You're not familiar with the story of Noah? Noah was a righteous man born during a time of great corruption, only he had to confront difficult obstacles in his life, both in his heart and in the real world. Like you, Noah was far from perfect, but he lived within a world so completely corrupted by avarice—the excessive desire for wealth—that he stood out from all the others. The Book of Genesis calls these people the Nephilim, the fallen angels, men of renown. Giants. Decode the passage, and we gain a clearer picture. To the common man they were giants, not in their physical size but in their influence. They were the equivalent of the power brokers who have corrupted Wall Street and Washington, using fear and warfare to make themselves even richer. That they considered themselves to be on a higher plane of existence defined their arrogance, and by their rule man was corrupted, all to appease their unquenchable thirst for power and possessions. The physical world became a very dark place, void of the Creator's Light. And so the Creator sought out the brightest light—Noah—warning him that He would wipe man from the face of the Earth unless things changed. Noah attempted to warn the people, but they refused to listen. And so the Creator instructed him to build an ark so he might save his family and repopulate the world with a new generation who would seek fulfillment through the Light . . . through the act of treating one another with kindness the way God had intended."

"It's a nice story, and you spin it like a true psychiatrist, but come on . . .

animals lining up in pairs. A flood that covered the world? I've never taken any of those Bible stories literally."

"The Bible stories were never meant to be taken literally. The entire Old Testament is encrypted, each Aramaic passage revealing a vital truth about man's existence, the ancient wisdom intended to instruct man on how to remove chaos through transformation by reconnecting with the endless Light of the Creator."

"How come I never heard of this ancient wisdom?"

"It remained hidden for most of the last four thousand years. Only now, as we approach the End of Days, has the knowledge become available to everyone."

"And the story of Noah . . . what's the hidden meaning there?"

"We could spend weeks on the subject, so I'll give you the broad strokes that relate to your particular situation. According to the encrypted wisdom, every person who comes into our lives represents an opportunity for growth, salvation, and fulfillment. Noah built the ark as the Creator commanded, but he did so seeking revenge against those who had wronged him. As such, he never attempted to convince God to allow him to save anyone besides his own family. Building the ark was a test of transformation, and Noah failed miserably, accepting the elimination of the world's populace, refusing to offer the fallen ones an opportunity at redemption.

"The story of Noah happened on two levels. In the *Malchut,* an Aramaic term that refers to our physical world, there was an actual cataclysm that wiped out the populace. On a spiritual level, Noah's entering the ark represented the Light of the upper worlds entering the physical universe, the positive energy destroying the negative energy."

"God wiped out evil, I get it."

"No, Patrick. The Creator never wipes out anyone. The Light of the Creator can only do good. What determines the outcome is the receiver. Think of God's Light as electricity. Plug in your appliances, and one renders power to the tools of fulfillment. Stick your wet fingers in the socket, and you can be electrocuted. Either way, the nature of the Light never changes. When Noah entered the ark, the Light of the upper realms destroyed the negativity and greed that had stained the Earth. Those who cared and shared and tried to change themselves into something better were protected. Those who didn't were destroyed."

"Whatever happened to Noah?"

"He died, impure."

"Wait . . . you just said—"

"The ark was built so that Noah and his family could hide inside a protective vessel when the Angel of Death arrived to smite humanity. The flood lasted twelve months, allowing time for Noah and his family to complete the purification process while the souls of the wicked were sent to *Gehenom.* But Noah made one last mistake, the same mistake Adam made. The fruit that tempted Adam was not an apple, but a grape, or the wine that comes from them. Wine can be abused, placing man in touch with levels of consciousness that cannot sustain a connection with the Light. When the floodwaters receded, Noah succumbed to temptation, consuming the fruit of the vine in an attempt to access the upper dimensions. Noah was born circumcised. When his son, Ham, the future father of the land of Canaan found Noah lying drunk and naked, he castrated him. That's why Noah cursed the land of Canaan."

"That was a bit severe, don't you think?"

"Again, the story requires a translation. Noah went from being a righteous man to a victim, at least in his own state of mind. He had borne witness to the deaths of every living soul in the world, save his own family, but he never truly understood the root cause of suffering. Noah's failure was that he built the ark, then, like all victims, assumed his own pain would purify his soul. Because he never felt the pain of those who had suffered, he couldn't grow in a spiritual sense."

They continued walking west on Riverside Drive, Shep deep in thought. "I've caused great pain, Virgil. How do I seek salvation for my sins? I mean, if a guy like Noah screwed up, what chance in Hell does a schmuck like me rate?"

"When a man seeks to cleanse his soul from difficult circumstances, he must first create an opening in his heart."

"You're saying I've grown cold. Unfeeling."

"Have you?"

Shep contemplated his response. "Sometimes cold is the only way to survive. There's a lot of evil in this world, Virgil. When fighting terrorists, one can't always be Gandhi."

"Gandhi said, 'Be the change you want to see in the world.' Violence only creates more violence."

"Fine words, but not very practical when you're dealing with enemy insurgents intent on killing innocent people."

"The difference between an insurgent and a freedom fighter is defined by whose side one happens to be on at the moment. Either way, it means nothing to the dead. Life is a test, Patrick. Noah failed his test, his soul denied access into the endless Light of the Creator. Like all souls who fail to complete their *tikkun*, his soul was redeployed on another mission."

"Redeployed? You mean reincarnation?"

"The process is known as *Gilgul Neshamot*—translated as Wheel of the Soul. A soul descends upon the physical world because it needs to make a correction, oftentimes from a sin committed in a past life. If a soul lives one lifetime without fulfilling its correction, it may return only three more times to complete its *tikkun,* its spiritual repair. Of course, for each lifetime a soul is recycled, it risks exposure to the negative forces that lie in wait."

"Let me get this straight: You're telling me that everything I'm going through now is punishment for sins committed in a prior life?"

"It's possible."

"No, it's crazy. I have zero recollection of living a past life."

"Do you recall every moment of your life, from birth throughout your childhood?"

"Of course not."

"Yet you obviously lived them. When it comes to past lives, your conscious memory is as limited as your five senses, which lie to you with every passing moment. Accept it or not, every soul that lives in the physical world today has lived before. Who you were is not as important as the *tikkun* you must complete for your spiritual transformation."

"Okay, fine. For the sake of argument let's say I accept what you're saying. What do you think my *tikkun* is?"

"I don't know. Often, the things that cause us to react in the most negative ways are the things that require the greatest correction. The pain you're experiencing, the pain that is blocking the Light from reaching you . . . I believe it has something to do with your separation from your wife. Resolve the cause, and you resolve the effect."

Rounding Riverside Drive, they came to the western gate of an ancient graveyard.

Trinity Cemetery: Twenty-four acres of historic hillside overlooking the Hudson River. In 1776, its earth had been bathed in the blood of British and Rebel forces during the Battle of Washington Heights. In 1842, an outbreak of cholera, typhoid, and smallpox had converted the land into grave plots. Today, more than thirty-two thousand deceased were buried in tight rows or held in mausoleums on the property.

Shep hesitated, unsure about entering the graveyard.

"It's all right. The Angel of Death has no interest in a cemetery."

Virgil entered first, leading him past hundred-year-old oaks, the trees' thick branches creaking in the wind, their knotty roots bursting through the broken cement walkway that ascended to its snow-covered summit. Shep helped Virgil up a narrow path bordered by ancient headstones aged with America's history. John James Audubon. John Jacob Astor. John Peter Zenger.

The slope steepened. The old man breathed heavily. "I need to rest."

"Over here." They sat together on a dry landing, the moon peeking between clouds.

"Virgil . . . the Grim Reaper, is he evil?"

"No. The Angel of Death is a neutral force that tailors his pitch to his audience. There have been cycles of darkness in the history of mankind where Satan has grown very strong, blocking the Creator's Light. When evil becomes widespread, when lust and avarice lead to a depravity that runs amok, then the wickedness of the world summons the Angel of Darkness to stalk the earth. These are trying times, but the darkest hours can yield the greatest Light."

"You lived during those times. Tell me about the Holocaust. How did you manage to survive?"

"Why is this suddenly so important?"

"I don't know. Something inside of me needs to hear it."

Virgil closed his eyes. For a long moment he said nothing, his expression appearing pained in the moonlight. "Like the Iraqi child you believed you had to kill, I, too, was only nine the night the Nazi soldiers dragged my loved ones from our beds and marched my family and the other Jews through our Polish hamlet to the train station. They squeezed us into cattle cars . . . it was so difficult to breathe. People were climbing on top of one another to reach a solitary air vent. I must have passed out; the train's whistle summoned me from my dreams when we arrived at our destination—Oswiecim—Auschwitz.

"I can still see the bright searchlights and the soldiers in black uniforms armed with machine guns. Like it is tonight, the air was frigid, the heat from the train's engines expelling whirling gusts of steam. Moving through this fog was a well-dressed man, an embodiment of evil. We later learned his name: Dr. Josef Mengele.

"That was the first time I saw the Angel of Death. He was dressed in a white robe and hood, hovering over Mengele's left shoulder. He looked at me, then he looked at my mother and my three sisters, each eye socket clamoring with dozens of fluttering eyes—witness eyes—eyes that had looked upon evil. As I watched, the green-tinged blade of his scythe began dripping fresh blood.

"Mengele motioned to me and my father, and we were separated from the women and led away to the right. The rest of the women, the mothers with young children, the sisters and daughters, the aunts and the elderly . . . all were sent to the left. I remember people screaming as families were separated. I remember one mother refusing to pick up her wailing infant, knowing the bond would seal her fate. I saw the SS shoot her on the spot.

"That was the last night I saw my mother and sisters alive. We would learn that they were taken to the gas chambers. Later, when the crematoriums were built, the children were tossed directly into the ovens or thrown into open burning pits."

Shep felt ill, his body trembling.

"The men and boys deemed strong enough to work were marched down a road bordered by fencing and barbed wire that led to the main gate. There was a sign posted in German, *Arbeit Macht Frei*—Work Brings Freedom. There was no freedom at Auschwitz-Birkenau. There was no Light, only darkness.

"Each morning began with roll call and the daily selections. We were forced to stand naked in the cold, sometimes for hours while the doctors examined us, determining who would live and who would die. I was instructed by my father to run in place to flush my cheeks and show them how strong I was. They fed us rations that would starve a dog—a piece of bread, a ladle of soup. A slice of potato was a good day. We became walking bags of bones—human skeletons, the muscle and fat gone, our pulses visible through the skin. My mouth became sore from abscesses, and the chronic hunger drove me insane. One day I found a patch of green grass, ate it, and became deathly sick, the diarrhea nearly ending my life. The clothes we wore were foul, the shoes were wooden clogs, impossible to move very fast in, but it was better to wear them than be naked. To be naked was to be defenseless. To be naked increased our shame.

"Things grew worse after the crematoriums were up and running. The furnaces ran night and day, funneling fumes through a single chimney that billowed a great column of black smoke, darkening the sky like a winding river. There were days I imagined Satan's face in the thick air, watching us, laughing. I saw the Angel of Death several times after that, only his garments by then were black."

"Did you fear the Angel of Death?"

"No. I feared the Nazis. I feared Mengele. The Reaper was death, and death was salvation, but the Nazis made the journey so horrible that you did whatever you could to stay alive. We had also made a pact, deciding it was our duty to our families to survive, if only to inform the rest of the world about the atrocities we had suffered.

"We labored on the dead. We became dentists, extracting metal fillings and bridges. We loaded possessions—luggage, women's purses, jewelry, clothing. We disinfected the hair of the gassed victims and dried it in the attics. We emptied gas chambers and fed the ovens, the furnaces fueled by the fat of the deceased. We ground the remains of our people into compost and used it to fertilize the camp fields.

"We were living in Hell, but as your friend, Dante, illustrated, Hell has many circles. The deepest was Block 10, the medical-experimentation block. This was Mengele's pathology lab, his personal chamber of horrors, where he conducted experimental surgeries performed without anesthesia. Sex-change operations. Fluid transfusions. The removal of organs and limbs. Incestuous impregnations. Mengele preferred to do most of his work on children, especially twins. Young Jews and Gypsies were castrated, others placed in pressure chambers or frozen alive. They were blinded, tested with drugs, and exposed to tortures too gruesome to speak aloud. You would think these horrors would cause revulsion among the German medical institutions. Instead, their physicians flocked to Auschwitz to take part in Satan's circus, relishing the opportunity to work on human cattle. And every day, the trains brought Mengele fresh victims."

"Didn't anyone try to escape?"

"A few tried. Most were recaptured. When someone did escape, all of us were ordered to stand at attention for hours on end in the courtyard while the escapee was tracked down, then humiliated and hanged. Remember, Patrick, we were Jews, exiled into Hell because no one else wanted us . . . where would we have escaped to? Even the Allies that eventually liberated the camps never entered the war to save us. We were told we were God's Chosen and God had abandoned us, as so many of us had abandoned Him at Mount Sinai.

"Prayer became intolerable, we were humans reduced to vermin. Still a few of us managed to find a speck of Light, one last shred of human dignity that represented our refusal to accept our fate. For me, it was cleanliness. Each night before I lay down on my bunk with four or five other living corpses, I found a way to wash my hands, to cleanse them of the grit and ash deposited from the day. This was the way I fought my oppressors. This was the small victory that kept me out of the darkness."

"Did you ever believe you'd be rescued? How did you manage to maintain any hope?"

"In Auschwitz, hope was a sin. Hope kept you alive another day, and to stay alive you were forced to think and act in ways that were inhuman. I saw mothers renounce their children in order to live, I saw women allow themselves to be raped by the guards in exchange for a slice of bread. I witnessed one man suffocate his brother to steal his rations. Evil begets more evil, Patrick, as well you know. And yet, through the madness of it all, yes . . . we held out hope that one day the world would be a different place, that our survival would usher in the change we yearned for."

Virgil opened his eyes. "Now you've heard my story. Does it set your misery in perspective?"

"To be honest, it only reinforces what I came to realize in Iraq—that there is no God, that this Light force you claim is part of all of us can't possibly exist. If God is so omnipotent, why is there so much evil in the world? If God is so loving, why didn't He stop the Holocaust? If you're saying He chose not to, then He's no God of mine, He's a monster."

Virgil struggled to his feet, his back aching. "I understand your feelings, Patrick. I've heard these same thoughts a thousand times a thousand. The answer goes back to the true purpose of life, which is a test for the soul—the completion of its *tikkun.* Evil exists so that free will can have a choice."

"What choice did you have when your mother and sisters were being gassed? If God was around, why didn't He answer your prayers?"

"God did answer our prayers. The answer was no."

"No?" Patrick shook his head, incredulous. "And that's acceptable to you? The Nazis were tossing children in ovens and God was cool with that?"

"Of course not. But who are we to judge the Creator's plan? You're one man, living in your own limited microcosm of time and space, your entire perspective of existence based on a single lifetime spanning three decades, lived in a physical dimension that represents less than one percent of what's really out there."

"Those people were innocent, Virgil! They were victims of rampant evil."

"Rampant evil, as you call it, has been around a long time. Just for argument's sake, what response would have sufficed? Another flood? Or maybe God should have killed the firstborn son of every German household like He did in Egypt? How about a new set of plagues? Or were you expecting more of a fire-and-brimstone response . . . like an atomic bomb? Wait, that came later, and thank God, because the world's a lot safer for it now, isn't it? Free will, Patrick. God gave us His laws; it's our choice whether to obey them or not. Or do the words, 'Thou Shalt Not Kill' appear with a special clause that says it's okay to murder hundreds of thousands of innocent people if you want to take over the Arabian oil fields?"

"Saddam was evil. We came as liberators."

"And who did you liberate the Native Americans from when your ancestors stole their land and wiped out their tribes?"

Patrick started to reply, then mulled it over. "Okay, point taken. We did this to ourselves, and I am as guilty as anyone."

"Yes you are, and like every soul, unless you complete your *tikkun,* you'll be coming back again . . . assuming there's something to come back to."

Reaching the crest, they could see acres of headstones spread out across Trinity Cemetery. Down the sloping hill to the east was Broadway, the main thoroughfare glowing from the light of hundreds of bonfires.

Virgil pointed. "We can follow Broadway all the way to Battery Park, but the journey will be dangerous. The plague has spread, the people are in a state of panic. Keep the vaccine concealed beneath your overcoat, or we'll have nothing left for your wife and daughter. Patrick, are you listening?"

Patrick was not listening, he was staring at the path ahead, the cracked concrete sidewalk bordered on the right by a row of mausoleums, on the left by gravestones.

"What is it?"

"I think I'm having a major déjà vu."

"You've been here before?"

"I don't know. But suddenly I'm very cold, like I just stepped into a deep freezer. Oh, no . . . it's him."

Standing on the path, pointing a bony finger at a tombstone topped by

the sculpture of an angelic child, was the Grim Reaper.

"Virgil, he's here."

"The Angel of Death? Where?"

"Can't you see him? He's on the path just up ahead. He's pointing to a grave. Virgil, what should I do?"

"Don't get too close, do not let him touch you. Can you see the name on the headstone?"

"No."

"Are you certain you've never been to this cemetery before?"

"Yes!"

The Reaper motioned again, this time more emphatically.

Shep could feel the Angel of Death's icy tentacles crystallizing upon his flesh—cold, bony fingers clawing at his scalp, seeking to penetrate his brain. He had never felt terror like this before, not in Iraq, not in his worst nightmare.

The fear was too much, unleashing waves of panic that curdled his blood.

Patrick Shepherd ran!

In four strides he was past the mausoleums, sprinting down the east side of the hill through a maze of graves, the route made more treacherous by the snow cover. His mangled prosthetic arm swung wildly by his side, the curved blade clipping headstones, each shearing contact generating a spark—a beacon that threatened to lead Death straight to him.

The walkway appeared on his right, an icy stretch of twisting tarmac that angled along the periphery, ending at the east entrance on Broadway. He headed for it—

—tripping over a snow-covered grave marker that launched him face-first down the hill like a human toboggan—spinning, rolling—the snow rushing down his open collar, the night sky whirling in his vision, until he landed in a heap against the ancient stone foundation that supported the eastern gate of Trinity Cemetery.

Shep rolled over on his back, sore and disoriented. He was no longer afraid, the Reaper's icy presence gone. Lying in the snow, he stared up at the night, the full moon having risen high enough to reflect its light behind a haze of clouds. *God, if you're really up there . . . help me please.*

He heard the reverberations—boots on snow. He closed his eyes, waiting for Virgil to arrive.

The voice belonged to another. "There's one."

"Leave him be, he's mine."

"Marquis, you promised me the last one."

"You tryin' to push up on me, *capullo*?"

"No man. It's cool."

"Yeah, that's what I thought you said."

Shep sat up—the night bursting into colors as the boot connected with his face.

FIFTH CIRCLE

The Wrathful

"No gloom of Hell, nor of a night allowed no planet under its impoverished sky, the deepest dark that may be drawn by cloud; ever drew such a veil across my face, nor one whose texture rasped my senses so, as did the smoke that wrapped us in that place."

—Dante's Inferno

DECEMBER 21

USAMRIID

FORT DETRICK-FREDERICK, MARYLAND

12:27 A.M.

(7 HOURS, 36 MINUTES BEFORE THE PROPHESIED END OF DAYS)

Colonel John Zwawa wore the day with a weariness that grew with each passing moment, every challenge magnified by the blood pressure intensifying in his veins.

Chaos had broken out at the United Nations. Scythe had killed Iran's Supreme Leader, the highest-ranking political and religious authority of the nation. The Council of Guardians had convened in an emergency meeting in Tehran, naming Ayatollah Ahmad Jannati their new Supreme Leader. Jannati, head of the hard line Council of Guardians and one of the biggest opponents of democratic reform in Iran—a man who once told worshippers that he wished someone would shoot Israeli Foreign Minister Tzipi Livni—now commanded Iran's new cache of nuclear-tipped Russian-made ICBMs.

The new Supreme Leader remained sequestered in a private suite somewhere in the Secretariat Building; only a handful of mullahs knew his location. Through an emissary, he was demanding to be taken by chopper to

JFK International Airport, where he would be flown by private jet back to Tehran. What Jannati didn't know was that his last encrypted e-mail to Tehran had been intercepted by the NSA and translated.

Upon his return to Tehran, Iran's new Supreme Leader would declare himself *Mahdi,* the prophesied redeemer of Islam, initiating the *Yaum al-Qiyamah,* the Day of the Resurrection, where he, as the "Guided One," would rid the world of terror, injustice, and tyranny. Translation: Jannati intended to unleash Iranian insurgents armed with nuclear suitcase bombs, targeting Tel Aviv, Jerusalem, Riyadh, and the Victory Base Complex that served as the US military's headquarters in Baghdad.

Briefed in his suite at the UN, President Eric Kogelo had immediately ordered all evacuation plans delayed until dawn while he and his advisors decided how best to handle the developing situation.

While the president's staff covertly organized an emergency meeting of the United Nations Security Council, it was left to Colonel Zwawa to clean up the mess in Manhattan.

The Big Apple was rotting from the inside. New estimates coming in from health officials at ground zero were placing the death toll at well over half a million people, with the dead and dying contaminating another hundred thousand every hour. Apartment buildings and high-rises were becoming Scythe incubators, the streets and alleyways repositories for the infected, and there was nowhere to escape except into the rivers.

To contain a potential mass exodus, the military had deployed another four armed Reaper drones, along with three more Coast Guard patrol boats. Fortunately, the river's currents were swift, with water temperatures dipping below forty-five degrees, making immersion a baptism into hypothermia.

But Zwawa knew that desperation fueled creativity, and by dawn legions of survivors with access to scuba gear could manage to elude the Reaper's thermal scans and find their way to the shorelines of Brooklyn, the Bronx, Queens, and New Jersey, their arrival unleashing a global pandemic. As a precaution, Manhattan's neighboring boroughs were being evacuated, along with the Jersey shoreline communities of Englewood and all parts south to Bayonne.

The question remaining was how to deal with Manhattan.

The facility was located six stories underground, its existence known only to a handful of non-black ops intelligence personnel. Exiting the elevator, Colonel Zwawa was escorted through two more security checkpoints before being led through a nondescript white-tiled corridor to a set of steel doors labeled DEPT. C.

The locks unbolted, the left door swung open, greeting him with a blast of INXS from the interior sound system.

John Zwawa entered the chamber, the room heavily air-conditioned. Seated alone at a rectangular light table was a man in his forties, his head clean-shaven, his complexion kept tan all-year-round by a UV bed. He was wearing an orange-and-white Hawaiian shirt, surfboard shorts, and Teva sandals. The sunglasses were prescription, the pipe tobacco laced with opium.

As the colonel approached, he realized that the tabletop was actually a 3D hologram, the image created by a real-time satellite view of Manhattan. "I'm Zwawa."

The man tapped his sunglasses, the stereo lowering. "Dino Garner." The physical chemist reached beneath the table to a small refrigerator, removing a can of soda. "Dr Pepper?"

"No thanks."

"Been analyzing your problem, Zwawa. You got lucky and screwed at the same time."

"How's that?"

"Got lucky in that it happened in Manhattan. If this had happened in any other New York borough, you'd be screwed six ways to Sunday. As an island, you were able to establish a quarantine, hence you got lucky. You also got screwed, being that Manhattan is also the most densely populated and expensive piece of real estate in the world . . . all of which complicates my job—cleaning up your mess."

Garner walked around the table, eyeing the skyline from different angles. "In essence, this comes down to incinerating every biological and organic contaminant, dead or alive. That means human, rodent, flea, tick, bird, and the family Chihuahua—all while maintaining the infrastructure. As we say around here, that's a simple complexity. I'm still calculating the minimal number of delivery systems, but the basics are sound. We do this in two phases. Phase I is to create a very dense cloud ceiling of carbon dioxide just above Manhattan's skyline, combined with a few other stabilizing elements. We've already commandeered three turbine jet engine Air Tractors from a Jersey pesticide company, with two more on their way. Chemical payloads should arrive at Linden Commuter Airport within three hours. Another hour to load up, then it's a quick flight over the New York Harbor to Manhattan."

"I'm sorry, Mr. Garner . . . why do we need a CO2 ceiling?"

"It's Dr. Garner, and you need the cloud ceiling to contain Phase II, the burn. Think of it as putting a tent over a house before you fumigate it for pests. In our case, we're going to fumigate the entire city, using a combination of white phosphorous, magnesium, and a few ingredients you don't want to know about, all to create enough heat to melt flesh off the bone.

"Oxygen will be the catalyst, the combustible gas that fuels the furnace. Once the fuse is lit, it'll torch every pocket of oxygen in the city—the subway tunnels, the ratholes, the apartments—it'll all go up in one massive flash fire that will smother itself as soon as the air burns up."

"Jesus . . ."

"Jesus only walked on water. Incinerating two million plague victims and three million rats requires serious ingenuity. Fortunately for you, this is how I make my living."

Colonel Zwawa felt ill. "This carbon-dioxide cloud, how long must it remain over the skyline?"

"No worries. It'll disperse when the incendiary charges go off."

"No, I mean . . . how long can it remain in place before we decide to . . . you know, to fumigate?"

"I'm not following."

"The president needs an excuse to delay the UN evacuation. Scythe is spreading rapidly through human contact as well as the rat population, specifically by way of infected fleas. My epizootic specialist is worried about these same fleas infecting birds, especially pigeons. An infected pigeon could deliver Scythe into New Jersey or the other four New York boroughs by first light."

"The carbon dioxide will kill any escaping bird. There's your excuse for releasing the CO2 cloud."

"And for delaying the UN evacuation."

"You're a blessed man, Colonel. To answer your question, in this weather the cloud should remain stagnant until dawn. We'd have to launch Phase II by then, or the sun's rays will gradually burn it off. Figure 8 A.M., give or take a few minutes."

Colonel Zwawa checked his watch. "Seven and a half hours. Can you pull everything together that soon?"

"It'll be done, and that's all you need to know. As for the infrastructure, it's gonna be three to five months before anyone can move back in, but that's your headache, not mine."

"May I ask you a personal question, Doctor?"

"You want to know how I sleep at night."

"Forget it." Zwawa shook his head, turning for the steel doors.

"Guilt is for civilians, Colonel, blame is for the pundits and politicians. Down here, we make choices . . . it's an old game we call us or them. You want my advice? Take a Vicodin and a shot of Captain Jack, and you'll sleep like a baby."

TRINITY CEMETERY
WASHINGTON HEIGHTS, MANHATTAN
12:33 A.M.

There were six of them, all Latinos, all in their teens, dressed in black jackets and red, white, and blue bandannas—the colors of the Dominican Republic's flag. A violent group, the DDP (Dominicans Don't Play) had carved out their territory in Washington Heights, Queens, and the Bronx, moving drugs through their connections in the Colombian crime cartel.

A cornrowed eighteen-year-old named Marquis Jackson-Horne straddled Shep, leaning in close. "No wallet or bling . . . whoa, what's dis? Got somethin' in your coat fo' me?"

He tore open Shep's jacket, revealing the polished wooden box. The gang leader grabbed it—

—Shep's prosthetic arm jumped to life, its curved blade pressing against the muscular youth's Adam's apple, his right hand grabbing a fistful of Marquis's leather coat, drawing him in close. "Sorry, friend, you can't have that."

Instantly, five 9mm handguns appeared, every barrel aimed at Shep's face.

"Remove the blade, nice and slow, whitebread."

"If they fire, I'll still manage to slice open your throat. Tell your crew to back off, and I'll let you go."

No one moved.

"There's no money in the box, just medicine . . . for my daughter. I know the world's gone insane, and you could give a rat's ass, but maybe just once before you meet your Maker, you and the homeboys here could do the right thing."

The gang leader's eyes widened, revealing an inner rage. "Do the right thing? You messin' with the wrong gangbanger, Spike Lee. I'm a hater. I'm fightin' a war."

"I just got back from fighting a war. Four tours' worth. Now I'm a hater, too, only you know what I just realized? Haters hate because they think they've been wronged, now all they want is justice . . . only justice and happiness don't mix very well. My family hasn't been in my life for eleven years. I blamed a lot of people for that. Now I just want them back."

Marquis's eyes lost their intensity. "Nobody move. You neither, Captain Hook." Gently, he unlatched the box, revealing the vials of serum. The gang leader turns to his crew. "*Ya stuvo.*"

The Dominican teens looked at one another, unsure.

"You heard me. Roll out!"

Tucking their guns back into their waistbands, the teens walked away.

Shep waited until they'd reached Broadway before releasing their leader. "How old are you?"

"Old enough to kill."

"I've killed, too. Trust me, there are better ways to live out your days."

"Fuck you. You don't know shit about me. My mother's dead. Cousins, too. My little sister's dyin' in her bed, spittin' up blood. Six years old, never did nuthin' to hurt nobody."

Shep reached inside the box, removing two vials. "Give this to your sister. Have her drink it, you do the same."

"You crazy."

"It's plague vaccine. Take it. Tell no one about it."

The gang leader stared at the vials. "This for real?"

"Yeah. Watch the side effects, it causes hallucinations. It probably won't bother your sister, but it makes you see things about yourself you may not want to see."

"Why you givin' me this?"

"I have a daughter."

"And me?"

"Call it a chance at transformation."

"Maybe I should just take the whole box."

"You'd never make it home. The military's after me, no doubt they're watching us by satellite as we speak. Go. Save your sister. The two of you find a way off this island."

Marquis hesitated. Then he jogged off.

Shep turned—

—confronted by Virgil. "That was dangerous. He'll come back with his gang to collect the rest of the vials. We have to go."

"What about the Grim Reaper?"

"Pray your act of kindness buys us some time before he finds you again."

UNITED NATIONS PLAZA

12:43 A.M.

Bertrand DeBorn waited in the back of the black Chevy Suburban, seated behind the driver. Both Ernest Lozano and the secretary of defense were wearing gas masks.

The former CIA operator glanced at his boss in the rearview mirror. The rebreather secured to DeBorn's face had left his silky white hair unkempt, revealing patches of scalp and liver spots near the head straps. His gray-blue upturned eyes appeared menacing behind the plastic shield as they stared, unblinking, out the rear window.

Lozano saw Sheridan Ernstmeyer reappear beyond the secured perimeter, escorted by a man wearing a white Racal suit. The female assassin double-timed it back to the Suburban and climbed in the backseat. She was breathing heavily behind her mask.

"Well?"

"It's bad. They gave up on containment twelve hours ago, now they're just trying to organize an evacuation."

"Can your contact get word to the president that I'm down here?"

"He's just local PD; there's no way he can reach him."

DeBorn slammed his fist against the back of the driver's seat. "I'm the damn secretary of defense!"

"Sir, all communications have been shut down, with the exception of a secured line between Washington and Kogelo's suite. No one's allowed on the president's floor, not even the CDC."

"Sonuvabitch." DeBorn's mask fogged up. He fought the urge to rip it from his face and heave it out the window.

"Sir, there's something else. Special Ops is organizing an assault team, my contact's one of the cops selected for their ground support. They're after Shepherd."

DeBorn's gaunt face paled.

"It's not what you think. Shepherd escaped the VA hospital with a case of Scythe vaccine."

DeBorn sat up, his mind racing. "We need to find Shepherd before they do . . . he's our ticket out." The secretary searched his jacket pockets, retrieving a piece of folded notepad paper with Beatrice Shepherd's address.

"Get us to Battery Park City . . . fast."

Ernest Lozano turned around to face him. "Sir, every street in Manhattan's stuck in endless gridlock. People have abandoned their cars–"

"Drive on the damn sidewalk if you have to, I don't care. We need to get to Shepherd's family before the military does."

MANHATTANVILLE/MORNINGSIDE HEIGHTS
1:37 A.M.

The buildings and streetlamps were dark, the densely packed neighborhood set aglow by hundreds of car fires and the streams of conflagration dispensed from the authorities' flamethrowers. Plague-infested corpses riddled the streets. Plague-riddled victims staggered along sidewalks and lay sprawled on curbs—their mouths and nostrils blotched in blood as if they had just finished cannibalizing the neighborhood. The surreal scene swept south down Broadway, as if taken straight out of a 1970s horror movie.

Homeland Security, dressed in storm-trooper black, their faces concealed behind gas masks, advanced in formation down the vehicle-littered avenue, herding the angry mob back inside their apartment dwellings. Sensing an ambush, a cop ignited a cluster of bodies with his flaming stream of propane and natural gas, chasing off a black woman and her two young children who had been hiding behind the remains of the deceased. The shrieking mother dragged her screaming kids down the sidewalk, all three engulfed in the blaze, the infested flesh dripping from their bones.

Shots were fired from the surrounding buildings' darkened recesses. Two officers went down; their comrades returned fire.

"Pull back!"

Dragging their wounded, they moved toward the safety of their fleet of Hummers.

A Hispanic woman, hysterical over the death of her infant, tossed her lifeless child from a third-story window. The fragile corpse struck one of the retreating storm troopers, who freaked out—

—his reaction compelling dozens of enraged, grief-stricken parents to hurl the infected remains of their dead offspring from their balconies and windows, pinning down the militia in the middle of Broadway's southbound lanes.

The change in tactics energized the revolt. Within minutes, hundreds of locals were streaming out of their apartment buildings, armed with baseball bats and knives, handguns and assault weapons. A final outburst of flames, and the battle was over, the masses victorious, their burning rage quelled, but only for the moment.

Reclaiming the streets, the multitudes scattered, unleashing their wrath upon local businesses, smashing windows as they looted their own neighborhood.

Virgil pulled Shep from the scene, leading him around rows of abandoned cars, the campus of Columbia University in the distance. "The breakdown of social order . . . it's always followed by chaos. We're bearing witness to a test of faith, Patrick. It appears as if Satan has won."

The Reaper hovered a thousand feet above Broadway, its scarlet eyes focused on the street below—

—its remote operator, thirty miles away, scanning faces in the crowd on his monitor. Each head shot was sent to a physiognomic range finder, which created a two-dimensional facial map using eighteen plotted points. The reciprocal points were then compared to a three-dimensional morphology of the targeted subject's face, already loaded into the computer.

The optical scanner zoomed in on the old man and his younger companion as they moved quickly south down Broadway. The younger man's image was acquired, pixelized, refocused, and plotted.

MATCH CONFIRMED: TARGET ACQUIRED.

"Major, we found him! Subject is heading south on Broadway, approaching West 125th Street."

Rosemarie Leipply leaned over the drone pilot's shoulder, confirming the match. "Well done. Lock onto the subject, then alert Captain Zwawa's people on Governor's Island. Be sure they're receiving the live feed."

"Yes, ma'am."

GOVERNOR'S ISLAND, NEW YORK
1:53 A.M.

The MH-60G Pave Hawk reverberated on its landing struts, the combat helicopter's rotors violating the cold December night. The nine members of the Army Ranger extraction team were already seated in back, waiting impatiently for the last recruit to climb aboard.

David Kantor willed his exhausted body to carry him and the forty pounds of equipment strapped to his back across the lawn to the waiting airship. As he approached the open side door, two Rangers reached down and dragged him on board, practically tossing him onto the far bench.

Major Steve Downey leaned in next to him, powering on the headset built into David's mask. "You Kantor?"

David nodded.

The Ranger offered a gloved handshake, shouting to be heard. "Major Downey, welcome aboard. I understand you're familiar with our target."

David grabbed on to the bench as the helicopter lurched into the air. "We served a tour together in Iraq."

"That it?"

"Yes, sir."

Downey pulled his mask and hood off, revealing spiked hair, a goatee, and harsh hazel eyes. "Your record shows you crossed paths on at least three tours. Your personnel records indicate you invited him to your oldest daughter's wedding, though he never showed. Don't screw with me, Kantor. There are lives at stake . . . the president's life, the UN delegates, and just maybe every person fortunate enough not to be in Manhattan. My mission is simple—get the vaccine. Whether your pal survives the night is up to him . . . and you. Am I being clear?"

"Yes, sir."

"Once we land in Morningside Heights, we'll divide the squad into two awaiting military vehicles. I want you seated next to me."

"Yes, sir. Wait . . . did you say Morningside Heights? I was told we'd be landing in the Battery."

"One of our drones spotted Shepherd in the vicinity of Columbia University, that's our new destination. The wife's strictly backup at this time. Is that a problem, Captain?"

David closed his eyes behind the tinted mask. "No, sir."

CATHEDRAL OF ST. JOHN THE DIVINE
AMSTERDAM AVENUE, MORNINGSIDE HEIGHTS
1:57 A.M.

There were thousands of them. Some had traveled miles on foot, others lived in the surrounding neighborhoods. Their government had abandoned them, the medical industry had no answers, and so they sought help from a higher power, pushing their infected loved ones in wheelbarrows and shopping carts. They pounded the sealed arched doors and shouted into the night, their pleas for last rites and salvation falling upon deaf ears . . . just as they had in Europe 666 years ago.

Inside the cathedral, the Reverend Canon Jeffrey Hoch moved through the massive hall, his face cloaked behind a red silk scarf. Several thousand people were scattered throughout the chapel, many asleep in the pews.

They had started arriving just before noon, senior citizens at first, as if they could sense the threatening storm. By two o'clock, hundreds were pouring in—angry families and frustrated tourists caught in the chaos, everyone seeking a warm place to wait out the hours, preferably one with a clean restroom.

The rush began an hour before dusk, when anger and confusion turned to desperation, desperation to fear. A mandatory curfew meant several hundred thousand people would be channeled into school gymnasiums, missions, and Madison Square Garden, the latter igniting memories of Hurricane Katrina and the chaos of the Superdome—only this time the desperate, destitute, and poor would be sharing space with the infected. As the multitudes began lining up along Amsterdam Avenue to be screened, Bishop Janet Saunders had ordered the clergymen inside, the cathedral sealed.

The Reverend Hoch paused to light a prayer candle, joined by Mike

McDowell, the dean of the religious school. "Reverend, this isn't right. How can we keep the public from sanctuary? How can we continue to deny the dying their last rites."

"I am no longer in charge. You must speak with Bishop Saunders."

"John the Divine is a multidenominational cathedral. I don't recognize the bishop's authority."

"Unfortunately, Mr. McDowell, I do."

The pounding on the three-ton bronze doors continued unabated, the sound dispersed throughout the cavernous 601-foot-long nave. McDowell headed down the center aisle for the apse, where Janet D. Saunders, the second woman elected primate in the Anglican Communion, was leading a small group of worshippers in prayer.

"Bishop Saunders, may I have a word with you in private?"

The sixty-seven-year-old Kansas native looked up. "Whatever you have to say, you can say it in front of my flock."

"With all due respect, Bishop, the majority of your flock are locked outside the cathedral, and they're terrified. St. John's can take them in; we can provide them with sanctuary."

"The Almighty has unleashed His plague upon this city, Mr. McDowell. Everyone outside these walls has been exposed. Open the doors now, and you'll condemn the few whom Jesus has chosen to survive the night."

Heads nodded in agreement.

McDowell felt his face flush. "And if we are being punished by the Almighty, is this not a prime example of our wickedness? Of our corruption? If we simply allowed those in need to seek refuge in our basement away from the uninfected, would this not convince God that we are worthy of being saved?"

The worshippers looked to the bishop for rebuttal.

"I considered this, Mr. McDowell. As the hour grew late, I consulted the Bible for answers. The first time God decided to strike down the wicked, he instructed Noah to build an ark, a vessel of salvation similar in size to the dwelling in which we now find ourselves. Noah warned the people, but they refused to listen. Once the rains began, no one else was allowed inside the ark, for the Angel of Death had come. The ark is now closed, Mr. McDowell. The Angel of Death shall not enter these premises."

Thirty-seven worshippers breathed a sigh of relief, a few actually applauding.

The thunder of the helicopter's rotors reached them seconds before the spotlight isolated them from the darkness.

Patrick and Virgil looked up, the Army chopper hovering overhead, preparing to land.

"We need to find cover . . . better yet, a crowd."

"This way." Virgil led him down West 113th Street past rows of candlelit apartments, the spotlight staying on them like an angel's halo. They emerged on Amsterdam Avenue, the Cathedral of Saint John the Divine looming across the street, the grounds a refugee camp for tens of thousands. They quickly melted into the crowd, ducking low as they gradually made their way around the Peace Fountain—

—the spotlight losing them as they cut across a snow-covered expanse of lawn, emerging on Cathedral Parkway.

The night swirled. Patrick's vision blurred. He looked up—

—shocked to see a black winged demon hovering eighty feet overhead, its unblinking scarlet eyes staring at him, as if looking through the void into his soul.

Virgil grabbed him by the arm, tugging him hard. The two men cut through an alleyway sandwiched between apartment buildings, only to find the passage blocked by stacks of human corpses. Retracing their steps, they zigzagged around abandoned vehicles.

The Pavehawk's searchlight picked them up again as they hurried down Amsterdam Avenue. Virgil bent over, out of breath. "Go on . . . without me."

"No." Shep looked around, desperate to find a place to hide—

—as a flock of winged demons dropped from the sky overhead. Time slowed to a crawl, each double cadence of his beating heart magnified in his ears, the night creatures descending from above, attempting to swoop him up in their talons—

The searchlight swiveled as the chopper battled a forty-mile-an-hour gust of wind, the airship's heavenly blue light illuminating a storefront sign:

MINOS PIZZERIA.

Every business on Amsterdam Avenue had been vandalized, every window broken, every store left in shambles *except* for Minos Pizzeria. As the light refocused on Shep, he could see sixty to eighty homeless people standing guard outside the premises—and not one looter dared cross their gauntlet.

Shep helped Virgil to the storefront, the ragged men and women blocking their way. "Please, we need a place to hide."

A stocky Italian man with salt-and-pepper hair and an unruly goatee and glasses pulled out a large bowie knife. "Walk away or die."

Shep saw the dog tags hanging around the man's unshaven neck. "Patrick Shepherd, Sergeant, United States Marines, LIMA Company, Third Battalion, 25th Marine Regiment."

"Paul Spatola, 101st Airborne."

"Who are you guarding, Spatola?"

"The owners of the pizzeria. They're good people."

"I can save them." Shep opened the polished wooden box, showing him the vials. "Plague vaccine. The government wants it to disappear. We need sanctuary—fast."

Spatola looked around, his eyes drawn to the helicopter's searchlight. Rangers were rappelling down to the street. "Come with me." He led them through the crowd of homeless, then banged on the rolled-up aluminum security gate covering the front glass doors.

The door opened a crack. The man inside remained hidden in the shadows, his voice muffled behind a painter's mask. "What's wrong?"

"This vet and his grandfather need to get off the streets. He says he has a vaccine for the sickness."

"A vaccine?"

Shep pushed in closer. "The military's right behind us. Help us, and we'll help you."

A woman's voice called out from inside the restaurant. "Paolo, don't!"

A flashlight passed over Patrick's face, the small box in his hand, then on Virgil. "Should I trust you?"

The old man nodded. "Only if you and your wife wish to survive this night."

On Amsterdam Avenue, heavily armed Rangers moved through the crowd, searching faces. "Inside, quickly." Unlocking the grating along its base, Paolo rolled the gate up high enough to allow the two strangers to enter.

Paul Spatola quickly slammed the security fencing back down so it locked, then passed the word, "No one gets through."

The pizzeria was empty. An aroma of Italian meat coming from the dark recesses of the kitchen set Shep's stomach to gurgle. He headed for the food—

—Paolo stopped him. "I need to check your skin for infection."

They lifted their shirts and lowered their pants, Paolo's light scanning their necks and armpits, legs and groins. Shep jumped as a cat nuzzled his left calf muscle from behind.

"You seem clean. Come with me." They followed the Italian past checkerboard-clothed tables back through the kitchen. Spread out on a row of aluminum tables were half-sliced salamis and bricks of cheese, loaves of bread and a tray stacked with already prepared sandwiches. "Take what you want; the homeless get the rest. Everything's spoiling anyway."

Shep grabbed a sandwich, consuming it in three bites. "Virgil, take something."

"I've eaten, and we don't have much time. The soldiers will—"

The aluminum door of the walk-in refrigerator swung open, revealing a pregnant Italian woman with jet-black hair. In her hand was a shotgun.

"It's okay, Francesca. They're clean."

"No one's clean. This plague will kill us all."

They heard men arguing outside. Shots were fired.

"Quickly, inside the cooler!" Paolo hurried Shep and Virgil inside the walk-in refrigerator, slamming the door closed behind them.

They huddled in the stifling darkness alive with meowing cats and the rotting stench of spoiling perishables. A dull circle of light from the woman's dying flashlight settled on her husband, who had pushed aside crates of lettuce and was kneeling by the exposed wet patch of wood floor. In his hand was a thin piece of bent wire. Feeding it through a knothole, he fished until he found a loop of rope. Standing, he pulled hard, dragging open a trapdoor set on hinges. The flickering light from an oil lamp below illuminated a ladder leading down to what appeared to be a basement.

Paolo climbed halfway down, waiting on a rung to assist his pregnant wife.

Virgil was next, followed by Shep. Paolo climbed back up and called for the cats, who scrambled down the hole. Resetting the trapdoor, he slid down the ladder, joining the others.

They were in an old wine cellar, the stone walls and mortar dating back several centuries. The room was stuffy but dry. Cardboard boxes and an old dresser were stacked against the far wall. "Please." The Italian handed the oil lamp to Virgil, then he began moving aside the stack of boxes, assisted by Shep. Hidden behind the chest of drawers was a small wooden door sealed with a padlock.

"The passage connects with the Eighth Avenue subway line. We can follow it south as far as 103rd Street, then cut through Central Park. Francesca's brother has a small boat in the Battery that can take us off the island."

"The Battery? My wife and daughter are in the Battery!"

"Then the vaccine for your safe passage."

"Yes, absolutely." Shep opened the box, removing two of the remaining eight vials.

Francesca snatched the lantern from Virgil. "How do we know it even works, Paolo? How do we know it won't kill your son?" Francesca shined the light on her belly, then at Shep. "Are you a doctor, Mr. War Vet?"

"The name's Patrick, my friends call me Shep. This is Virgil. I have no medical training, so I can't even guess whether the vaccine will affect your baby. So far, the only side effect I've experienced are hallucinations—"

"—which is why I haven't taken it yet," adds Virgil.

"No medical training, huh?" She held the clear elixir up to the light while her husband opened the padlock sealing the small door. "Three years ago I was studying to become a registered nurse, only I had to quit. Now, instead of working in a hospital with a decent insurance plan, I get to serve pizzas and care for the homeless."

"Darling, now is not the time. Forgive my wife, she's due any day now."

Virgil squinted against the raised lantern. "For what it's worth, Francesca, I was at the VA hospital earlier with Patrick. They had a pregnant woman infected with plague in an isolation tent. I suspect all who worked there are probably dead by now. As for the homeless, it seems they have repaid their debt."

Paolo dragged open the wood door, unleashing a howling gust of cold air into the basement. "The homeless are no match for assault weapons, Francesca. Yes or no, should we take the vaccine?"

"For the baby's sake, I'll wait. You take yours."

"Yes, that's wise . . . my wife is the wise one." Paolo loosened the cork, then drained one of the vials of vaccine. Lantern in hand, his wife crawled through the opening, followed by Virgil, Shep, and the cats.

Tossing aside the empty vial, Paolo dropped down on all fours and crawled in after them.

UNITED NATIONS

2:11 A.M.

They were connected to one another via audio headsets, their spoken words translated into text on their monitors in French, Russian, Chinese, and English—the languages of the five permanent Security Council nations.

President Eric Kogelo drained his bottled water, waiting for the President of the Security Council to take roll.

"Hello. This is Rajiv Kaushik, the Assistant Secretary General. I regret to inform you that the President and Secretary General were both exposed to plague; neither is well enough to participate on this call. Unless there are any objections, I will be fulfilling their duties during this emergency session. Is the gentlemen from France on the line?"

"*Oui.*"

"The gentlemen from the Russian Federation?"

"*Da.*"

"The gentleman from China?"

"This is Xi Jinping. President Jintao has taken ill. Since I am the senior member of our party, the Standing Committee has requested my presence at this meeting."

"Thank you, Mr. Jinping. Is the gentle lady from Great Britain with us?"

"Yes, I'm here."

"The gentleman from the United States?"

"Present."

"Then let us begin with the gentleman from the United States. We have been repeatedly promised that an evacuation is imminent. Why does it seem we are purposely being left here to die?"

"My apologies if it feels that way. This situation is very serious. Our goal is to commence the airlift at dawn."

A flurry of Russian shot back at President Kogelo, the translated text coming up on his screen in spurts. "This is a disgrace. Entire delegations have been wiped out. You cannot keep us quarantined, it is in direct violation of the United Nations charter."

Kogelo took a deep breath, refusing to lose his cool. "President Medvedev's concerns are shared by all of us, my own staff included. But let us be clear. We are facing an outbreak that could easily turn into a global pandemic if the quarantine is not 100 percent secured. The death toll in Manhattan has now exceeded half a million people. All of us have lost colleagues, allies, loved ones, and friends. The last thing any of us wants is to rush the evacuation without proper precautions and end up being the carrier who unleashes the plague in your own countries, and across the globe."

"We have heard reports that this plague originated in your CIA-run bio labs."

"Again, a half million people have died, more are suffering, and the vast majority are Americans. There will be a proper time to investigate and assign blame. For now, our priority is to safely transport United Nation diplomats and heads of state to a secure medical facility on Governor's Island. To accomplish this requires each evacuee to wear a self-contained environmental suit, which will prevent any infected individuals from passing the plague on to others. The environmental suits are en route as we speak, they will be brought to your suites as soon as they arrive. I am also being told that a vaccine has been located that can not only inoculate but reverse the effects of the plague."

Kogelo waited for the delayed murmurs as his words were translated. "While this is good news, there is another issue that must be discussed. Mr. Kaushik?"

The acting Security Council President took over. "President Kogelo has strong reason to believe Iran's new Supreme Leader, upon his return to Tehran, will provide Iranian insurgents in Iraq, Israel, and possibly the United States with nuclear suitcase bombs. The transmission you are about to hear comes from a private conversation between Ayatollah Ahmad Jannati and a general who oversees the Qods training centers, which have been linked to insurgent activities."

Everyone listened intently, their eyes scanning the text as it appeared in their own languages on the monitor.

The senior Standing Committee member from China was first to speak. "I do not hear a threat. I hear only Mr. Jannati's intention to declare himself *Mahdi.*"

"With all due respect, Mr. Jinping, our intelligence agencies have provided us with a far more lethal interpretation of his intentions. We are requesting the Security Council to issue stern public warnings to Mr. Jannati, the foreign minister, and Iran's hard-line clerics that any nation providing enriched uranium to terrorist organizations shall, in the event of an attack, suffer the same fate as the perpetrators."

"And how are we to know, in the event of such an attack, whether the Iranians were responsible?" the Russian president retorted. "There are factions within your own government, Mr. President, that have been pushing for an invasion of Iran since Vice President Cheney was running the White House. How can we know if a nuclear explosion was not intentionally detonated by the CIA or Mossad in order to instigate war?"

"My administration seeks peaceful solutions to the conflicts in the Middle East."

"If this is so, why are your troops still occupying Iraq and Afghanistan? When will your military bases in the region be closed? Your new secretary of defense continues to ally himself with Georgian officials, pushing them to challenge our own nonaggression pacts with Abkhazia and South Ossetia. These actions send quite a different message."

"Secretary DeBorn was chastised for his actions. Our plan is to continue to reduce our troops in Iraq, reaching our targeted goal of fifty thousand by next August. An act of war by Mr. Jannati would undermine these efforts, fuel a neoconservative agenda in both Washington and Tel Aviv, and force us to respond in kind."

"And what of this plague that has killed off so many, including most of the Iranian delegation. Would this not be considered an act of war in Tehran?"

Eric Kogelo fought to maintain his focus through the headache and fever. "A half million Americans have died. Our largest city has been rendered unlivable. If this were an act of war, then America was the target. Let me again assure you, we shall investigate and bring to justice all those responsible for the plague. What we cannot do is allow these radical factions to succeed in pushing our nations into nuclear war. That is why all of us agreed to come to New York this week—to prevent another war."

But the Russian was far from done. "Mr. President, in August of 2001, President Putin sent a Russian delegation to Washington, DC, to brief President Bush about an al-Qaeda plot to hijack commercial airliners and fly them into the World Trade Center. We were not the only nation issuing warnings. There were at least a dozen other intelligence agencies that sent warnings, including the Germans, who provided the dates of the attacks. Why were those warnings ignored? The reason became obvious to all—the Bush administration wanted the attacks to succeed so they could justify a second invasion of Iraq. Now here we are, a decade later, only this time the desired target is Iran. Mr. President, if you really want to avert a nuclear holocaust, do not ask us to issue threats against the Iranians. Instead, show the world you mean business by policing the radical elements within your own country that continue to undermine your efforts to bring about peace."

MINOS PIZZERIA
AMSTERDAM AVENUE
2:19 A.M.

Rubber bullets and tear gas had dispersed the homeless, a grenade tearing the steel security gate from its tracks. Major Downey stepped over broken glass and debris, entering the dark storefront. "They're in here somewhere. Find them."

The Rangers in black moved through the deserted pizzeria, tossing aside checkerboard-clothed tables and ransacking closets and cabinets, searching every square foot of space that could conceivably hide two grown men.

"Sir, someone was in the kitchen making sandwiches. Looks like they're gone."

"The homeless weren't guarding sandwiches. Search the apartments upstairs."

Two Rangers exited the walk-in refrigerator, pushing gruffly past David Kantor. The medic entered the warm enclave, the beam of his flashlight revealing containers of pizza dough and grated cheese. He sat down on a crate of tomatoes, his body weary, his nerves on edge. *Got to find a way to separate myself from the group and get to Gavi's school.*

He heard the cat meowing somewhere in the darkness, but could not locate it. Saw the crate-shaped wet stain. Tapped on the floorboards with the butt end of his assault rifle. The sound was hollow. He checked the kitchen. Heard the Rangers in the apartment upstairs.

Returning to the wet mark, David stomped on the floorboards with his boot—

—caving in the trapdoor.

SUBWAY PASSAGE
2:35 A.M.

Three stories beneath a dying city, through a maintenance shaft bored fifty years ago, the fluttering illumination of Paolo's lantern was all that kept the claustrophobia at bay. Light danced on concrete walls riddled with pipes and graffiti. Shoes scuffed cement against a backdrop of dripping water that nourished unseen puddles cloaked in perpetual darkness. Francesca squeezed her husband's free hand, her mind burdened with fear, her lower back and shoulders by the unborn child that might never be.

After ten minutes, the shaft intersected the Eighth Avenue subway line. Rails cold and traffic-free made for new obstacles in the shifting light, along with the dead rats. The vermin were everywhere, black clumps of wet fur. Sharp teeth beneath pink noses lathered in blood.

Francesca crossed herself. "Paolo, maybe you should give me the vaccine."

Paolo turned to Virgil, uncertain. "What do you think?"

"It's your decision, son. Perhaps you should pray on it."

Patrick scoffed. "After the story you told me about Auschwitz, how can you possibly suggest prayer?"

"I simply said prayer might help Paolo find the answer. It's their child. They need to decide, not you."

"And if God ignores them, like he ignored you? Like He ignored six million of your people during the Holocaust?"

"I never said the Creator ignored our prayers. I said His answer was no."

"Apparently, He's still saying no. Think any of those families stranded in their cars on the parkway were praying tonight when the plague took them? Or those people dying on the street?"

"God is not a verb, Patrick. We must be the action. Prayer was never intended to be a request or plea. It is a technology that allows communication into the higher spiritual dimensions, helping to transform the human ego into a more selfless vessel to accept the Light. The Light is the—"

"We don't have time for the whole Light dissertation. Francesca, take the damn vaccine."

"Not yet." Paolo turned, the lantern's light swimming in Patrick's eyes. "I think Virgil's right. In times like these, we must have faith."

"You know what faith is, Paolo? Faith is nothing more than belief without evidence, a waste of time. The vaccine's real."

"Faith is also real," Virgil retorted. "Or perhaps we are wasting our time trying to find your wife and daughter."

A sickening rush of anxiety dropped Shep's blood pressure. "That's different. You said you spoke with her."

"Yes, but that was long before so many people got sick. For all we know, she may be dead. Maybe we should head straight for the boat."

"Bea is not dead."

"And you know this how?"

Patrick struggled in his skin to remain calm. "Pray your damn prayer, Paolo."

"O Lord, You have made us for Yourself, and our hearts are restless until they rest in You . . ."

The sensation felt like ice water running down his spine. Shep turned around slowly, his eyes focused on the maintenance shaft. Peering at him from the darkness was the Grim Reaper. Arms raised, scythe frozen in mid-swing. Hooded skull and empty eye sockets aimed at Paolo, the devout man's words were clearly agitating the supernal being.

"—grant us the grace to desire You with our whole heart, that so desiring You, we may seek and find You, and so finding You, we may love You and share equitably with our neighbors—"

The Reaper screamed in silence, melting back into the shadows of the underground passage.

"—through Christ Jesus we pray this. Amen."

Shep wiped beads of cold sweat from his forehead, his right hand shaking. "Amen."

CHINATOWN
2:47 A.M.

She was dragged from her nightmare by her hair, the pain forcing Gavi Kantor from her drug-induced stupor and onto her feet. Using her hair as a leash, a wiry man drenched in aftershave pulled her through a basement maze lit by candles. Past doorless bathrooms and into a hallway bordered by a dozen curtained stalls. The sour air reeked like old onions, the grunting sounds coming from these recesses more animal than human. In her delirium, she caught glimpses of male predators forcing naked girls to perform acts that caused her to scream.

The silhouetted man punched her in the back of the head, the glancing blow felling her to her knees.

"Enough!"

The Mexican madam's rotund mass outweighed the silhouette's by a good sixty pounds. "Give her to me, she is mine. Come here, *Chuleta*. Did Ali Chino hurt you?"

Good cop—bad cop. The thirteen-year-old crawled into the woman's embrace, bawling her eyes out. The madam winked to her associate.

Human trafficking was not prostitution. Human trafficking was the multibillion-dollar global business of kidnapping and purchasing children and young adults to be used as sex slaves. It was the third-most-profitable criminal enterprise in the world. Controlled by organized crime. Dominated by the Russians, Albanians, and Ukrainians, who trafficked women into Western Europe and the Middle East.

America remained a major consumer. Thirty thousand foreign women and children were trafficked into the United States each year. Smuggled across the Mexican border, they were sold to sex rings and transported to stash houses and apartments, some in major cities like New York, Chicago, and Los Angeles, others in smaller suburban towns, where they hid in plain sight.

But the highway that ran slavery into the United States was far from a one-way street. American children and teenagers were in high demand overseas. A six- to thirteen-year-old could be sold at a six-figure premium. Many end buyers included Saudi princes, "allies" the State Department was loath to crack down upon. When it came to human trafficking, corruption remained the lifeblood of immorality, the public's indifference its pulse.

The chamber was windowless. A dozen bare mattresses covered the concrete floor. Shared by twenty-two girls, ages ten to nineteen. Working in shifts. Business was rampant at the End of Days.

The "harvest" was mostly Russian and Hispanic. Halter tops and cheap makeup covered emaciated flesh. Bare arms sported track marks and bruises. The victims' eyes were vacant, as if the light of their souls had been sealed in amber—a result of having been gang-raped and beaten, forced to service twenty to thirty men a day.

The madam kicked a Romanian girl off a mattress, shoving the American teen down in her place. As "surrogate mother," the matriarch's job was to psychologically torture her charges before passing them off to male trainers who would repeatedly rape and beat each new recruit into submission. After two weeks, the American merchandise would be drugged and exported to Eastern Europe for sale to the highest bidder. For this, the madam would receive $3,000.00.

"Please let me go! I just wanted to buy a watch—"

The obese woman backhanded Gavi across her face, drawing blood. "You will wait here until I come for you. If you try to escape, the other girls will tell me, and Ali Chino will return. Ali Chino kills many girls. Do you wish to be killed?"

Gavi Kantor's body shook uncontrollably, her eyes blind with tears. "No."

"Then do as I say. I am here to take care of you, but you must listen." She scanned the room, pointing to a Russian girl. "You. Teach her how to use the penicillin."

With that, the Hispanic overlord left, locking the door behind her.

CENTRAL PARK WEST
2:45 A.M.

Central Park West defined the western border of Central Park, running from 110th Street south to 59th Street.

Dousing the lantern, Paolo exited the deserted subway station, leading Francesca, Virgil, and Patrick across Frederick Douglass Circle to Central Park West, darting between abandoned cars.

The moon was cloaked behind endless clouds, its veiled light revealing the high-rise buildings bordering Central Park. Home to some of New York's wealthiest, the structures had been rendered dark and foreboding. But far from silent. The cries of the destitute and suffering pierced the night, joined by the occasional sickening *thud* of a body as it plunged from an open window, striking the snow-covered sidewalk below.

Reaching 106th Street, Paolo led his entourage to the Stranger's Gate, a modest park entrance composed of a black slate stairway that deposited them in a wooded area. Moving beneath a canopy of American Elms laid bare by winter, they headed east across a hilltop meadow until they came to the tarmac path that was West Drive.

Closet psychotics and sexual deviants roamed the periphery—wolves wearing human flesh whose whispered cravings added another layer of terror to the night. Francesca pulled her husband closer. "We're too exposed out here. Take us along the ravine."

Two hundred feet overhead, the Reaper drone hovered, silently tracking its quarry.

The information was relayed over Major Downey's communicator, the target's coordinates visible in his right eyepiece. "They're in Central Park. Let's move!"

"Sir, we're missing a man . . . the National Guardsman."

Downey cursed under his breath as he switched radio frequencies in his headpiece. "Control, I need a track on Delta-8."

"Delta-8 is four meters south of your present position."

Downey looked around, confused. He entered the walk-in refrigerator—

—locating David Kantor's communicator lying in an open container of mayonnaise.

Paolo's eyes scanned the dark field, searching for the blotch of shadow. "This way."

Spanning ninety acres of Central Park's northern quadrant, the North Woods was a dense woodland so thick, it obliterated any trace of the

Hudson River
Riverside Drive
110th Street
Central Park North
Stranger's Gate
North Woods
Ravine
MEER
Central Park West
Henry Hudson Parkway
Broadway Ave.
West Drive
North Meadow
East Drive
5th Ave.
Reservoir
Museum of Natural History
Great Lawn
Belvedere Castle
Metropolitan Museum of Art
79th St. Transverse
Lincoln Square
LAKE
Strawberry Fields
Park Ave.
59th Street
Central Park South
Pond
FDR Drive
East River

surrounding metropolis. Running through the forest was the Ravine, a stream valley encompassing the Loch, a narrow lake that cascaded into five waterfalls before flowing into a brook that paralleled a southbound trail.

Moving quickly across the snow-covered lawn, they reached the forest edge. A frigid wind whipped at their backs, setting the trees to dance. Paolo knelt in the damp grass, shielding his lighter as he attempted to ignite the lantern. The flame would not catch. He tried again and again until his frozen fingers burned. "The wick's gone. The lantern's useless. Francesca, try your flashlight."

Francesca aimed the beam, but it was too faint to penetrate the trees. "Now what?"

"Shh." Paolo listened, his ears homing in on the rushing sound of water. "Hold hands. I can get us to the trail." Taking Francesca's hand, he stepped over brush and entered the woods.

The darkness was so encompassing, he could not see his groping hand in front of him. Through leaves and stumbling over logs, past unseen branches slicing their coats and cheeks, they continued on until the forest floor yielded to a narrow tarmac trail. Somewhere in the pitch ahead was Huddlestone Arch, a natural underpass consisting of huge schist boulders held in place by gravity. Inching forward, ducking their heads, they felt their way through the arch, carefully progressing along the steadily descending path.

A sliver of moonlight revealed the southbound trail. It looped to their right, leading to a small wooden bridge that crossed a stream.

Standing on the bridge was the Grim Reaper.

"Paolo, my feet . . . I need to rest a moment." Oblivious to the Angel of Death, Francesca approached the bridge, leaning back against its wooden rail.

Shep attempted to shout a warning, only his voice constricted, as if a weight were pressing against his throat. His eyes widened in terror as he watched the Reaper silently raise its scythe high over its right shoulder, the curved metal edge targeting the back of the pregnant woman's frail neck!

Francesca shivered, her exhaled breath thick and blue in the moonlight. "Suddenly it's so cold."

Death grinned at Shep as its cloaked arms—bone wrapped in decaying ligaments, tendons, and flesh—sent its olive-tinged blade arcing downward.

Shep pushed past Paolo in two quick strides, unfurling a backhand strike with his steel prosthetic. The metallic arm caught the Reaper's scythe mid-strike, the *clack* of metal meeting metal generating a brilliant orange spark that briefly illuminated the entire ravine.

Temporarily blinded by the light, Shep dropped to one knee, his body trembling.

"What was that?" Francesca whipped her head around, staring wide-eyed at her husband.

"What was what?"

"You didn't see that flash?"

"No, my love. Virgil?"

The old man was kneeling by Shep. "Son . . . are you all right?"

"The Reaper . . . it's after Francesca."

Virgil stared into Shep's constricted pupils. "Paolo, give your wife the vaccine."

"But you said—"

"Do it now."

Francesca took the vial from her husband and drained it, choking on the clear elixir.

Shep stood, the purple spots in his vision gradually fading. "I met his blade with mine. Tell me you saw the spark of light."

"No, but Francesca obviously saw it. You must have pulled her from the tunnel."

"The tunnel?"

"The passage every soul must travel through when leaving *Malchut,* the physical world. The tunnel leads to the Cave of Machpelah, where the patriarchs of all humanity are buried."

Shep pulled him aside. "The plague . . . all this death—it's like bait to him, isn't it?"

"It's not death, Patrick, it's the negativity . . . the reactive behavior that is increasing the power of Satan. In a way, the Angel of Darkness is a barometer of man's psyche. The transgressions of the world have tipped the scales beyond a critical mass, granting Death a free reign. The End of Days is upon us, and this time even the souls of the innocent will not be spared."

GOVERNOR'S ISLAND
3:29 A.M.

The biohazard lab had been set up in one of the island's former military residences. Powered by a portable generator growling in the open garage.

Doug Nichols handed Leigh Nelson a mug of coffee. The lieutenant colonel had arrived seven hours earlier from Fort Detrick to supervise the analysis and replication of the Scythe vaccine. The square-jawed veteran smiled at the pretty brunette. "Are you all right?"

Leigh's lower lip quivered. "I'd be much better if you allowed me five minutes to contact my husband."

The smile waned. "You can use my cell phone . . . after we've identified the vaccine."

"You're a real sport."

"You say you held the box containing the serum? Think you could identify it if you saw it again?"

"Probably."

Nichols opened his laptop. Typed in the address of a secured Web site. "These are standard field carrying cases Dr. Klipot would have had access to. For instance, these packs are used to transport influenza vaccine."

"No, it wasn't metal. This was a polished wood case, fitted with foam packing for twelve vials, each about three fluid ounces."

"Any identifying marks on the box? Serial numbers? Department logos?"

"None that I can remember. But there was a warning inside the lid. Something about the vaccine containing a powerful neurotransmitter that could produce temporary hallucinogenic effects."

"You're sure about this?"

"Positive. The Klipot woman wigged out on me shortly after I gave her the antidote. I remember thinking—"

The lieutenant colonel clicked through several pages, searching the site.

"Was this the box?"

Leigh stared at the image. "Yes. That's it, I'm sure of it. What's wrong?"

"This is a shipping case used for antimicrobic therapies, including tetracyclines, chloramphenicol, or streptomycin. AMTs are grown in artificial media from organisms inactivated with formaldehyde and preserved in 0.5 percent phenol. For that reasons and others, serum antibodies need direct access into the bloodstream. You of all people should know that digestible antimicrobic sera can't cross the brain-blood barrier, they must be injected."

"You think I'm making this up?"

"The Klipot woman escaped under your care. So did Sergeant Shepherd. Now you're deliberately lying about the nature of the cure. Either everything's just an inconvenient coincidence, or you're working with the terrorist groups responsible for infecting Manhattan."

"That's insane."

"Guard!"

An MP rushed in from the next room. "Yes, sir."

"Dr. Nelson's been lying to us. Have Captain Zwawa question her . . . under suitable duress."

CENTRAL PARK, NEW YORK
3:51 A.M.

They had made their way through the North Woods. Circumnavigating the North Meadow and the orgy of shadows segregated by bonfires, they crossed the bridge at 97th Street, where they stopped to rest by the life-sized bronze statue of Danish sculptor Albert Thorvaldsen.

Patrick had left them there to do reconnaissance along the eastern border of the park. Remaining concealed behind a four-foot stone wall, he had surveyed Fifth Avenue. Vehicles clogged the artery. Shadows stirred beneath dark awnings. He was about to leave when a disturbance shook the night.

The two black Hummers were weaving their way south on Fifth Avenue, avoiding the gridlocked lanes by veering onto the extra-wide sidewalk bordering Central Park. Screams cut through the frigid night air as the military vehicles ran over civilians sprawled out along the walkway, crushing limbs and skulls beneath the Hummers' double-wide tires.

Patrick hurried back through the park, locating the others on the East 96th Street playground. "They're coming. We have to move."

Francesca moaned, her feet aching. "How did they find us so quickly?"

Shep glanced up at the overcast heavens. "Probably using aerial drones to track us down. Come on."

"Where are we supposed to go?" Paolo asked, annoyed. "We came from the north, there's nothing to the west but athletic fields, and everything to the south is blocked by the reservoir. They'd overtake us long before we could get around it."

"We were safer at the pizzeria," Francesca complained. "I told you not to let them in, Paolo. I begged you."

"Francesca, please." Paolo knelt by the frost-covered sliding board, closing his eyes to pray. "God, why have you led us here only to kill us? Lead us out of here safely . . . show us the way!"

"Help us, God, show us the way." Virgil mimicked Paolo, his inflection dripping with sarcasm.

"Virgil, please—"

"And Moses whined to God, 'God, do something. We have the Red Sea in front of us and Egyptians in back of us.' And God answers back, *ma titzach alai*—why are you yelling to me?' That's right, Paolo, Moses was screaming to God, 'help us' and God was screaming back, "Why are you yelling to me?'"

Paolo stood. "I . . . I never read this Bible passage before."

"That's because the King James version removed it, and no rabbi or priest will ever discuss it. Few could accept that God would answer Moses like this, after all, God is good . . . God is just. What God was telling the Israelites was that they held the power to help themselves."

"I don't understand. How could the Israelites cross the Red Sea without God's help?"

"The answer lies in the verse itself, Exodus verse 14, the most important passage in the entire Torah. By pulling letters in a specific order from lines 19 through 21, you are left with seventy-two three-letter words—the very triads that God had engraved on Moses's staff."

"What were they?" Paolo asks.

"The 72 names of God. Not names in the ordinary sense but a combination of Aramaic letters that can strengthen the soul's connection to the spiritual realm and channel the unfiltered Light. Abraham used the 72 names in his youth to keep from being burned alive by Emperor Nimrod when he was tossed in an oven. Moses used the energy to control the physical universe."

"Virgil, I'm sorry . . . but how can any of this help us now?"

"Paolo, if you truly believe God is all-knowing and all-seeing, then it's insulting to think He needs to be reminded to help you. 'Hey, God, I need you down here, and don't forget my soul mate, my money, my food.' That's why God the Creator, God the Light said to Moses, *ma titzach alai*—why are you yelling to me? What God was saying was, 'Moses, wake up, you have the technology, use it! It's the concept of mind over matter."

Shep paced, his eyes focused in the direction of the approaching engines. "Virgil, this really isn't the time for a sermon."

The old man grimaced. "Patrick, the connection fostered by the 72 names won't work when your thoughts and actions are impure. Moses doubted, so the sea didn't part. But one man never wavered in his belief. One devout man took Moses's staff, engraved with the 72 names, and walked straight into the Red Sea until the water was up to his chin . . . and that was when the waters parted. You see, Paolo, when it comes to faith, there can be no doubt, no ego, only certainty. There are twenty-two letters in the Hebrew alphabet. One key letter is missing from the 72 names of God—the gimel, which stands for *ga'avah*—the human ego. If you truly believe in God, there can be no room for doubt."

Shep turned away from the conversation, his adrenaline pumping as he waited for the military vehicles to appear. *Nowhere to run, nowhere to hide . . . slowed down by a crazy old man and a pregnant woman.*

He looked out at the reservoir. So vast was the waterway that its borders stretched nearly from one end of the park to another, its ten-block horizon disappearing in a fog bank.

Fog?

"Paolo . . . we need to find a boat!"

The Jacqueline Kennedy Onassis Reservoir was a forty-foot-deep, 106-acre body of water encircled by a 1.58-mile jogging track and tall chain-link fence. The reservoir's maintenance shed was located off the bridle path.

Shep kicked open the door. Paolo peered inside with his light. The yellow inflatable raft was hanging from the ceiling, secured to the wooden beams by two pulleys. Shep cut the lines with one swing of his prosthetic arm. Grabbing an oar, he helped Paolo drag the rubber craft outside.

"Over here." Virgil and Francesca were waiting by the jogging track's public bathrooms. The old man had pulled a section of fencing loose from where it attached to the edge of the brick facing, allowing them access to the water.

The building's facade was covered in spray-painted graffiti, representing everything from gang insignias and messages of love to colorful artistic endeavors that would put Peter Max to shame. Appearing along the top of the wall, painted in black letters, was a prophetic message:

YOU ARE UNDER SURVEILLANCE.

Below that, represented in four-foot-high stylized white letters was a rock fan's homage to his favorite band:

Shep stared at the stylized graffiti, a distant memory tugging at his brain.

"Patrick, we need you." Virgil and Paolo had pulled back the loose section of fence, allowing Shep to maneuver the raft through the opening and into the water. Paolo climbed down into the boat first, then reached up to assist

Francesca and Virgil.

Squeezing through the opening, Shep dragged the fencing back into place and lowered himself into a kneeling position in the stern next to Virgil. He gripped the middle of the oar in his right fist but could not secure the top with the mangled pincer of his prosthetic left arm.

"Allow me, my friend." Paolo took the oar from Patrick and stroked, guiding the raft away from the reservoir's northern wall. The water was dark and murky, though noticeably warmer than the frigid night air, the temperature differential the cause of the dense fog bank.

The shoreline gradually disappeared from view, along with the night sky.

Paolo continued paddling, quickly losing all sense of direction. "This isn't good. I could be taking us in an endless circle."

Virgil held up his hand. "Listen."

They heard a crowd cheering somewhere in the distance.

"Head for the sound, Paolo. It will guide you to the southern end of the reservoir."

Altering their course, he paddled, the sound of the water crisp in the December air, the fog thickening with each stroke.

The smell reached them first, the putrid scent similar to an open sewer.

The bow struck an unseen object. Then another.

Paolo abruptly withdrew the oar. Snatching the lantern from Francesca, he again attempted to light the wick, succeeding on his third try. He held the lamp out over the side, the fog-veiled glow revealing what lay upon the surface. "Mother of God."

There were thousands of them, floating like human flotsam. Some drifted facedown, most were facing up, their red-rimmed eyes bulging in death, their mottled flesh bloated and pale, their necks festooned with grapefruit-sized purplish black buboes, swollen even more from their immersion in water. Men and women, old and young—the cold water having combined with the plague to disguise their ethnicity, their body compositions determining their ranking within the reservoir. The heaviest among them, being the most buoyant, occupied the surface of the man-made lake. The thin and muscled, unable to float, had been relegated to the mid and deeper waters, along with the infants and children.

Paolo cupped his hand over his wife's mouth before she could scream. "Close your eyes, look away. Scream, and the soldiers will find us."

Virgil wiped at cold tears. "Paolo, douse the light and work your oar . . . take us across this river of death."

"River of death . . . Styx." The words of the *Divine Comedy* cracked open another sealed chamber of Shep's memory, Dante's hellish prose laid out before him. *The water was a dark purplish gray, and we, following its somber undulation, pursued a strange path down to where there lay a marsh at the slope's culmination—*

—Styx was the name that swamp bore.

Shep's eyes widened as the vaccine-created hallucination gripped his mind, the flock of floating corpses spinning in his vision—

—the dead suddenly animating!

Limbs gyrate. Waterlogged hands paw blindly at one another, stripping clothing from skin in the process. Growing steadily more restless, the awakening dead reach out to tug at their neighbors' hair and gouge their eyes. Several of the more feisty corpses actually propel their ghastly heads from the frigid water, sinking their bared yellowed teeth into another plague victim's rotting flesh as if they were zombies.

As Shep watches in horror, bizarre flashes of bluish white light ignite randomly from somewhere within the depths, each strobe-like burst revealing haunting glimpses of more plague victims—a submerged army of the dead fighting their way to the surface. Suddenly, Shep finds himself looking out onto a sea of faces—Iraqi faces—all staring at him in judgment, their silence deafening.

"Ignore them, Shepherd, they're nothing but godless heathens."

Patrick looks down, stunned to find Lieutenant Colonel Philip Argenti. The clergyman is floating on his back next to the raft, his body dressed in his long, flowing black cassock, his corpse towed by the boat's moving current.

"War is hell, Shepherd. Sacrifices had to be made in order to achieve our objectives. We did what was necessary."

"Necessary . . . for who?"

"Freedom comes with a price."

"And who pays that price? We killed families . . . entire villages. These people never asked to be bombed and invaded."

"Whoa there, Sergeant. People? They're Muslims, scourge of the earth. Bunch of no-good Arabs hell-bent on destroying Western society."

"You're wrong. The majority of these people simply wanted to live in peace."

"No one asked for your opinion of the mission, Sergeant. You were trained to defend America against those who seek to destroy our way of life. Instead, you took the coward's way out, you cut and ran. In doing so, you shamed your family, you disgraced the uniform . . . but most of all, you betrayed our Lord and Savior, Jesus Christ."

"Jesus was a man of peace. He'd never support any act of violence."

"Wake up, Sergeant! America is a Christian nation. One nation, under God."

"Since when is America a Christian nation? Since when does God need man to fight His holy wars? Invoking God's name in our military actions does not sanctify violence any more than al-Qaeda proclaiming Jihad. Take a good look at them, Colonel. These are the lives we've butchered in God's name, the people we vilified as an excuse to bomb their cities, the children we've slaughtered in order to—"

"Save your speech, traitor. Would you stand by and allow these Islamic extremists to strike our shores again? What kind of an American are you?"

"One who refuses to be your tool any longer. Linking 9/11 with Saddam, weapons of mass destruction, democracy on the march . . . it was all a lie. All you fanatics ever wanted was an excuse to gain control of Iraq's oil supply. War is nothing more than a cash cow for the military-industrial complex. Who's next? Iran? Venezuela? Is that all part of God's plan, too?"

"Who are you to preach to me? We both know why you went to Iraq—you were looking for a target . . . an enemy combatant, someone you could line up in your crosshairs and blow away, reaping sweet revenge. We gave you that opportunity, Sergeant, and this is how you repay us?"

Shep gazes upon the multitude of mottled brown faces staring at him in silence. "You're right. No one forced me to go. It was my decision, I wanted justice . . . revenge. I killed innocent people, convinced that God was on my side . . . until I took my first life. My actions never brought justice, they only brought more pain and suffering. I allowed my anger to tarnish my soul, and the blame is all mine."

Another burst of luminescent light appears, this one a spark that ignites directly below the raft, illuminating the faces of the dead. Instead of fading, the light rises, circling Colonel Argenti like a hungry shark.

The clergyman senses the supernal being's approach. "The Angel of Death! Don't let him take me, Shepherd . . . in the name of all that's holy—"

"It's time, Colonel. It's time you and I both reaped what we've sown."

"I am an ordained minister . . . an ambassador of Christ our savior!"

The light circles closer, its luminous energy shearing the cassock and undergarments from the clergyman's body. Philip Argenti screams as his naked form suddenly heaves out of the water onto the raft. His lifeless limbs thrust forward, his dead hands somehow managing to hook themselves around the lapel of Patrick Shepherd's coat. "I . . . am a man . . . of God!"

"Then go to Him." Wielding his mangled prosthetic arm like a scythe, Shep slashes Argenti's throat. The colonel flails backward, the gash in his neck spurting black ooze as he plunges back into the water—

—the spectral glow dragging him below the frothing surface with one final, sizzling flash of light.

A thousand Iraqi faces—men, women, and children—close their eyes and sink beneath the corpse-littered surface . . . satisfied.

Wild-eyed, Patrick Shepherd stood in the raft, slashing his steel appendage through the empty fog-ridden night.

"Stop him! He'll slice through the raft!" Francesca held on to the sides of the roiling vessel, commanding her husband to act.

Virgil reached for Shep's right hand, squeezing it. "Son, it's all right. Whatever it was, it's gone."

Shep shook the vision loose. Confused, he allowed Virgil to guide him to his seat. The old man turned to Paolo. "He's all right. Continue on."

"No . . . this is all wrong. We're disturbing the holiest of the holies. We shouldn't have come—"

Francesca took her husband's hand. "Look at them, Paolo . . . they're all dead. Your son, on the other hand, he wants out."

"My son . . ." Returning the oar to the water, he paddled in the direction of the crowd noises.

Virgil placed a hand on Shep's shoulder. "What did you see? Was it the Reaper?"

"No. I saw people . . . victims of warfare. They rose from below . . . only—"

"Go on."

"Only I didn't kill these people. And yet, somehow I felt responsible for their deaths. There was a detached sense of familiarity to everything. Like a bad déjà vu."

"Accepting responsibility for your actions is the first necessary step in reconnecting with the Light."

"You're not hearing me. I didn't kill thousands of people."

"Maybe you didn't kill them in *this* lifetime."

"Virgil, I already told you, I don't believe in the whole reincarnation thing."

"Whether you believe in it or not doesn't make it any less true. Our five senses cause us chaos—the misperception that there are no connections. In fact, everything is connected. Déjà vu is a past incarnation experienced by the present. Whatever you did in your prior lives, I suspect that this may be your last chance to make things right again."

"Make what right? How am I supposed to know what to do?"

"When the time comes, you'll know. Trust your gut, your instinct. What does your intuition tell you?"

"My intuition?" Shep looked to the south.

The fog thinned as they neared the reservoir's shoreline. Half a mile away, the night was aglow with the orange haze of a thousand fires.

"My intuition tells me things are about to become a lot worse."

PART 4

LOWER HELL

SIXTH CIRCLE

The Heretics

"And we our feet directed tow'rds the city, after those holy words all confident. Within we entered without any contest; and I, who inclination had to see what the condition such a fortress holds, soon as I was within, cast round mine eye, and see on every hand an ample plain, full of distress and torment terrible."
—Dante's Inferno

DECEMBER 21

CENTRAL PARK

MANHATTAN

4:11 A.M.

(3 HOURS, 52 MINUTES BEFORE THE PROPHESIED END OF DAYS)

Their arrival at the southeastern end of the reservoir had presented the journey's next hurdle, for the fence separating the jogging track from the southern retaining wall offered no exit point or weak link. Paolo continued paddling, following the stone barrier as it circled to the west. Francesca's light finally revealed a break along the wall—a small boat ramp—the incline partially blocked by a large flatbed truck.

Climbing out first, Paolo dragged the bow of the raft up the cement ramp, then helped his pregnant wife out of the boat.

The truck's rusted metal flatbed was tilted at a thirty-degree angle to the reservoir, stained in frozen blood. Francesca wrapped her scarf across her face. "They must have used the truck to collect the dead, dumping them right into the water. Why would they do such a thing?"

Paolo peered inside the window of the empty cab. "The more important question is, why did they stop?"

"The plague must have spread so fast, they couldn't dispose of the dead quickly enough." Shep searched the night sky. "We need to keep moving, before another drone tracks us down."

They continued on, following a snow-covered bridle path, the bonfires glowing somewhere up ahead.

CENTRAL PARK WEST
4:20 A.M.

David Kantor made his way south along Central Park West. Gun drawn, he moved in the shadow of stalled vehicles. Cloaked in darkness, he was surrounded by death. It was slumped in the cars and sprawled on the sidewalk, rained from apartment windows to mangle awnings and decorate snow-covered lawns. Every fifteen seconds, he paused to make sure he was not being followed. The paranoia allowed him to stretch his hips and lower back, already aching from hauling his life-support equipment. *I'll never make it to Gavi's school like this. I need to find another way.*

He rested again. His stifling face mask collected a pool of sweat. Pulling open the rubber chin piece, he emptied the excess, his eyes locked in on the bizarre buildings on his right. The Rose Center for Earth and Space cast a diamond-shaped void against the lunar-lit heavens. The Museum of Natural History blotted the night like a medieval castle, its drawbridge guarded by the bronze statue of President Theodore Roosevelt on horseback.

The sight of the Rough Rider brought with it a memory of his youngest daughter's first visit to the facility. Gavi was only seven. Oren had come along, too, David's son insisting they skip the train and drive into the city so the boy could listen to the Yankees game on their way home. The day germinated in David's mind.

Checking the periphery in his night scope, he jogged up the museum steps to the sealed main doors, arguing internally whether he was wasting valuable time.

The doors were locked. He looked around again, determined he was alone, and shot out one of the plate-glass doors with his sidearm.

The museum was dark inside, save for the fading glow coming from an emergency light. David moved quickly through the Theodore Roosevelt

Memorial Hall, the deserted entry unnerving. Diverting past the Rose Gallery space exhibit, he searched for a visitor sign he knew was posted somewhere in the dark corridor up ahead.

"There." He followed the arrow to the parking garage, praying for a small miracle.

The spots reserved for motorcycles were located just past the handicapped row. His heart raced as the beam from his light revealed a Honda scooter and a Harley-Davidson, both vehicles still chained to their posts. He contemplated hot-wiring the scooter, but worried that the vehicle's engine would draw the attention of the military.

Then he saw the ten-speed bicycle.

CENTRAL PARK
4:23 A.M.

The bridle path ran past Summit Rock, the highest elevation in Central Park, before descending into a forest valley. Ahead was Winterdale Arch, a twelve-foot-high sandstone-and-granite underpass buttressed on either side by a retaining wall that extended east and west through the park. Illuminating the underpass were a dozen steel trash barrels, their contents set ablaze.

Beyond the fires, guarding the entrance of the granite tunnel, were a dozen men and women. Self-appointed gatekeepers. Heavily armed. Each wearing a fluorescent orange and yellow vest removed from the back of a deceased construction worker.

A procession of people milled about outside the guarded portal—families, lost souls, streetwalkers, displaced businesspeople, and the indigent—all waiting to be allowed to pass through the Winterdale Arch.

Paolo turned to Virgil. "This is the only way through, unless you want to risk the main roads again. What should we do?"

"Patrick?"

Shep continued watching the night sky, anticipating another aerial assault. "We're safer in a crowd. Let's see if they'll allow us through."

They approached the last person in line, a big man in his mid-fifties.

Despite the frigid temperatures, he was wearing a ski vest over a tee shirt, his bare arms covered in tattoos of the United States Marine Corps. The words: *Death Before Dishonor* were emblazoned across his upper right biceps. He was holding a woman wrapped in a blanket. From her stiffness and body position, Shep could tell she had cerebral palsy.

"Excuse me—"

"Welcome, brothers, welcome sister. Have you come to witness the glory of God?"

"What glory is there in so much suffering and death?" Shep asked.

"The glory comes from the Second Coming. Isn't that why you are here?"

Paolo pushed in, his eyes wide with excitement. "Then this really is it? The Rapture?"

"Yes, my friend. The twenty-four elders have assembled. The Virgin Mother herself is said to be inside the park walls, preparing to grant immortality to the chosen among us."

Paolo crossed himself, trembling. "When the plague was first announced, I had a feeling . . . How do we get inside?"

"They're bringing us up in small groups. They need to determine who is clean."

"We're clean." Paolo pulled Francesca to his side. "No plague, you can check us."

The big man smiled "No, brother, by 'clean' I am referring to the soul. Everyone must be escorted inside, at which point the worthy will be separated from the heretics. No sinner shall be granted access by the Trinity."

Shep looked to Virgil, who shook his head.

"What about the plague?" Francesca asked "Aren't you afraid of being contaminated?"

"Sister, it was Dis that summoned Jesus's return."

"Dis?"

"The disease," the woman said, straining to adjust her blanket so she could see. "Vern, explain it to them the way Pastor Wright explained it to us at the mission."

"My apologies. We're the Folleys, by the way. I'm Vern, this is my wife,

Susan Lynn. We flew in Saturday night from Hanford, California, for a two-day medical conference. We were scheduled to fly home this afternoon, only they shut down the city before we could leave. We wandered the streets for hours, somehow ending up at the mission."

"It was God's will," Susan Lynn chimed in.

"Amen. When we arrived, Pastor Wright was telling hundreds of people that he had just spoken with the Virgin Mother. She had incarnated herself as a Christian woman. The Virgin told him that Manhattan had been selected as ground zero for Revelations because of all its wickedness."

"What made him believe she was the Virgin Mary?" Francesca asked.

"There can be no doubt, sister. Pastor Wright actually witnessed a miracle when the Virgin cured the infected. Seeing the pastor, the Holy Mother instructed him to gather his flock in Central Park for the Rapture, that Jesus would be coming before the dawn. The Virgin would determine who would be saved and who would be cast out into Hell."

Paolo turned to Virgil, tears in his eyes. "Then it's true, this is the End of Days."

The old man gave him a wry look. "There is spirituality, Paolo, and there is religious dogma. The two are rarely compatible."

Vern's expression darkened. "Stay your tongue, old man. Any words perceived as blasphemy may burn you and your flock."

"It's time!" A bank security guard wearing a fluorescent orange vest waved his handgun at the crowd. "Single file, stay together. If the Furies ask you a question, answer honestly. Each of you will be instructed where to go once you reach the amphitheater."

The crowd jostled one another, several pushing past Shep to secure their place in line. "Vern, who are the Furies?"

"It's Judgment Day, fella, and the Furies are the judges. All three Furies are women personally selected by the Virgin Mary."

"But what is the Furies' purpose?"

"To administer the Lord's vengeance. One of the guards told me they're especially hard on anyone who raped or killed women and children. Once the Furies begin their process of vengeance, they won't stop, not even if the guilty party repents."

The crowd moved quickly through the arch, the armed detail signaling for Shep and his entourage to join the line.

Paolo pulled Shep aside. "No hallucinations. You need to find a way to control yourself. Francesca and I must be among those chosen for salvation." Before Shep could argue, the Italian and his pregnant wife fell in line behind the Folleys, trailing the couple through the Winterdale Arch.

Shep and Virgil looked at one another before joining the moving herd. They passed through the granite tunnel, following the bridle path up a steep slush-covered hill, accompanied by a howling wind that bit deep into their exposed flesh.

Patrick was operating on autopilot. His feet were numb from the cold, his legs moving just enough to keep pace with the faceless bodies in front of him. He felt lost, physically and spiritually, as if he had been transported into a waking, disorienting nightmare.

This is a wasted effort, an intentional walk before the manager visits the pitcher's mound, takes the baseball, and pulls you from the game. Just lie down now. Lie down in the snow and the cold of night and die. How bad can it be?

"Ow . . . damn it!" Lost in thought, he had walked headfirst into an immovable object. It was a bronze statue, Romeo caressing Juliet in a loving embrace. Shep stared at the immortalized figures, his heart yearning again for his soul mate. *Was that supposed to be a sign?*

"Let's go! Keep moving!"

The path circled through pitch-darkness, sending hands to grope the brick facing of a large building. Another sixty feet, and the forest suddenly yielded to a spectacle of religious fervor gyrating across the Great Lawn.

The assembled were everywhere, their numbers revealed by the glow of tangerine flames dancing from a thousand torches. It was an orgy of faith—forty thousand lost souls—all competing to gain entry into Heaven. Some scrambled atop the timeworn crags of Vista Rock, others pushed forward in random tides of desperation, drawn to the base of Belvedere Castle, the Gothic mansion rising above an undulating sea of humanity . . . the modern-day equivalent of the Israelites waiting for Moses's return from Mount Sinai.

The building Shep and the others had just circled was Delacorte Theater. The horseshoe-shaped arena that had once hosted Shakespeare in the Park now served as the pit for a raging bonfire. The remains of a large vinyl banner hung over the amphitheater stage, its CITY OF N.Y. PRESENTS DISNEY ON ICE message purposely torn to read:

CITY OF DIS

Situated on a blanketed perch of rock, silhouetted by the crackling bonfire that raged warmth at their backs were three women, each clad in a black robe taken from the quarters of a circuit court judge.

The "Fury" seated on the left was Jamie Megaera. Five-foot-one-inch tall, endowed with a thirty-eight-inch D-cup, the twenty-five-year-old single mom had given up custody of her daughter three years earlier to pursue an acting career in the Big Apple. The closest she had come to performing onstage was dancing nude from the birdcage hanging from the strip club where she worked.

Jamie's identical twin sister, Terry Alecto, was seated on the right. As a high-class prostitute, Terry earned three times more money than her sibling, $500 a trick. Like her sister, she was also separated from her family, her husband serving a nine-year prison sentence for promoting the prostitution of his wife (Terry having been a minor at the time of his arrest). The twin had no qualms about her line of work. In fact, she saw herself as providing a service, just like the local hairdresser or manicurist. She had had sex three times since she first noticed the swollen buboes on her neck.

Situated between the twins was sixty-five-year-old Patricia Demeule-Ross Tisiphone.

A product of alcoholic parents, Patricia had married when she was seventeen and spent thirty-nine years in an abusive relationship. Her daughter was addicted to pain pills, brought on by the suicide of her husband. Her sister and best friend, Marion, had moved in with Patricia after finally divorcing her own alcoholic husband, who had physically and verbally abused her since she was twenty. The two elderly women had been subletting an apartment to the twins, having "adopted" the girls as granddaughters.

By three in the afternoon, all four had been stricken with plague.

Feverish, infected by painful buboes and coughing up mouthfuls of blood, the four women had made their way to Central Park to "die in peace with nature." Marion had gone first, succumbing in front of her favorite spot, the Bethesda Fountain's Angel of the Water sculpture.

Patricia and the twins lay dying by her side, all three holding one another, trembling in the cold and pain but not in fear.

Pastor Jeramie Wright had administered last rites from a safe distance when the former biker had observed a woman approach the fallen females. Clad in white, she knelt on the ground and kissed all of the infected women on their open mouths, inducing them to swallow her "spit."

Within minutes, the three dying women were sitting up. Reborn.

Having witnessed the miracle, Pastor Wright approached the woman in white. "Who are you? What is your name?"

"I am Mary the Virgin. Baby Jesus has been born. Assemble the flock, for tonight, Revelations shall come."

Word of the Virgin's miracle had spread quickly. By nightfall, tens of thousands of frightened, abandoned New Yorkers were flocking to Central Park to be saved.

"**Each one of** you shall bow before the Furies, so that they may determine your place at the Rapture. You . . . state your name and occupation."

A tall woman with an hourglass figure bowed her head. "Linda Bohm. I'm visiting from California. I work as an assistant buyer at Barnes and Noble—"

"Why are you here?" the older Fury asked

"I was visiting a friend. We were on a bus. One of the passengers was coughing. None of us knew about the plague."

"You've got Dis?"

She nodded, wiping back tears. "Can the Virgin cure me?"

"Yes."

"Sorry, but I don't think so." The twin on the right brushed her long, wavy, brown hair, smacking her gum. "Bohm sounds like a Jewish name.

Linda doesn't believe in the Virgin Mother, and that makes Linda a heretic. The Virgin Mother specifically told us to purge all heretics into the arena."

"Are you a Jew?" asked the twin on the left.

"No. I'm . . . Episcopalian."

"She's lying. Mother Patricia?"

The older woman scrutinized the frightened tourist. "It's so hard to decide. Still, I suppose it's best to err on the side of caution. Toss the heretic into the flames."

Shep's eyes widened in horror as two orange-vested guards dragged the screaming California woman toward the amphitheater. Before he could react, a third guard doused her with gasoline and she was coldly heaved into the mouth of the conflagration, her flailing body igniting in an ethereal white flame.

Shep swooned, the black smoke rising from the pyre—not over the amphitheater but over a brick enclave surrounded by wood barracks and barbed wire herding living skeletons wearing striped uniforms and despair.

Auschwitz . . .

"Who's next? You . . . one-armed man. Tell us your name."

Shep shook the vision of the Nazi death camp from his mind, only to find himself staring at the voluptuous twins. Wind swirled around the jagged rock, whipping up the conflagration—

—loosening Jamie Megaera's and Terry Alecto's outer garments. The twins smile seductively at him, exposing their ample breasts as they stand to perform, gyrating in place.

"Come closer, Patrick Shepherd."

"Yes, Patrick. Come closer so that we might taste you."

He takes a step closer—

—his face battered by a blinding gust of sleet that whipped through the park, dousing torches and swirling bonfires, sending the Furies crawling down from their perch to seek cover.

Thunder rolled in the heavens, followed by a blast of trumpets that cut through the night like a scalpel. Having been officially summoned, the swell of forty thousand followers pushed forward as one, crowding the base of

Belvedere Castle.

Virgil yelled at Paolo, shouting above the wind to be heard. "Find us a car, anything that's mobile! Patrick and I will watch over your wife!"

"No! It's the Second Coming! I need to be here!"

"Remain here, and your son shall never see the dawn. Tell him, Francesca!"

She looked at the certainty in Virgil's eyes. "Paolo, do as he says!"

"Francesca?"

"Go! We'll meet you at the 79th Street Transverse."

Unsure, Paolo looked around, got his bearings, then pushed through the crowd, heading for the stretch of tarmac known as West Drive.

A slice of spotlight cut across the Great Lawn's periphery. For a moment, Patrick feared it was an Army helicopter, but the beam was coming from atop the Delacorte Theater. It settled on a lone figure standing on the third-story balcony of Belvedere Castle—a pale woman, dressed in a hooded white robe.

Loudspeakers crackled to life, powered by two backup generators. Cheers rose across the Great Lawn as the white-clad figure took the microphone from its stand to address her flock.

"Then the seven angels with the seven trumpets blew their mighty blasts. And one-third of the people on Earth were killed by this mighty plague. But the people who did not die still refused to turn from their evil deeds . . . refusing to repent their murders or their witchcraft or their thefts."

The woman in white retracted the garment's hood, revealing herself to her followers. Her frightening appearance elicited gasps from those standing closest to the castle's foundation. A moment later, her image materialized on the theater's big screen for all to see.

Beneath a shock of greasy candy-apple red hair was a face plagued hideously pale. The tip of her nose was blotched grayish purple, matching the circles beneath her olive green eyes. Scythe had rotted her teeth and gums black, and her psychotic expression was more demon than deliverer.

Virgil pulled Shep closer. "Patrick, I've seen this woman. She was in the VA hospital. They were moving her into an isolation ward."

"Isolation?" Shep stared at the figure, recalling his last conversation with

Leigh Nelson as she dragged him up the stairwell to the VA hospital's roof. *"One of my patients, a redheaded woman we had in isolation, she released a man-made plague . . ."*

Mary Louise Klipot moved to the edge of the Victorian balcony, the crowd silencing itself to listen to the woman's words. "Babylon has fallen. Our once-great city has fallen because she was seduced by the nations of the world. Babylon the great . . . now mother of all prostitutes and obscenities in the world, hideout of demons and evils spirits, a nest for filthy buzzards, a den for filthy beasts. And the rulers of the world who took part in her immoral acts and enjoyed her great luxury will suffer as the smoke rises again from her charred remains . . . the heretics who sought to destroy her . . . who sought to destroy America shall suffer God's wrath."

Yellow-tinted lights illuminated the second tier of the castle directly below Mary's perch, revealing three hastily constructed gallows. Lined up in rows, held at gunpoint, were several hundred people, their wrists bound behind their backs, their mouths duct-taped shut. Gays and lesbians, Muslims and Hindus. Old and young, men, women, and children . . . all predestined to be sacrificed . . . at least in Mary Klipot's jumbled thoughts.

"Bring forth the first group of heretics!"

The first three people in line—a Hindu family—were segregated from the condemned.

Manisha Patel convulsed in the grasp of hooded men adorned in the robes of the archdioceses. She screamed through her gag. Her knees buckled, her bridled angst sending her body writhing in contortions as she witnessed men grab her daughter, Dawn, and forcibly shove the girl's head through the noose on her right.

The rope on her left was occupied by her husband, Pankaj, who was being wrestled into submission by four men dressed in religious robes.

The crystal dangling around Manisha's neck sparked with static electricity as her own head was forcibly thrust through an awaiting noose. The rope was tightened around her jaw, forcing her up on her toes in order to breathe. "God, please spare my child. Spare my child. Spare my child!"

As Manisha moved, her hearing dulled, muffling the voice of the redheaded witch as she drove the crowd into a feverish frenzy. Barely conscious, the necromancer grunted each painful breath—an arctic inhalation that burned her throat while causing her nose to run. Her entire body trembled as she danced on the rope, waiting . . . waiting—

"Stop!"

Manisha opened her eyes, her dilated pupils too blurred with tears to focus.

She found him on the big screen. He was standing atop the third tier directly above their gallows, his face partially concealed within the dark hood, his right fist holding the witch upright by her hair, his bloodstained scythe poised at her neck.

Patrick Shepherd dragged Mary Klipot past the two skinhead "elders," who lay bleeding on the stone deck, and leaned over the microphone to speak, the blinding spotlight glistening on his steel prosthetic arm. "And then another angel appeared . . . the Angel of Death. And the Grim Reaper said, Release those innocent people now, or I'll cut off this ugly bitch's head and send her and the rest of you straight to Hell."

The moon slipped behind storm clouds, once more casting him from West Drive's snow-covered tarmac into darkness. Unseen branches tore at his clothing and face, unseen roots caused him to stumble and fall. He was hopelessly lost, separated from his wife, exiled from deliverance. Regaining his feet, he groped his way forward another eight paces—

—only to run into fencing along the edge of a partially frozen wetland. The impasse unleashed a wave of panic. His bearings gone, his faith diminishing rapidly, he knelt in the snow and prayed, more an act of desperation than of salvation.

The wind died down. Then he heard it . . . the gentle strumming of an acoustic guitar.

Wiping back tears, he followed the sound, finding his way through rows of American Elms before coming to a clearing that intersected with a vaguely familiar path.

The man was in his forties, seated alone on one of a dozen benches situated around a circular mosaic. Oily brown hair hung past his shoulders. A gaunt pale face, framed by long sideburns. The signature wire-rimmed glasses were slightly tinted. He was wearing worn jeans, a denim jacket over a black tee shirt, and appeared not the least bit concerned about the cold. The guitar rested on one knee. He was measuring each chord as he felt his way through an acoustic rendition of a song recorded nearly four decades earlier:

". . . playing those mind games forever, some kinda druid dudes . . . lifting the veil. Doing the mi . . . ind guerrilla. Some call it magic . . . the search for the grail. Love is the answer, and you know that—for sure. Love is a flower . . . you got to let it . . . you got to let grow."

John Lennon looked up at Paolo Salvatore Minos and smiled. "I know what you're thinking, lad. Truth is, I thought about singing "Imagine," but that would have been a bit clichéd, don't you think?"

Paolo knelt by the Imagine mosaic, now visible in the returning moonlight, his body shaking with adrenaline. "Are you real?"

The deceased Beatle tuned a string. "Just an image in space and time."

"I meant . . . are you a ghost, or is it this damn vaccine?"

"Don't believe in ghosts, don't believe in vaccines either." A roar grew louder in the distance. "Listen to them . . . murderous bastards. Praying for Jesus to arrive on his white steed like some rock star . . . as if Jesus would have any part of that chaos."

"They're not sinners. They're just looking to be saved."

"Yes, but salvation, according to John the bloody Apostle, is a right reserved only for Christians. Ironically, that would exclude Jesus, too. Toss Rabbi Jesus into the fire pit on the right, lads, the Muslims, Hindus, Buddhists and the rest of the lot into Satan's pit on the left. Once they're gone, we can reserve the infighting strictly among the Catholics and Protestants, the Lutherans, Episcopalians, Pentecostals, Mormons, Baptists . . . who am I forgetting? Wait, I know, we can call for another war in the Holy Land, this one to sort out whose church is the real church of God."

Paolo grabbed his head. "No, I can't hear this . . . not now, not on Judgment Day. You were such a hero to me, but this . . . this is heresy."

"Aye. And be sure to count Rabbi Jesus among the heretics."

"Stop . . . please!"

"Paolo, listen to me. We're all God's children. All of us. The real sin is man's refusal to become what we are. Spirituality isn't about religion, it's about loving God. Two thousand years of bickering, persecution, hatred, and war, all caused by some silly competition over who Daddy loves best. All we have to do is love unconditionally. When each man becomes his brother's keeper . . . that's when everything changes. It's not too late. Look at me. I grew up angry, then I found my purpose."

"Your music?"

"No, lad. Music was merely a channel, a means of delivering the message." He strummed a chord. "Love is the answer . . . Sorry, I'm a bit off-key."

"John, I need to know . . . is this it? Is this the end?"

The former activist put down the guitar. "Destruction is a self-fulfilling path, but so is peace. Murder has become a billion-dollar industry, with greed and selfishness leading mankind toward oblivion. It must be stopped. As a Christian taught to believe out of fear, you need to decide what it is you want more—the destruction of the world and the so-called promise of salvation, or the peace, love, and fulfillment that transforms every human being on the planet."

"But how can one man . . . I mean, I'm not you."

"You mean you're not an insecure, egomaniacal, angry musician who abused drugs and alcohol?"

"Come on, John. You risked your career . . . your life to speak out against the Vietnam War. You mobilized millions, you saved lives—"

"And how many lives have you saved by feeding the hungry? If history has taught us anything, lad, it's that one man, one voice, one mantra can change the world. Now tell me, what is it you really need?"

Paolo wiped the tears streaming down his face. "I need . . . a car."

John Lennon smiled. "Follow the path across West Park Avenue to my old building, the Dakota. There's a parking garage next door . . ."

With the spotlight in his eyes he could not see the crowd, but he could feel their negative energy, their hatred. For a fleeting moment Patrick Shepherd was on the mound at Yankee Stadium, forty thousand hometown fans booing him unmercifully.

A thousand feet overhead, the night lens of the Reaper drone's camera zoomed in on his face.

"Listen to me! Those people . . . they've done nothing wrong."

"Liar!" Tim Burkland was standing on the back of a WABC radio van loaded with speakers. The former punk rocker and talk-show blogger was a self-described "polemic journalist," his radical views, wrapped in religious dogma, helping to secure a New York cable show in which he battled "the lies, injustice, and cruelty of American socialism and the systematic destruction of the Church."

"You listen, freak. Christ died for our sins, for our imperfections. Jews need to be perfected. Homosexuals need to be perfected. Muslims need to be perfected. Not all Muslims may be terrorists, but all terrorists are Muslim. Allowing these people to exist within our Christian society is a sin against our Lord and Savior!"

Burkland's supporters roared, chanting, "Hang the heretics! Hang the heretics!"

The redhead squirmed in Shep's grip, turning to face him. "And He shall destroy all who have caused destruction on Earth."

"Shut up." Shep yanked her head away from the microphone, catching a whiff of her foul, diseased breath. "All of this hatred, all of this negativity . . . it's fueling the plague. Hundreds of thousands have already died, none of us may live to see the sunrise. Every one of us here has wronged our fellowman. Is this really the last act you want to commit on Earth before you're to be judged? Whose side would Jesus defend if He were here? Would He support the hatred spewing from the mouths of these false prophets of the entertainment world who desecrate His message of peace so they can earn millions in book royalties and over the airwaves? Would Jesus be so easily deceived that He would stand by and allow innocent children to be hanged? Mark my words—if one of these people dies tonight by your action or inaction, then all shall be judged!"

The crowd grew silent, contemplating Shep's words.

Dozens of men and women wearing fluorescent orange vests approached from either side of the balcony, aiming their guns. Pastor Jeramie Wright stepped out from the group, the big man pushing his followers' shotgun barrels toward the ground. "Strong words, son. It'll mean nothing if you harm the Virgin Mary. Let her go."

"This woman is not the incarnation of the Virgin Mary. She's Typhoid Mary, the one who unleashed the plague."

"Now that's a lie. I witnessed the miracle myself."

"What miracle?"

"I saw her spit into the mouths of the inflicted and cure them."

The armed men raised their shotguns.

Shep tightened his prosthetic arm around the redhead's chest, freeing his right hand so he could pat her down.

"Rape! Murder!"

The crowd surged forward.

"Stop, or I'll slit her throat!" He pressed the blade of his mangled prosthetic until he drew a ring of blood around her neck, halting the armed men's advance—

—while his right hand felt for the plastic vials located in an internal pocket of the redhead's hospital robe. Removing several, he tossed one to Pastor Wright, holding the rest up to the crowd. "This is what your so-called Virgin Mother used to cure the inflicted—plague vaccine. The sickness is called Scythe. This woman helped develop it for the government, then she unleashed it in Manhattan. And now you want to worship this murderer?"

The mob on the balcony looked to Pastor Wright—unsure.

A murmur rose from the thousands watching the big screen.

Her moment of transformation stolen, Mary Klipot struggled to free herself, growling at Shep like a rabid dog—

—while on the balcony below, Manisha Patel strained to remain on her toes, the rope's friction peeling away the skin along her throat.

A few catcalls rose from the crowd. "Give us the murderer!"

"Give us the vaccine!"

Shep reached beneath his overcoat, pulling out the wooden case. "You want the vaccine? Here it is!" He flung the case into the crowd, then turned to face Pastor Wright and his followers. "There's more in her pocket—you deal with it." He shoved the redhead toward the security detail—

—as Tim Burkland and his followers reached the second-floor gallows directly below his balcony, the radical talk-show host intent on hanging the roped victims himself.

"No!" Patrick Shepherd jumped down from the third-story ledge, landing feet first on the wooden gallows. He swung his steel appendage wildly toward Burkland and his mob, backing them away—

—while on the ground, thousands of plague-infected men and women tore into one another in an attempt to grab the wooden box.

And then all hell broke loose.

The heavens bellowed, the frozen ground reverberating beneath the sonic rumble generated by five turbine jet engine Air Tractors. The industrial crop dusters rolled overhead in a standard inverted-V formation a mere two thousand feet above the park. The crowd never saw the planes or their dispersing payload—a partially frozen mist laden with carbon dioxide, glycerine, diethylene glycol, bromine, and an array of chemical and atmospheric stabilizers.

The fighting ceased, all eyes gazing at the heavens as the gas elixir mixed with the moist air, causing a chain reaction. Frozen CO2 and bromine molecules expanded rapidly, creating a dense, swirling reddish brown cloud that coagulated as it sank, reaching neutral buoyancy a mere 675 feet above Manhattan.

To the amped up crowd, the Rapture had arrived. Thousands already swooning with fever collapsed and fainted. Those still conscious dropped to their knees in fear.

The noose around Manisha's throat loosened, the sliced rope falling across her shoulders. She bent over, wheezing, as Shep cut through her duct-tape bonds, freeing her arms.

Daughter and husband rushed to her side, the family weeping and hugging one another in an emotionally spent embrace, the kind that comes only from death's reprieve.

Shep grabbed Tim Burkland by his coat collar, dragging the radical TV host to his feet. The blade of his mangled steel pincer pressed alongside the man's Adam's apple, drawing blood.

"Please don't! I was wrong. I'm asking for absolution."

"I'm not God, asshole."

"You're the Angel of Death . . . the Grim Reaper. You have the power to spare me."

"You want to live? Free these people—every one of them."

"Right away! Thank you . . . bless you!" Burkland crawled off—

—as an explosion of white-hot pain stole Patrick Shepherd's thoughts in a frothing wave of delirium—the blade of the axe buried deep inside his left deltoid, tearing muscle and nerve endings before being blunted by the coupling of his steel appendage. Crying out, he collapsed to his knees in agony, his body wracked in spasms, the wound gushing blood.

The encapsulated night sky ignited to the east and north, turning what was left of the heavens into a rose-colored aurora. The military flares illuminated the face of Patrick's attacker, who stood over him, the axe poised above her forehead, the blade dripping his blood.

"And the first angel blew his trumpet, and hail and fire, mixed with blood were thrown down upon the earth!"

Shep's eyes widened—

—as Mary Klipot's red hair thickens into coiling serpents, her eyes pooling with blood until the overflow pours down her stonelike face, the Medusa screeching at him.

Paralyzed in shock, Shep remained frozen in place as the axe plunged toward his skull—

—its wooden shaft intercepted by Pankaj Patel, who tore the weapon loose from Mary Klipot's hands. "Begone, witch, before I chop off your ugly head and feed it to the ducks!"

As if tossed from a trance, Mary stumbled backward, then dashed from the gallows, disappearing down the stone stairwell.

Manisha Patel knelt by Shep. "Pankaj, he's in shock. Look at his arm. She cut clear down to the bone."

Dawn Patel gathered strips of torn duct tape, the ten-year-old attempting to seal the gushing eight-inch-long wound. "Mom, hold that in place while I wrap his shoulder with my scarf."

An old man with long, silvery white hair tied in a loose ponytail bounded out of the open stairwell. "Patrick, we have to go, the military's coming."

"He can't hear you," Manisha said, her hands covered in blood. "He's in shock."

Virgil looked at the Patels, his blue eyes kind behind the tinted teardrop glasses. "We have a car waiting for us on the other side of this castle. Can you get him on his feet?"

"This man saved our lives, I'd carry him through Hell if I had to." Pankaj slid his left shoulder beneath Shep's good arm, hoisting him off the ground. Manisha wrapped the scarf tightly around the duct-tape bandage, then assisted her husband in carrying the unconscious one-armed man down the Victorian temple's steps.

They exited Belvedere Castle to the south by Vista Rock, where Francesca was waiting. "Virgil, what happened to Patrick?"

"He'll survive. Where's Paolo?"

They turned as gunfire erupted to the north.

"Francesca?"

"He's down below, on the 79th Street Transverse. This way."

The two black military Hummers bounded across the Great Lawn, their four-wheel-drive vehicle with its bulletproof tires tearing up the snow-covered softball diamonds. Turret-mounted guns spit lead-laced tracer fire above the crowd, scattering the multitudes like bleach sprayed upon a fire ant's nest.

Major Steve Downey was up front in the lead vehicle, relaying instructions from the Reaper drone's crew to the second Hummer. "He's leaving the castle, heading south. Head southeast past the Obelisk and Turtle Pond. We'll head west around the castle, trapping him at the 79th Street bridge."

In order to create an uninterrupted natural flow of lakes, streams, glades, woodlands, and lawns, Central Park's engineers had had to sink the roads that crossed the venue so that they actually ran below the landscape. Their biggest challenge had been the 79th Street Transverse, a section of road that connected the Upper West Side with the Upper East Side at East 79th Street. To submerge the street meant carving a tunnel out of Vista Rock, the remains of an ancient mountain that became the foundation of Belvedere Castle.

Completed in January 1861, the rock tunnel was 141 feet long, 18 feet high, and 40 feet wide. To access the transverse from inside the park, pedestrians descended a hidden stairway by the 79th Street bridge, which overlooked the subterranean roadway.

A swarm of humanity pushed, prodded, and shoved past Francesca in the darkness as she led Virgil and the Hindu family carrying Shep away from Belvedere Castle and through the Shakespeare rock garden. Disoriented, swallowed by the fleeing masses, she quickly lost her way.

Flares exploded in the distance. The pink glare illuminated the surreal brown ceiling of clouds, the surreal light revealing the 79th Street bridge. Feeling her way along the stone wall, Francesca located the 150-year-old niche and stairwell. Reaching for the iron gate, she was shocked to find it padlocked. "No . . . no!" Francesca yanked hard on the shiny new combination lock, unable to free it from its rusted hardware.

The roar of the military vehicles grew louder, drawing Patrick Shepherd from his stupor. He was leaning against a stone wall covered in ivy. Through a haze of pain, he gazed at the ten-year-old brown-skinned girl perched three steps above him. He blinked away tears, unsure if what he was seeing was real.

Hovering over Dawn Patel was a spirit. The luminescent blue apparition appeared to be playing with the girl's braids as it whispered into her ear.

Pankaj Patel ushered the pregnant woman aside, his right hand wielding a rock.

"Dad, wait, you'll only jam it. Let me, I can do it." The girl grabbed her father's wrist, attempting to stop him from smashing the lock.

"Dawn, we don't have time—"

"Let the girl try."

All heads turned to Patrick, who was now standing on wobbly legs.

"Go ahead, kid. Open the gate."

Dawn slipped past her father. She spun the tumbler several times, her ear to the lock as she slowly turned the numbered dial, the spirit clearly guiding her.

Headlights appeared behind them, the military vehicles within a hundred yards.

With a metallic *click,* the lock's shackle miraculously popped open.

"You did it!" Pankaj hugged his daughter.

"No time for that." Francesca pushed the iron gate open, its rusted hinges squealing in protest. Carefully, the pregnant woman made her way down a winding set of stone steps to 79th Street and a white Dodge Caravan, parked on the street below.

Paolo saw his wife and hurried to assist her. "What happened? Are you all right?"

"We're being chased. Get in the car and drive—wait for the others!"

Manisha and her husband helped Patrick down the steps, followed by Dawn and Virgil. They climbed inside the van, Paolo accelerating east into the darkness, using only the parking lights to guide him through the 79th Street tunnel.

The two military Hummers skidded to a halt by the 79th Street bridge. Receiving instructions through the communicator in his mask, Major Downey quickly located the concealed stairwell leading down to the 79th Street Transverse. "Damn it all!"

The iron gate was sealed shut . . . as if it had been welded in place.

Lost Diary: Guy de Chauliac

The following entry has been excerpted from a recently discovered unpublished memoir, written by surgeon Guy de Chauliac during the Great Plague: 1346–1348. (translated from its original French)

Diary Entry: May 18, 1348

(recorded in Avignon, France)

I am infected with sickness.

Perhaps I thought God had other plans for me, that He would keep me safe so I might tend to his flock. Perhaps he has stricken me with plague so that I might better understand the malady? Regardless, I remain bedridden and weak, the fever a constant companion. The carbuncles (Author's Note: buboes) have sprouted red below my left armpit and, more alarming, within the crease of my genitalia. I have not yet begun spitting up blood, but I can detect the beginning of a strong stench in my sweat.

Diary Entry: May 21, 1348

An observation to whoever discovers this diary after my death: It seems there may be two variations of the mortality. The more severe was clearly prevalent in winter, the victims usually dying within two to three days. The second type, a warm-weather variation (?) appears to allow its victims time to linger. It appears I am blessed with the latter . . . or condemned.

Diary Entry: May 25, 1348

Awoke to church bells and singing in the streets. Was it a wedding? My own funeral? Delirious, I summoned my servant, who delivered the bad news—the Flagellants have arrived in Avignon.

Dressed in soiled white cloaks and bearing large wooden crosses, these troupes of religious zealots move from village to village seeking to cure the Great Mortality through self-inflicted penance. Armed with thorn-covered whips and iron spikes, they publicly flog themselves in order to earn salvation from a wrathful God, transforming Christianity into an almost erotic spectacle of blood.

And how the people do follow! In an era dominated by plague, pestilence, and corruption, fear has replaced sanity, allowing the self-righteous to impose their idiocracy upon Avignon's surviving populace. The zealots expel the priest from his church and drag the Jews from their homes . . . burning them alive.

I was wrong. It is evil that rots humanity, plague merely our salvation.

Dying hard, I grow ever envious of those who perished in winter.

Diary Entry: May 27, 1348.

Fever. Abdominal pain worsening. Bouts of chills. Cannot eat. Bowels . . . diarrhea, traces of blood. Death close now. Clement absolved my soul before he abandoned Avignon.

Let the Reaper come . . .

(end entry)

SEVENTH CIRCLE

The Violent

"I thought the universe was thrill'd with love, whereby, there are who deem, the world hath oft been into chaos turn'd and in that point, here, and elsewhere, that old rock toppled down. But fix thine eyes beneath: the river of blood approaches, in the which all those are steep'd, who have by violence injured. 'Oh, blind lust! Oh, foolish wrath! Who so dost goad us on in the brief life, and in the eternal then thus miserably o'erwhelm us."

—Dante's Inferno

DECEMBER 21

GOVERNOR'S ISLAND

5:17 A.M.

(2 HOURS, 45 MINUTES BEFORE THE PROPHESIED END OF DAYS)

The cloak over her head paralyzed. It constricted each breath. It turned her blood into lead. Her body became a corpse, supported beneath each arm and carried away into oblivion.

Down the basement steps. Dragged by the two MPs.

Leigh Nelson's heart jumped as punk rock music suddenly blared from speakers, the Ramones' "Blitzkreig Bop" assaulting her inside the black hood. She twisted against unseen foes forcibly pressing her body down upon a hard surface, her head angled lower than her feet.

"Oh God oh God, please don't do this! I swear I had nothing to do with that woman!"

She kicked blindly at powerful hands that restricted her legs, her assailants duct-taping her ankles to the backboard. When they taped down her chest, the terrified physician and mother of two expelled a bloodcurdling scream into the black hood.

Hey ho, let's go . . . shoot 'em in the back now—

A hand pinned her skull to the board while raising the hood above her mouth and nose.

What they want . . . I don't know. They're all revved up and ready to go–

In the frightening darkness in the dank basement in her worst nightmare a thousand light years from home, the suddenness of cold water poured into her upturned nostrils sent the bound woman into a full-body convulsion. Liquid suffocation. No breath to hold or release. The terror a hundred times worse than drowning in an ocean or pool.

The board was raised. The music lowered.

She vomited up water, her purged lungs struggling to gasp a life-sustaining breath. Finally, her esophagus cleared as she wheezed air and tears.

Captain Jay Zwawa spoke slowly and clearly into her right ear. "You helped the Klipot woman escape, didn't you?"

Leigh sobbed and choked, unable to find her voice.

"Lower her again–"

She shook her head emphatically, buying precious seconds, the confession rasped. "I helped . . . I planned everything!"

"Did you inject her with vaccine?"

"Yes! Ten cc's into her IV."

"What was in the vial?"

"Tetracycline . . . other stuff."

"What other stuff?"

"I don't know, I can't think–

The board was lowered.

"Wait! Get me inside your lab, I'll figure it out!"

Zwawa signaled his men to cut her loose, ending a performance necessitated by Lieutenant Colonel Nichols and the Pentagon Nazis who still insisted torture yielded valuable field intelligence. The fact that Leigh Nelson had been cooperating up until then was a moot point, as was the reality that the terrified physician would have confessed to the Kennedy assassination and the Lindbergh baby kidnapping had it meant avoiding another waterboarding session.

"Get her warm clothes and clean sheets for her mattress."

"Sir, shouldn't we take her to the lab?"

Heading up the basement stairs, the captain ignored the MP.

CENTRAL PARK/UPPER EAST SIDE

5:24 A.M.

The white van raced east through a tunnel of rock nature had made impervious to the all-seeing eyes of the Reaper drones. The pitch-darkness forced Paolo to use his headlights. He powered them off the moment the vehicle cleared the tunnel, and the billowy brown sky reappeared overhead, the light from the luminous pink flares dimming as he distanced them from Belvedere Castle.

Ahead was Fifth Avenue. Central Park's eastern border was blocked by a wall of cars and buses.

Paolo swerved onto the sidewalk, bulldozing his way south in the darkness.

Thump . . . thump! Thump . . . thump! Each collision rocked the van like a speed bump. Francesca was seated up front between her husband and Shep. With outstretched arms, the pregnant woman braced herself, using the dashboard. "Paolo, those are people you're running over!"

"Dead people."

"Get off the sidewalk."

"And drive where? The streets are blocked."

Manisha was in the second seat, holding Dawn's head in her lap. Her daughter was coughing violently, expelling specks of blood. The necromancer turned to her husband, desperation and anger in her eyes. "We should have never left the cab."

"Easy to say now," Pankaj retorted. "How much longer could we have remained there?" The van lurched again, the jarring blow forcing everyone into seat belts.

"Paolo, enough!"

"They're dead, Francesca. We're still alive."

"Excuse me," Manisha interrupted, "but how are you still alive? None of you even looks sick."

Francesca motioned to Shep. "Patrick has plague vaccine. At least he had it. He threw what was left into the crowd."

Shep struggled to turn around, the pain coming from his severed left deltoid pushing him in and out of consciousness. "I still have vaccine left." He half grinned at Virgil, seated behind him. "I emptied the box into my pocket before I stormed the castle."

Reaching into his right jacket pocket, he retrieved three small vials of the clear elixir.

Virgil stopped him before he could pass them back. "What about your wife and daughter? Have you forgotten the reason we're trying to cross Man hattan?"

Manisha's expression of hope vanished, her mouth quivering. "Your family . . . where do they live?"

"Battery Park." Shep grimaced as he searched his jacket pockets again.

"When did you last . . . I mean, are you certain—"

"Manisha!"

"I am so sorry, forgive me. My husband is right. I cannot take from your family to save mine. You've already risked your life–"

"No wait, it's okay. There were eleven vials to start, I still have six left, two for Bea and my daughter, one for Virgil. Virge, maybe you should take yours now?"

"Hold on to it for me."

Shep passed the three vials back to Manisha. She trembled as she accepted the gift of life, kissing Patrick's hand. "Bless you."

"Just be careful, the drug causes wicked hallucinations. Back in the park . . . I imagined something hovering over your daughter. I swear, it looked like an angel."

Dawn raised her head. "You saw her?"

"Saw who?"

Her hands shaking, Manisha hurriedly uncapped the vial. "Dawn, swallow this. It will make you feel better." She poured the liquid into her daughter's mouth, fearing the one-armed man's line of questioning.

"*Her?* Are you saying what I saw was real? What did I see? Answer me?"

Dawn looked to her mother.

"My name is Manisha Patel, this is my husband, Pankaj. I am a necromancer, a person who communicates with the souls of the dead. The spirit you saw hovering over Dawn, she shares a special bond with our daughter."

The van lurched again, the impact nearly popping a shock absorber.

Francesca screamed, slapping Paolo on his arm. "What's wrong with you? She just said she speaks to the dead. Stop running them over!"

"Sorry." Spotting a break in the wall of cars, he veered across Fifth Avenue, working his way east along 68th Street.

"Manisha, this soul . . . you called it a she?"

The necromancer nodded at Shep, swallowing the tasteless vaccine. "She has been my spiritual guide ever since we moved to New York. She warned us to leave Manhattan, but we were too late. How is it you were able to see her?"

Shep winced as the van rocked wildly, the pain in his shoulder excruciating. "I don't know. Like I said, the vaccine causes hallucinations. To be honest, that's all I thought it was."

"What you glimpsed," Virgil interjected, "was the veiled Light of the soul. Remember what I told you back in the hospital, that our five senses lie to us, that they act as curtains that filter out the true reality of existence. In order to be visible, light requires an object to refract upon. Think of deep space. Despite the presence of countless stars, space remains dark. Sunlight only becomes visible when it reflects off an object, like the Earth or the moon. What you saw was this companion soul's Light reflecting off the girl."

"Why her?"

"Perhaps the girl possesses something very special, like her mother."

"And what is that?" Pankaj asks.

Virgil smiled. "Unconditional love for the Creator."

Manisha gazed up at the old man, tears in her eyes. "Who are you?"

The high-rise apartment was heavy with the scent of aroma candles. The dying flames flickered within designer glass jars aligned across the granite kitchen table, reflecting off the stainless-steel surface of the Sub-Zero refrigerator. Powerless, the double-sized doors lacked the vacuum to remain sealed.

Forty-four-year-old Steven Mennella moved through the condominium as if he were wearing a lead suit. Steven was an NYPD sergeant, his wife, Veronica, a career nurse who had recently taken a job at the VA Hospital.

Steven grabbed a scented candle from the kitchen and carried it into the master bedroom. Leaving it on his bedside table, he stripped off his uniform, meticulously hanging it up in the walk-in closet. Searching by feel, he removed a recently pressed collared white shirt from a hanger, along with his favorite gray suit. He dressed quickly, then selected from a tie rack the patterned tie his daughter, Susan, had given him on his last birthday. He knotted the silk tie, slipped on his leather belt and matching dress shoes, then did a quick check in the closet mirror.

For a brief moment, he contemplated making the bed.

Leaving the bedroom, he returned to the living room. The apartment was situated on the thirtieth floor, twenty feet above the dense layer of an ominous brown maelstrom. At the moment, the night sky above the balcony was starry and clear, offering a bizarre view of a cloud city—Steven imprisoned in this penthouse nightmare . . . alone.

Veronica was lying on the U-shaped leather couch. The Veterans Administration nurse's pale face was no longer pained, her blue eyes fixed in a glassy, red-rimmed open stare. Steven had washed the blood from his wife's lips and throat, covering the frightening black tennis-ball-sized welt on her slender neck with the wool blanket.

Leaning over, he kissed his deceased partner on her cold lips. "I left the kids a letter, along with instructions . . . just like we talked about. Wait for me, hon. I'll only be a minute."

Steven Mennella blew out the candles. Clearing his throat, he strode toward the open French doors leading out to the balcony. The full moon was low on the horizon, revealing the thick bank of mud-colored clouds gyrating below. A frigid wind greeted him as he gracefully stepped up onto his favorite chaise lounge, balanced himself on the aluminum rail—

—and stepped off the balcony.

Icy crystals formed on his flesh as he plummeted through the noxious man-made chemical cloud, the wind howling in his ears . . .

There was no warning. One moment, Paolo was veering around a mailbox—

—the next, the van was struck by a human meteor.

The hood detonated, the impact crushing the engine block and bursting both front tires. Paolo jammed on the brakes, sending the crippled vehicle skidding sideways into a light pole. Antifreeze exploded out of the damaged front end, soaking the windshield, which looked like a burst watermelon across the spiderweb shattered glass.

The horn wailed and died, yielding to the whimpering chorus of hyperventilated breaths. Francesca palpated her strained swollen belly. "What the hell was that?"

"Everyone out of the car." Shep kicked open the passenger door, ventilating the van with toxic steam from the antifreeze. For a moment, he stared at the remains of Sergeant Steven Mennella, the corpse embedded in the hood, face-up. Then he turned away. "We need to find another vehicle that runs."

Not waiting for the others, he sloshed down East 68th Street, his legs calf deep in a moving stream of cold water by the time he reached the intersection of Park Avenue. *Main must've broken. Maybe a fire hydrant?*

Then he saw the nightmarish scene and prayed it was the vaccine.

Park Avenue's six-lane boulevard resembled a scene straight out of Hades. High-rise office buildings and condominiums formed an ominous corridor squeezed beneath a ceiling of roiling brown clouds. Functioning as insulation, the man-made atmosphere had encapsulated the heat from dozens of car fires, the rising temperatures melting the snow that had been piled high along the curbs, transforming one of Manhattan's major arteries into a river. Contaminated with gasoline, the floodwaters sprouted pockets of flames that burst and receded across the hellish scene.

Whomp.

The distant sound was somehow familiar, causing the hairs on the back of Shep's neck to stand on end.

Whomp. Whomp . . .

His eyes locked onto an object as it dropped out of the clouds a block away. He never saw the impact, but he heard it as it struck a parked vehicle, setting off a car alarm.

Another object dropped, then two more. Shep swooned, having realized what he was witnessing.

Manhattan was raining its dead.

But not every object was corpse. Plague-infested suicides leapt from candle-lit apartment windows, dancing in free fall before pulverizing the roofs and hoods and trunks of the countless vehicles that clogged Park Avenue, their insides splattering on impact.

Paolo joined Shep, the two men dumbstruck. "Is this an illusion?"

"No."

The flood became a swiftly moving current as it swept around Park Avenue onto 68th Street, dragging an object with it. The glow from a burning vehicle revealed the body of a small child.

The image triggered a collage of remembered images that staggered Shep. His heart raced, his senses blinking in and out of reality until suddenly he was no longer in Manhattan—

—suddenly he is back in Iraq, standing along the banks of the Shatt-Al-Arab waterway.

It is dusk, the horizon purging sunlight into orange flames, squelching the heat of day into a tolerable climate. David Kantor is with him, the medic assisting an Iraqi physician. Dr. Farid Hassan drags a headless body from out of the shoreline's weeds.

David inspects the remains. "Looks like more of al-Zarqawi's work. Dr. Hassan?"

"I would agree."

Patrick Shepherd, two months into his first tour of duty, responds with a belch of acid reflux. "What I wouldn't give to line those bastards up one at a time."

The Iraqi physician exchanges a knowing look with the American medic. "Dr. Kantor tells me this is your first time in Iraq, yes?"

"Yeah." Shep searches the weeds for more dead.

"He says you played professional baseball. My son, Ali, he also loved sports. A natural athlete, my son."

"Hook us up. I'll teach him how to throw a slider."

"Ali died four years ago. He was only eight years old."

"Oh. I'm sorry."

"But these are just polite words. Are you really sorry? How can you possibly feel the sadness in my heart?"

A cramp-like stitch grips Patrick's chest. He winces in pain, yet neither David nor Dr. Hassan seem to notice.

In the distance, a small boat approached. A lone figure stood in the bow, its cloaked outline silhouetted by the setting sun.

"If you were truly sorry, Sergeant, you would be home playing baseball, telling your many American fans that the war is wrong. Instead, you are in Iraq, carrying an assault rifle, pretending to be Rambo. Why are you in Iraq carrying an assault rifle, Sergeant Shepherd?"

An internal switch flips, his blood again running cold. "In case you didn't get the memo, we were attacked."

"And who attacked you? The September 11 hijackers were Saudis. Why aren't you in Saudi Arabia, killing Saudi children?"

"American soldiers don't murder children. I mean, with all due respect, no one ever means to hurt a child. Help me out here, Dr. Kantor."

"Sorry, rook, it's time you opened your eyes. There is no Santa Claus, the Easter Bunny's dead, and everything you think you learned about war from Hollywood and Uncle Sam is bullshit. You think Cheney and Rumsfeld give a rat's ass about WMDs or Iraqi freedom? Newsflash, Shep: This invasion was strictly about money and power. Our job is to control the populace so Washington can control the oil and make a bunch of rich people a whole lot richer. And those billions allocated for reconstruction? The money's being spent on military bases, lining the pockets of private contractors like Haliburton and Brown and Root. Bechtel was given the contract to control the Tigris and Euphrates Rivers, and they're reaping a fortune while the locals are left with water that's no longer potable. Money and power, kid, and the real casualties of war are the children. Of course, I doubt that story will ever air on the nightly news."

"Again with the children? Sir, with all due respect . . . what are you talking about?"

"Half a million dead children, to be precise." The Iraqi physician's dark eyes fill with rage. "When you invaded our country back in '91, your military purposely targeted our civil works, a calculated yet immoral act that violated the Geneva Convention. You destroyed the dams we used for irrigation. You destroyed our pumping stations. You destroyed our water-purification plants and sewage-treatment facilities. My little boy was not killed by a bullet or explosive, Sergeant Shepherd. My son died from diphtheria. The drugs I would have used to treat Ali's inflamed heart were banned from entering my country, thanks to American and British sanctions imposed by the United Nations."

The flatboat moved closer. Shep could make out a hooded figure standing in the stern. Paddling slowly.

"We are not a backward nation, Sergeant. Before the first American invasion, Iraq possessed one of the best health-care systems in the world. Now we are fraught with cholera and typhoid, diarrhea and influenza, Hepatitis A, measles, diphtheria, meningitis, and the list goes on and on. Five hundred thousand children have perished since 1991. Hundreds more continue to die every day because we no longer have access to safe drinking water. Human waste is rampant, leading to infectious diseases."

Shep spots the body, submerged in weeds . . .

"—one in eight Iraqi children now dies before its fifth birthday, one in four is chronically malnourished."

He lifts the seven-year-old girl's drowned corpse to his chest, his body convulsing as he recognizes her face—

"So please, do not tell me you are sorry for my son's death. You have no idea what it feels like to lose a child."

—Bright Eyes.

"Patrick, watch out!"

Flames flared up as a pool of gasoline ignited. Shep staggered back, clutching his face.

"Are you okay?"

He nodded at Paolo, pulling his hands away. His blood ran cold. The flatboat from his daydream was moving slowly down Park Avenue.

A lone figure stood in the wood boat, the Grim Reaper using the stick end of his scythe to guide his craft along the flooded thoroughfare.

Shep backed away as the current swept the craft down Park Avenue and onto 68th Street. The Angel of Death turned its wretched face to him as he passed. The supernal creature nodded, beckoning him to follow.

Shep slogged through the flooded street after him.

The flatboat spun out of the current and over the submerged curb, coming to rest along the sidewalk leading up to the darkened entrance of a neoclassical limestone structure. Nearly a century old, the four-story building, located on the northwest corner of East 68th Street, had large arched windows that wrapped around the first floor and octagonal windows on the upper floor, all situated below a cornice and balustrade roofline.

An engraved sign reads: COUNCIL OF FOREIGN RELATIONS.

The floodwaters were washing down the curbside gutter, which inhaled everything the rapids drew into its orifice. Including the remains of the dead.

The Grim Reaper stared at Shep. The two orbital cavities within its skull were filling with dozens of fluttering eyeballs, the unnerving image resembling a honeycomb overflowing with bees. The Death Merchant waved the olive green blade of his scythe at the sewer.

The flooded crevice widened into a massive sinkhole. Tainted water swirled down the oval gullet as if it were a drain, the aperture twenty feet across and still growing. Pools of gasoline ignited, illuminating the subterranean depths below in a fiery orange radiance.

The Reaper pointed a bony index finger at the void, silently commanding Shep to peer into the abyss.

Patrick refused.

The Angel of Death raised its scythe, pile driving the blunt end of the staff against the flooded sidewalk. The resounding tremor unleashed a ring of foot-high waves that cascaded down 68th Street.

Shep glanced around. Paolo, Francesca, Virgil, and the Patels stood rigid as statues, as if they now existed in an alternative dimension from his own. *It's just the vaccine . . . it's just another hallucination.*

He moved to the edge of the breach. Knee deep in water, he braced his quadriceps muscles against the tug of the icy current as he looked down.

"Oh, God . . . no. No!"

Patrick Shepherd was peering straight into Hell.

BATTERY PARK CITY
5:27 A.M.

Stone Street was a narrow avenue in Battery Park, its road paved with ancient cobblestone, the ground level of its buildings serving as storefronts to many popular eateries. Seventeen hours earlier, locals and tourists had been ordering lunch at Adrienne's Pizzeria and buying desserts at Financier's Pastries. Five hours later, they were crowding the Stone Street Tavern, the pub one of many public refuges for out-of-towners with no place to go to escape the mandatory curfew.

By 7 P.M., the free-flowing alcohol had transformed Stone Street into a raucous block party. Music blared from battery-powered CD players. A doomsday "anything-goes attitude" had paired women off with men they had just met, converting the backseats of parked vehicles into temporary bedrooms.

Families with young children abandoned Stone Street, initiating a pilgrimage up Broadway to Trinity Church.

By 10 P.M., the music had stopped playing. By ten thirty, the inebriated turned violent.

Fights broke out. Windows were smashed, businesses vandalized. Women who had consented to sex hours earlier were gang-raped. There was no police, no law. Only violence.

By midnight, Scythe had delivered its own version of justice to the debauchery.

Five and a half hours have passed since the calendar date changed to the dreaded twenty-first of December, the winter solstice transforming Stone Street into a fourteenth-century European village.

There were no lights, just the orange glow of embers smoldering from steel trash cans. A ceiling of mud-colored clouds churned surreally overhead. The cobblestone streets and alleyways were littered with the dead and dying. Melting snow had drenched their remains. Thawed blood flowed again from their nostrils and mouths—drawing rats.

Rats outnumbered the dead and dying sixty to one. High on fleas infected with Scythe, the vermin converged upon the fallen in cannibalistic packs, their sharp teeth and claws gnawing and stripping away husks of flesh, each meal contested, igniting another blood-frothed frenzy.

The black Chevy Suburban turned slowly onto Stone Street. For the last five hours, Bertrand DeBorn's driver had squeezed and bulldozed and maneuvered the truck around endless avenues of abandoned vehicles that had restricted their speed to six miles an hour. Reaching another impasse, Ernest Lozano swerved onto the sidewalk, the truck's thick tires rolling over human speed bumps, crushing rodents refusing to abandon their meals.

Sheridan Ernstmeyer was seated next to him, riding "shotgun." The female assassin had killed anyone approaching within ten feet of the Suburban.

Bertrand DeBorn stirred in back. The secretary of defense's glands were swollen, the low-grade fever building in his system. Eyes closed, eyelids fluttering, he rasped, "Are we there?"

"No, sir. We're about a block away."

"What the hell's taken so—" DeBorn succumbed to a twenty-second-long coughing fit, his rancid breath filling the vehicle. The two bodyguards readjusted their own face masks.

Lozano turned right on Broad Street, New York Bay coming into view. The street was completely gridlocked with vehicles, the sidewalks clogged as well.

"Sir, we're blocked. But the apartment building's just up on the right."

"The two of you bring her to me. Shepherd's daughter, too."

The two agents looked at one another.

"Is there a problem?"

"No, sir." Ernest Lozano shifted the gear into PARK. Exiting the vehicle, he followed Sheridan Ernstmeyer down the corpse-laden, rodent-infested street, heading for the apartment building of Beatrice Eloise Shepherd.

UPPER EAST SIDE

For Patrick Shepherd, time appeared to have stopped. The floodwaters, the flames, the members of his entourage—everything within the physical dimension Virgil had referred to as the *Malchut wa*s frozen.

Several hundred feet below his Park Avenue curbside perch was another reality.

The widening aperture reveals three distinct levels of the seventh circle of Hell. The first, running beneath the CFR Headquarters for as far as his vantage will allow, is a vast river of blood, as long and as wide as the Mississippi, fed in part by the gradually progressing waterfall sweeping its refuse from the Sixty-eighth Street gutter.

The stench of the river is as unbearable as the plight of those caught in its chop. Somehow, Shep can sense their aura—a deep, slowly reverberating malevolent pulse of energy, its negative frequency as asphyxiating as Hell's stink. Men and women. Naked and bleeding.

The souls of the violent.

Countless thousands, their faces appear, then disappear, like tainted baptized meat within a broiling vermillion broth. Gasping desperate sustaining breaths before being forced to submerge once more. Clawing over one another, their focus is on saving themselves rather than on working together to charge the shoreline.

Patrolling the shallows and shoreline are the Centaurs. Half man, half horse, the creatures greet every emerging soul with the business ends of their pitchforks, stabbing the condemned until they are forced to retreat back into the river.

It takes Shep a moment to realize that these wretched men and women are surfacing en masse not just to breathe; they appear to be attracted to the Light coming from above—

—his Light!

Patrick shudders, terrified. Tyrants and murderers . . . is this the fate that awaits me?

"Help me. Please."

Shep's eyes track the plea to a crater-sized hole just beyond the shoreline. The vent reveals a second level beneath the first—an alien forest, the trees leafless, bearing only thorns. The voice is coming from a man in his forties, wearing a gray business suit, collared white shirt, and patterned tie.

Shep recognizes him. It's the guy who landed on the van . . . the suicide.

As he watches, the man's feet become rooted in the ashen soil. His limbs stiffen into branches, his fingers sharpening into thorns.

Flapping their way from branch to branch on this newly formed suicide tree are Harpies. Half female, half bird, the creatures are searching for leaves, plucking each green growth the moment one sprouts from the human/tree appendage.

Shep cannot see what is happening below the Wood of the Suicides and into the third level, but he can hear the echoes of screams, accompanied by tortured shouts of blasphemy, all aimed at God.

A now-familiar sensation causes Shep to look up. The Reaper is staring at him through eyes composed of hundreds of fluttering pupils, the creature's grin curdling Patrick's blood. A bony hand reaches out from the dark robe for him—

—another hand forcefully dragged him away from the seventh circle of Hell.

Shep shouted as he wheeled around to face Virgil.

"Are you all right? No, you're not, I can see it in your eyes."

Dumbfounded, Shep looked around for the Grim Reaper. Both the Angel of Death and the aperture were gone.

"Patrick?"

"I can't take it anymore, Virgil. The hallucinations . . . the guilt. But worse, far worse, is the loneliness . . . always feeling empty inside. It's like a poison that slowly eats away at every cell in my body. Only the fear of what happens to suicides in the afterlife has kept me from killing myself all these years. I feel so lost . . . surrounded by darkness."

"It's not too late, Patrick. There is still time to change, to bring Light into your vessel."

"How? Tell me!"

"Allow yourself to feel again. Where there's love, there's always Light."

"All I feel is emptiness."

"That's because you're afraid to feel. Stop bottling up your emotions. Allow yourself to experience pain and suffering. You must be willing to face the truth."

"The truth about what? What do you know, Virgil? What did your buddy, DeBorn, tell you about me?"

Paolo rushed over to join them, his eyes wild, his mind in the throes of his own hallucination. "Look! In the sky! Do you see it? A demon!"

Shep and Virgil looked up.

The Reaper drone was hovering just below the swirling brown clouds, its crimson camera lens spying on them from above.

Virgils squinted at the flying object. "It's not a demon, Paolo; it's a military drone. Where are the Patels?"

A gray Volkswagen van swerved around the sidewalk, its tailpipe belching exhaust as it skidded to a halt, the mechanical beast's heavy idle scattering waves across the flooded street. Pankaj was driving, his daughter and wife up front. Francesca was lying down in the third seat.

Pankaj rolled down his window. "Soldiers are coming. Get in!"

Shep yanked open the sliding back panel, ushering Paolo and Virgil inside. The relic bashed and squeezed its way south along Park Avenue, heading for Lower Manhattan.

EIGHTH CIRCLE

FRAUD

"Already we'd climbed as high as we were able to in order to observe the next burial place, standing midway on the bridge with an aerial view over the ditch. Oh Supreme Wisdom, how you embrace the heavens, the Earth, and even Hell with high art, and how justly your power dispenses grace! The sides and bottom were punctured by a myriad of round holes scattered over the livid-colored rock; each was as wide as I, and similar in depth and diameter to those basins found in my cherished San Giovanni, within which the baptizer would stand. From the mouth of every opening a sinner's legs protruded out, from the feet up to the thigh, the rest of the sinner remaining inside the hole."

—Dante's Inferno

DECEMBER 21

TRIBECA, NEW YORK

6:07 A.M.

(1 HOUR, 56 MINUTES BEFORE THE PROPHESIED END OF DAYS)

The stairwell was empty, a good sign. David Kantor reached the second-floor landing, his legs dead tired, his quadriceps burning with lactic acid from the long bike ride.

Running out of time . . . come on!

Grabbing the rail, he dragged himself up the steps, each exhaled breath crackling in his headpiece.

The journey through Manhattan on the ten-speed bicycle had been treacherous. David's military equipment had played havoc with his balance, his boots barely able to remain on the pedals. But the bike's narrow width had given him the ability to maneuver through gridlocked streets, and the quiet ride helped keep him from being noticed by the military.

As it turned out, they were the least of his problems.

Racing through the Upper West Side, he had made the mistake of following the Avenue of the Americas. The CBS Building. The Bank of America Tower. W.R. Grace. Macy's. The stretch of city blocks known as "skyscraper alley" had been transformed by the roiling brown clouds hovering below the glass-slab structures into a gothic scene resembling something straight out of a Wayne D. Barlowe nightmare. Burning cars, flooded streets. Bodies falling out of bizarre clouds . . . flying sacks of flesh and blood. A woman nosedived onto the roof of a yellow cab. Not from high enough to kill her, so she lay moaning, broken and disfigured.

The sudden jolt of adrenaline had quelled his fatigue. He sprinted past Rockefeller Plaza, refusing to gaze at the multitudes of dead piled high on the ice rink. He continued on through the Garment District and Chelsea. Passing through the arch at Washington Square, he entered Greenwich Village, a Bohemian neighborhood where he had spent most of his college years. He cut across the sidewalks of his alma mater, New York University's campus deserted, its student body thankfully on Christmas break. He diverted past his parents' old row house, traversing by the familiar basketball courts on Desalvio and Bleecker Street, where he had logged thousands of hours of pickup games. Like the ice rink, the asphalt rectangles had become drop-off points for Scythe's unburied dead, the adjacent playgrounds a battleground for unbridled gang members determined to turn the Village into a shooting gallery.

Without warning, machine-gun fire erupted from out of the pitch, and suddenly he was back in Iraq, the unseen assassins seemingly nowhere and everywhere. One bullet grazed his shoulder, another ricocheted off a manhole cover and struck his bike, forcing him to take cover between rows of abandoned cars. Remaining low, wheeling the ten-speed through the narrow spaces, he managed his way out of the contested turf into SoHo.

The trendy shopping area named for its location South of Houston Street resembled a demilitarized zone. Eight hours earlier, waves of locals had run amok, looting and vandalizing the neighborhood's shops. They had been met by SWAT teams wearing environmental suits and little tolerance. Bullet-ridden remains had been left over shattered store windows beneath the colorful tattered awnings as a warning to other curfew violators.

It had taken David Kantor almost ninety minutes to finally reach Tribeca.

Situated between SoHo and Manhattan's Financial District, just west of Chinatown, Tribeca derived its name from its location—the Triangle below Canal Street. Once an industrial district, the neighborhood had become one of the Big Apple's wealthiest areas, its warehouses having been converted into residential buildings and lofts, many providing second homes to some of Hollywood's biggest stars.

Claremont Prep was located just south of Wall Street in the former Bank of America International Building. The private elementary, middle, and high school consisted of 125,000 square feet of classrooms, art studios, laboratories, a library, café, gymnasium, outdoor play areas, and a twenty-five-meter swimming pool. The student body came from New York's five boroughs as well as New Jersey. Well-to-do parents, seeking the best education for their offspring. Twelve hours earlier, the entire school had been in lockdown.

Now it was left to David to see if anyone had survived.

Having accessed the Bank of America building's stairwell, the Army medic continued climbing. He was panting heavily by the time he arrived on the third-floor landing. He tried the stairwell's fire door. Locked. He banged on the steel barrier, using the butt end of his assault rifle. No answer.

Standing back, David aimed the gun barrel at the lock, then squeezed off a round, shredding the mechanism. Terrified over what he might find, he yanked open the door and entered the dark confines of his daughter's school.

LOWER EAST SIDE, MANHATTAN
6:16 A.M.

They had driven without lights, cruising along sidewalks and tearing through store awnings. Leaving Park Avenue, Pankaj had tried to avoid the major thoroughfares, finding it easier to maneuver south down the less con-gested northbound streets.

Midtown East was especially dangerous, the military presence still heavy surrounding the United Nations. Diverting west again across Park Avenue, Pankaj managed to work his way through Murray Hill before cutting back to the southeast through the quiet, older areas around Gramercy Park.

Entering the East Village, he had had little choice but to head south on the Bowery.

The crystal around Manisha Patel's neck immediately began to vibrate. "No, this is the wrong way."

"What choice do I have? Traffic is backed up from the two bridges; there's no place to drive."

"My spiritual guide says no. Find another way. Take us south through Chinatown."

The Minoses were in the third seat. Paolo comforted his pregnant wife, who was lying down with her head in his lap, her swollen belly contorting. "Your son is abusing his mother."

"Look how well he kicks. He will be a great soccer player."

"He wants out, Paolo. I was afraid to tell you. My water broke back in the park while we were waiting for you to return."

Overwhelmed, feeling utterly helpless, Paolo could only muster enough strength to squeeze Francesca's hand. "Try to hold on, my love. We'll be at the docks soon."

Virgil was seated in the middle seat next to Shep. Exhausted, the old man snored in his sleep.

Patrick Shepherd leaned against the driver's side back door, his injured left shoulder throbbing, the constant pain keeping him awake. Through heavy eyelids, he gazed at the young Indian girl seated up front between her parents, his psyche somehow drawn to her aura.

Ever alert, she sensed him staring. "Are you in terrible pain?"

"I've hurt worse."

Unbuckling her seat belt, the girl turned around, kneeling on her seat to face him. "Give me your hand." She smiled at his hesitancy. "I promise I won't hurt you."

He reached out with his right hand, allowing her to take it in her soft, delicate palms. Palpating his flesh, she closed her eyes, her fingertips resting on his pulse. "So rough. So much pain . . ."

"I was a soldier."

"This is much deeper . . . a pain that comes from a prior journey made long ago. A terrible misdeed . . . so many dead. The burden weighs you down."

"A prior journey? What kind of—"

"—something else . . . a great disappointment, all-consuming. Your actions haunt you."

"Dawn!" Manisha turned around, apologetic. "Patrick, my daughter . . . she is young—"

"No, it's . . . all right." He looked at the girl. "Your name is Dawn?"

"Yes."

"You have such pretty brown eyes. When I first looked into them back in Central Park . . . well, never mind."

"Tell me."

"It's just . . . they remind me of someone I knew."

"My mother says the eyes are the windows to the soul. Perhaps we knew one another in a prior life."

"Perhaps. And what do you see when you look into my eyes?"

She made eye contact, staring easily at first, then deeper.

Patrick felt himself trembling.

The girl's expression changed. Her lower lip quivered. Losing her composure, she suddenly released his hand and hugged her mother.

Shep sat up, trying hard not to freak out. "What is it? What's wrong?"

The sobbing girl buried her face in Manisha's lap.

"Come on, kid, don't leave me hanging."

"Forgive my daughter, Patrick, she didn't mean to upset you. Reading a person's face is tiring work on a good day. Dawn is exhausted, but there is nothing to fear. Dawn, tell Patrick you are sorry for upsetting him."

"I'm sorry for upsetting you, Patrick. Please forgive me."

"Yeah . . . sure, no worries." Unnerved, he turned away, staring coldly out the driver's side backseat window. Somewhere in the distance was FDR

Drive, beyond that the East River. There was only darkness out there, save for two towering infernos—the Manhattan Bridge to the north, the Brooklyn Bridge to the south. The two expanses had been destroyed seventeen hours earlier, yet the incendiary thermite used in the blasts still burned, the chemical compound melting right through the steel girders—

—just as it had on September 11, 2001.

Three buildings had collapsed at near-free-fall speed. Two had been hit by hijacked planes, the third building—Building-7, a forty-seven-story structure—had folded like a deck of cards hours later, floor after floor, the skyscraper having been hit by nothing more than debris. While most Americans never questioned what their eyes had seen, scientists and engineers were baffled by events that defied every known law of physics, engineering, and metallurgy known to man.

In the end it came down to a simple numbers problem: How could jet fuel, which burned off rapidly at 800 to 1200 degrees Fahrenheit liquefy steel girders, which melt at 2500 degrees, more than twice the jet fuel's highest recorded heat? There was no doubt steel had melted; molten steel was videotaped pouring from windows moments before the collapse, and a lake of molten steel had burned beneath the World Trade Center foundation for months after 9/11, despite firefighters' best efforts to quell the fire with millions of gallons of water and Pyroccol, a chemical-fire suppressant.

Homeland Security had shut down all access to Ground Zero, effectively preventing any close inspection of the debris; still, resourceful engineers had managed to collect plenty of particle samples—their analysis revealing the presence of a foreign substance that should not have been in the wreckage: Thermite. A pyrotechnic material used by the military and construction engineers to collapse steel structures, thermite generated temperatures at a superhot 4500 degrees. Thermite also burned for extended periods of time. And it could be applied as a paint.

In response to independent experts' unsettling discoveries, the National Institute of Standards and Technology released a thousand-page report containing explanations that contradicted every known case study of high-rise-building fires. The report never accounted for thermite residue; nor did it acknowledge the mysterious lake of molten steel. NIST officials also refused to address the series of explosions reported by hundreds of eyewitnesses moments before the towers collapsed. Or the videotape evidence of Building-7's collapse, which clearly showed squibbs—puffs of smoke created by demolition explosions—coming from each floor as the tower pancaked at near-free-fall speed.

More than four hundred independent architects and engineers disputed the NIST findings—to no avail. America had been attacked, and Americans wanted retribution, not ridiculous conspiracy theories.

It was during Patrick Shepherd's second deployment that he first learned of the controversial 9/11 Truth Web sites from a fellow soldier. The accusations infuriated him. So what if the towers were known health hazards, filled with asbestos? So what if Building-7's collapse was reported by the BBC forty minutes before it actually happened? Or that the tower housed the second largest covert CIA station in the country, as well as the SEC offices investigating Enron's and WorldCom's frauds. True, Larry Silverstein, the new owner of the World Trade Center, had shut down a few of the Twin Towers' elevator shafts for "upgrades" a month before 9/11, but so what? How could any loyal Americans believe that elements within their own government could have aided and abetted such a nefarious terrorist attack, using the event as an excuse to invade Iraq? It was utter nonsense.

The mainstream media refused to buy into it, and most Americans, Patrick among them, refused as well. But as the years went by, and the deployments mounted, Patrick's mind began to warm to the evidence, and the toxic thoughts turned his heart stone-cold.

He learned that modern history was littered with false-flag events—acts of violence, organized by ruling elites designed to direct blame at an enemy in order to amass the public's support. In 1931, the Japanese blew up sections of their own railway as a pretext for annexing Manchuria. In 1939, the Nazis fabricated evidence of a Polish attack against Germany to justify their invasion of Poland. In 1953, the United States and Britain orchestrated "Operation Ajax," a false-flag event that targeted Mohammed Mosaddegh, the democratically elected leader of Iran. Nine years later, President Kennedy stopped Operation Northwoods, a Department of Defense plot that would have blamed Cuba for a rash of incidents, including the hijacking and crash of a US commercial airliner. Years later, another false-flag operation—the Gulf of Tonkin incident—escalated the Vietnam War.

Three thousand innocent people had been murdered on September 11. As horrific as it was, the numbers were almost negligible when compared to the history of modern warfare. Hitler had exterminated six million Jews. Pol Pot had systematically eliminated over a million Cambodians. The Chinese were massacring Tibetans on a daily basis. Genocide had wiped out a million in Rwanda. The US invasion had killed a million Iraqis . . . even though Saddam had had no weapons of mass destruction, and Iraq considered Osama bin Laden and al-Qaeda a sworn enemy.

To the military-industrial power brokers and Wall Street's elite, three thousand casualties were nothing compared to Iraq's oil reserves and a trillion dollars in no-bid contracts and military expenditures.

Seated in the backseat, Patrick recalled the moment the truth about September 11 had finally clicked. It was the last day of his fourth and final deployment, the day he had realized that the country he loved had been taken over by the corporate elite, that he had killed innocent people to support their empires of greed, and that he was destined to burn in Hell for his actions, never to see his soul mate again.

Staring at the burning bridges, Patrick registered the familiar copper taste of hatred in his mouth. It was a hatred that had blinded him for the better part of eleven years, an anger so deep that it smothered every ounce of love he had ever felt, destroying every decent memory, blocking every speck of Light. And in this sudden moment of clarity, another truth surfaced its ugly head . . .

"They're going to incinerate Manhattan."

His fellow passengers turned to face him.

Paolo gripped his wife's hand. "Who's going to incinerate Manhattan?"

"The feds. The Department of Defense. It'll happen soon, probably when the sun comes up. It might have happened hours ago had they gotten hold of this vaccine."

"How do you know this?" Pankaj asked.

"Back at the VA hospital, I overheard Bertrand DeBorn threatening to spill the beans about anthrax and the attacks back in 2001."

"Kogelo's secretary of defense?"

"What does anthrax have to do with—"

"The anthrax originated from CIA-run labs. I'm guessing Scythe was designed in a similar lab."

"For what purpose?" Paolo asked.

"To invade Iran. Since we lack the manpower to take over another country, the intel guys came up with a new plan. We unleash a biological like Scythe, gut the country's militia, then ride in with the vaccine and negotiate peace."

"I don't believe that," Francesca stated emphatically. "I refuse to believe it. This is Manhattan, the Big Apple. No one's going to incinerate the most populated city in America."

"They don't care," Shep said, closing his eyes. "We're simply numbers on a ledger sheet, acceptable losses. They'll incinerate Manhattan, blame Scythe on a bunch of terrorists, and the next thing you know, it'll be World War III."

GOVERNOR'S ISLAND
6:20 A.M.

Alone in the darkness, marooned on the moldy mattress on the damp concrete floor, Leigh Nelson's body convulsed as she heard someone cross the first floor directly overhead. Terror gripped her mind as the heavy-footed soldier descended the wooden steps.

She cried out as he approached.

"No more waterboarding, I promise. I brought you something to calm your nerves. Can you sit up?" Jay Zwawa helped Leigh Nelson into an upright position, the female physician's muscles trembling. He handed her the open bottle of whiskey.

She forced it to her lips and drank. Drained a third of the bottle before he could take it from her. Her insides were on fire, the internal heat soothing her frayed nerves.

"You okay?"

"Why did you torture me?"

"Why? Because I was following orders. Because the world's gone crazy. Because common sense got tossed out the window the day presidents decided chicken hawks like Cheney and Rumsfeld and DeBorn knew more about running the military than men who had actually served in the armed forces."

"I hate you and your damn wars, and your insane biowarfare programs. I hope and pray every maggot and warmonger involved burns in Hell."

"I suspect you may get your wish."

She cowered as he reached into his jacket pocket—

—withdrawing a cell phone. "Call your family. Tell them you're okay. Nothing more."

With a trembling hand, she took the device and dialed.

"Hello?"

She broke into a sob. "Doug?"

"Leigh! Where are you? Did you get out of the city? I've been calling you all night!"

She gazed up at Captain Zwawa through a pool of tears. "I'm okay. I'm at an Army base on Governor's Island."

"Thank God. When will you be home? Wait . . . are you infected?"

"I'm okay. Are you okay? Are the kids safe?"

"We're all here. We're okay. Autumn's right here next to me. Autumn, you want to say hi to Mommy?"

A groggy child's voice said, "Hi, Mommy."

Leigh burst into sobs. Her throat constricted as she talked. "Hi, baby doll. Are you taking good care of Parker and Daddy for me?"

"Yes, Mommy. Are you taking care of Patrick for me?"

Leigh's heart pounded in her ears.

Jay Zwawa's eyebrows rose, his expression darkening.

"Honey, Mommy has to go. I love you." She powered off the phone, terrified. "I took him home to meet my family. He bonded with my little girl."

The captain pocketed the cell phone. Without another word, he trudged up the bare wooden steps, locking the door behind him.

Leigh Nelson crawled off to a corner of the basement and retched.

BATTERY PARK

6:21 A.M.

Ernest Lozano followed Sheridan Ernstmeyer into the apartment building lobby, their guns drawn. The small marble foyer was dark, save for a lone yellow emergency light blinking along the ceiling.

Shadows crawled. Moans rose from coughing victims. Muffled screams reached out from first-floor dwellings. The foul air reeked of death.

Lozano was losing his composure quickly. "This is bullshit. DeBorn's infected, he could be dead before we even make it back outside."

"Shut up." The female assassin searched for a stairwell, her cardiovascular system amped up on adrenaline and amphetamines. "Over here." She yanked open the fire door, releasing a cat. The skittish house pet scurried past them into the darkness.

"Floor?"

"Huh?"

"Shepherd's wife, what floor is she on?"

"Eleven. Sheridan, this is a fool's errand."

Turning to face him, she aimed the barrel of her 9mm at his mask. "DeBorn's a survivor, he'll make it out of here alive. Will you?"

"You're crazy."

"You mean I'm a crazy bitch. That *is* what you were thinking, isn't it, Ernie? Go on, make a menstrual reference. We'll see who will be the one bleeding."

The eyes peering at Lozano from behind the woman's mask were frenetic. "Let's just find Shepherd's wife and get the hell out of here."

She poked his chest with her index finger. "Yeah, that's what I thought you said." Backing away, she turned and headed up the concrete stairwell.

TRIBECA, NEW YORK
6:24 A.M.

The death of a child was profoundly unnatural, a perversion of existence. Children were simply not supposed to die before their parents. When it happened, it unleashed boundless grief, a pain so intense, the emptiness so encompassing that it could spiral the bereaved parent into oblivion.

David Kantor had been to war. He had treated children missing limbs. He had held their lifeless bodies in his arms. After five deployments spanning two wars, the medic had never grown immune to any tragedy involving children. Only this was different. A sight so heart-wrenching that only the overwhelming need to find his daughter prevented him from a mental breakdown.

David staggered from one classroom to the next, the beam of his flashlight uncloaking Scythe in its most evil form. Infected by plague, the youngest had huddled together on the floor like a newborn litter of puppies, drawn to one another's body warmth. Human snowflakes stained in blood.

She won't be here. These are the elementary-school students. Find the seventh graders.

David heard someone moaning. Moving quickly toward the sound, he cut across the corridor into the library, his flashlight homing in on the source.

The headmaster was lying on the carpeted floor, his head propped on an encyclopedia. Rodney Miller opened his eyes, each labored gasp exhaling a breath of blood.

"Miller, it's David Kantor."

"Kantor?"

"Gavi's father. Where is she? Where are the older kids?"

The headmaster struggled to form words. With a final gasp, he muttered, "gym."

CHINATOWN
6:26 P.M.

A driving wind whipped the East River into a rabid chop, stirring the muddy cloud bank hanging over Manhattan into an atmospheric maelstrom. Below the toxic ceiling of carbon dioxide and chemical compounds, the survivors of Scythe huddled on rooftops, each patch of elevated asphalt a refugee camp, the buildings' apartments having long been abandoned to the dying, the streets to the dead.

Pankaj Patel ground the gears of the gray Volkswagen microbus as he drove southwest along Henry Street, the bonnet of the clunky five-speed relic sideswiping awnings and everything else littering the tight sidewalks. He passed beneath the remains of the Manhattan Bridge. Turned right on Catherine Street. Drove another two blocks before he was forced to stop.

The north–south thoroughfare known as the Bowery was a virtual pileup of cars, buses, and trucks that occupied every square foot of asphalt and sidewalk as far as the eye could see. Most of the passengers caught on the Bowery had long since abandoned their vehicles, seeking bathrooms and food. Those few who had steadfastly remained inside their cars managed to avoid the pandemic into the night, only to find themselves trapped on their island of sanctuary with nowhere to go.

The silhouette of Chinatown's redbrick buildings and rickety fire escapes loomed beyond the Bowery's moat of vehicles like a medieval castle.

Pankaj turned to the others. "We have two choices: Remain here and die, or attempt to pass through Chinatown on foot. It's a short walk to the Financial District from here, then it's clear on to Battery Park and Paolo's brother-in-law's boat. Manisha?"

"My crystal has calmed. My spiritual guide is in agreement."

"Virgil?"

"Agreed."

"Paolo?"

"Francesca's water broke, she just had her first contraction. What happens when the baby starts coming?"

"We'll have to make do . . . find a cart or something to wheel her around in. Patrick?"

Virgil nudged Shep awake. "Your wife and daughter are close. Are you ready to continue on?"

"Yes."

Exiting the minibus, the seven survivors made their way across the Bowery on foot, climbing and sliding over the hoods and trunks of cars until they reached an eighteen-wheeler. The produce truck was lying on its side, blocking their entrance into Chinatown.

Sixteen hours earlier, the Asian enclave had been a crush of humanity, thousands of tourists filtering through *dim sum* restaurants and bargain hunting along the cluttered narrow streets. By mid-afternoon, the tourists had fled. By dusk, the Asian ghetto had segregated itself from the rest of Manhattan. Organizing quickly, Chinatown's leaders had cleared the streets of vehicular traffic as far north as Canal Street, ordering access into the community sealed off from all outsiders, the borders barricaded with overturned delivery trucks.

Pankaj signaled them to follow, the psychology professor having located an accessible fire escape. "We'll climb up to the roof, then make our way south to Columbus Park." Scaling a trash bin, he reached up and grabbed the lowest rung of a steel ladder, drawing it down from its slide axis.

Minutes later, the group was ascending the side of the building, the rusted slats of the fire escape's steps creaking beneath their weight.

UNITED NATIONS SECRETARIAT BUILDING
6:32 A.M.

The emergency generator had been powered on, its tentacles rewired to distribute electricity only to the building's six elevators. In the lobby, the process of disseminating Racal suits began, the self-contained hazardous-environment apparel loaded onto carts and sent by military escort to the suites still harboring survivors.

On the thirty-third floor, President Eric Kogelo and his staff had already received their suits. The leader of the free world has been awake for almost thirty hours, under enormous pressure. Throughout the long night, he had been assured by CDC physicians that his fatigue and low-grade fever were simply a result of exhaustion and not Scythe. Kogelo had pretended to accept their verdict but had chosen to isolate himself inside his private office "just as a precaution."

That the buboes had swelled along his groin and not his neck had helped hide the truth from the rest of his staff. Only John Zwawa at Fort Detrick knew that the president had been infected, the colonel hell-bent on delivering a cure by the time Kogelo arrived at Governor's Island.

"Mr. President, the vaccine is in Manhattan, being acquired as we speak. If the buboes only appeared six hours ago, then we still have time. I know it's difficult, sir, but try to remain calm."

For a while, Kogelo had remained calm, tasking himself to leave video messages to his wife and children, his vice president, Congress, and the American people. Internal hemorrhaging had forced him to stop, each blood-drenched cough raking his lungs with pain.

Now, as he lay on the leather couch in his Racal suit, he prayed to his Maker that he be allotted a little more time . . . to see his kids again, to hold his wife—

—and to forestall the war that would end all wars.

CHINATOWN
6:37 A.M.

One level after another, they continued their ascent on the rickety fire escape. Manisha kept a watchful eye on Dawn, Pankaj assisting Virgil. Paolo helped Francesca up the narrow trellis-like steps, his wife's progressing labor forcing her to pause every eight to nine minutes to "ride" a contraction.

Patrick was the last to step off the fire escape onto the eight-story building's summit—an expanse of tarmac and gravel that revealed a disjointed maze of silhouetted rooftops. Some were flat, others angled, almost none equal in height, creating a labyrinth of shadows that concealed brick ravines and interconnecting bridges, pipes and heating ducts, air conditioners and chimney stacks, antennae and satellite dishes—all jutting out at varying degrees in the darkness.

"This way," said Pankaj, certain of the direction yet unsure of the path. Ushering them to the west, he resumed the lead—

—when the asphalt suddenly rose before him in undulating waves, the shadows becoming people. Huddled beneath blankets, hundreds of Asian men, women, and children awaken to greet the invaders with utter silence, the dying light from their lanterns casting an unworldly aura upon the confrontation.

A boundary had been violated. Weapons were drawn.

Before Pankaj could react, before Manisha could register the vibrations of her crystal, before ten-year-old Dawn could scream or the Minoses pray, the mob cowered back into the shadows, dropping to their knees in fear.

Patrick stepped forward, his head and face concealed within the shadow of his ski jacket's hood, his prosthetic arm held aloft as if it were the Angel of Death's scythe.

"Paolo, I think it's time I took the lead." Pushing past the stunned psychology professor, Shep ventured forth, his presence parting the terrified sea of survivors.

TRIBECA
6:38 A.M.

The gymnasium was located on the ninth floor. David tried the doors—locked. Using the butt end of his assault rifle, he banged on the small rectangle of glass, shattering it. "Hello! Is anybody in there?" He shined his light inside. Heard rustling . . . whispers. "Who is it?"

"David Kantor, I'm Gavi's father. I am not infected."

Someone approached. A heavy chain was removed from the inside of the door. It was pushed open, and David entered. Dark inside, save for a fading emergency light. The students were spread out on the hardwood basketball court, silhouetted in blackness.

"Who's in charge here?"

"I am . . . sort of." The young man was sixteen. "There are eighteen of us in here. No one's infected, as far as we can tell. We locked ourselves in around two in the afternoon."

"Is Gavi Kantor in here? Gavi?"

"She's not here." A seventh grader stepped forward, an African-American girl wrapped in a blanket. "She wasn't in school today."

She wasn't in school! Did she cut classes? Maybe she's not even in Manhattan . . .

"Dr. Kantor, do you have enough environmental suits for all of us?"

A young boy in first grade tugged on his pant leg. "I wanna go home."

Home? David ground his teeth. *If they leave, they'll become contaminated. If they stay, they'll die anyway. What do I do with them? Where can I take them? There's no way off the island . . .*

They gathered around him like moths to a flame. "Please don't leave us."

He looked down at the seven-year-old boy. "Leave you? Now why would I do that? I'm here to take you home. But before we can leave, everyone needs to cover their mouths and noses with something. Use a scarf or a towel, even a sock . . . anything you can find. You older kids, help out the little ones. Once we leave the gym, you can't touch anything . . . you need to breathe through your scarves. Leave your belongings here, you don't need them. Only your jackets, gloves, and hats."

CHINATOWN

6:39 A.M.

The sudden reverberation of her crystal caused Manisha to jump. She looked around with a mother's paranoia. "Pankaj, where's Dawn?"

Her husband pointed ahead to where their daughter was walking hand in hand with the hooded figure of Patrick Shepherd. "She insisted. Is something wrong?"

"Everything is wrong," Manisha whispered, trembling. "Our supernal guide is close."

"**Patrick, can we** stop for a moment, I need to rest." Dawn released his right hand and sat on an air vent, using the back end of her coat for padding against the frosted surface. "Sorry, my feet hurt."

"Mine, too." He leaned against the corner of the rooftop's five-foot ledge, gazing below at Mott Street. "Columbus Park is only a few more blocks. Would you like me to carry you? I can put you on my back, just like I used to do with my own little . . ."

His voice trailed off, his eyes focused on the street below.

"What is it, Patrick? What do you see?"

The Chinese were efficient, he had to give them that. As the plague-infested bodies began multiplying, they had moved quickly, disposing of their dead directly into the sewers in the most efficient way possible—by dropping them headfirst down the open manholes. At some point, the seemingly endless procession of corpses had piled up below, clogging the makeshift burial ground. As a result, every manhole on Mott Street was stuffed with bodies, the legs of the last deceased protruding out of each open aperture upside down.

Inverted bodies, protruding feet first from the earth . . . The Scythe vaccine latched on to the long-extinct memory as if hooking a fish, dragging it up from the abyss and reeling it to the surface.

Wisps of gray mist rolled over Mott Street—

—revealing a muddy landscape that stretches for a thousand miles in every direction. The dead are everywhere—mottled, rotting corpses. Most lie in layers in the muck, others remain buried headfirst up to their waists in the bog. Prolonged exposure underwater had peeled the drowning victims' clothes from their flesh, in some cases the flesh from bone.

It is a valley of the dead, a fermenting graveyard of tens of thousands, the aftermath of an unimaginable natural disaster . . . or an act of God.

Shep snapped awake, his body trembling, his mind still gripped by the terrifying images. Instinctively, he dropped to his knees and hugged Dawn with his one good arm, his shaken spirit somehow soothed by her aura.

"Patrick, what is it? What did you see?"

"Death. On a scale I could never imagine. Somehow . . . it was my fault."

"You must go."

"Yes, we have to leave this place."

"Not us. Just you."

"What are you talking about?" He pulled away—

—and that was when he saw the spirit. The luminescent blue apparition appeared to be hovering over Dawn, whispering in her ear, instructing the child as she spoke. "You must leave us to tend to another flock."

"What flock? Dawn, is your spiritual companion telling you this?"

"Ten levels below us is *Malebolge*, a pouch of evil where the innocent are being accosted. Go to them, Patrick. Free them from servitude. We will meet you outside this circle of death when you have completed the task."

Patrick regained his feet, his eyes transfixed on the Light as he staggered backward—

—nearly toppling over Virgil. "What's wrong, son? Not another vision?"

"This was something different. Something much worse. Genocide. Destruction. The End of Days. Somehow, I was there for it, only it wasn't me. But I caused it. I was directly involved!"

The others gathered around.

"Try to remain calm, we'll sort this out."

"I have to go."

"Go where?" Paolo asked. "I thought you needed to find your family?"

"I do." He looked from Virgil to the girl, the spirit's light fading behind her. "But first I need to run a quick errand."

MALEBOLGE

6:53 A.M.

She was drifting between the pain of consciousness and the finality of darkness, the terrifying presence of the three circling predators ultimately keeping her from passing out.

She was bent over the tabletop, her jeans pushed down around her ankles. Her body trembled, her skin crawling as they moved in for the kill.

She squeezed her eyes shut, but could not escape the abusive aftershave of the one called Ali Chino. The lanky Mexican lurked before her; still she refused to look at him. She gagged as he licked her neck. She trembled as the blade of his knife glided past her throat and down her blouse. He removed each button with a flick of his wrist. She involuntarily jumped back, discovering Farfarello.

The Sicilian was twenty. He tore off her bra and groped her breasts from behind, his hands as callused and cold as his soul. Her mind blotted out the Sicilian and Mexican, the two followers having been relegated to leftovers at the feast. It was the alpha male who caused her to tremble, the demon pulling down her panties, groping her from behind.

Wanting her for himself, Cagnazzo shoved Farfarello aside. The Colombian was a psychopath. A monster who lived to inflict pain and suffering. Gavi Kantor cried out as the twenty-seven-year-old's blistered fingers probed her with one hand, readying himself with the other. He leaned forward. Whispered in broken English, "This is going to hurt. It's going to hurt bad. And when I'm done, I'm going to do it again with my gun."

For thirteen-year-old Gavi Kantor, there was nothing left. No more fear, no more spent nerves, no emotions or prayers. The butterfly had been broken on the wheel, the last hours of her existence taking with it her identity, her future, her past.

The Colombian bent her over the desk, getting no resistance.

And then, suddenly, there was another presence in the room—another predator.

There are three of them . . . and the girl. She is in her early teens, her shirt torn open and bloodied, her lower body naked, stretched belly down across a desk. Dark eyes greet him as he enters the den of iniquity. The teen cries out. The garbled words need no translation.

"This is not our battle, Sergeant. Leave the premises now!"

"Not this time."

Cagnazzo looked up, startled. "Who the fuck are you?"

Patrick Shepherd's eyes widened, his nostrils flared. "Don't you recognize me? I'm the Angel of Death."

The prosthetic arm whipped through the air, its curved blade slicing cleanly through the front of Cagnazzo's neck and esophagus until the steel edge lodged between the Colombian's fourth and fifth cervical vertebrae. Shep kicked the dead man loose from his scythe, then turned his attention to the other two slave traders.

Farfarello, pale as a ghost, crossed himself and fled.

Ali Chino, his body paralyzed in fear, watched the bloodstained blade loop upward from the ground, splitting the inverted V between his legs—tearing through his jeans as it sliced open his testicles. The castrated Mexican youth screamed in agony, then fell forward, clutching his gushing privates . . . knocking himself out on the desk.

Gavi Kantor covered herself, her body trembling. "Whoever you are, please don't hurt me."

"I won't hurt you." Shep retracted his hood, revealing himself to the girl.

The teen dressed quickly, staring at his face in the flickering candlelight. "I know you. . . . How do I know you?"

"You're shivering. Here, take my coat." He slipped off the ski jacket, handing it to her.

"My name is Patrick. We need to get out of here." He searched the dead Colombian, removing a .45 caliber Smith & Wesson from his waistband.

"They kidnapped me . . . they were going to . . . oh my God—"

He put his arm around her as she lost it. "Shh, it's okay. I'm going to get you out of here. Is there anyone else here? Any other girls?"

"They're locked up in a room. Down the hall."

"Show me."

BATTERY PARK

7:04 A.M.

Sheridan Ernstmeyer arrived at the eleventh-floor landing first, sweat pouring beneath her rebreather mask and down her face. For a well-deserved moment, she luxuriated in the intense burning sensation in her quadriceps, the endorphin high always accompanying a good workout.

Turning back to the stairs, she looked down—Ernest Lozano lagged two floors below. "Anytime, Mr. Y-Chromosome. Preferably before the apocalypse."

No answer.

"What's the apartment number? I'll handle this myself."

"Eleven-oh-two. Why didn't you tell me that nine floors ago?"

"You needed the workout. Man up while I grab Shepherd's wife." She yanked open the fire door, gun in hand.

The apartment was close to the stairwell, second door on the left. She knocked loudly several times. "Mrs. Shepherd, open up! Hello?" She banged again, readying herself to kick down the barrier.

Someone inside approached. "Who is it?" The voice belonged to a woman in her thirties.

"I'm with the military, Mrs. Shepherd. It's very important I speak with you." She held her identification up to the peephole.

A dead bolt was retracted. The door opened—

—revealing a thirty-two-year-old African-American woman dressed in a flannel bathrobe.

"Beatrice Shepherd?"

"No, I'm Karen. Beatrice is my mother."

"Your mother? No, that can't be right. Your husband . . . your estranged husband, Patrick . . . he needs to see you."

"I'm not married, and my mother has been a widow for twenty years. I think you have the wrong person." She attempted to shut the door, only Sheridan's boot was in the way.

"You're lying. Show me some ID."

"You need to leave."

The assassin aimed her gun at the woman's face. "You are Beatrice, aren't you?"

"Karen?"

The voice came from somewhere in the dark living room. Sheridan pushed her way in. Candlelight revealed a figure sprawled out on the sofa.

Fifty-seven-year-old Beatrice Eloise Shepherd lay in a pool of her own sweat and blood, the woman's body wracked with fever. An obscene dark bubo, the size of a ripe apple, protruded above the neckline of her silk pajamas. She was clearly on death's door—

—and she was clearly *not* the estranged wife of Sergeant Patrick Ryan Shepherd.

The female assassin backed away, then turned and left the apartment—

—running into Ernest Lozano in the corridor. "So? Where's Shepherd's wife? I thought you were handling it, hotshot."

Raising the 9mm pistol, Sheridan Ernstmeyer calmly and coldly shot the agent three times in the face, bone shrapnel and blood spraying across her mask. "We had the wrong person."

Stepping over the corpse, she hurried for the stairwell, enjoying the fleeting rush of endorphins flowing in her brain.

"This is the end . . . beautiful friend
This is the end . . . my only friend, the end
Of our elaborate plans, the end
Of everything that stands, the end
No safety or surprise, the end
I'll never look into your eyes . . . again."
—THE DOORS, "THE END"

NINTH CIRCLE

TREACHERY

"We silently climbed the bank which forms its border. Here it was less than day and less than night, so that my vision could hardly reach farther than a few yards. But if I was limited in sight I heard a high horn which made such a loud blast that the effect of thunder would have been slight by comparison. Immediately my eyes passed back along the path of the sound to its place of origin. Not even Roland's horn surpassed its dreadful wail. Not long after I'd turned my face to follow the sound there appeared to my eyes a number of high towers, or so I believed, and I asked: "Master, what is that city which lies before us?" And he explained: "What you've perceived are false images which come from trying to penetrate the shadows too deeply. You'll see how you're deceived once we get closer, so try to accelerate."

—Dante's Inferno

DECEMBER 21

GREENWICH VILLAGE, MANHATTAN

7:11 A.M.

(52 MINUTES BEFORE THE PROPHESIED END OF DAYS)

Major Steve Downey sat in the front passenger seat of the black military Hummer, his gaze focused on the live video feeds coming from the two Reaper drones hovering over Chinatown. For nearly two hours, his team of Rangers had maneuvered their military vehicles along sidewalks littered with the dead and dying, progressively working their way south as they tracked their quarry through Lower Manhattan. And then, somehow, Shepherd and his entourage had evaded them. By the time the Reapers had reestablished contact, Downey's crew had reached Houston Street.

The east–west thoroughfare that separated Greenwich Village from SoHo was a wall of vehicles that could not be negotiated. With chopper extractions banned because of the cloud cover and the UN evacuation set for seven thirty, time was running out quickly.

"Base to Serpent One."

Downey grabbed the radio. "Serpent One, give me some good news."

"The ESVs have landed. ETA for ESV-2 is three minutes."

"Roger that." Downey switched frequencies to speak with his second-in-command. "Serpent Two, the road's being paved, prepare to move out."

While the backbone of the US Army's ground forces remained the Abrams and Bradley tanks, these heavily armored vehicles, weighing upward of sixty-seven tons each, often required months to transport to the battlefield. For assignments requiring rapid deployment, the Defense Department developed the Stryker Force, eight-wheeled attack vehicles that weighed only thirty-eight thousand pounds, could be airlifted via a single C-130 aircraft, and possessed enough armor to stop small-arms fire.

The two vehicles that had been off-loaded from flatbed barges in Battery Park and Hudson River Park were M1132 Stryker Engineer Support Vehicles, each fitted with a seven-foot-high, two-foot-thick arrowhead-shaped steel tractor blade mounted to the Stryker's front end, converting the ESVs into fast-moving bulldozers.

Having deployed at Pier 25 in Tribeca, ESV-2 plowed its way east along Houston Street doing thirty miles an hour, its driver viewing Manhattan through night-vision and thermal-imaging cameras as he rammed his V-shaped blade into the gridlocked avenues, pushing vehicles aside and flipping buses as the Stryker cleared a twenty-foot-wide path through Lower Manhattan. Reaching Broadway, the all-terrain vehicle turned right, obliterated the wall of cars blocking the two black military Hummers, then headed south, the two Ranger teams following in its wake.

TRIBECA

7:17 A.M.

David Kantor exited the building's southwest stairwell, the seven-year-old boy in his arms, the rest of the students in tow. The older teens looked around, in shock. "What happened?"

"Oh my . . . there are dead people everywhere."

"Eww!" Children screamed, panicking the rest of the herd.

"It's okay. Stay calm." David looked around, desperate to find a means of transportation, even as he realized the futility of the task. "Kids, do you know where the school keeps its buses?"

"I do!" The sixth-grade girl pointed west down 41st Street.

"Good. Okay, everyone stay together now and watch where you're walking." He followed the middle schooler through a tight passage between rows of cars, the older teens plying him with questions.

"Did these people all die of plague?"

"How are you gonna drive a bus? The streets are jammed."

The sound was faint popping sounds—like distant firecrackers.

"Manhattan's been quarantined. How're you going to get us off the island?"

"We were safer inside. Maybe we should go back?"

"Quiet!" David stopped to listen.

The disturbance was growing louder, approaching from the north, the popping becoming more of a bashing of metal on metal, accompanied by a deep, rumbling sound.

"That's an ESV. The military must be clearing an evacuation route. Kids, come on!"

BATTERY PARK
7:19 A.M.

Sheridan Ernstmeyer heard the eruption of metal on metal the moment she exited the building lobby, the sound resembling a demolition derby. She approximated the location, then hustled back to the SUV. "Bert?" She shook the secretary of defense awake.

"Where's Shepherd's wife?"

"Dead," she lied, "but the military's here. There's an ESV moving north on Broadway. Must be an extraction team."

Bertrand DeBorn sat up, his mask spotted with specks of blood. "Get us out of here."

CHINATOWN

7:22 A.M.

The survivors—seven foreign girls wrapped in blankets—followed their one-armed angel and the American teenager through pitch-dark corridors and up a set of creaky wooden steps to the first floor of the Chinese souvenir shop.

The brothel's 270-pound madam was standing before the store's front door, the Mexican woman's rotund mass blocking the exit. "And where do you think you are going, *Chuleta?*"

Patrick Shepherd stepped in front of the girls, aiming the dead Colombian's gun at the madam's head. "Move it or lose it."

The madam smiled through bloodstained teeth. "You do not frighten me. I am protected by *Santa Muerte.*"

"Never heard of her." Raising his right knee, Patrick launched a front-thrust kick into the obese woman's belly, sending her crashing backward through the store's plate-glass window.

The girls scampered over the body of their former keeper and into the night.

COLUMBUS PARK

7:25 A.M.

Pankaj Patel led his family and fellow plague survivors down Bayard Street to the perimeter fence. Columbus Park's asphalt basketball courts and synthetic baseball field were covered in snow, the reflective alabaster surface offering a peek at the extent of Scythe's infestation upon the rodent population.

Hundreds of black rats moved as one in a symbiotic dance of tug-of-war. Rendered mad by the perpetual bites of ten thousand starving fleas, competing packs of rodents swarmed and retreated across the basketball court like schools of fish. At the center of this blood-laced scrum were the remains of an elderly couple, their ravaged torsos left recognizable only by their tattered outer garments, which provided grappling materials for tiny claws and teeth.

The visceral battle caused the six survivors to back away from the fence.

Francesca moaned, her contractions coming more frequently with every passing minute. "Paolo, do something!"

"Virgil, my wife's having our baby."

"And what would you have me do?"

"Lead us away from this horrible place. Get us to the waterfront and my brother-in-law's boat."

"What about Patrick?"

"We can't wait for him any longer. If what he said was true, then we're running out of time."

Manisha nodded at Pankaj. "He's right. We cannot wait any longer."

"Mom, no!"

"Dawn, sweetheart, whatever he's doing, he'll find us when he can."

"Perhaps you should build a golden calf?"

The four adults turned to face the old man.

"Pray to the idol, perhaps it will grant you the salvation you seek."

"Virgil, my wife is about to have a baby. We're surrounded by death—"

"—and who led you across this valley of death? Who inoculated your wife and child from plague? Manisha, who was it who risked his own life to save your family from the hangman's noose? Yet here you are, ready to abandon your leader as easily as the Israelites abandoned Moses at Sinai. Faith is easy when things are going right, when the challenges remain negotiable, not as much so when faced with your own mortality. But what if this is the very purpose of the physicality? To test one's faith, to battle the ego, to trust the system."

Pankaj broke into a cold sweat. He could hear the rats growling thirty feet behind him as they tore into morsels of human flesh. "What system, Virgil? What are you advising us to do?"

"Act with unquestioning certainty."

Dawn pointed. "There he is!"

Shep was jogging toward them, accompanied by a small group of girls, ages ten to eighteen. The youngest—a Mexican child, clung to his chest.

Manisha burst into tears of shame, immediately connecting Patrick's "errand" to the sex slaves he had just liberated. She took the child from him, allowing Shep to catch his breath. "We need to hurry, the sun'll be up soon."

Nodding at Virgil, the one-armed man led his growing flock west on Worth Street toward Broadway.

UNITED NATIONS PLAZA

7:29 A.M.

The Boeing CH-47F Chinook commercial transport helicopter flew low over New York Harbor, its tandem rotors kicking up the frigid waters, its pilots purposely avoiding the ominous layer of brown clouds swirling several hundred feet overhead. Reaching the East River, the heavy-lift airship headed north, following the narrow waterway to Lower Manhattan, landing at the United Nations Plaza.

A procession of delegates exited the lobby of the Secretariat Building, each survivor dressed hood to boots in an environmental suit. The ambulant occupied the permanent seats situated in the center of the Chinook. Those on stretchers were secured in the cargo area—

—President Eric Kogelo among them.

FOLEY SQUARE

7:32 A.M.

The sound reached them first—booming metallic collisions that rattled the night. The lights appeared next, blazing and bright, silhouetting a wave of vehicles tossed from the monster's path as it crashed its way east on Worth Street.

"This way!" Shep led them south into Foley Square.

Engines growled in the distance. Strobe lights illuminated the columns of the surrounding civic buildings. A Reaper drone loomed overhead, its camera catching Shep as he attempted to lead his followers up the US courthouse steps—the same steps Bernard Madoff had trod years earlier. As with the captured Ponzi schemer, there was no escape.

A midnight wave of Rangers swarmed in from all sides. They pinned

Patrick Shepherd to the concrete, their flashlight beams blinding his eyes as they pawed every square inch of flesh and stripped the clothing from his body. He screamed in agony as two Rangers wrenched his steel prosthetic from his lacerated shoulder, tearing nerve endings and tendons as they amputated the limb by force.

Patrick writhed on the ground, his wounded body in spasms, his mind set on fire. He heard Dawn cry out in pain. He registered Paolo's protests as gloved hands performed a cavity search on his laboring spouse.

The terror ceased, its victims left naked and shivering on the snow-covered lawn. Major Downey stalked the area. "Report."

"Sir, we found three vials of Scythe vaccine on Sergeant Shepherd, nothing more."

Downey straddled Patrick, pressing his boot to the amputee's bleeding left deltoid. "Where's the rest of the vaccine?"

"I sent it to your mother as a thank-you for last night."

The Ranger wound up to kick Shep in the face when Virgil, lying on the ground beside him, grabbed his ankle. "He inoculated these survivors. Take them with you, they remain plague-free."

"No one's going anywhere, old man." Downey activated his internal headset. "Serpent to base, we've acquired the Scythe vaccine."

"Well done. We'll meet you at the extraction point in five minutes."

"Roger that. Okay, people, let's move!" The Rangers double-timed it back to their vehicles—

—as a black Chevy Suburban skidded to a halt in front of the Hummers, causing the men to aim their assault weapons. A woman wearing a cloth mask climbed out of the driver's seat, her hands raised. "Don't shoot! I'm with the Secret Service. I have Secretary of Defense Bertrand DeBorn in back. We're to be part of your extraction."

Downey opened the back door of the Suburban, gazing at the white-haired man, who appeared to be unconscious. "It's him all right. And he's got full-blown Scythe. Load him on board, we'll get him into a Racal suit back at the docks."

"What about her?" One of the Rangers pointed to Sheridan Ernstmeyer.

"She goes, too."

The female assassin breathed a sigh of relief.

Across the park, a slight figure in a white Racal suit stepped out from behind a statue. The Tibetan monk removed his hood, his opaque eyes glittering like diamonds at Bertrand DeBorn.

The secretary of defense gurgled on a larynx full of blood, tumbling from the open rear door of the Suburban.

One of the Rangers checked for a pulse. "He's done."

"Leave him, we're running out of time." Major Downey climbed into the front seat of the lead Hummer.

"Wait!" Sheridan Ernstmeyer grabbed at the closing door. "What about me?"

"Sorry, lady. Looks like your ticket out of here just croaked."

Before she could react, the two military vehicles executed wild U-turns across the snow-covered park lawn, skidding their way back down Worth Street.

To the east, the slice of horizon beneath the false brown ceiling of clouds had turned gray, summoning the dawn. Retrieving their clothing, the accosted survivors dressed quickly, shivering in the cold.

Patrick dressed, his mangled left shoulder on fire. With his bare right hand, he gathered a clump of snow to press against the wound—revealing a small in-ground plaque:

"THESE ARE THE TIMES THAT TRY MEN'S SOULS . . ."
THOMAS PAINE.

Paolo comforted his wife, covering her with his overcoat. "It's all right. God will not abandon us in our hour of need."

"Wake up, Paolo. Look around you. God *has* abandoned us."

"You should restrict your tongue from negativity. Especially with a child to be born."

Francesca turned to see the bizarre-looking Asian. "Who the hell are you?"

Gelut Panim offered a slight bow. "A humble servant of the Light."

Pankaj looked up. Seeing the Elder, he rushed over. "How?"

"It's not important." The monk scanned the group. "I seek the righteous one. Where is he?"

Heads turned as a yellow school bus barreled around Centre Street, skidding to a halt.

The front door squeaked open, releasing an ominous figure dressed in black.

The women screamed.

David Kantor removed his face mask. "It's all right, I won't hurt you. I saw the military vehicles drive off, and–"

"Dad?"

David turned, his heart pounding in his throat as his eyes sorted through a crowd of scantily clad women—

—finding his lost lamb. "Gavi? Oh, God, thank you." He rushed to her, sweeping her up in his arms like a rag doll, crushing her in his embrace, his daughter weeping uncontrollably. "I was so scared. I've been looking for you! I went to your school—"

"They kidnapped me! They beat me. Daddy, I was so scared—"

"Who beat you?" He looked at her face. "Are you okay?"

"I'm okay. That man saved me. The man with one arm." She pointed at Patrick, sitting slumped over on a park bench.

David stared at the gaunt figure. "Shep?"

"Daddy, you know him, don't you? I saw a picture of you with him in Iraq."

"Gavi, get on the bus. Get all these girls with you aboard, too." David watched her go, then walked over to the bench, pushing past a small Asian and an old man.

"Shep, it's D.K."

Patrick looked up, his eyes swimming in pain. "Who?"

"David . . . Dr. Kantor. Don't you recognize me? We spent three deployments together."

"David?" Shep sat up, the pain snapping him awake. "What are you doing here?"

"The Guard sent me here looking for you. For the vaccine. That girl you rescued, she's my daughter. Buddy, I owe you big-time."

Patrick wiped back tears. "Wish I could have saved my own daughter. Bastards took the vaccine before I could get it to her."

"Your daughter? Oh, geez." David turned to the old man. "Are you a friend of his?"

"I'd like to think so. Patrick's memory isn't so good. Maybe you could help him?"

David sat on the bench next to his fellow vet. The others gathered around. "Shep, how could the vaccine help Donna?"

"Donna?"

"Your daughter."

Shep's eyes grew wide in recognition. "Donna. My little girl's name . . . is Donna. I remembered Beatrice, but for the life of me—"

"Who's Beatrice?"

"My wife. You know that."

"Shep, did you get married while you were in the hospital?"

"David, come on . . . Beatrice! The only woman I ever loved. The mother of my child . . . my soul mate."

David looked to the others, then placed his arm on Patrick's good shoulder. "The surgeon said the explosion damaged your memory, but there was no telling how bad. Shep, I don't know who this Beatrice is, but the woman you told me was your soul mate . . . her name was Patty. Patricia Segal."

Patrick paled, the blood draining from his face.

"You used to call her Trish. I suppose it sort of sounds like Beatrice. Shep, the two of you never got married. You were engaged . . . there were wedding plans, but then her dad—your high-school baseball coach—he got sick. The cancer took him right before the Red Sox called you up. Right before the accident."

An icy shiver ran down Patrick's spine. "What accident?"

Across the park, the Grim Reaper stared at him . . . waiting.

David looked to Virgil, who nodded. "Go on, he needs to hear it."

"Shep, Trish and Donna were aboard the flight from Boston . . . the one that struck the World Trade Center. Buddy, you lost your family on September 11."

Francesca clutched her husband's arm, doubling up with a contraction. Dawn swooned. Manisha grabbed her daughter before she fainted.

Patrick Shepherd's chest constricted so tightly, he could not breathe.

And in that moment of revelation, a decade of pent-up psychological trauma suddenly released, freeing the synapses within his damaged cerebral cortex as if they were the clogged gears of a clock—

—and suddenly he remembered.

He remembers sprinting down Trinity Place after the second tower was hit.

He remembers thick brown smoke pouring into the heavens. People falling from the sky.

He remembers Trinity Cemetery and the funeral for his soul mate and his young daughter. He remembers filling their empty coffins with their belongings . . . everything put to rest beneath the sculpture of an angelic child . . . the very tombstone the Grim Reaper had been motioning at hours earlier.

There was one piece of the puzzle left . . . one final memory—the day he had realized the truth about September 11, the day he had pieced together the treachery—

—the day he had walked out of his barracks in the Green Zone and into the sunshine, the pin in his right hand—

—the live grenade in his left.

From across the lawn, the Grim Reaper opened his cloaked arms wide, beckoning an embrace. Shep leapt off the bench, sprinting awkwardly toward the Angel of Death, ready to end it all.

The Reaper smiled, disappearing into the shadows.

"Shep, wait!" David started after him—

—the old man blocked his way. "You are a doctor?"

"Huh? Yeah—"

"We have a pregnant woman in labor. Paolo, this man is here to deliver your son. Pankaj, get these people to Battery Park."

"Virgil, what about you?"

"Patrick needs me. Now hurry, there's not much time." The old man patted Pankaj on the cheek, offering a wry smile to a transfixed Gelut Panim before following Patrick's tracks through the snow.

David, Pankaj, and Paolo helped Francesca onto the awaiting vehicle, the interior of the bus fifty degrees warmer. Manisha escorted Dawn. But at the last moment, Dawn slipped past her mother and dashed across the lawn, retrieving Patrick's mangled steel prosthetic from the short Asian man.

"Are you coming with us?"

"I'd like that." The Elder turned, looking for the old man.

Virgil Shechinah was gone.

The horizon had turned a light gray by the time Shep reached Ann Street. Ahead was Broadway. Looking up, he saw the Reaper beckon from atop a flipped vehicle, the olive green blade of his scythe again dripping blood.

"Bastard!" Gathering himself, Patrick crossed Broadway, continuing east to the corner of Trinity Place and Vesey Street—

—the World Trade Center construction site loomed ahead.

Pankaj Patel raced the school bus south on Broadway, following the path cleared by the second Stryker. Morning's first light lifted the veil of a long night, exposing the true horrors of the runaway pandemic. Bodies lay everywhere, strewn across Manhattan as if the Big Apple had been struck by a thirty-story tsunami. Some hung from shattered windows, others still occupied the hundreds of vehicles that clogged every city block. Every sidewalk was a morgue, every building a tomb. Men, women, and children, old and young, ethnic and Caucasian, domestic and foreign—Scythe had spared no one.

The bus passed Trinity Church and the New York Stock Exchange, heading for the southernmost tip of Manhattan—Battery Park.

Francesca leaned back against Paolo's chest. Her husband entwined his fingers around hers as David Kantor worked between her spread legs, the Army medic having shed his bulky environmental suit aboard the heated vehicle.

"Okay, Francesca, looks like you're fully dilated." He turned to his daughter, Gavi assisting him from the next bench seat. "Find me something clean. A towel or blanket would be great."

Francesca trembled, her body exhausted, her nerves overwrought with fear. "You really are a doctor, right?"

"With all the degrees. I gave up my practice to go into business. Maybe I should have gone into pediatrics, this'll be my second delivery today."

Paolo forced a nervous smile. "See, my love, God has taken care of us. The first child you delivered, Dr. Kantor . . . what was it?"

David swallowed the lump in his throat. "A healthy little Hispanic girl. Okay, slight push on the next contraction. Ready . . . steady . . . push."

"Ugh!" Francesca bore down, her unborn infant sliding farther down her stretching birth canal, the pain excruciating. Looking up, she saw the strange-looking Asian man watching her from across the aisle. "Why don't you take a picture, it'll last longer!"

"My apologies. I am simply honored to bear witness to your miracle."

"Miracle? You call this a miracle! I'm on a school bus, giving birth in a plague-infested city in front of a bunch of strangers."

"Exactly. In a city taken by so much death, you and your husband have defied the odds and managed to survive. Now, out of the darkness, you bring forth a new spark of Light. And this is not a miracle?"

David looked up. "The man's got a point. Okay, one more time—"

Hunched down in one of the rear seats, Sheridan Ernstmeyer watched the medic deliver the Italian woman's child, her anger mounting.

WORLD TRADE CENTER SITE
7:42 A.M.

The site had been sanitized. The crime scene scrubbed. Every ounce of rubble inspected, yielding everything from family photos to personal belongings to the smallest traces of DNA used to identify air passengers and office occupants. Everything *except* the virtually indestructible black boxes that had been aboard the two aircraft safeguarding the in-flight recordings.

Tons of steel shipped overseas. Replaced by gleaming fortified structures rising from Ground Zero's excavated graveyard. *Out with the old, in with the new . . .*

Patrick slipped through a detached section of aluminum fence and entered the construction area, marking the first time he had returned to the site where his fiancée and daughter had been incinerated alive, along with three thousand other innocent people.

Trembling with emotion, he moved to the edge of a massive pit—the foundation of what would soon be another mammoth structure. A gray morning fog had rolled in off the Hudson, obscuring the partially constructed buildings looming across the site.

He registered the now-familiar presence and turned to his left. The Grim Reaper was standing beside him on the overlook, staring into the pit.

"Why have you brought me here?"

The Angel of Death raised its scythe to the heavens. The Manhattan sky was concealed behind a dense layer of swirling brown clouds—just as it had been on that day of treachery.

A dizzying bout of vertigo. Shep dropped to one knee as a sizzling wave of energy rattled his brain and extremities as if he had touched a live wire. Gasping a breath, he opened his eyes, disoriented and beyond confused.

The sky is a maelstrom of swirling dark storm clouds, the rain that pelts his exposed flesh as frigid as droplets cast from a frozen lake and as fierce as a monsoon. He is standing upon a raised wooden structure, towering fifty feet above a vast forest of cedar rendered into acres of stumps and saplings by the axe. The valley below is flooded. The floodwaters rising.

Advancing toward the wooden structure are people. Thousands of them. Carting children and possessions. Desperate and angry and scared. Standing in frigid water up to their knees, shouting at him in a Middle Eastern dialect.

His attention is diverted to a new discovery—he now has a left arm! Only it's not his. He examines his left hand, then the right . . . both weathered. Knotty, and arthritic, his flesh bears a Sephardic tan. He palpates a gaunt face, the leathery skin pruned in wrinkles. He grips a handful of shaggy white hair and strokes a matching beard. His rail-thin body is cloaked in damp robes bearing the heavy scent of animal musk.

What's happening to me? Is this another hallucination? I'm an old man . . .

The cries of the mob demand his attention. He walks to the edge of the wooden structure and realizes he is standing on the deck of an immense boat.

A crash of thunder rattles heaven and earth. The ground trembles, then the mountainside opens, the fissures belching molten rock, the magma setting the flooded landscape to boil.

The crowd screams. Many attempt to board, climbing atop one another, only the coracle's steep sides and rounded bottom render the feat impossible. The raging current from the flooding Tigris River sweeps the ark from its pilings, the scalding waters searing the flesh of every man, woman, and child.

Shep bellows an old man's wail—

—returning his consciousness to the edge of the construction pit.

Hyperventilating, his chaotic mind struggled to surf this last wave of anxiety, even as a new vision took form before his eyes.

From out of the gray mist appeared the Twin Towers. Scorched, yet still standing. The two World Trade Centers had shed their concrete facade, revealing floor after floor of steel beams. Standing in unified silence within the framework of every bared perch of exposed office space were the victims of September 11, their identities silhouetted in the shadows.

Shep turned, registering the heavy presence of these lost souls through the supernal being standing on his left. The Angel of Death gazed at him through three thousand fluttering irises rotating within his hollow sockets like percolating molecules. Dark blood poured from the upturned curve of his olive-tinged scythe—a steady stream that rolled down the wooden shaft, pooling and dripping from the creature's bony right fist.

Without warning, the Grim Reaper dropped feet first into the pit, the entity's gravitational vortex dragging Patrick Shepherd with it . . . into the Ninth Circle of Hell.

PIER A

BATTERY PARK

7:45 A.M.

Pankaj Patel drove the school bus over the curb and across an expanse of snow-covered lawn. Reaching the waterfront, he jammed on the brakes, the front end of the skidding vehicle smashing through the construction fence surrounding Pier A.

The younger children screamed. Francesca Minos swaddled her newborn to her chest, shielding him from the jolt. "Paolo, find Heath. Help him launch the boat."

Still overwhelmed with emotion over the birth of his son, Paolo exited the bus, Pankaj and David Kantor in tow. Pushing through the battered gate, the three men made their way to the southwest entrance of the pier, entering the dilapidated building.

The scent of plague was overwhelming.

Heath Shelby lay beneath the suspended hull of his ten-foot Cuddy Cruiser, the deceased still partially dressed in his Santa Claus outfit. His complexion was bluish-pale, his lips stained in blood. A plum-colored bubo was visible along his neck.

Paolo turned away in horror.

David repositioned his environmental hood and mask, then knelt beneath the boat by the dead man. "Your brother-in-law . . . he was repairing the hull?"

"Yes. He said . . . he promised he'd finish before we arrived."

"I don't know if these patches are going to hold."

"You'd better pray they do." Pankaj inspected the winch. "Paolo, how do we launch?"

"Start the winch, and the hatch will open beneath the boat."

Pankaj activated the generator, then started the winch. Two steel doors beneath the boat slowly swung open, revealing the water eight feet below the pier. They watched as the Cuddy Cruiser was lowered into the harbor. It bobbed gently along the surface. Exhausted, the three men looked at one another, smiling at death's reprieve.

And then the ten-foot passenger boat lurched to starboard, its bow heaving as its aft end filled with water—

—salvation sinking to the bottom of New York Harbor.

WORLD TRADE CENTER SITE

He was falling into darkness, the sensation accompanied by a rush of voices—distant memories—echoing in his ears. *Sewer ball! Go fetch, German Shepherd . . . Not our battle, Sergeant . . . Well, you gonna stay down there all day . . . You pitched a helluva game today, son . . . Damn IED. Arm's gone, skull's fractured pretty badly . . . You said your good-byes three weeks ago . . . It's a lot of gear, but you'll be glad you have it . . . I love you, Shep . . . Blood pressure's dropping! I need another pint of blood . . . I thought I was your soul mate? . . . Now pitching for the Red Sox—*

God, why am I here?

"Life is a test, Patrick . . ."

The speck of light raced up at him from below, growing larger . . . wider—

—and suddenly he plunged through, submerged in clear, blue water. He panicked, disoriented . . . unable to breathe. He struggled, then kicked and stroked to the crystal azure surface, his bare arms tan, muscular, and intact. Swimming to the ladder, he hoisted his bathing-suit-clad body out of the swimming pool. Disoriented, he knelt on the slate patio deck.

An oceanfront beach house. The sun, warm on his face. Water rolled off his physique. The Atlantic Ocean pounded softly a hundred yards to the east beneath a cloudless blue August sky.

This isn't real, it's the vaccine . . .

"Hey, baby. How was your swim?"

He turned as she stepped out onto the patio, her body curvy and tan and irresistible in the skimpy red bikini, the wavy-haired blonde as gorgeous as the last day he had set eyes upon her.

"Trish? Oh God . . . is it really you?"

"It's okay, baby. Everything's gonna be all right." She held out the hooded bathrobe for him.

He slipped it on, feeling light-headed. "You're not real. None of this . . . it's all in my mind, I'm hallucinating again."

"Not this time, baby. This was the life the Creator stole from us . . . all to teach you a lesson."

"A lesson? What lesson?"

"Humility. The pain of losing a loved one."

"But the war . . . all that came after you and our daughter died. It doesn't make any sense."

"Apparently, these were transgressions from a prior life."

"This is insane. Why am I being punished for something I can't even remember? Why am I responsible for some other guy's mistakes? And why am I here . . . now? Is God rubbing it in my face?"

"This isn't God's doing, Shep. We're in the eleventh dimension, a far-more-livable realm that plays by a different set of rules. All of the filtered Light here is controlled by the Adversary."

"The Adversary? You mean Satan."

"Relax, baby. There is no devil, no demonic force. In the eleventh dimension, we're not required to jump through hoops or endure endless suffering. All we have to do is want. Don't look so worried. Every one of us is born with the desire to receive, that's the entire reason we were created in the first place. Lucifer isn't the devil, Shep, he's an angel who left Heaven to help man be happy. Our desire to indulge brings the Creator's Light into the eleventh dimension—an endless existence of fulfillment without all the needless pain and suffering."

A flash of light—

—and he was standing on the pitcher's mound at Fenway Park, facing the Philadelphia Phillies in Game 7 of the World Series. The sellout crowd is going wild, chanting his name. The score is 1-0 Red Sox, top of the ninth inning, two outs, two strikes on the batter.

The scoreboard revealed that he was throwing a perfect game.

He wound up, launching a 106-mile-an-hour fastball that the batter missed by three feet.

His teammates rushed to him from all sides, their boundless joy intoxicating his soul. Fans poured out from the bleachers, delivering scantily clad women who pawed at his uniform—

"Enough!"

They were back at the pool, Shep lying outstretched on a cushioned lounge chair. Trish hovered over him, her oiled cleavage tantalizingly close.

"Baby, what's wrong? Isn't this what you wanted?"

"No . . . I mean yes, but I didn't want it handed to me. I wanted to earn it."

"Shep, honey, you did earn it. You earned it all . . . only He took it away. He took me away. He took our daughter away. It wasn't right. It wasn't fair. And do you know why He took it from you?"

Shep felt the blood rush from his face. "Because I took it for granted. I didn't appreciate it."

"Nonsense. Of course you appreciated it. Sure, there were moments you slipped, but who doesn't? Even the fight we had over this house . . . I knew you still loved me. We're soul mates, after all."

"We are soul mates. I swear it."

"The truth is, I was the lucky one. Look at how you suffered after we died. All that pain, all that emptiness. Have you experienced a single moment of joy since we were taken away?"

He pinched away tears. "No."

"War . . . famine. Endless suffering. Is that how a loving parent is supposed to treat his children?"

"No, it's not."

"Life isn't about suffering, it's about indulgence. Ask the rich and powerful if they're suffering. This beach house is a perfect example. Had I listened to you and allowed you to buy it, your daughter and I would have never been on that plane. You were right and I was wrong, and you paid the ultimate price for our ignorance."

"Oh, God . . ."

"Forget God. God is nothing but a concept . . . a fictitious figure sitting upon a throne, always asleep at the wheel. We never needed God. The Adversary has grown strong in His absence. The Adversary offers us his gift of immortality without any of these hidden tests."

"What do I have to do, you know . . . for us to be together again?"

"For one thing, stop worrying. There's no violence involved, you don't have to kill anyone. Simply join me in a toast." She reached for a carafe of wine, pouring the red liquid into a gold goblet.

"A toast? To who? Lucifer?"

"Baby, you have got to stop watching so many horror movies." She straddled him, still holding the goblet of wine in her right hand. "Remember that course in Latin we took together as sophomores? Do you know what Lucifer translates to in Latin? Light-bringer. Lucifer wasn't a fallen angel, Shep, he was sent to bring Light into our world through our actions. I mean, seriously, baby, does this look like Hell to you?"

"No."

"Drink with me. Let us get drunk together from the fruit of the vine and connect with the Light."

Connect with the Light . . .

Shep's heart raced as his mind replayed a similar conversation he'd had with Virgil hours earlier in the cemetery. *"Noah made one last mistake, the same mistake Adam made. The fruit that tempted Adam was not an apple, but a grape, or the wine that comes from them. Wine can be abused, placing man in touch with levels of consciousness that cannot sustain a connection with the Light . . ."*

He pushed the goblet aside. "And when I'm lying here, drunk, will you castrate me?"

She forced a smile. "Shep, honey, what are you talking about?"

"You know . . . the way my son, Ham, castrated me when he found me lying drunk and naked on the ark."

Her expression hardened, her eyes spewed daggers. "Drink the wine, Patrick."

"You drink it, *soul mate.*" He stood, tossing her from his lap, the goblet spilling wine across her face and down her neck and cleavage—

—the liquid melting the flesh, exposing an ancient skull, darkened with age, the eye sockets fluttering with a thousand eyes!

Their surroundings shattered like a hall of mirrors, revealing a dark, massive pit, the skeletal remains of the World Trade Center looming overhead. Shep was standing on a frozen lake, surrounded by thousands of animated heads, the bodies trapped beneath the ice. Treacherous traitors of humanity, babbling in tongues. Each garbled word generated a tiny spark of light that floated through the rank air like a firefly, the accumulated specks absorbed by the massive creature frozen dead center in the lake.

Lucifer was being held chest high in the ice, and still his shoulders and three heads towered ten stories above the frozen surface. The winged demon was terrifying to behold, yet it appeared oblivious of its surroundings, as if it were a front—a giant balloon puppet. Animated by the sparks of negativity generated by the babbling heads of the tortured.

Hovering over Lucifer's left wing was the Grim Reaper.

On the demon's right was the Reaper's soul mate.

Santa Muerte was dressed in purple satin robes, her hooded skull adorned with a wavy ebony wig. The abomination snarled as she saw Shep. Gripping her scythe in her bony fists, she advanced, swinging the deadly blade like a pendulum.

Shep attempted to run, only he slipped on the ice and fell. He looked up as the curved blade looped downward from its arc, slicing through his deltoid and lopping off his new left arm in one brutal motion.

He dropped to his knees on the frozen lake, the searing pain pushing him toward unconsciousness—only *Santa Muerte* was far from finished with him.

Raising the scythe once more over her bony shoulder, she swung the instrument of death downward, the bloodstained blade whistling through the air—

—its lethal blow intercepted by the scythe belonging to her male counterpart. The Grim Reaper stood over Shep, protecting him from the assault.

And then a golden beacon of Light reached down from the unseen heavens—

—whisking his consciousness out of Hell.

PART 5

TRANSFORMATION

DAY'S END

DECEMBER 21

NEW JERSEY/NEW YORK AIRSPACE

7:50 A.M.

(13 MINUTES BEFORE THE PROPHESIED END OF DAYS)

The three MH-53J Pavelow-III Air Force helicopters flew east in a staggered formation over Jersey City, en route to Manhattan. Large and unwieldy, the "Jolly Green Giants" specialized in rescuing downed pilots and providing support to Special Operations troops. Their selection for this morning's mission was based on their ability to operate in bad weather—along with the airship's rear ramp, a deployment feature that allowed for the dispersal of a special payload.

First developed in 1958, the neutron bomb was opposed by President Kennedy and later postponed by Jimmy Carter, only to be jump-started again in 1981 under Ronald Reagan. Designed as a tactical weapon, the bomb's purpose was to eradicate troops while maintaining the targeted area's infrastructure. Unlike standard enhanced radiation weapons, the three ERWs loaded aboard the Pavelows were chemical incineration bombs designed for underground bunkers. Formulated to combust on contact with oxygen molecules, the conflagration would burn out every square inch of airspace before suffocating itself.

At precisely 8:03 A.M., the three helicopters would drop their payloads at their designated locations above the carbon-dioxide cloud hovering over Manhattan. Passing through the man-made insulating ceiling, the neutron bombs would detonate—

—incinerating every biological—dead or alive—in New York City.

BATTERY PARK
7:52 A.M.

A frigid wind whipped across New York Harbor, driving the dark surface into froth. Liberty Island was visible in the distance. The statue beckoned.

They had gathered by a concrete boat ramp close to the water's edge. The Patels and the Minoses. David Kantor and his daughter. The frail Tibetan monk who seemed bothered by nothing, and the female assassin who was angry at the world. The students and freed sex slaves stayed warm in the school bus. A Scythe incubator rendered moot by the arrival of dawn.

Francesca Minos clutched her swaddled newborn inside her coat, using her body heat to warm her son. "What are we supposed to do now?"

Paolo shielded his wife and child from the wind. "We'll just have to find another boat."

"There are no other boats," yelled David. "There's no way off the island short of swimming, and you wouldn't last two minutes without a wet suit."

Dawn Patel was seated on a park bench next to her mother, the girl examining Patrick Shepherd's detached prosthetic arm. "Mother, this is so strange. Look at how these Hebrew letters are grouped together in threes."

"May I?" The Tibetan monk offered a disarming smile. Pankaj joined him, looking over the Elder's shoulder at the engraved letters. "This is most amazing. The letters are not written in Hebrew, this is Aramaic."

"Who cares?" Manisha retorted. "Pankaj, come and be with your family."

"In a moment. Elder?"

"Pankaj, Aramaic is a metaphysical tool used by the Creator. It is the only language that cannot be understood by Satan."

"These letters . . . they were not there earlier."

"You are certain of this?"

"I helped carry Patrick from Belvedere Castle after he saved my family. The engraving was not there, I am quite sure. Can you read the message?"

"It is not a message, Pankaj, nor are these translatable words. What has been inscribed upon the steel are the 72 names of God."

"What did you say? Let me see!" Paolo left his wife and newborn son to join them. "How do you know they're the 72 names?"

"I scan these words every day. Each of the letters comes from three encrypted verses in Exodus 14, lines 19 through 21. The Torah portion describes Moses's parting of the Red Sea."

Paolo took the steel limb from the Tibetan. Stared at the pattern of letters. "It wasn't Moses. Virgil said it was actually a man of deep faith who parted the Red Sea."

"You are correct. The true story of the Israelites escaping bondage had nothing to do with slavery, it was all about escaping chaos and pain and suffering. The parting of the Red Sea was not a miracle, it was a manifestation, an effect caused by the ability to use the 72 names engraved on Moses's staff as a supernal tool to control mind over matter."

"Elder, do you think Patrick was the righteous one chosen by God to offer mankind salvation?"

David approached with Gavi. "What are you two talking about?"

"Your friend's involvement with the End of Days may serve a higher calling," Pankaj explained.

"Look, fellas, I don't know anything about this End of Days stuff, but I knew Patrick Shepherd, and trust me, he was far from a righteous man."

Paolo stared at the steel limb. His body trembled. His mind raced . . . deliberating.

Francesca approached with the baby. "Paolo, what is it?"

"Wait here." Gripping the prosthetic device, he headed for the water.

"Paolo, what are you doing? Paolo, are you crazy?"

The survivors gathered around Paolo, who held the prosthetic steel arm to the heavens. He hesitated. Then walked resolutely down the concrete boat ramp and into the harbor.

The near-freezing water hit him like a jolt of electricity, driving the air from his lungs, turning his blood and limbs to lead. He floundered in waist-deep water, then abruptly stepped off an unseen ledge and plunged underwater.

Francesca screamed.

Her husband's head reappeared seconds later. Paralyzed by the cold, he gasped for air as he struggled to swim back to the ramp. David and Pankaj reached out for him, dragging the devout man to safety.

Gavi ran back to the bus to fetch blankets.

Sheridan Ernstmeyer laughed. "So much for divine intervention."

The Tibetan monk approached Paolo, who was kneeling by the water's edge, struggling to catch his breath. "Mr. Minos, why did you attempt to part the harbor's waters? What made you believe yourself worthy of such a task?"

"The 72 names . . . I believed the story to be true." The Italian was shaking uncontrollably, his face deathly pale, his lips purple. He looked up at Gelut Panim, completely lost. "I did as Virgil said. It didn't work."

"The crossing was a test of certainty, not faith."

"I don't understand?"

"You have faith, my friend, but your moment of hesitance revealed that you expected to fail. Certainty is more than prayer, it is knowing. There is a story of a man of faith who was climbing down from the face of a mountain at night when his strength gave out. Hanging by his two hands, freezing to death as you are now, he called out to God to save him. God answered by instructing him to let go. The man released one hand, but he was too afraid to obey. Instead, he called out into the night for help from another. The villagers found him the next morning, frozen to death, hanging five feet off the ground."

Gavi handed a wool blanket to the shivering man. "Who are you to judge the depths of my faith? I walked straight into the water. I let go with both hands!"

"I meant no insult. When God asked Abraham to sacrifice his son, Isaac . . . that was a test of certainty. You merely went for a foolhardy swim."

"Dad, look!" Gavi pointed to the southwest over Liberty Island, where three military helicopters had appeared on the horizon. "Are they coming to rescue us?

David swallowed hard. "No honey. Not this time."

GOVERNOR'S ISLAND

7:55 A.M.

Leigh Nelson was yanked from her sleep, the physician violently dragging her off the Army cot and onto her feet, where she was confronted by Captains Jay and Jesse Zwawa.

"What is it? What's wrong?"

"You lied to us, lady."

Leigh felt her blood pressure drop. "Lied about what?"

"The Scythe vaccine. We analyzed it." Jay Zwawa thrust a half-empty vial into her hand. "It's nothing but water."

"What? That's impossible—"

Jesse Zwawa signaled to the guard. "Take this traitor outside and shoot her."

BATTERY PARK

7:56 A.M.

Marquis Jackson-Horne had shed his gang colors but not his gun. The eighteen-year-old cornrowed Latino gang member and his seven-year-old sister joined the survivors of Scythe, everyone watching the western horizon as three dark gunships began a long circle, following the New Jersey coastline to the north.

Marquis nodded to Pankaj. "Ya'll here to get rescued?"

"I'm sorry."

"You're sorry?" He glanced at the shivering Italian wrapped in a blanket. Saw the prosthetic arm lying in the snow by his side. "Yo, what happened? Where's the one-armed man?"

"You knew Patrick?"

"He gave me the vaccine. Cured me and my little sis. Where he at?"

Pankaj looked the gang leader in the eyes. "He's with his family."

Paolo was with his family, but his thoughts were occupied by the sting of the Asian man's words. All his life he had lived by the laws of the Catholic

Church. Attended Mass. Taken communion and tithed when he could barely afford it. He had fed the homeless and confessed even his most minor transgressions. Now, in the last moments of his life, to be told he was not worthy . . . to be told he harbored doubts!

Leaving Francesca and his infant son, he stalked after the Tibetan monk. "I don't know who you are, but I know you possess knowledge of the 72 names. Use them to save us!"

"Sadly, I cannot. Long ago, I made the decision to abuse the knowledge for my own selfish needs. As such, I am far from righteous."

"Then teach me! Tell me what to do!"

"I already have." The Elder's opaque eyes glistened. He placed a reassuring hand on Paolo's shoulder. "Think of it as a baptism."

Paolo was shaking uncontrollably. His eyes darted from the three military choppers to the Asian man to the frail infant swaddled in his wife's arm.

Defying his greatest fear, he shed the blanket, returning to his loved ones. "Francesca, give me our son."

She saw the look in his eyes. The steel arm in his hand. "No!"

"Francesca . . . please."

The others gathered around in silence.

The Elder watched, fascinated and humbled by the unfolding events.

"Francesca, it is a miracle that brought us here, now we must trust the cause of that miracle."

Her eyes swelled with tears.

"My love, God has given us the tools, now it is up to us to act."

She hesitated, then handed the blanketed newborn to her husband. "Go on. Sacrifice your son. Sacrifice yourself, too. I can't handle this anymore."

Gripping the steel limb in his right hand, his infant son cradled in his left, Paolo strode down the concrete boat ramp and into the harbor . . .

WORLD TRADE CENTER SITE
7:57 A.M.

The brown maelstrom swirled overhead, blotting out the dawn. A cold

December wind whipped up construction garbage and dirt into miniature tornadoes, then died.

Patrick Shepherd sat by the edge of the construction pit, alone, frightened, and lost.

The wind picked up again, howling through rivet holes in the bare steel girders.

Patrick . . .

The whispered voice was male and strangely familiar. Shep looked up, unsure.

You've endured a helluva journey, son. Now we need to start working on your mental game.

"Coach? Coach Segal? Is it really . . . what am I saying?" He gripped a handful of his long brown hair and pulled, doubling over in agony. "Get out of my head, get out of my head! I can't take it anymore!"

I'm no hallucination, Patrick. You knew that the first time I communicated with you. On the roof of the VA hospital.

Shep's skin tingled. He stood, facing into the wind. "You're the one who stopped me from jumping?"

You trusted me then, son, trust me now. Everything you've experienced was real, except for the demon's deception using my daughter. But you knew better. By trusting your instincts, you saw through the ruse.

"It's true. I knew it wasn't Trish, I knew it couldn't have been her. When I'm with her, I feel . . . I feel—"

"Fulfilled."

Shep spun around, his eyes searching for the owner of the new voice. He heard the sound of boots approaching on gravel and turned.

Virgil Shechinah stepped out from behind an earthmover and into a beacon of sunlight coming from a small break in the clouds. "And they said, come, let us build us a city and a tower, whose top may reach to heaven, and let us make ourselves a name. So Master Dante, did you enjoy your excursion through Hell, looking for your beloved Beatrice?"

The mention of Dante's deceased lover angered Shep even more. "You know, you're a liar, old man. You told me you spoke with my soul mate.

She's dead. She died with my daughter in this very spot, eleven years ago."

"Yes she did. And she's very worried about you."

"What's that supposed to mean? Are you some kind of medium, channeling her spirit? Or maybe you're an angel? Is that what you are, Virgil? An angel, hired by Bertrand DeBorn to drive me crazy?"

"Not an angel. And I never claimed to be a psychiatrist, nor was I referred to you by the late Mr. DeBorn. That was your assumption."

"Okay, so you're not a shrink. Then who are you? Why did you come see me in the VA hospital? Wait, I forgot . . . my dead soul mate was worried about me, so she sent you."

Virgil smiled. "The eyes are the windows of the soul. Look into mine. Tell me what you see." He removed his rose-colored glasses. "Go on, I won't bite."

Shep moved closer, gazing into the old man's blue eyes—

—his consciousness suddenly overwhelmed by a squall of ethereal white light, its warmth seeping through his brain, bathing every cell in his body with a healing energy that was so soothing, so loving, that it caused him to giggle.

He awakened, disoriented and lying on the ground, smiling as he opened his eyes. "God, what a rush."

"Let's just keep it to Virgil for now, shall we?"

Shep sat up. Incredibly, the fatigue from his long night was gone, the cold no longer affecting him. "I don't know what you just did, but if we could bottle it, we'd make a fortunate."

"What you experienced was *Keter,* the Light from the uppermost *Sefirot* . . . the highest of the ten dimensions of existence. The energy is only accessible to man once a year, on the dawn following forty-nine days of internal cleansing after Passover. The date commemorates a connection to the immortality that existed on Mt. Sinai thirty-four hundred years ago."

"Great, more riddles." Shep stood, shaking his head. "Look, whoever you are, you've been a friend these last twenty-four hours, but maybe just once you could give me a straight answer, seeing as how we're probably only a few minutes away from being incinerated by the Defense Department."

"Time has no place in the supernal realm, Patrick. Look around you. Time has ceased to exist."

Patrick looked up. For some strange reason, the brown clouds were no longer moving, as if frozen in place. "What the hell? Okay, wait, I get it. This is another hallucination brought on by that damn vaccine."

"Everything was real. As for the vaccine, it was water."

"Water? Come on."

"Water is the essential component to existence in the physical world. Long ago, water was imbued with the essence of the Light, giving it the power to heal and restore, protecting man at the cellular level. Life spans were far greater. It was humanity's overwhelming negative consciousness that tainted water's nature after the flood. The process is reversible through certain blessings and meditations, which return the water to its primordial state. The vaccine was a highly concentrated form of this cleansing water, called Pinchas Water. The Defense Department confiscated a supply that had been used by those possessing the knowledge to help clean up parts of Chernobyl. A noble effort, silenced once again by man's ego. The Klipot woman gained access to the water while at Fort Detrick."

"And that's what kept us safe from the plague?"

"What kept you safe was your belief. The water was simply the medium used to mobilize your thoughts. To coin a phrase, it was mind over matter."

"This is insane . . . or maybe I'm insane." Shep paced back and forth, unable to process everything at once. "Maybe I'm not insane, maybe I'm just delusional. Wait . . . that's it! It all makes perfect sense now. This whole little Wizard of Oz adventure . . . it all began when the chopper crashed in the forest. Everything I experienced from that moment on . . . you, miraculously showing up in Inwood Park, me, living out Dante's Nine Circles of Hell while I attempted to get back home to my family, the 'helper characters' we conveniently managed to pick up along the way . . . even that wicked Grim Reaper witch waiting for me down in Hades . . . it was all just a dream, none of it actually happened. In reality, I'm still unconscious in the chopper, or better yet, I'm lying in a drug-induced coma in some hospital bed in the Bronx. And that rush I felt when I looked into your eyes . . . that was probably a B-12 shot the nurse just injected into my IV." Shep beamed a smile. "That's it, isn't it? God, I'm good. I didn't mean you, Virgil, that was just an expression, you know, like I was talking to the man upstairs. The real dude."

"The guy asleep at the wheel?"

"Exactly."

"Tell you what, let's do a test." Virgil reached for Patrick's face and pinched his cheek.

"Ow! That's your test?"

"You seem wide-awake to me. Still, it pays to be sure."

Shep jumped as a phantom sensation suddenly oozed a healing warmth from his butchered left deltoid muscle. As he watched in stunned amazement, the protrusion formed a humerus, the bone miraculously extending down from his shoulder, followed by a progressive web of nerves and blood vessels, tendons and muscles, the growing appendage extending into a forearm, wrist, hand, and fingers, the newborn limb atomizing flesh before his spellbound eyes into a fully formed and functional left arm.

Shep fell to his knees, flexing his fingers . . . giddy. Unlike the experience in the Ninth Circle of Hell, he could instinctively tell that this limb was real. "How?"

"Stem cells. Amazing things. It's a shame mankind waited so long to begin using them. Imagine the boundless joy that could have been spread across the world by harvesting new limbs for amputees, spinal cords for the paralyzed, organs for the decrepit, or cures for diseases—all of which were intended to challenge man's ability to better himself. Unfortunately, the Adversary bound you to organized religion. That was Satan's trump card, and man's ego embraced it like opium."

Shep stared at Virgil, as if seeing the old man for the first time. "You really are God, aren't you?"

"God is a concept of man, a digestible image of a ruler on a throne, a divine entity one petitions when one wants to hit the lottery or is faced with death. I am the Creator's desire to reveal Himself to you within the Light of Wisdom, appearing to you in a reflected finite image your mind can accept and absorb."

"The Light of Wisdom?"

"The essence of existence." Virgil's blue eyes danced behind his rose-colored spectacles. "You wish to know how all this came to be."

"Please."

"Very well. But what I explain now are supernal matters—matters that occupy neither space or time, nor material manifestations—the very elements that dominate your senses and surroundings. There are things you may not be able to accept or grasp, yet instinctively your soul will know them to be true. Try not to fight your gut reaction by using finite logic."

"You're telling me my brain's too small to handle this."

"I am saying your senses are hardwired into the *Malchut,* the physical world. The Upper Realm is a completely different reality. It's like you, a three-dimensional being, having to explain existence to a two-dimensional cartoon character. You'd have to limit yourself to two-dimensional vernacular in order to describe three-dimensional concepts."

"This is algebra, and I'm only in first grade, got it. Anything else I should know?"

"As I said, time and space do not exist in the spiritual realm. Therefore, if I use the word 'before,' it refers to cause. If I say 'after,' it is the effect."

"Understood. Now tell me . . . what's really out there? How did this all come to be?"

"In the reality of the infinite, there is the Creator, there is the unknowable Essence of the Creator, and there is the Light that comes from the Creator. The Light exists in the Endless. The Light is perfection. And though you can never know the Creator, at His essence is the nature of sharing. But because there was nothing upon which to share, a reciprocal energy was necessary to complete the circuitry, in this case a Vessel to receive the Creator's infinite Light.

"And so the Vessel was created, and its entire purpose was to receive. And the Vessel was the unified soul. And now there were two types of Light in the Endless: The Light of Wisdom, which was the essence of existence that simply gives, and the Light of Mercy, or the Vessel, which desired only to receive. Remember the example I gave earlier? If the Light of Wisdom was the electricity circulating throughout your home, the Light of Mercy, the Vessel, would be a lamp that plugged into a wall socket to receive the energy. Without the lamp, you have no illumination, without the Light of Mercy the Light of Wisdom cannot reveal itself."

"Like you said earlier with Dawn, it's like the sun. The sun radiates energy, and yet its radiance can only be seen when it reflects off a body in space . . . like the Earth." Shep paused, his mind racing. "Virgil, you said you were the Creator's desire to reveal Himself to me within the Light of Wisdom. Does that mean you are reflecting . . . off my Light of Mercy?"

Virgil smiled. "Let's return to the story of creation. In the infinite Endless that filled the entirety of existence, there was the Creator's Light that gave unconditionally and now, through cause and effect, there was the Vessel, a repository of the unified soul and the only true creation that has ever occurred. The Torah encodes the Vessel with a name: Adam. But the Vessel Adam, like a battery, was composed of two aspects, or energies. Its male energy, positively charged protons, and its negatively charged female aspect—the electron, so named Eve in the encoded Creation story. And the Vessel had only the desire to receive, and the Light only gave, and so there was boundless fulfillment. Still, Adam lacked an awareness of its own fulfillment, for how does one appreciate a sunny day if every day is sunny? More important, how does one come to know and appreciate God if one never experiences the absence of God?"

"So what happened?"

"Cause and effect. As the Light continued to fill the Vessel, it passed along the Essence of the Creator, His desire to share. The Vessel, created only to receive, now desired to share, to be the cause of its own fulfillment . . . in essence, to be like the Creator. But the Vessel had no way of sharing; furthermore, it felt shame because it had not earned the endless Light and fulfillment it was receiving. And so, in order to be like the Creator, the Vessel shunned the Creator's Light.

"This act of resistance caused the *Tzimtzum,* the contraction. Without the Light, the Vessel contracted into a singular point of darkness within the endless World—the infinite giving birth to the finite. Suddenly without the Creator, the Vessel expanded to allow the Light back in. This sudden contraction and expansion, what you refer to as the Big Bang, was the cause that led to the physical universe, giving Einstein his time-space continuum. And yet this bubble of existence is not true reality. The true reality of existence is in the 99 percent . . . the Endless. What's wrong?"

"It feels right, it's just hard to get my mind around this. But go on . . . please."

"When the *Tzimtzum* occurred, the constriction formed ten dimensions, or *Sefirot.* Six of these ten *Sefirot* compacted, enfolding into one superdimension, the *Ze'ir Anpin.*"

"Why ten dimensions? What is their purpose?"

"The *Sefirot* filter the Creator's Light. The upper three realms, known as *Keter, Chochmah,* and *Binah,* are closest to the Creator and do not exert direct influence in man's physical realm. The bundle of six that remain just beyond man's limited perception is the source of all knowledge and fulfillment available to mankind in this physical world. The physical world, the lowest of the ten *Sefirot,* is called *Malchut.* As immense as the universe appears, it represents a mere 1 percent of total existence, and it is a reality based upon deception, reinforced by the limitations of man's five senses."

"Incredible. What about the soul?"

"Every soul is a spark from the shattered Vessel, Adam. When the Vessel shattered, it separated the male principle, Adam, from the female principle, Eve. Just as conception in the womb is followed by the division of the cell, so too did the shattered Vessel divide, its sparks becoming male and female souls. Lesser sparks filtered down into the animal kingdom, trees, vegetation, and so forth, all the way down to every aspect of matter and energy that makes up the cosmos."

"But my soul is not whole, is it, Virgil? It remains divided. You promised me—"

The Light appeared before him as a luminescent blue apparition—the same apparition he had witnessed communicating with Dawn Patel. As he watched, it constricted into the human form of a woman. She was wearing the same outfit she had worn in the scorched Polaroid, her wavy blond hair falling past her shoulders down to the small of her back.

Patricia Ann Segal smiled at her long-lost soul mate. "Hey, baby."

"Oh God . . ." Patrick collapsed to his knees, tears flowing from his eyes as he hugged her about the waist, the emptiness in his heart instantly replaced by boundless joy.

Virgil beamed a cherubic smile. "The reunification of soul mates is a force of Light that cannot be denied, greater even than the parting of the Red Sea."

Trish drew Shep to his feet. He kissed her face. He inhaled her pheromones, the flesh of his whiskered cheeks warmed by her touch.

The old man watched the couple like a proud parent. "Women tend to complete their spiritual correction sooner than their male counterparts. A woman's soul may reside in the Upper Realm while she attempts to assist her soul mate in his own correction."

Shep pulled back from his embrace. "What about our little girl?"

"She has already returned." Trish gazed into his eyes. "What does your heart tell you?"

"Oh gosh . . . it's Dawn! The Patels' daughter . . . she harbors our little girl's soul."

"I've kept a watchful eye on her . . . and you."

"Trish . . . I've done such terrible things. I joined the military to avenge your death. I committed murder. I brought darkness into the lives of others." His body trembling, Shep turned to Virgil and prostrated himself, hugging the old man's boots to his chest. "I'm sorry, God, please forgive me!"

"Your repentance has been accepted, my son."

Shep wiped back tears. Regaining his feet, he took his soul mate's hand. "Will we be together?"

"Soon. Your soul must be cleansed before it reenters the Upper Realm, but the burden has been lessened by your selfless actions over the last twenty-four hours. The more Light a soul desires and receives, the higher it ascends. Everything you see around you, all that exists and that evolved to exist in the physical world of time and mortality was created so that the soul could spiritually transform itself from a receiver to a giver and earn its immortality and fulfillment in the Endless. This is the reality you requested as the Vessel, Adam, the request granted by the Creator because He loves His children unconditionally."

"If He loves us so much, why is there so much hatred in the world? So much violence? So much pain and suffering."

"As we discussed earlier, in order to earn the endless fulfillment, there must be free will. To challenge free will, there must be an Adversary. An opposing team. And the game cannot be fixed, or the prize has no meaning. The Adversary is the human ego at the genetic level, referred to in the Creation story as the consumption of the forbidden fruit from the Tree of Knowledge. Lust, gluttony, avarice, wrath, violence, fraud, greed, and treachery . . . all are symptoms of the ego, every selfish act diverting the Creator's Light to Satan. Sin is man's refusal to become what man was destined to be. If man would simply expand his own vessel by using the tools he was given, there would never be suffering in this world again."

"And how do we do that?"

"By expanding your vessel to allow more Light in. By loving thy neighbor as thy self in the same way the Creator loves each of His children—unconditionally. Love is a weapon of the Light, it has the power to eradicate all forms of darkness. Spirituality isn't about just being nice, Patrick, it's about transforming one's not-so-nice qualities. When you offer love even to your enemies, you destroy their darkness and hatred. What's more, you cast out the darkness inside yourself. What is left in the aftermath are two souls who now recognize the spark of divinity they both share. Think about that. It is not the positive trait that flips on the Light switch; the Light goes on when one identifies, uproots, and transforms their own reactive negative characteristics. When a mass majority of people reach this magnitude of understanding, then endless fulfillment and immortality shall be had for all. Conversely, when collective negative actions rise to a critical juncture, the Angel of Death is granted free rein, and even the righteous shall suffer."

"Is that what's happening here, Virgil? Has evil run so amok that humanity needs another do-over?"

The old man turned somber. "The generation of Noah was stubborn and bold enough to sin openly. The generation of the flood has returned."

"Then . . . I really was Noah?"

"The soul that inhabits your existence as Patrick Shepherd also shared the physical being that was Noah, a righteous man born in a time of greed and corruption. You and your soul mate, Naamah, have returned to witness the end of another generation."

Shep squeezed Trish's hand, his face flushing red. "You're not really going to wipe out 6 billion people?"

"Six million or 6 billion, in either case the Creator does not destroy. Man has become his own instrument of destruction. His desire to feed from the Tree of Knowledge without restriction, his insistence on receiving for the self alone . . . it is these acts that have summoned the Angel of Death to stalk the Earth, just as it did 666 years ago during the last pandemic."

"But you could stop it, you could end the insanity. You talk about mankind being proactive, what about you? What about that Holocaust story you told me!"

"The story was yours."

Patrick's face paled. His body trembled. "The boy you spoke of?"

"It was your life, Patrick, your second deployment, as you call it. What you experienced was the severity of Noah's *tikkun.* You lost your entire family at Auschwitz. Your soul mate perished there as well."

"And you did nothing? While innocent children were being tossed into ovens. While planes were being flown into buildings—"

"—and innocent families were being slaughtered by American soldiers? As I said, God is not a verb, Patrick. The Light flows, regardless of intent. It's all about free will. Those who live their lives by the Creator's laws remain protected. A miracle of salvation at this juncture would be interpreted as a religious happening. In the end, it would lead to the very war you seek to avert, serving Satan, who continues to grow stronger through these acts of darkness."

"I don't care! Noah may have stood idly by while you drowned the world, but I won't. You and I . . . we had a covenant after the flood. The ark was our covenant. You promised never to destroy humanity again!"

"It is not the Creator that will destroy humanity, Patrick. Behold."

The brown swirl of clouds parted to the west, revealing three dark helicopters frozen in time over the Hudson River. "Man is responsible for this flood. And through his actions, Satan's power grows."

Virgil pointed to the edge of the construction pit, where the Angel of Death had materialized. The male Grim Reaper had been impaled by his female counterpart's scythe, the blade buried in the base of the being's barren skull.

"What happened to him? How can you slay . . . an angel?"

"Every element of creation maintains a male and female aspect. So it is with the Angel of Death. Each Reaper, both male and female, was born human into the physical world. When it is time for a Reaper to move on, they select their replacement from among the living. The female aspect of death, strengthened by the corruption of man, no longer remains held in check. Unless humanity is terminated, she shall walk the Earth unabated and poison the *Malchut* so that no Light can ever be again revealed in this dimension."

Shep stared at the male Reaper. The supernal creature was vibrating, its eye sockets fluttering, its life force diminishing rapidly.

"I never completed my *tikkun,* did I, Virgil? Not as Noah or in Auschwitz. Not now, as Patrick Shepherd. You said each soul has four deployments."

"This was your last."

"Who else was I? A mass murderer? An alcoholic, like my father?"

"Actually, you were a poet, a man inspired by the Light, yet lacking the discipline to keep from getting perpetually drunk on the forbidden fruit. James Douglas Morrison. His friends called him Jim."

"Wait . . . Jim Morrison of *The Doors*?" Patrick turned to Trish. "I was Jim Morrison?"

The former Pamela Courson squeezed the deceased rocker's hand.

The old man placed his hand on Patrick's shoulder. "Are you ready to continue your journey, son?"

"No . . . just wait, wait one second. You said every soul must complete its *tikkun* before moving on to the Upper Realm. How can I be reunited with my soul mate in the Upper Realm if I haven't completed my *tikkun*? And how can I complete my *tikkun* if you're allowing this pandemic to wipe out humanity?"

"Mankind has chosen to move away from the Light. The generation of the plague shall have no share in the World to come."

"So you're simply going to allow Scythe to wipe out everyone? Just like that?"

"God is not mankind's servant. God just is. It's man who needs to take action, not the Creator. This was the test of existence."

Shep balled his fists in frustration. "You know what, *God*? You really suck as a parent!"

"Shep—"

"No, Trish, He needs to hear it. You say we're moving away from the Light? Maybe that's your fault. Maybe we could have used some more spiritual guidance? Or how about a sign every once in a while that you're not asleep at the wheel? Hell, it'd be nice to see a little justice in this world, too."

"Every soul is judged at the appropriate time. The Creator no longer micromanages, Patrick. That just leads to more religious dogma, more false prophets . . . more chaos."

"Then appoint someone who will micromanage. Give me one last deployment. Let me fulfill my *tikkun* . . . as him!" Shep pointed to the Grim Reaper.

"Baby, no. You don't know what you're saying."

"He's been following me throughout Manhattan, Trish. I think he chose me. Humanity needs someone to keep the Grim Reaper's old lady in check . . . the Upper Realm needs balance to be restored in the *Malchut*—well, I'm volunteering. What I'm not going to do is stand by and allow all those people to die. Not this time around . . . no way."

"Know the ground rules, Patrick, before you volunteer for yet another war. The Angel of Death is a supernal being, able to access both the higher and lower worlds. There are demons out there . . . entities of existence that even Dante dared not imagine. Unless you remain vigilant, the forces of darkness will easily corrupt your soul."

"My soul mate will protect me; she'll keep me anchored to the Light." Shep squeezed Trish's hand. "It's the only way we can be together again. It's the only way I can protect our daughter."

"You request this of your own free will?"

"I do."

Virgil looked at Patricia, who nodded.

"Then the covenant is made. All those you choose to save shall be fruitful and multiply, all those you choose to condemn shall perish. And when the world regains its balance, your *tikkun* shall be completed, and you shall be reunited in the Upper Realm with your soul mate."

Shep hugged Trish, holding her tight. "I love you."

"I love you."

Virgil waited patiently until they separated.

"One last question . . . why me? I'm about the farthest thing from a righteous man."

"As were all the great sages. The greatest Light, Patrick, comes from the greatest transformation."

Shep maintained his grip on his soul mate's hand. "There are no accidents, are there, Virgil. You set this whole thing up."

"No, son. You did." He took their entwined hands in his. "Just remember, free will works both ways. Noah failed to restrict himself in the *Malchut* and was castrated. Should you fail to restrict yourself in the supernal realm, the forces of darkness will corrupt you so that even the Light and love of your soul mate will not be enough to rescue you from this self-induced purgatory."

Patricia squeezed his hand . . . then let go, her aura fading into the light.

"Are you ready?"

"Yes." Shep swallowed hard. "Any last spiritual advice you want to impart, Virge?"

The old man took him by the hand and led him toward the Reaper, the being's body now bathed in the light of a rainbow. "Always remember, your soul is forever connected to the Light of the Creator. At times, your actions can veil this connection, but it can never be severed. Never."

"Thanks. Hey, about that lousy parent remark—"

"Unconditional love is unconditional, Patrick. Embrace the chaos. Use it to eradicate the negative traits within you, and you will hasten your transformation into a true *tzadik* . . . a holy man."

Shep took a deep breath. Then, reaching out, he touched the Grim Reaper's bony hand . . .

BATTERY PARK

7:58 A.M.

Armed with his newborn son, his certainty, and a mangled steel prosthetic limb, Paolo Salvatore Minos reentered the frigid waters of New York Harbor. So focused was his mind that he no longer registered the cold. The water rose past his knees . . . still nothing happened.

Think of it as a baptism. He continued on up to his chest, the thirty-seven-degree surface mere inches from the baby's blanket—

—sound and sky were suddenly blotted out as he stepped off the unseen concrete ledge and plunged underwater!

His heart pounded in terror as his left hand felt for the baby's nose, his fingers pinching his son's nostrils. He forced a panicked stride—

—his left foot relocating the perch. Using the steel arm as a crutch, he regained his balance and headed back up the ramp to save his child. But as his head cleared the surface, and he released the infant's nose, he saw that he was not standing on the concrete boat ramp; he was standing on a hunk of ice!

The harbor had not parted; instead, it was progressively freezing all around him, at least some of it is—a ten-to-fifteen-foot-wide swath that appeared to be stretching southwest across New York Harbor.

He exhaled a frozen breath, his body trembling, tears pouring from his swollen red eyes. Turning back to shore, he was met by his teary-eyed wife, who gathered the crying infant in her arms, wrapping him in a dry blanket. "Paolo . . . how?"

"Certainty."

David and Pankaj looked at one another, unsure of what to do.

The Tibetan monk gripped them both by the elbow, jerking them back into the moment. "Do not analyze the manifestation; use it to get everyone off the island!"

"Take Gavi, I'll get the others!" David sprinted back to the school bus to awaken the children while Pankaj and Manisha helped Dawn and Gavi climb onto the edge of the ice floe, which bobbed yet managed to maintain its buoyancy.

The children hurried off the school bus, racing to the water's edge, as the three helicopters crossed the Hudson a mile to the north.

"Let's go, let's go, everyone move! We have to hurry!"

David and Marquis Jackson-Horne passed the children to Pankaj and Manisha, everyone holding hands, forming a line behind Paolo and Francesca, who quickly led the exodus across the harbor. The middle schoolers and former sex slaves helped the younger children, hustling them across the slippery surface. David climbed onto the floe, rejoining his daughter.

The Elder stopped Marquis. "Choose the course for the rest of your days now."

His little sister nodded.

Reaching into his waistband, the gang leader removed the 9mm and tossed the gun into the harbor. He followed his sister onto the ice.

The Elder climbed after him, bringing up the rear.

Sheridan Ernstmeyer waited until the thirty-six men, women, infant, and children were a good thirty yards offshore before she convinced herself to follow, gingerly stepping onto the frozen surface. "This is crazy."

Ahead, Paolo and Francesca slid their feet along the slippery opaque surface as if skating. Liberty Island was less than a quarter mile ahead, the Statue momentarily disappearing from view behind a white mist that formed around the frozen path, concealing the exodus from Manhattan—the frigid fog serving to obliterate their heat signatures from the Reaper drones' thermal sensors. Paolo focused on the advancing ice floe as it continued to form and harden several yards ahead of him, even as he registered a sudden bone-deep chill that raced down his spine, causing him to shiver.

Glancing to his right, he saw the dark form appear out of the haze, standing along the path like a sentry.

The hooded figure was cloaked in black, the scythe held within the bony grip of the being's left hand. The Angel of Death was standing on the edge of the newly formed ice, signaling for them to advance.

Averting his gaze, Paolo led his procession past Death, gripping the prosthetic arm even tighter. "Keep moving, keep your eyes on the path! Look at nothing else."

Ignoring the warning, Dawn looked up at the Grim Reaper and smiled. "Thank you, Patrick."

David Kantor's eyes widened. The Elder swept the former Army medic and his teenage daughter along, restricting his own gaze, though he sensed the supernal being's weighty presence.

Sheridan Ernstmeyer did not see the Grim Reaper until she was almost upon it. "What the hell are you supposed to be?"

The Angel of Death grinned—

—as the ice beneath the female assassin's feet cracked open, and she plunged feet first into the unforgiving depths of the Hudson River.

GOVERNOR'S ISLAND

8:01 A.M.

Her legs were moving, but she could not feel them, the numbness of fear making her trek across the compound feel like an out-of-body experience. The two guards half carried, half dragged her past the courtyard and out a small gate in the fortress wall.

Leigh Nelson stared at the fog-enshrouded harbor, her limbs trembling uncontrollably. She thought of her husband and children. She prayed they would remain safe from the pandemic.

The guard on her left placed the gun to the back of her skull—

—and collapsed . . . dead. The second man's eyes bulged out of their sockets in terror, then he, too, joined his comrade in death.

Leigh looked around, giddy with relief—

—her legs buckling, her mind taken aback by the tall figure in the hooded cloak, his eye sockets aflutter with three pairs of seeing eyes. Floundering on all fours along the frozen ground, she looked up, terrified. "Please . . . don't . . . hurt . . . me."

The Reaper spoke, his voice a familiar rasp. "I have a basic rule: I never take a good soul after Wednesday."

"Shep?" Leigh Nelson's eyes rolled up into her head as she fainted.

High over Manhattan, the three military helicopters reached their designated drop zones. Praying for forgiveness, the distraught pilots released their payloads . . .

VA HOSPITAL

8:02 A.M.

The corridors, rendered powerless, were vacated and dark. The interior was autumn cold, disrupted by an occasional chorus of coughs and moans coming from wards harboring the forgotten. Shown respect in words but never compensated for their sacrifice, the veterans of foreign wars remained yesterday's problem—a burden to society, like the crazy uncle who never received an invitation to the wedding or mourners at his funeral. Dealing with amputees and cancer-ridden returning soldiers was a depressing reality to the "patriotic masses" and remained a very low priority for the members of Congress, who receive greater "fulfillment" by funding a new weapon of mass destruction than by cleaning up the "mess" left over from their two ongoing wars.

Of course, those who made it their life's work to bring light into a wounded veteran's life know different. And yet Scythe had chased even these stalwarts of spirituality away.

Having emptied the hospital of its staff, the plague had stalked the antiseptic halls like a hungry wolf. Desperate to feed, it had acquired new life when a fleeing member of the maintenance crew had failed to secure the vacuum seal on the doors leading into the VA's wards, summoning the beast to the banquet.

Open wounds and immobilized victims. Fresh meat lined up like sausages.

Twelve hours later, there was nothing left but incubators of death.

The life sign resonated like a flower blooming on a desert pampa, its isolated bubble energized by a self-contained battery pack. The newborn, an auburn-haired girl less than twenty-four hours old, slept peacefully under the watchful eye of her mother.

Mary Louise Klipot stared at her daughter, yearning to hold her . . . to give her the love and affection that she was denied by her own parent. She looked up as a dark silhouette reflected off the neonatal intensive care unit's Plexiglas incubator. "Go away, Death. You're not stealing my baby. *Santa Muerte* protects her."

The Grim Reaper slammed the wooden handle of his scythe upon the tile floor, the sledgehammer-like impact opening an eight-inch fissure that divided the room in half.

"What is it you want? Not my child!"

"You must answer for the ten thousand infants your actions stole this day. You shall reap the pain you've sown through all eternity, and your child shall be part of the harvest."

"No!" She threw herself over the incubator, begging for mercy. "Please don't compound my sins by stealing another innocent life! God, I know you are out there . . . please forgive me . . . have mercy on my daughter's soul."

The Reaper stared at the innocent newborn. "Renounce *Santa Muerte,* and I shall spare your child."

Mary looked up as a brilliant white light filled the city outside her room—

"I renounce her!"

—the intense heat melting the scream from her larynx, liquefying the flesh from her bones.

Paolo and Francesca gingerly stepped off the ice and onto the pier at Liberty Island. The teens and children ran past them, everyone hurrying up a paved sidewalk leading to the Statue of Liberty.

David Kantor kicked open the sealed doors at the base of the monolith, and they entered the pedestal's observation level—

—as a brilliant white burst of heat ignited to the northeast like an expanding bolt of lightning.

GOVERNOR'S ISLAND
8:12 A.M.

President Eric Kogelo opened his eyes. The pain that had wracked his head and internal organs over the last six hours had ceased, the fever gone.

He stole a prolonged moment in bed, enjoying the sheer joy of simply feeling well again, until an overwhelming sense of dread forced him into action. He sat up, disoriented and still a bit weak, surprised to find himself alone in the isolation room, the door bolted from the inside.

A sudden jolt of icy fear sent the president scrambling over the side of the bed.

The gaunt figure in the ragged hooded robe was standing in the corner of the room, watching him through eye sockets flitting with hundreds of tiny pupils. The being's scythe, held upright, dripped blood from the curvature of its olive green blade.

The skeleton animated, approaching the foot of his bed.

"Help! Somebody get in here!"

A burst of frigid air emanated from the Reaper's mouth as the ancient skull spoke. "There is no one here to help you. The ark your people built to isolate your failed leaders has been breached. Plague has taken every living soul on this island, save one."

"Oh . . . God." The president gasped to catch his breath, then gathered himself and stood in defiance of his impending death. "Just tell me one thing before you take me . . . will humanity perish as a result of our stupidity?"

"That remains to be seen."

"Will my death serve a greater purpose?"

"No. But your life can still bring Light to the world."

Kogelo's skin tingled with adrenaline. "You're sparing me?"

"You are a righteous man born in a time of greed and corruption, tasked by the will of the masses to bring peace. You have not gone far enough. You have struck deals with the dark forces and been manipulated in the process. To unveil the Light, you must end war. To end hatred, you must make peace with your enemies."

"It's not that easy. Ending two wars . . . there were loose ends in Iraq. Afghanistan is complex, we're dealing with Pakistan. There are issues . . . we're making progress. I could set a new timetable—"

"Should ten more innocents perish in Iraq, the eleventh shall be your wife."

"What?"

"Should ten more innocents perish in Afghanistan, the eleventh shall be your child. This is *my* timetable."

Kogelo collapsed to his knees. His throat constricted. "Please don't do this. Take my life, I don't care. Not my wife and daughter. I beg of you."

"Cause and effect. You hold the power over life and death. Reap what you sow."

Fueled by desperation, the president stole courage. "I will end the war. But there are enemies about . . . entities who prefer the darkness. How do I bring peace when all they want is war?"

"For those who seek to harm others, Judgment Day has arrived. This is my covenant to you."

The Grim Reaper extended its skeletal right hand—

—the bony appendage instantaneously wrapping with blood vessels and nerves, tendons and muscles, all sealed within a layer of warm Caucasian flesh.

For a brief second, Eric Kogelo swooned, then he willed himself to shake the offered hand, gazing up into the face of its owner.

The man who looked back at him was in his thirties, bearing Jim Morrison features, his long brown hair matching his eyes. The dog tags around his neck identified him as a US soldier. Kogelo squinted to read the inscription. *Sgt. Patrick Ryan Shepherd . . .*

Shep pulled back, releasing the president's hand . . . and his own humanity—

—casting his soul to the underworld.

"Greatness is not what you have achieved
but what you have overcome."
—Eliyahu Jian

"Are you going to get any better or is this it?"
—Earl Weaver, Baltimore Orioles manager, to the home plate umpire.

Lost Diary: Guy de Chauliac

The following entry has been excerpted from a recently discovered unpublished memoir, written by surgeon Guy de Chauliac during the Great Plague: 1346–1348.
(translated from its original French)

Diary Entry: September 13, 1348

(recorded in Avignon, France)

Time has passed. So much has happened, and yet I am at a loss to account for everything. Perhaps that is best.

When last I recorded an entry, I was worse than dead . . . a hapless soul, drifting in and out of torturous pain. In my delirium, I prayed to my Maker to take me.

Death finally paid its visit one wretched night in May.

My confines were stifling, my fever refusing me a moment's respite. Perhaps it was an incessant blood-soaked cough, perhaps divine intervention, but at some juncture I opened my eyes to the night. At that moment, the cloaked figure emerged from the shadows of my bedroom, his ragged garb blending with the darkness. The candlelight flickered in his presence, its orange glow revealing a scarred skull tinged brown with age, as if the bone had been left to rot in a pond. Or, by its overwhelming stench, perhaps a cesspool.

The room cooled noticeably as he spoke, his French twisting in an Asian accent. "I was once like you, a slave of the flesh, born in a time of greed and corruption. In my early years I bore witness to unaccountable bloodshed delivered by my own father's blade, and many a man suffered by my family's rule. But I turned away from the violence following my first battle as Emperor in order to pursue the mysticism of the spiritual realm. Instead of war, I waged peace, and in doing so, I changed our sworn enemies into allies, bringing prosperity to our entire region. But the knowledge I sought eluded me. And in my final hour, I was visited by Death, and he, too, offered me what I now offer you—the secrets of creation . . . the path to immortality. Agree to my terms by your own free will, and I shall extend your days in this world, and the knowledge of the ages that abandoned me shall be yours, bringing joy to the rest of your days . . . and beyond."

I sat up in my deathbed, my mind waging a war with my own sanity. "And if I accept your offer . . . what then? What is to be my end of this covenant?"

"When the natural end of your days transpires, and you have taken your final breath, you shall relieve me of my burden as the Reaper of Souls. Complete this spiritual task, and you shall be forgiven all your earthly sins and be guaranteed a place in Heaven's endless fulfillment."

"And how many days," I asked, "must I wander the Earth as Death?"

"Time is not measured in the spiritual realm, *monsieur.* But fear not, for a worthy soul, tarnished by his own past deeds, even now awaits his next rebirth. Together with his soul mate, they shall relieve you of your future burden as you shall relieve me of mine."

He left me then, this Angel of Death, to ponder whether his visit was real or a delusion brought on by the fever. But soon after, my symptoms improved, and by summer's end, I was my old self.

But while I was gone, how the world had changed.

More than half the European population that existed a mere two years earlier were dead, entire villages wiped out by the plague. Religion was brought to its knees by its own corruption. Papal rule was forced from its partnership with the Royals, who gradually lost their own coercive hold on the masses when food and land proved plentiful in the sudden absence of more than 45 million people.

I, too, have changed. Titles no longer have any meaning to me. I wish now only to serve mankind, sharing my acquired knowledge of the human condition with others.

Then this!

No sooner had I begun penning a manuscript that would become *The Inventory of Medicine* than I was visited by a peculiar fellow of Asian descent. That he knew of my encounter with death was outweighed by his most unusual gift—a journal accumulating the greatest medical wisdom of the ages, authored by Aristotle and Plato and Pythagoras, as well as some of the most renowned sages in history.

The bounty of knowledge this strange-looking Tibetan monk offered was as mind-boggling as his opaque eyes and the asking price: "Accept our Society's invitation, and the knowledge is yours to preside over as caretaker."

From darkness the Light, from sickness and death . . . a level of joy and accomplishment I could never have imagined. I no longer fear death, knowing that the promise of immortality awaits.

And so, I live out my days to help others, each act of kindness seeding an everlasting fulfillment . . .

Let the Reaper come indeed!

—Guigo

LAMERICA

Clothed in sunlight
Restled in waiting
Dying of fever

Changed shapes of an empire
Starling invaders
Vast promissory notes of joy

Wanton, willful & passive
Married to doubt
Clothed in great warring monuments
of glory

How it has changed you
How slowly estranged you
Solely arranged you

Beg you for mercy.

—Jim Morrison

EPILOGUE

AUGUST 6

CHARTRES, FRANCE

12:03 A.M.

The medieval town rose above undulating fields of golden wheat like an ancient Gothic island. Thousand-year-old walls, the mortar worn smooth, dated its baronial fortification. Narrow cobblestone streets weaved through rows of half-timbered houses. Ancient bridges traversed the Eure River, the inky waters of its three tributaries winding beneath archways of stone.

Chartres. Located sixty miles southwest of Paris, the French commune was a magnet of history, bearing witness to some of humanity's darkest days.

Black Death: The Great Mortality.

Crowning the hill upon which the village had been erected was Our Lady of Chartres, one of the most magnificent cathedrals in all of Europe. Two towering spires, their unique designs representative of the architecture of the eleventh and sixteenth centuries, soared more than 350 feet into the heavens, rendering them visible for miles in every direction. Flying buttresses highlighted a Romanesque basilica and massive crypt, its foundation encompassing 117,000 square feet. Gothic carvings adorned its facade, stained glass its portals.

It was just after midnight, and the streets surrounding the cathedral were deserted. The word had been passed—not a soul ventured outside, lest one tempt the wrath of God.

They approached the church on foot, each member having been sequestered in the village earlier in the day. Entries were purposely staggered, made through an earthen passage concealed within a dense patch of foliage adjacent to the church grounds.

Nine men: Each cloaked in a heavy hooded monk's robe that concealed his face.

Nine men: Their names never spoken, their identities kept hidden lest one of their comrades be apprehended or tortured.

Nine Unknown Men.

The subterranean war room lay three stories beneath the church, its walls seven feet thick. The chamber contained its own power generator, and was equipped with sixteen-channel night-vision surveillance monitors and three wraparound computer security stations. One member of the Nine occupied a console, the other seven were situated in comfortable high-backed cushioned chairs that surrounded a circular oak table. Eight men, transformed by recent events. Awaiting the arrival of their leader.

Pankaj Patel was seated in the seventh chair. The psychology professor appeared to be speed-reading from an ancient Aramaic text.

Yielding to his curiosity, Number Five, a thirty-seven-year-old Austrian technowizard sharing the same bloodlines as Nikola Tesla, left his security post to speak with the sect's newest member. "You are reading the Zohar?"

"Actually, I'm scanning."

"What happened, Seven? Did you lose a bet with the Elder?"

"I've seen things, Five. I walked on water."

"I thought it was ice?"

"It was a miracle, plain and simple. Now I am a changed man. I pray. I scan. I am even writing a spiritual book, with the proceeds going to the new Children's Hospital in Manhattan."

"Admirable. Tell me, Seven, when you pray, do you pray for the soul of Bertrand DeBorn?"

"Blow me, Five."

"Seven!" The Elder entered the chamber, his opaque eyes scolding Patel. "Remember, my friend—restriction."

"My apologies, Elder."

The Nine men took their assigned places around the oval table. The Elder began. "Number Three, so good of you to be here, especially in light of your new responsibilities within the Politburo. Will our Russian friends agree to President Kogelo's new disarmament plan?"

"If you had asked me two days ago, I would have emphatically said no. Since then, four of the communist hardliners have suffered fatal heart attacks."

"Must be something in the water," quipped Number Eight, a Chinese physicist in his sixties. "Two of our more radical communist leaders also died last week. No foul play is suspected, but, as the Elder likes to say, there are no coincidences."

"You wish to comment, Number Seven?"

"It's got to be Shepherd," Pankaj stated. "Look at what happened to those neocons in Israel . . . the hardliners in Hamas. And don't forget the two radical clerics in Iran who died before the election."

"Every action has a reaction," responded Number Six, a Mexican environmentalist bearing a Zapotec heritage. "While Shepherd attempts to micromanage the physical world, *Santa Muerte* grows stronger in the darkness below."

"How do you know this, Number Six?"

"Somehow, the female Reaper managed to open a fissure that allows her access from Hell into the physical world. Two weeks ago, she exhumed the remains of a priest who had died in Guadalajara of swine flu and danced his contaminated remains at a local wedding."

The Elder laid his head back against his chair. "Mr. Shepherd must learn to restrict himself as Emperor Asoka and Monsignor de Chauliac before him. We must find a way to communicate with our new Angel of Darkness. Number Seven, has your wife had any supernal communications since you and your family moved back to Manhattan?"

The professor looked uncomfortable. "None, Elder."

"What about . . . your daughter?"

TRINITY CEMETERY
WASHINGTON HEIGHTS, MANHATTAN
12:03 P.M.

August roasted New York's five boroughs in a midday broil, the heat rising off the sidewalks transforming the cement into a baking stone. The Hudson River, its surface stagnant to the naked eye, cascaded a subatomic tsunami of water molecules upward into the atmosphere, contributing humidity to the parade of cumulus clouds already forming to the west.

In the city below, a lunchtime crowd sweltered. Businessmen hustled between air-conditioned enclosures, red-faced vendors sought relief from umbrella-drawn shade and portable fans.

After forty days of inspection and 153 days of construction, debris removal, and public Masses, the Big Apple once more had a pulse. Manhattan's population now approached six hundred thousand, with lower rent ceilings promising even more transplants.

The cemetery's caretaker was sleeping off a hangover in his office. Venetian blinds were pinched closed above a window-unit air conditioner that had outlived its warranty. There were no graveside ceremonies on the schedule, and the summer heat had kept the visitors away—

—save two.

On a lonely summit beneath a relentless sun, a mother and daughter stood amid a metropolis of mausoleums and ancient graves, staring at a polished headstone. After ten minutes, the child asked, "Is this really where Patrick's buried, Mommy?"

Leigh Nelson played mental dodgeball with the answer, debating which threads of truth would satisfy her child's curiosity without leading to nightmares. "Patrick's with God now. The headstone's just a place where we can tell him how much we love him and miss him"—she tears up—"and how much we appreciate what he did."

The Range Rover parked by the gated western entrance blared its horn.

Leigh smiled at Autumn. "Daddy misses us, we'd better go."

"I want to stay."

"I know, but it's Tuesday and daddy needs to get back to work. We'll come back another time, maybe on the weekend. Okay, baby doll?"

"Okay."

Hand in hand, they made their way back down the steep hillside along the broken-slated path. Halfway down, Leigh saw the eleven-year-old Hindu girl seated in the shade of a concrete tomb. *Waiting patiently for a private audience.* Leigh waved.

Dawn Patel waved back. Then she hurriedly ascended the steep hill, her route through the grave sites guided by the headstone adorned with the sculpture of an angelic child.

She laid the first of two white roses on the older grave as she read the inscription silently to herself:

PATRICIA ANN SEGAL
AUGUST 20, 1977–SEPTEMBER 11, 2001
BELOVED MOTHER AND SOUL MATE

DONNA MICHELE SHEPHERD
OCTOBER 21, 1998–SEPTEMBER 11, 2001
BELOVED DAUGHTER

The adjoining headstone was new, erected by the thirty-six survivors discovered plague-free in the Statue of Liberty Museum two days after the horrors of the December Mortality.

The two adult inscriptions were eerily similar:

PATRICK RYAN SHEPHERD
AUGUST 20, 1977–DECEMBER 21, 2012
BELOVED SOUL MATE—BLESSED FRIEND

The girl placed the second rose on the tomb, the buried casket of which contained the prosthetic left arm of its deceased owner. Backing away, she sat on the edge of a nearby stone, its heated surface barely tolerable through her denim shorts.

After a few moments, she felt the female presence of her guardian angel on her left, the chill of the darker male force on her right. "The two of you were born on the same day. I think that's so romantic."

Dawn's scalp tingled as the supernal female being played with the girl's hair.

The Grim Reaper remained partially obscured in the shade of an oak tree.

"School starts soon. They say we'll be combining grade levels until more people move back to the city."

Thunder rumbled in the distance. The western sky took on a bizarre appearance—the cloud's low-hanging ceiling undulating like a forty-foot sea, the distant horizon appearing lime green.

"Oh yeah, remember the miracle baby . . . the newborn girl they found alive in a neonatal enclosure at the VA hospital? She's finally been adopted, only no one's saying who the parents are. They think her mother was the one who released Scythe. God, can you imagine having to grow up with that hanging over your head?"

The upper leaves on the oak trees blew skyward. Telltale sign of an impending afternoon thunderstorm.

"Anyway, I wanted to come by and wish you guys an early happy birthday. I probably should go. My mother thinks I stopped by Minos for a slice of pizza. You know they named the baby after you. Patrick Lennon Minos. I thought that was pretty cool."

The atmospheric change was sudden and electric, the static charge coming from behind the girl. Before she could turn to the source of the disturbance, the female spirit launched her sideways from her grave-site perch—

—a split second before the blade of the materializing scythe struck the vacant slab of concrete!

Regaining her senses, Dawn turned in horror to see the witch flying out at her from the iron-gated mausoleum, the female Grim Reaper wearing a wavy black wig and matching satin dress. The force from Hell reached for her with its ten fleshless fingers—

—only to be intercepted by her male counterpart.

The midair collision between the two guardians of death unleashed a bolt of violet lightning that shot skyward from the ground, splitting the century-old oak tree in half—

—the otherworldly charge inhaling the two figures into another dimension!

Dawn's spiritual companion pushed and prodded the girl down the east side of the summit, her supernal mother refusing to allow her to rest until she reached Broadway.

Then she, too, disappeared.

The girl gathered herself, sweating heavily in the August heat. Overhead, the undulating olive green cloud formation has dispersed.

For the first time in this life, Dawn Patel felt alone.

The consciousness that was Patrick Shepherd awakens.

He is kneeling on a flat, rocky summit, enshrouded by darkness. Purple lightning illuminates the valley below, offering brief glimpses of *Gehenna*. A spark ignites a bush into an orange incandescent flame, the fire expelling sulfurous smoke but not burning.

The woman steps out of the shadows and into the light . . . revealing her nude form.

Her skin is composed of keratin, the fingernail-like substance as pale as reflected moonlight, her long, wavy hair as ebony as the abyss. Her naked body is the definition of sensuality, the raw musky scent of her pheromones releasing an involuntary paroxysm within her male counterpart's being.

Her voice is deep and soothing. "Today is the ninth of Av, a time of reckoning. Reveal yourself to me."

Within seconds, the male Reaper's skeletal frame entwines in blood vessels, nerves, muscles and tendons, wrapped in the flesh-covered epidermis of Patrick Shepherd. "Who are you? Why have you summoned me to this place?"

She approaches slowly, each measured stride causing his pulse to quicken. "I am the tempest that awakened Adam, the spirit embodied in the Tree of Knowledge. I am a newborn's giggle that haunts its sleep . . . the desire that causes adolescent males to pleasure themselves. And when the semen is spilt, it finds its way into my loins to father my demons. I am darkness personified, a black hole of existence where the Upper Light can never dwell—

"—I am Lilith, and you, Noah, are my soul mate."

The story continues in...

To contact Steve Alten go to:
www.SteveAlten.com

To learn more about the ancient wisdom of
Kabbalah go to:
www.uKabbalah.com

FINAL THOUGHTS

By Nick Nunziata

Grim Reaper wasn't as much a book as it was a pilgrimage. Like most pilgrimages, it has had its ups and downs, trials and tribulations, and became less about the destination than the journey. The process certainly has left an indelible mark on how Steve and I now approach our material. I think we carried this thing with us like a malicious hitchhiker; it left a film on each of us both in its subject matter and its seeming desire to reach the world at any cost. *Dante's Inferno* is so deep and dark and timeless on its own but when coupled with real world dangers that have a distinctly modern hue, it takes on a far deeper meaning. Many of the things happening in our own lives and in the real world around us affected the story's evolution, taking us on unexpected turns and avenues on its way to the book in your hands. It's as if certain plot points waited for us in the shadows, seeping into Steve and me on the sly. In the night. Scythe at the ready. It just wouldn't die.

The seed for the series was planted back in 2005 at a time when the *MEG* movie (currently unmade) had just been optioned for the second time, and Steve and I were aching to collaborate on something new and different. During long conversations into the night, we shared a lot of great ideas that seemed to have merit for a script or book. Suggestions flew fast and furious, a few of which eventually made their way onto paper. The idea for *Grim Reaper* started quite innocuously but quickly evolved from a generic horror script into something much more dense and disturbing. In pursuit of the story, we met in New York. We walked Manhattan like Shep. We paid attention to the nooks and crannies. We went deep beneath the surface of the city and saw places that seemed out of . . . well, a book. As time went on it, became apparent that *Grim Reaper* was far too deep a story to make its debut as a screenplay.

Like a man possessed, Steve dove into the novel. He reached into places you haven't seen in his other books, though in many ways this is a soul mate to some of his best work. The book grew and evolved, on the way seemingly ripping at us to decipher it and solve its riddles. Eventually, after a very long time, many discussions, many edits, it was finally considered done. That said, part of me wonders if there's not some parasite in Steve's head screaming different little things he can tweak and add to this day. And if you thought this book was epic and filled with harrowing and visceral moments, just you wait. So many of the big ideas and deep mythology we have fueling this story have to wait until books two and three. How fortunate for us that the *Divine Comedy* wasn't just a singular story.

With *End of Days* complete, I think we're now in a position to dig deeper into Dante's world and the stuff nightmares are made of while still carrying that golden light through it. I hope you agree, because as far as Steve Alten books go, this is a step in a new and more epic direction, and if you know the guy, once his sights are set on something, there's no turning back. Part of that is his tenacity, and part of that is his loyal and truly special readership. Hopefully I can carry my weight in this and do my part in keeping you awake late at night when you shouldn't be tempting the fates.

Grim Reaper was not an easy tale to tell, nor was it is the easiest book to sell at a time when publishers prefer simpler easier-to-market fiction. Still, as an avid book reader, I'll always consider *End of Days* as a mainstream page turner. It certainly speaks to me in the same way Dan Simmons's amazing *Carrion Comfort* did and, of course, King's *The Stand.* Those great books of the seventies and eighties managed to avoid being caught up in a business model. They were stories that ripped your heart out, asked difficult questions, and took their readers through places both familiar and alien, their plots and characters sinister yet filled with the darkest thoughts we could muster. They were also frighteningly relevant, with a relevance that has taken on a different meaning as time has progressed. In their own way, these books were a living thing with horrors most people could relate to, both real and supernal. I'd like to think *Grim Reaper* fits into this same mold.

As much as I love movies, there's still nothing like a good book. I hope you've found this one worth keeping in your collection, wearing down the pages of, and recommending to others. Because *He* is watching you, you know. That scythe at the ready. Those eyes sparkling in the night.

Nick Nunziata
March 25, 2010

Many thanks to the Hal Leonard Corporation for providing permissions to the following:

COMING SOON...

PHOBOS:
MAYAN FEAR

Part three of the DOMAIN series

by
NY Times best-selling author

STEVE ALTEN

SNEAK PEEK

AUTHOR'S NOTE:

Phobos is the third book in the Mayan Doomsday Prophecy series that began with the release of *Domain* in 1999 and continued with *Resurrection* in 2004. Back in 1999, few people knew about the 2012 prophecy and fewer still probably cared. Nevertheless, over the years I have often been asked, "Do you think humanity will really end on the winter solstice of 2012?" My answer is always to explain that both natural disasters (asteroid strikes, Yellowstone caldera eruptions) or man-made threats (biological weapons – see Ft. Detrick & Battelle Labs) could do the job. As the 2012 date approaches and man's ego gave us runaway greed, corruption, and new lows in human morality, I sometimes wonder if we'll even make it to 2012.

Phobos simply scares me. Had I known about this very real threat when I penned *Domain* I would have written the book you now hold in your hands back then. But this threat didn't exist back then and ultimately the series is better for it. Still, *Phobos* gives me nightmares, just as its conclusions scare a small minority of scientists attempting to use legal action to shutdown a $10 billion science experiment. Sadly, unless the silent majority gets behind their gallant effort, far worse than the Mayan prophecy may come true. Theoretically, it may already be underway.

Whenever possible, I seek out the advice of experts whose opinions can improve key parts of the story. Upon reading the original conclusions I put forth in *Phobos*, a quantum physicist far smarter than this former Penn State physical education major rendered the following comment:

> Steve, I'm "wowed." Aside from the story-line a-la Cern-Hadron; if {IF!} your scenario were a naturally occurring phenomenon (and I perceive that very well might be fact) then the posit that your description makes is indeed the very process of planetary expansion with the "monster" rather becoming a quasi-white-hole a.k.a. balanced gray hole---->Core-Star---->making the very planet a version of a plasma-breach trans-dimensional-bleed through reactor---->AND these reactors DO EXIST and the SUPER-COLLIDERS are "inadvertently" COPIES of the "general" ELECTRO-MAGNETIC RING that these

Plasma-Breach Hyper-Gravity-Lobe bleed-through Reactors actually are. . ."

Let me make two points abundantly clear: I have no idea what the hell that means, and my brain hurts when I read it. What I do know is that, as a writer of science-based "faction" I take pride in researching my topic to exhaustion before penning digestible conclusions designed to entertain my readers while standing up to the scrutiny of experts. And that's why *Phobos* scares me, first because I know the scenario is plausible; and second because anytime you combine man's ego with atom splitting or colliding, bad things are apt to happen (see Kabbalah).

As you read this passage they are happening right now.

In Geneva.

–Steve Alten

"All should leave Geneva, Saturn turns from gold to iron. The contrary positive ray will exterminate everything. There will be signs in the sky before this."

—Nostradamus 9 44:

"The Large Haldron Collector (in Geneva) is certainly by far, the biggest jump into the unknown."

—Brian Cox, CERN physicist

THE FINAL PAPERS OF JULIUS GABRIEL, PH.D.

CAMBRIDGE UNIVERSITY ARCHIVES

August 23, 2001

Phobos:. A Greek term meaning "morbid fear."

Fear: A state of mind, inducing anxiety. The trepidation preceding an unwanted outcome. Fear is the mind-killer that disrupts the higher aspects of brain activity, overruling common sense.

It is argued that modern man suffers from six basic phobias: Fear of poverty. Fear of old age. Loss of love. Criticism. Poor health. And, of course, our most overwhelming fear – fear of death.

My name is Julius Gabriel. I am an archaeologist, a scientist who investigates humanity's past in search of the truth. Truth is the light that eliminates the darkness induced by fear. Conversely, lies are the weapons of darkness, designed to spread fear.

What you are about to read is the culmination of more than half a century of research that reveals startling truths about man's existence, our intended purpose, and our prophesied demise. The evidence that follows has never been made public, for to do so would have violated a dozen non-disclosure agreements that would have resulted in my incarceration and very likely a quiet execution made to look like a suicide – ramifications rendered moot following a recent visit to my cardiologist.

In truth, my decision to finally go public with these papers was based more on anger than my own intended exit strategy. I am sickened by an illegal and unconstitutional black ops program that exists solely to empower and enrich members of the military industrial complex and the fossil fuel industry. These pseudo-emperors have committed high-treason against our entire species. They have lied to Congress and continue to operate outside the bounds of the Constitution of the United States, thereby voiding the previously mentioned non-disclosure agreements. Worse, they have murdered one president, disrupted the administration of another, and have refused to be held accountable by any office, though they are funded with an annual budget that exceeds $100 billion. In order to preserve their secrets, they have killed people of fame and fortune and innocent bystanders alike, and have orchestrated false flag events that have led to wars. Of most importance to mankind's future, they covet and have bottlenecked advanced technologies in the field of energy and propulsion that would not only provide free endless power for all, but avert a looming global catastrophe.

To ensure the survival of their "Ivory Towers of Power" they are prepared to unleash a final false flag event that will lead to planetary fear and eventually the weaponization of space. Before that happens, or perhaps as a result, every living being on this planet shall die.

Am I being overly dramatic? Keep reading and you too will know what real fear is.

Within these pages I am going to reveal everything to you, the good, the bad, and the mind-boggling truth – from the very secrets of existence that predates the Big Bang to the Big Bang that shall eradicate our species. In the process, you will come to understand that the universe is not what it seems, nor is human existence, and that this ticking clock of physicality that begins at conception and terminates with our final breath is neither the end nor the beginning, but an elaborate ruse constructed by our Creator. . .as a test.

And we are failing miserably.

Judgment Day is coming, and we have reaped this destruction upon ourselves. Greed, corruption, hatred, selfishness, avarice . . . most of all sheer ignorance—all brought about by the one human weakness that continues to define and poison our species even as it lures us toward the precipice of our very demise . . . our ego.

The pages you are about to read will unveil forty years of lies and deception, but enlightenment comes with a price: Do not covet the truth. Seed the information to the four winds, be the cause of your own hard-won salvation. For what hangs in the balance is nothing less than a fate prophesied by every ancient civilization and every major religion . . . the End of Days.

Phobos:: Fear.

Fear is the elephant in the living room. To overcome the mind paralysis of fear, you must master it, you must, in a sense, consume it. But how can one consume something as large as an elephant?

The answer, of course, is one digestible bite at a time.

To digest the Doomsday Event requires that I not only deliver the facts, but that I do so in their proper context lest you dismiss this document as merely a work of fiction—a source of entertainment. It is neither! Question the author, take nothing within these pages for granted. Research every fact. Cross-reference any statement and every conclusion that draws your ire. Only then will your mind begin to accept the truth; only then will you realize that there are evil entities lurking in the shadows playing with matches, and unless you open your eyes and act they will incinerate the world.

Like it or not, accept it or not, a Doomsday Event is coming. How can I be so sure? Because, dear reader, the event has already happened! Even more bizarre – some of you reading these very words were there to witness the end.

Confused? So was I, until I stopped thinking like a third dimensional creature entrapped by our own perceptions of time and unraveled the truth.

Before rendering a verdict, allow me to present my case.

As previously stated, I am an archaeologist. In 1969, having earned my doctorate degree from Cambridge University, I set out on a journey of discovery, motivated more by curiosity than fear. My inspiration was the Mayan Calendar, a 2,000-year-old instrument of time and space that predicted humanity's reign to end on December 21, 2012.

Doomsday.

Let us pause a quick moment and make that fork-full of elephant meat more digestible. A calendar, by definition, is a device used to measure time, in this case the amount of time it takes for our planet to revolve once around the sun. Somehow a society of jungle-dwelling Indians managed to create an instrument of time and space that—despite being 1,500 years older than our modern-day Gregorian Calendar—remains one-ten- thousandth of a day more accurate.

The Mayan Calendar is a device comprised of three cogged wheels operating in a fashion similar to the gears of a clock, plus a fourth calendar—the Long Count—which details twenty year epochs, called Katuns. Each Katun is a prophecy in its own right, detailing happenings on Earth in accordance with the astrological ebb and flow of the cosmos.

The Doomsday event is aligned with precession. Precession is the slow wobble of our planet on its axis. It takes the Earth 25,800 years to complete one cycle of precession – the exact amount of time that defines the Mayan Calendar's five great cycles, the current and last one terminating on the day of 4 Ahau, 3 Kankin – the winter solstice of 2012.

How were the Maya, a race of Indians who never mastered the wheel, able to create such an advanced scientific instrument that prophesied events over thousands, perhaps millions of Katuns? How were they able to plot our precise position in the cosmos, comprehend concepts like dark matter, or fathom the existence of the black hole at the center of our galaxy? Most important: How were the ancient Maya able to describe events that had yet to happen?

The simplistic answer is they couldn't. In reality, it was their two mysterious leaders who possessed the knowledge.

The first was the great Mayan teacher, Kukulcan, who came to the Yucatan Peninsula a thousand years ago. Described as a tall Caucasian man with silky white hair, a matching beard, and intense azure-blue eyes, this "messenger of love" who preached against the blood sacrifice remains a paradox of existence, for not only does his knowledge of science and astronomy dwarf our own, but his presence in Mesoamerica predates the arrival of the first white explorers (invaders) to the Americas by 500 years.

Still convinced you are reading fiction? Travel to the Yucatan and visit Chichen Itza. Harbored within this long-lost Mayan city is the Kukulcan Pyramid, a perfect ziggurat of stone, stained with the blood of ten thousand human sacrifices intended to stave off doomsday in the wake of the great teacher's passing. Ninety-one steps adorn each of the temple's four sides; add the summit platform and you have three hundred and sixty-five, as in the days of the year. Arrive on the fall or spring equinox and you'll witness the appearance of a serpent's shadow on the northern balustrade, a thousand year old special effect constructed to warn modern man of the cataclysm to come.

The second mysterious Mayan was Chilam Balam, the greatest prophet in Mesoamerican history. Chilam is the title bestowed upon a priest who gives prophecies, Balam translates to Jaguar. The Jaguar Prophet was born in the Yucatan in the late 1400s and is known for his nine books of prophecies – one of which foretold the coming of strangers from the east who would "establish a new religion."

In 1519, Cortez and his invading Spanish armada arrived in the Yucatan, armed with guns, priests, and bibles just as Chilam Balam had prophesied.

Though he is not credited for it, I strongly suspect Chilam Balam to be the author of the Mayan Popol Vuh, the Mesoamerican equivalent of the Bible, at the heart of which is the Mayan Creation Story. Much like the Old Testament, the Popol Vuh's stories contain historical mythology that strains the boundaries of credibility. Like our own Judeo-Christian Bible, the Mayan Creation Story was never intended to be taken literally (more on that later). Instead, it was encrypted with an ancient knowledge that unveils the truth about mankind's future and past.

Following decades of work, I managed to decode the Mayan Creation Story. And therein lies yet another paradox, for the deciphered text reveals incredible details regarding *Homo Sapiens'* mysterious ascension as an intelligent force of nature – only the evolutionary events described in the Popol Vuh took place millions of years ago!

In archaeology, we call this a paradox. In layman's terms, one might call it a déjà-vu. By definition, déjà-vu is the uneasy feeling that one has witnessed or experienced a new situation previously – as if the event has already happened.

It has.

As incredible as it sounds, I have discovered that our physical universe is caught within a temporal time loop that begins and ends with our destruction on the winter solstice of 2012, and the very instrument that once more shall be responsible for the doomsday event has been constructed on our watch—

—funded by our tax dollars.

—JG

Note:

Professor Gabriel's final papers were subsequently banned from publication or public review as per ruling of the Massachusetts superior court (Borgia v. Gabriel estate; Hon. Judge Thomas Cubit presiding). The Cambridge University archaeology department petitioned and received the papers following Professor Gabriel's death on August 24, 2001, and his son, Michael's incarceration at the Bridgewater State mental facility for the criminally insane. The Pentagon successfully appealed the ruling to the British courts, who ordered the papers sealed and not to be reviewed. They remained archived until 2032.